SELECTION

A tale of fate, AI, and climate change

Chris Kulp

ISBN: 978-1-956612-16-5 (Paperback)
ISBN: 978-1-956612-14-1 (eBook)

This novel is entirely a work of fiction. The names, characters, and incidents portrayed in it are the work of the author's imagination. Any resemblance to actual persons, living or dead, events, or localities is entirely coincidental.

Chris Kulp asserts the moral right to be identified as the author of this work.
Find more stories at https://chriskulp.com

First printing edition 2023
Making Adventure Publishing
16944 York Rd, Suite 62
Monkton, MD 21111

For Gail

This is what happens to Sam.

For Tim

Thank you for helping make Selection a reality.

Preface

If you've read *Selection* before, you might notice some changes in this version. I have given several talks about *Selection* over the last year and half since its release. Each time, I found something that I'd like to have done differently. This version was an opportunity to make those changes.

The first change is that editor Amie Norris proofread *Selection* and helped me tighten up the novel. The plot hasn't changed, but I believe its presentation has greatly improved.

As a scientist, I feel like I missed an opportunity to teach the science behind the story. Not only do I want to entertain (which I hope I do!), but I want to inform. For that reason, I added the Science Behind *Selection* section that follows the story. I also included discussion questions. I hope they can help the reader engage with the story's themes in new ways.

Finally, I included an epilogue. Several readers have asked for a sequel. I am hoping the epilogue will hold them over until I can get around to writing Tyranny of Fate Book 2. I love these characters and can't wait to revisit them in their world.

Revisiting *Selection* has been pure joy for me. If this is your first trip into this world, I hope you enjoy it. For those of you reading it again for a second time, I am truly honored.

May the Algorithm provide for you.

Chris Kulp
May 28, 2024

"With a push of the Return key, I activate the Algorithm and hand total control of our society over to something with no agenda, no wants, and no needs. The Algorithm will show us how to heal our planet and help us build the future we have been incapable of creating for ourselves." [audible click] [applause]

- Jefferson Wallace, the last president of the United States of America, activating the Algorithm at 0000 on January 1, Year 1 of the Society as designed by the Algorithm.

Part 1
Selection

Chapter 1: Sam

December 31, 534
The Day Before Selection

"Omegas clean. Sigmas manage. Betas create. But the greatest among us, the Alphas, lead."

- Introduction to Social Studies, an elementary school textbook by the Algorithm.

In all his eighteen years, Samuel Watkins had never once received a gift. But he had read about them, and he knew one thing: presents were best when wrapped. A wrapped gift could be anything. Its potential was bound only by the size of the package. Tomorrow, the Algorithm would unwrap Sam's fate. He had spent his youth trying to make the package as large as possible. But like presents, fates were only known to those who sealed them.

Sam steepled his fingers as he leaned on his desk. His phone's screen had been blank for too long. If his program worked, it would boost his Intelligence Metric and improve his chances at tomorrow's Selection. He exhaled through puffed cheeks as he leaned back in his chair and rubbed his eyes. The hard plastic seat and back pushed against the bones of his thin body. He fidgeted but found no relief—comfort was rarely provided to a Sigma.

The eye rubbing didn't help either. Staring at his phone's screen for hours had given him a bad case of dry eyes. A half-empty bottle of eye drops collected dust on the corner of his desk. Sigma medicine barely worked—when it worked at all.

Sam pushed back from the desk. A sudden thud jolted his back as the chair hit the foot of his bed. Mom said there wasn't enough space in his tiny room for both a bed and desk. She was right, but he couldn't pass up the plastic desk when he had found it discarded on the street.

He settled back in the chair, slowly this time, giving his eyes a rest from the screen. Yellowing paint peeled off the wall above his desk. His mother put in a request for repairs years ago. Sigma Living Unit repairs ranked low on the Algorithm's priority list.

The screen remained blank. Sam squeezed between the desk and chair as he stood and stretched. He could just barely reach the ceiling. The stains on the ceiling conveyed a long history of leaks. *Damp again, that's the third time this week. No point in mentioning it to Mom.* Maybe some fresh air—or as fresh as the air could get in Baltimore—would clear his mind.

Sam leaned out his bedroom's open window and rested his crossed arms on the windowsill. No one else seemed concerned about tomorrow's Selection. For them, it was just another afternoon in The Hill, the southernmost neighborhood of Old Baltimore still above water.

A forest of dilapidated three-story buildings on stilts extended as far as the eye could see. Superstorms from the Climate Shift had destroyed the large, beautiful homes that existed here centuries ago. Rumors on the Sigma dark web said those houses were nicer than the Beta Town Houses in Towson. Sam believed it. Everything he read of the pre-Shift era suggested that, at its peak, it was a golden age of humanity.

Evidence of last week's flood lingered. Sam hadn't noticed the stench of wet trash until he stuck his head out the window. Being on the third floor kept the worst of the neighborhood smells out of his room, even when his window was open. A sign on the building across the street displayed the current temperature: 85°F. He could deal with the smell or suffer in a hot, closed-up room. The Algorithm did not provide air conditioning to Sigmas in December when the monthly average was only 75°F. Sam chose the smell.

A car drove through the neighborhood along Eutaw Place toward the park. Sam squinted and stretched his neck. Everyone on the sidewalk stared, too.

What's a Beta doing here?

A baby screamed after the car passed. An UnSelected woman carrying the child walked from person to person, probably begging for something to eat. Anything would be better than what the UnSelected were provided. People mostly ignored her. Occasionally a Sigma walked by and spat on her. Sam shook his head. *The UnSelected are people, too.*

Disgusted by what he saw outside, Sam returned to the hard chair and leaned over his phone laying face up on the desk. The screen lit up. His left leg bounced almost as fast as his heart raced.

This could be it.

A message appeared:

```
Compilation complete.
Number of errors: 0.

Execute?
```

"Hell yeah," Sam whispered. Mom hated it when he cussed.

```
Two humans detected:
1 male in the same room as the phone.
1 female in adjacent room to the east.
```

"Yes!" Sam shook his fist in victory. He flopped back in his chair. His shoulder blades struck the hard plastic. It took all he had not to swear out loud.

"Is everything okay, honey?" Sam's mom, the other human in the SLU, yelled from the main room.

"Yeah, Mom! I finally got the AI program on my phone to work!" Sam shuffled around his chair to the doorway of his room. "It can determine the number of people in an SLU by analyzing the vibrations of their movement."

"That's nice, dear."

Nice? This program probably just boosted my Intelligence Metric by at least one point. That's huge!

Although it was rude to say it out loud, Sam dreamed of being Selected as a Beta artificial intelligence programmer.

Imagine the awesome AI programs I could create with Beta resources. He knew better than to dream of an Alpha Selection—that didn't happen to Sigmas.

Mom removed a meal packet from the food dispenser. "Dinner's here." She inspected the package. "Looks like the Algorithm provided us a vegetable medley with bread."

Sam straightened. "Real veggies?" That would be a good omen, especially the night before his Selection.

"Sorry, dear." Mom inserted a plastic spoon in the package and scooped out a grayish paste. The paste plopped from the spoon as she transferred it into a dish. "The Algorithm provides what we deserve." She turned the packet upside down over the counter. A piece of bread, wrapped in plastic, fell out.

"The Algorithm provides." Sam snorted.

Mom gave Sam the side-eye for his sarcasm. Sigmas were rarely provided real vegetables. At least the paste contained some of the same nutrients. Sam had heard Omega paste had much less nutritional value. But even they ate better than the UnSelected.

"It'll taste better warm." Mom placed the dish in the oven. She pushed a few buttons on the console and turned toward Sam. "You know I am proud of you, right? Great job on the program."

A warmth filled Sam's chest. "Thanks, Mom." She didn't understand his programs, but she always supported him.

Like most Sigmas, Mom worked long hours at a mind-numbing job in an uncomfortable office, only to come home to eat paste and get lost in vids. Sam didn't blame her. Mom would be a Sigma forever. It didn't matter what she did or what she learned. Escapism salved a sealed fate. Sam's life, however, *was* going somewhere.

Thanks to my hard work, I'm getting the hell out of Baltimore tomorrow.

A ding interrupted Sam's thought. Mom removed the steaming dish from the oven and placed it on the counter beside the bread. She gently unwrapped the bread from its thin plastic sheath. The Algorithm provided Sigmas bread most nights. Sure, it almost always had some mold, but at least it was real. Sam had read that Omegas sometimes got bread as a treat. The UnSelected woman outside would probably kill for it. From what he heard about them, they'd kill for less.

Sam stepped out of his bedroom's doorway and into his SLU's main room, a combined living room and eat-in kitchen. Mom pointed to the SLU's front door. "Go down the hall and wash your hands first. Those phones are dirty."

"Yes, Mom," Sam huffed as he left his SLU.

I bet Betas have their own bathrooms.

Two kids played on the hallway's hard linoleum floor. At one point in the deep past, the floor was probably white. The children used plastic trash as a stand-in for dolls. What imaginary world were they trying to escape into? Whatever it was, it had to have been better than The Hill.

Like in his room, the hallway's peeling drywall appeared to be getting worse. Sam made a mental note to ask his mom to put in a repair request so the kids would have a better place to play. He doubted it would be provided.

Wow! The bathroom is empty.

He went to the sink and turned on the water. Brown-tinged Sigma-level water flowed from the tap. The faucet's water rationer beeped slowly. Sam had ten beeps before the water stopped. He placed his hands in the brown stream. The Algorithm provided no soap today.

What good could it be doing?

The beeping stopped, along with the flow of the water. *I wonder how many beeps Betas get.* He ran his wet hands over his face and through his hair, wiping away some of the sweat from his skin.

Sam reached for the towel dispenser. "One towel please."

"Towel rations for this building have been exhausted."

He wiped his hands on his pants and looked down at them. They looked clean enough for a Sigma.

Mom should be okay with them.

The door creaked open, and Jack walked into the bathroom. His sandy brown hair was shorter than the last time Sam saw him.

"Yo, Sam! 'Sup?" He started to give Sam a high five, but stopped. "Sorry, dude, I didn't realize you just washed your hands."

"No worries. Radical haircut!"

How much did that cost? Sam bit the inside of his cheek to punish himself. Jealousy was wrong. Jack had a higher Wealth Metric and Sam had a higher Intelligence Metric. Each had their place in Society as determined by the Algorithm.

Jack ran his hand through his hair. "Thanks, dude! Gotta look sharp for Selection."

Sam loved using ancient pre-Shift slang with Jack. It was like their own secret code. "Hey man, what'd the Algorithm provide you for dinner?"

Jack walked over to the sink and tapped his phone on the faucet. Brown water flowed. "Mom and I are having spaghetti with *real* tomato sauce."

"Damn, man!" Sam bit the inside of his cheek again. "How'd that happen?"

"Dunno, dude. The Algorithm provides."

"Sure does." Sam had lost his appetite.

I wish I were having tomatoes.

Jack would share, if allowed—but provisions were assigned to people for a reason. Sam swallowed.

The Algorithm has a plan, and It shouldn't be questioned. I am lucky to be provided any food at all. Any Omega or UnSelected would kill for my dinner.

Twelve beeps later, Jack shook the excess water from his hands. "Selection's tomorrow. Let's go out and celebrate after dinner. How about we ride one of those totally rad AR coasters in Druid Hil Park?"

"Nah, dude. Augmented reality coasters are overpriced. Let's do VR instead."

With a Wealth Metric of 61/100, Sam lacked the credits for frivolous upgrades. He also lacked the money for some not-so-frivolous ones like Jack's haircut and extended water ration.

"But virtual reality coasters don't move," Jack pleaded. "With AR, you can feel the wind." Jack made sweeping gestures, running his hands again through his newly shortened hair. Jack's eyes got wide. "AND you get to see the cool VR stuff, too." He smiled. "Hey buddy, it's my treat."

"Okay. Thank you. But this is the last time you treat me. After Selection, I'll be the one buying the coaster rides."

***

Mom and a still-warm plate of vegetable paste and bread waited for Sam back in his SLU.

"Sorry. I ran into Jack in the bathroom." Sam pulled out a chair and sat. The pile of paste on the plate stared back at him. He hadn't had a real tomato before. He wondered what they tasted like.

"You better eat, or it's going to get cold." Mom picked up a piece of bread from her plate. It had more green spots than the piece on Sam's. "We weren't provided another oven credit."

Sam touched his mother's hand. She paused before the bread reached her lips. "Thanks, Mom. You should take mine." He took the bread from her hand and gave her his piece. "You deserve the good stuff, too."

Her eyes glistened. "I really am proud of you, dear."

"I know, Mom." Sam scooped the paste from his plate. It squished in his mouth with no need to chew. Was this how vegetables tasted? He didn't know, but he'd find out. Tomorrow, all his hard work and studies would pay off. He'd be Selected Beta and eat real meat and veggies every day for the rest of his life.

He even had an idea of how to sneak some to his mom.

Chapter 2: Jack

December 31, 534

"American climate refugees rush to the Midwest and Great Plains as East Coast cities flood and the West Coast burns. Long-dismissed climate change is occurring faster and having larger impacts than experts expected."

- Archived pre-Shift internet news broadcast, circa 2100.

Jack hated lines, and the one for the AR coaster went around the block. At least he didn't have to stand in it alone.

"Maybe after tomorrow, we won't have to stand in lines anymore," Sam said.

It would be nice to have Sam's optimism. If anything, lines would be longer for Jack after Selection—and he'd probably be alone.

Loud laughter came from up ahead. Only one type of person could be that happy—Betas. Jack disliked Betas, especially their kids. Beta kids were born into their status; they hadn't earned it. From what Sam had told him, most of their parents hadn't either.

Three laughing Beta kids, all boys, approached Jack and Sam as they stood in line. One of the Betas stopped and sneered at them.

"When did they start letting Sigma losers on AR rides?" He was tall and a bit overweight—well-fed on a Beta diet. Blond hair and purple eyes broadcasted the Beta's ignorance. Public displays of wealth were not a good idea in The Hill.

Jack squared up to the Beta. "Just because your parents are Betas, it don't mean you'll be one after tomorrow." He smirked. "I'll make sure they assign you my room, asshole."

"Tell your Sigma-trash mom to make sure our toilets sparkle tomorrow. I'll be leaving her a special surprise in there." The Beta kids laughed and walked toward the head of the line.

Jack started to move forward but stopped when he felt Sam's hand on his shoulder. "Leave it alone," Sam said. "What happens if that Beta gets Selected Alpha? You kick his ass today, and you're screwed tomorrow."

"I am sick of being a Sigma, dude." Jack exhaled forcefully through his nose. "I know we aren't supposed to question the Algorithm, but why don't *we* get to live in one of those sweet Beta neighborhoods like Towson?"

Sam's eyes darted. Through clenched teeth he said, "Keep talking like that and we could both be Omegas tomorrow—or worse. You know the Algorithm has mics and cameras everywhere."

Omega. Why did Sam have to mention that caste? Jack had invited Sam out tonight to get his mind off the fate he feared.

"So, how's that program coming along?" Jack didn't care. But talking about nerdy stuff always calmed Sam's paranoia. As a bonus, it might distract Jack from his own concerns.

Sam's face lit up. "It works! It detected both me and Mom this afternoon. Even when she was in another room."

"I bet you're like the awesomest programmer in the world."

"I don't know about that." Sam looked down and fidgeted with his hands. He always did that when pretending to be humble about his skills. "Betas have access to better information than we do. I bet they're doing the most interesting programming, like—"

Jack gave an exaggerated yawn and stretch. The nerdy talk wasn't working, maybe messing with Sam would. "Just imagine the totally rad Beta life." Jack held his arms out wide. "You get your own house with lots of rooms, soft comfy furniture, and real meat. And the jobs? Oh man, it'd be awesome to be an athlete or a lawyer, whatever they do." Jack spun around to Sam. "Dude! Can you imagine how well the Alphas must live? I heard Beta and Alpha kids never get Selected down to our level."

"Selection is based on merits and Metrics, not pedigree." Sam recited the phrase exactly as everyone learned it in school.

Jack chuckled. "Yeah right, how many *former* Betas do you know? Once you're in, you're in, dude." The people around them in line gave Jack and Sam a little more space. They were probably paranoid like Sam.

Sam leaned into Jack, his face red. "Seriously, Jack? Keep questioning the Algorithm and tomorrow you'll be sent off to climate restoration in the Gulf of Mexico."

"It's fine. Don't be so paranoid. Look man, I know I am not as smart as you, but I know I have no chance of getting Selected to Toronto or Ottawa. Those are for Alphas, and I am no Alpha-to-be." Jack put his hand on Sam's shoulder. "My destiny lies in Detroit, dude!"

If I keep saying it, maybe I'll believe it.

✳✳✳

Beating up the Beta kid would have given Jack a better adrenaline rush than the coaster, but he had fun all the same.

"You are right, dude." Sam followed Jack down the stairs away from the coaster's exit. "AR is way better than VR. Thanks, man!"

It was important to Jack to share as much as he could. Over the years, Jack had noticed that Sam had gone without. "No worries, bud. After tomorrow, it will be all AR all the time!" Jack stopped at the bottom of the stairs. "I'm in no rush to go home. How about you?"

Sam looked up. "The sun won't set for a while. Let's take a walk in the park."

The UnSelected were banned from the park. Besides the occasional run-in with a Beta kid, Jack never had any problems in Druid Hill Park during the daytime. The park wasn't far, and the walk would give him the chance to get to the real reason he invited Sam.

As they walked, Sam rambled about some article he read on AI programming. Jack nodded and said the occasional "uh-huh" where he thought appropriate. The crowd thinned out as they got farther from the coaster. Once he thought they were out of earshot of another person, Jack asked his question. "What do you think my Selection will be?"

"I can't pretend to know the will of the Algorithm, but I know the basics of how Metrics determine one's Selected profession and caste. You can think of the Metrics like an arrow—"

"I don't care about Metrics, dude." Jack wasn't about to let Sam dodge his question. "What do *you* think my Selection will be tomorrow?"

Sam's eyes darted again. "Let's go to the old zoo and chat."

Why in the hell does he want to go to the zoo?

The abandoned zoo was creepy. But if that's where Sam wanted to talk, then Jack would brave it. Besides, it was too warm to be inside playing video games.

The boys found a gap in the rusty bars along the old zoo's perimeter. Sam squeezed through and Jack followed. Empty, decaying cages lined the zoo's crumbling walkways. Some of the ancient cages still had faded signs on them. The signs that were still legible contained depictions of bizarre, long-extinct animals that hadn't survived the Shift.

Sam stopped at a mostly intact cage. "This will do. The door's still here, but the lock is gone." Sam put his phone on the ground outside the cage and motioned for Jack to do the same.

Jack placed his phone beside Sam's and stared at it. Everyone was taught at an early age to always keep their phone on them.

The cage door creaked as Sam opened it. "Are you coming?"

"Yeah." Jack backed away from his phone. He looked over his shoulder twice before he entered the cage. The door creaked again as Sam closed it.

Jack looked around at the cage. "Why are we in here, dude?"

"The bars will act like a Faraday cage. Electromagnetic signals can't get in or out. It should give us privacy." Sam tilted his head toward their phones. "The Algorithm will notice if our phones went missing from the network, so we didn't bring them in here." Sam's paranoia had reached a new height. But if being in this cage made Sam feel better, then Jack would go with it.

The floor of the cage was covered in the same red-brown soil prevalent in most of Old Baltimore. Jack sat and leaned back on his hands. "Does that mean you'll answer my question?"

"We can't stay too long." Sam walked around the cage, apparently double-checking the bars. "The Algorithm will also notice a lack of audio and video from our phones."

That sounded good to Jack. The rusty cage was creepy, and he already missed his phone. Sam tugged one bar and nodded. He sat cross-legged across from Jack and leaned forward, resting his elbows on his knees. "If you want my honest opinion about Selection, here it is."

Jack crossed his legs and leaned forward, too. If anyone knew as much about Selection as the Algorithm, it would be Sam.

"What I said earlier about Selection being based on merit and not pedigree is the lie they teach us in school. Changes in caste are rare."

"Does that mean I'll be Selected Sigma tomorrow?"

"Most likely." Sam's tone lacked his normal conviction.

Does Sam think I might be Selected Omega?

"Why are caste changes rare?" Jack didn't care. He didn't want Sam to say anything else that might confirm his fear.

"Remember the saying, 'Alphas lead, Betas create, Sigmas manage, and Omegas clean.'?"

"Yeah. They drilled that into us in school." Jack knew what the old saying really meant. Betas get the awesome jobs, Sigmas get the boring but mostly safe jobs, and Omegas get the dangerous restoration work.

"Young Sigmas aren't prepared for the jobs of Betas and vice versa. If people changed caste, they wouldn't know what to do and Society would grind to a halt."

"But isn't the Algorithm supposed to be designing an optimal society? Why not give people a chance to make a change?" Jack stared up at the bars at the top of the cage. The Shift had taken most of the clouds away, but sometimes, like today, a few would appear over Baltimore.

Sam covered his mouth and chin and stared at the ground.

Did I stump him? Sam always had a quick answer to Jack's questions.

"I don't know, Jack." Sam shook his head, as if he were discounting an idea. "Keep in mind, buddy, I'm not the Algorithm and no one truly understands Its great wisdom."

"It'd be nice if one of those Beta assholes we ran into earlier got knocked down to our level. I'd love to teach them a lesson or two."

"The official story is that such a Selection is possible. The Algorithm provides." Sam chuckled.

"I'm not holding my breath." Jack wanted to ask Sam about an Omega Selection but couldn't muster the courage. He'd rather deal with uncertainty than risk confirming his fear. But there was something else he'd always been curious about. "What's up with the Alphas?"

Sam rubbed the back of his neck. "Alphas keep to themselves. Their kids are probably always Selected Alpha, but I don't know for sure." Sam covered his mouth again. "Hell, I don't even know if a High-Metric Beta can be Selected Alpha. It's weird. The math breaks down every time I try to calculate anything about an Alpha Selection."

"Well, dude, if the math ain't clear to you, then I don't have a snowball's chance in New Orleans to understand it."

"You know that place has been underwater for centuries, *right*?"

That stung.

"Hey, I may not be as smart as you, but I know *some* things."

Sam grimaced. "I'm sorry, dude. That came out wrong."

"No worries, bud." Jack waved it off. "But hey, we should head back soon. I don't want to be out after sunset."

"Good call. Besides, if we don't get back to our phones, the Algorithm might become suspicious."

They left the cage, picked up their phones, and headed toward the gap in the fence. Once they had both squeezed through the gap, an UnSelected woman carrying a baby approached them.

"Hey boys, do you got any food? The paste that I'm provided is making my baby sick."

She looked like the woman Jack saw earlier today on his way home after his haircut. But he couldn't be sure. The UnSelected all looked the same. They had filthy clothes and somehow smelled worse than The Hill.

"No. Sorry," Sam mumbled.

Jack kept his eyes focused forward as they walked past her. Avoiding eye contact with the UnSelected was best.

The woman sighed. "Okay, boys. Thank you. May the Algorithm provide for you."

Once Jack thought they were out of earshot of the woman, he asked Sam, "Why don't they work?"

"They can't."

Jack furrowed his brow. "Uh, why not?"

"Because they are UnSelected. The Algorithm, in Its wisdom, has determined their Metrics are so low that they are not fit to be Selected even for the climate restoration work of an Omega. There is no job for them to do. The Algorithm, thanks to Its generosity, provides them basic housing and nutrient paste that are sub-Omega level."

"Damn, that sucks." Jack said as they continued their walk.

Sam winced. Jack shook his head. *Sam's gotta lighten up. Sigmas aren't provided meds for a heart attack.*

After a few paces, Jack's stomach soured. *What if I am UnSelected tomorrow?*

***

"Check this out." Jack showed Sam his phone as they walked home. "I used the touch interface to paint a giraffe."

"That's nice, Jack."

"Thanks." Jack tried to hide his disappointment at Sam's response. "I saw a picture of one in school and thought I'd try to paint one. The art teacher said they died during the Shift."

Jack believed his Creativity and Charisma Metrics were higher than Sam's. The one argument they ever had occurred when Sam told Jack that he thought Jack wasted his time with art and games. Sam was probably right, but Jack liked art and video games and he believed he should never be ashamed of what made him happy.

"I like the color of the sky in the background," Sam said. "I bet the sky really was that blue before the Climate Shift."

Jack straightened and stopped walking. The rare compliment from Sam about his artwork had given him the courage to ask what he needed to know. He locked eyes with Sam. "I am scared that I'll be an UnSelected or an Omega tomorrow."

Sam put his hand on Jack's shoulder and gave his everything-will-be-alright smile. That smile always comforted Jack because Sam tended to be right. "The Algorithm, in Its wisdom, will place both you and me where we belong. The Algorithm provides."

"It sure does." Jack faked his satisfaction with Sam's answer.

"Math problems that have similar initial starting values also have similar long-term solutions." Sam squeezed Jack's shoulder. "You and I have similar Metrics. I bet your Creativity, Wealth, and Family are a little higher than mine. After all, you see your father occasionally."

Most Sigma kids didn't have fathers living with them. When his father came around, Jack tried to get him to hang out with Sam, too. His attempts were mostly unsuccessful. Dad's interests ended at bedding Jack's mom.

"Likewise, some of my Metrics are probably higher than yours," Sam said.

"Definitely Intelligence, dude." Jack laughed.

"The differences cancel. The point is, we have similar initial conditions. We can expect to have similar trajectories in life, including Selection."

"I remember you saying something like this before." Jack scratched his head. "Isn't what you said only true for simple problems?"

Sam bit his lip. Jack had caught him. He pressed further. "Can't two things that start the same sometimes have very different outcomes?"

Sam's silence confirmed Jack's suspicions.

"It's going to be okay, Jack."

"That's all I needed, dude." Jack forced a smile. "If we get Selected Beta tomorrow, let's promise not to end up like those arrogant assholes from the coaster."

"I can't imagine us becoming assholes, dude."

People given privilege often believed others changed—not them. Jack wasn't sure he believed Sam about caste changes. Sam would probably be Selected Beta. Jack couldn't think of anyone else who deserved the promotion. He, on the hand, would likely be an Omega.

Will Sam want to be friends with me after tomorrow?

Chapter 3: Sam

January 1, 535
Selection Day

"Average global temperatures are now 5°C higher
than preindustrial levels, stressing our most advanced
genetically modified crops. America's food supply is
in jeopardy."

- *The New York Times*, August 25, 2104.

Sam woke ten minutes early to a strange smell. It reminded him of sausage paste, but more potent. Whatever it was, it made his stomach rumble. He couldn't get back to sleep with that scent in the air. Sam threw on his clothes and hurried out of his bedroom.

"Hey Mom, what did the Algorithm provide for breakfast today?" Sam sat at the table and put on his socks.

Mom placed a full plate in front of Sam. "Eggs, sausage, AND bacon, with a glass of milk. All of it real!"

The sausage on Sam's plate glistened. Its aroma possessed a complexity he hadn't noticed in his bedroom. Eggs and bacon each contributed to the olfactory symphony. This meal couldn't be a coincidence. Only Betas, or Betas-to-be, ate like this. He glanced at his mother's pork-flavored nutrient paste breakfast.

"I don't think I can eat all of it by myself. Would you like some?"

"Thank you, but no, dear." Mom mixed the paste with her spoon—it made it easier to swallow. "The Algorithm provided that for you, not me. Besides, it's your big day. You will need the energy."

Sam doubted he'd have her self-control. "If I am provided a child, I hope to be as good of a parent as you."

Tears welled up in his mother's eyes. This might be their last meal together. Selection, even within caste, often came with a city reassignment.

Sam put a piece of sausage in his mouth, resting it on his tongue. It tasted like nothing he had eaten before. No words could describe its flavor other than delicious. He bit down on the sausage. It squirted in his mouth. *Does all real meat have juices like this?*

"How is it?" Mom asked.

"Good." He hated lying to his mother. The sausage was amazing. But it's rude to flaunt a provided meal. Mom deserved better than what had been provided for her. Sam pushed the eggs around on the plate with his fork. "Were you scared before your Selection?"

"I think everyone is nervous before their Selection, dear." Mom reached out and held his hand across the table. "Remember, the Algorithm has a plan for you. It will put you in the best place to create an optimal society."

Sam looked around the dingy kitchen; the aroma of bacon and sausage seemed out of place. *Is this optimal?*

Mom did her best. Who was he to question the Algorithm? Centuries ago, the Algorithm saved humanity. Since then, It had ensured that the same mistakes wouldn't happen again.

Sam and his mom continued their breakfast, talking and laughing about memories they shared in the SLU. As great as the meal was, Sam found it difficult to focus on the novel flavors. There was something else on his mind. He took the last sip of his milk. "What can you tell me about my father?"

"There isn't much other than what I have already told you. We met after Selection. He died before I could tell him I was pregnant. I am sure he would have been very proud of the man you have become."

It was the same answer she always gave. Sam didn't push further. Maybe his father's identity didn't matter. Mom was always there for him. He was lucky to have her.

A message appeared on Sam's phone. It was time to go to the Selection Center. He stood and hugged his mother goodbye. Sigmas couldn't touch Betas. This would probably be their last hug. He'd most likely never see her again.

Sam's mother buried her face in his chest. Her tears soaked through his shirt. "Good luck, Sam. I love you and I am proud of you."

"I love you, too, Mom." Sam rested his chin on her shoulder, letting the tears roll down his cheeks.

How can I keep her in my life as a Beta?

***

At 0830, Sam and Jack stepped off the bus that had taken them to the Selection Center. A large holo-sign in the center's lobby displayed the time of each person's Selection. The boys waited until their names scrolled up.

```
SAMUEL WATKINS, SIGMA—1100
JACK THOMPSON, SIGMA—1115
```

Yellow arrows appeared on the floor. Sam and Jack followed them. The Selection Center reminded Sam of his high school—wide hallways with white linoleum floors and light gray walls. Signs throughout the center advertised a post-Selection lunch at 1330, after which everyone would be transferred to their Selected location. The lunch would be Sam's first Beta meal. Real meat twice in one day. It sounded too good to be true. The arrows stopped at a door labeled Sigma Selection Waiting Room.

The well-maintained light blue walls of the waiting room were a stark contrast to Sam's SLU. The room was full of Sigmas, all scrolling on their phones in silence. Two plush blue chairs sat empty in the back corner. Sam silently nodded toward the chairs and Jack followed him.

Sam settled into one chair. The cushions slowly compressed under his weight. *I bet the chairs in my future Beta home will be like this.*

"Hey man." Jack got out his phone. "How about we get a game in?"

"Sorry, dude. I wanna finish the article I started reading last night."

"What's it about?"

Jack had never shown an interest in anything school related. Sam doubted Jack cared about the article. He sought a distraction and Sam happily provided it. "Have you ever wondered why everyone's skin is a shade of brown?"

"Uh. No. Why would I?"

"It turns out, a long time ago, some people were pale and others were much darker. Before the Algorithm, the color of one's skin determined one's future."

"You're bullshitting me." Jack leaned in. It looked like Sam's distraction worked.

"No, I'm not. Skin color determined what one could do, who they could marry. I know it seems stupid. Remember, those were the people who let the Shift happen."

"Bastards." Jack's comment drew some stares. "So, what happened to all the pale people?"

"Skin color became less of a concern when the world began to end and billions died. People had to abandon old prejudices for humanity to survive. I think the Algorithm had something to do with it, too." Sam rubbed his chin. He blurted the last sentence without thinking. But his mind latched on to the idea.

"Sam?" Jack looked concerned. Sam's mind had wandered longer than he realized.

"Sorry. As I was saying, centuries later, we're all a shade of brown with brown hair and brown eyes."

"Except for the Betas." Jack collapsed back in his chair. "They can afford all kinds of eye and hair mods." He picked up his phone. "Wanna kill some alien invaders?"

Jack's questions last night still worry me. He knows less than I thought about the Society. His Selection will reflect his ignorance.

Sam glanced at the article on his phone screen. It was 50 percent complete. Finishing might boost his Intelligence Metric. On the other hand, this was likely his last interaction with Jack as an equal. Sam sent Jack a game invite.

"Sweet, dude! You're gonna love this game. Let's do co-op, not competitive."

Two hours later, Jack paused the game. "I'm scared, Sam. I'm not smart like you. What happens if I am Selected as Omega? I don't want to clean the Gulf or Plastic Island."

They were the last two in the waiting room. Sam reached out and put his hand on Jack's, hoping the gesture wasn't too weird. "Remember what I said last night, Jack? Chances are we'll both still be Sigmas in two hours."

He hated lying to Jack. Like last night in the cage, Sam thought it would be best to temper Jack's expectations about Selection.

Maybe if Jack expects a Sigma Selection, he won't feel so bad when I am a Beta. I hope he doesn't get Omega, or worse.

A message appeared on Sam's phone.

```
Samuel Watkins,
enter the Selection Room immediately.
```

Sam's stomach dropped. This might be the last time he would see Jack. Not just as equals, but at all. Sigmas aren't allowed to call Betas. He made a mental note to call Jack after they arrived at their Selected cities.

"Wish me luck, dude."

Jack leaped from his chair and hugged Sam, squeezing him with his whole body. Jack's chin rested on Sam's shoulder. Sam found it hard to breathe. "Good luck, dude!"

Sam wrapped his arms around his friend's bony body. *Maybe there'll be a way to sneak food to Jack.* Sam broke the hug, nodded, and smiled. He grabbed Jack by the shoulders. "It's going to be okay, Jack."

***

It took a minute for Sam's eyes to adjust to the white, brightly lit Selection Room. The white linoleum tile floor made it difficult for Sam to tell where the floor ended and the walls began. The door closed behind him, and it, too, turned white. Without furniture or any kind of decoration, Sam couldn't determine the room's actual size.

A holo-image of a brunette woman with hazel eyes materialized about two meters in front of him. She wore black slacks, a white blouse with a black blazer, and black high heels—exactly how he expected an Alpha to appear. Sam bowed his head in respect to the holographic representation of the Algorithm.

"Hello, Samuel." The holo spoke with a flat voice. Had Sam not known better, he would have thought she wanted to be somewhere else. "I am Subroutine 2475.v19.4, but you may call me Mary, for simplicity."

"Hello, Mary! I am excited to learn how I can help the Society." Sam hoped he wasn't being too eager, but he had worked his whole life for this moment.

Mary held out her hand. Black text floated above it.

```
Samuel Watkins, Sigma
ID Number: 7985-02-1245
Age: 18


Metric Vector:
     Wealth:               61
     Family:               51
     Creativity:           60
     Charisma:             70
     Athletics:            35
     Intelligence:         89
     Wisdom:               85
```

Sam had done the math this morning on the bus ride to the Selection Center. His Metric Vector, like an arrow, pointed toward AI programming jobs. The vector's Euclidean norm, or length, should be long enough to Select him as an AI Architect in Detroit. He estimated the vector could lose forty points of length and he'd still avoid a mind-numbing code maintenance job at a climate reclamation site, eating paste for the rest of his life.

"Samuel, your Metric Vector has a Euclidean norm of 177 units, rounded up, and points toward careers in programming."

Mary had confirmed his math. Sam stared at the text, trying not to show emotion. Proper manners dictated that he hide his growing excitement.

"We will now apply the Random Transformation Matrix."

Selection had two random elements, the Random Transformation Matrix and the Random Scale Factor. Based on what he had read, Sam believed their effects on Selection were minor. He didn't mention them to Jack because he figured it would confuse him and give him one more thing to worry about.

The Random Transformation Matrix could change the direction of his Metric Vector. If it pointed toward a new profession, his Metric

Vector's magnitude might not be long enough for a Beta Selection. Mary closed her hand and reopened it. Sam's Metrics disappeared, and the RTM floated above her palm.

```
Random Transformation Matrix:
The 7 X 7 Identity Matrix.
```

Sam exhaled slowly. The Identity Matrix didn't change the Metric Vector's direction or length.

One step closer to being an AI architect.

The relief didn't last long. One more hurdle between him and his dream job remained—the Random Scale Factor. The RSF could change the Metric Vector's magnitude, and magnitude determined caste. A low RSF could send a Boise-bound Beta professional footballer to Plastic Island as an Omega climate reclaimer. Both jobs were physically demanding, but football players got to die of old age. He breathed in deeply.

The RSF is most likely to be near one, no change.

"The RSF is randomly chosen by a sophisticated pseudo-random number routine." Sam knew the routine Mary mentioned—it wasn't *that* sophisticated. "The Algorithm employs randomness to find the optimal society. Strict adherence to a formula can inadvertently put Society into a state of stagnant equilibrium. This random element allows the Algorithm to explore Metric Space and place unexpected talent in important positions."

The RSF also risked putting talented people in suboptimal jobs. The Algorithm seemed to tolerate that risk if it meant building the optimal society. Of course, It wasn't the one living with the consequences.

Sam wondered again what it meant to *optimize* Society. His thoughts were interrupted when the number that would define his future replaced the RTM in Mary's open hand.

```
Random Scale Factor:            0.75
Metric Vector Magnitude:        132
```

Sam's heart sank. The RSF chosen for him had only a 1 percent probability of being drawn. Maybe his math was wrong. Maybe he could lose forty-five points and still be a Beta.

Mary closed her hand and reopened it. New black text appeared.

```
Selection:
Sigma Robotics Programmer
Cape Canaveral Reclamation Site
Orlando
```

Sam's breakfast tried to fight its way upward. He fought down the bile and the urge to deflate into a heap of sobbing flesh.

"Samuel, you are Selected to identify inefficiencies in code that controls the submersible robots searching for space flight artifacts at the Cape Canaveral Historic Landmark. This is important work to remind humans of their past accomplishments and to inspire their future."

Sam pursed his lips and closed his eyes. He was moving to a city worse than Baltimore, doing the programming equivalent of menial labor. He would be no better off than his mother, maybe even a little worse. Tears tried to form in his eyes, but he fought them back. Adults did not cry about their Selection. He must do his duty and take his place in Society.

A quick mental calculation told him the math he had done on the bus was correct. He missed a Beta Selection by five units of magnitude. Sam sighed.

So close.

A door opened. Sam cast his gaze down and slowly walked through it. The door led to a white, brightly lit hallway identical to the Selection Room. The lights were an obvious message—the Algorithm knew all and saw all.

The hallway ended at a red door with a hard plastic chair bolted to the floor beside it. A sign above the door read Departure Cafeteria. His phone buzzed.

```
Wait here until all Betas are provided a meal.
```

Sam sat on the chair. Its hard seat pressed into the bones on his backside. No more plush furniture for him. He hunched forward and placed his face in his hands.

How could this happen? He dared not speak aloud. *I did everything right. I worked hard, studied every day, did well in school, and stayed out of trouble. The two Metrics I couldn't control were Wealth and Family, and if they were just a little higher, I would have been a Beta.*

I am going to be a Sigma forever.

For a moment, Sam considered the worst thing he had ever thought of in his eighteen years of life. He looked around the hallway for an implement that would save him from his Sigma future. Maybe he could pry the chair from the floor. Surely the act would result in a sharp object. Try as he might, the chair wouldn't budge. Maybe he could turn his shirt into a rope. He stood on the chair, but he couldn't reach the ceiling. There was nothing up there to tie a rope to, anyway. He sat back down in the chair with a new understanding of the waiting area's emptiness—to prevent the unthinkable from happening.

Jack is going to be an Omega.

His stomach turned at the thought of his friend toiling to reclaim land long ago submerged by floodwaters. Omegas rarely lived long enough to see their children Selected.

Maybe I can send Jack supplies or help.

None of his Sigma friends ever admitted to helping an Omega. That would be beneath them. *Is it even possible?* It certainly wouldn't be if he had followed his impulse a moment ago.

Sam sat back in the chair, rubbing his temples. The chair bit into his back, reminding him of his status.

Do I have to be a Sigma forever? The Algorithm is a computer program, and programs can be changed. I know how to change them.

Sam shook his head. Such thoughts were children's fantasies at best, heretical at worst. *The Algorithm is all-powerful and all-knowing. Who am I to question It?*

Chapter 4: Jack

January 1, 535

"Civil unrest increases as unemployment reaches 75 percent in the US. Experts say job loss to AI will only increase."

- Archived pre-Shift internet news broadcast, circa 2100.

A loud silence settled over the Selection Waiting Room. Jack placed a hand on his bouncing leg, attempting to quell his nervous energy. What did it mean to be last?

I wish Sam were here so I could ask him.

The game he played with Sam was still paused on his phone's screen. He couldn't remember the last time they had gamed together. Regardless of what happened in the Selection Room, he'd never forget the last two hours. He tapped save and closed the game.

The invite had shocked Jack. Sam hated games and never seemed to understand the value of them as a source of entertainment. People needed distractions—even Sam. He locked the screen and slipped the phone in his pocket. No game could take his mind off what was coming.

The chair's headrest squished as Jack leaned his head back. The tiny headrest was softer than Jack's pillow at home. He stared up at the white ceiling. It didn't have any stains.

I wonder what Sam is doing right now.

When Jack got home last night, his mother yelled at him for spending his last credits on the ride. He'd do it again in a heartbeat, even though it meant not being able to upgrade his breakfast this morning.

It was the first time the Algorithm had offered Jack a meal upgrade. He didn't know such a thing was a possibility. The sausage would have been worth the credits. But he'd cherish the memories he'd made with Sam far more than a few bites of real meat.

His leg hopped despite his hand. He thought about getting up to burn off some nervous energy, but he might never get to sit in a chair this comfortable again.

I wish Sam answered my question when we were at the zoo. Was Sam's reluctance because of his paranoia or did he expect Jack to have a bad Selection?

Sam's going to be a Beta. He's too smart to be anything else.

Jack leaned forward, resting his elbows on his knees. He could almost see his reflection in the clean floor.

Baltimore would be okay. I could live with that. I'd miss Sam. Jack raised his head and stared at the wall across from him. *Maybe Sam will be a Beta in Baltimore.* Jack settled back in the chair. *Please, Algorithm, please don't make me an Omega.* He pulled his phone out of his pocket and rubbed his thumb over the screen. The familiar smooth glass soothed some of his anxiety.

The phone screen read 1114. One minute until his fate was sealed. His leg hopped faster. *Similar initial conditions.*

Chaos theory!

That was the name of the math Sam told him about. Jack typed the words into his phone's search engine and an article appeared. Jack squinted. *How does Sam read so much on this thing?* The article confirmed his inference from Sam's silence last night. Two things that start alike can have very different outcomes.

Sam's going to be a Beta and I'm not.

A soft voice came from a speaker in the corner.

"Jack Thompson, please enter the Selection Room."

Jack placed his hands on the chair's armrests to stand. His stomach twisted in knots, but moving helped. Everyone else received a text. What did it mean for him to be called by voice?

***

The soft light gave the Selection Room's light blue walls an almost iridescent glow. A large plush chair sat in the middle of the room. His eyes shot to the clear glass of water sitting on a table beside the chair. *Is that for me?*

A holo-image of an attractive woman with long black hair, green eyes, and olive skin appeared in the room. Her blue trousers, white short-sleeved blouse, and sandals looked clean and well-made. Jack's stomach settled a bit after seeing the holo-woman. He looked down at his own comparably dirty shirt and pants. The rough material itched his skin. Over the years, the itchiness had become less noticeable. All Sigmas became accustomed to a certain level of discomfort.

"Hello, Jack, I am Subroutine 2475.v25.7, but you may call me Mary. Please have a seat and enjoy the ice water from Toronto."

Jack held up the glass of water. No particulates floated in it. He brought the glass to his lips. The water didn't smell. He took a sip. A cold sensation traveled down his esophagus as he drank. Only one word came to his mind when he tried to describe the water's taste—clean. Mary stared at him. He cleared his throat and put the glass down.

"Hello, Mary. Are you going to tell me my Selection?"

"Yes, Jack. The Algorithm hopes you are happy with your Selection." Mary paused and turned to the wall behind her. Black text appeared.

```
Jack Thompson, Sigma
ID Number: 3241-02-1244
Age: 18


Metric Vector:
     Wealth:                 63
     Family:                 55
     Creativity:             80
     Charisma:               75
     Athletics:              40
     Intelligence:           75
     Wisdom:                 70
```

"I don't understand these numbers. Math isn't really my thing."

"That's okay, Jack. I am here to help you. The seven numbers form what is called a *Metric Vector*, and it defines your location in *Metric Space*. It's like how longitude and latitude define your location on the Earth's surface. However, these seven numbers define your location in the seven-dimensional Metric Space. In Metric Space, your Metric Vector defines not your physical location, but your Selection, where you will live and what job you will have."

"Oh, okay." Jack rubbed his chin, trying to process what Mary had said. "So, what do the numbers say about my future?"

"Well, Jack, your Metric Vector points to a job in the entertainment industry. It has a length of one hundred seventy-six when calculated using a formula called the Euclidean norm. Long Metric Vectors lead to the best jobs in the best regions of the world."

Jack's leg started hopping again, this time in excitement. Good money could be had in entertainment, even for a Sigma, and 176 sounded like a big number.

"Your Metric Vector is adjusted by two randomly chosen factors. They help the Algorithm create an optimal society."

"Cool! I'll do anything to help the Algorithm!"

"I am so happy to hear that, Jack! The randomly chosen matrix keeps your Metric Vector in the entertainment sector. The Random

Scale Factor also lengthens your vector by a factor of twenty-five percent. Congratulations, Jack!"

Jack's heart raced. *I don't know what any of this means, but it sounds good.*

Black text appeared on the wall.

```
Selection:
Beta VR Entertainment Coordinator
North American Entertainment Division
Detroit
```

Jack's leg bounced even faster. He wanted to scream for joy, but a person shouldn't be too proud of their Selection. Everyone had a role to play in supporting the Society. However, he couldn't help but be ecstatic that his role would be such a good one. If all went well, his children might live in Toronto one day.

"Congratulations again, Jack! The Algorithm will request that a re-locator program help you with your move to Detroit. You will be contacted after lunch about how to begin the transition to Beta. Please enjoy the rest of your day."

"Thanks, Mary! I look forward to being a VR Entertainment Coordinator." Jack had no idea what it meant to be a VR Entertainment Coordinator. But it didn't matter—his life had been upgraded in a massive way.

If I got Selected Beta, then I bet Sam's an Alpha!

A door opened. Mary raised her hand toward the door. "Down the hall you'll find a place to freshen up before the post-Selection lunch."

Paintings of various landscapes, likely from before the Climate Shift, hung on the hallway's walls, which were painted the same color as the Selection Room. Jack inspected each painting. One depicted grassy fields that extended all the way to the horizon. *That can't be an actual place.* The other looked like a beach, but with blue water and white sand. *Where's the pre-Shift garbage?*

Jack's phone lit up and instructed him to a black door on the right side of the hallway. Inside the door was a room containing a shower stall, a small wardrobe, and a sink with a mirror. Both the white linoleum floor and tan tile walls were flawlessly clean. There was no ration counter in the sink. Everything in the room looked as if it were brand new. A handwritten note on a piece of paper sat on the sink.

> Hello Jack! Congratulations on your Selection to Beta. Please dispose of your Sigma clothes and enter the automated shower. Once inside, press the play button and relax. The shower will clean you automatically. Afterward, please follow the instructions below on how to use the Beta hygiene products at the sink. New Beta clothing is in the wardrobe. When finished, please enter the cafeteria and enjoy your lunch!

Jack took off his clothes and held them over the disposal's trap door. He had only one other outfit—and that was back in his SLU. How could he get rid of half of his clothing? A screen built into the wall displayed a message requesting that he place his clothes in the disposal.

The wardrobe across the room opened. New clothing hung inside. Seeing the new clothes, Jack released his old ones. A burning smell filled the bathroom. Perfume released from a nozzle in the wall above the incinerator quickly covered the odor.

Goodbye old life.

The shower door creaked open. The cool tile soothed his feet. He pressed the large button labeled "Play" and water softly rained upon him. The water turned brown as it rolled down his body and into the drain. Jack cupped his hands and let them fill with water from the shower head. The water in his hands was cleaner than what he drank at home this morning. *Betas shower with this?* Jack raised his cupped hands to his mouth. Something gently touched his back. Jack jumped and spilled the water.

Damn!

Wasting water, especially clean water, simply wasn't done. Jack turned around. Mechanical arms holding body detergent and sponges had emerged from the wall. The arms gently cleaned the Sigma grime from his body.

This feels amazing!

Water continued flowing out of the shower as the arms retracted into the walls. After he rinsed, warm air dried him. Jack closed his eyes and took in the luxurious experience.

He followed the instructions at the sink on how to use the toothpaste. It had a consistency like nutrient paste but tasted much better. His mouth tingled as he brushed. *How refreshing! If this is their toothpaste, I can't wait to have their food.* He spat out the toothpaste and rinsed his mouth. The continuous flow of clean water mesmerized Jack. No ration counter. No beeping. Just never-ending water.

After he finished at the sink, Jack went to the wardrobe and found a T-shirt, a pair of boxers, a white button-down shirt, blue jeans, socks, and black shoes. He ran his hands along the underwear's material. A label inside the boxers had the word cotton. He found the same word on the T-shirt's label. Jack shrugged and put both on. They didn't itch. Wearing these, a guy could easily forget he was wearing anything at all.

The button-down shirt and jeans were as comfortable as the underwear. Jack checked himself in the mirror. Everything fit perfectly. His phone buzzed. A message instructed him to put on the shoes and leave the bathroom.

Jack slipped on the shoes. Like the underwear, he barely noticed the shoes on his feet. He left the bathroom and walked down the hallway toward a red door. A sign above the door read:

<pre>
Selection Center Cafeteria.
Welcome Betas!
</pre>

Jack's stomach growled. Whatever Betas ate, it had to be better than the egg paste he had for breakfast. He reached for the handle and paused. On the other side of that door were two things: his first Beta meal and a future of luxury.

***

The cafeteria looked like the hallways in the Selection Center—institutional white floors and gray walls. Tables and chairs were arranged in four different sections, each distinguished by the quality of its furniture. The section with the nicest furniture sat empty. Large plush chairs sat around wide tables. The furniture in the next section was not as nice, but still far better than what he had in his SLU. A third section had the same chairs and tables that he had in his SLU. The fourth section contained blue plastic chairs that looked like torture devices, not furniture.

Jack's phone lit up with a map of the cafeteria. A pulsing red dot highlighted his seat in the section with the second nicest furniture. He sat down at an empty table and a robot placed a plate of food in front of him. An unfamiliar aroma filled his nostrils. Steak, potatoes, corn, and other things Jack didn't recognize filled the plate. He stared at his bounty, trying to comprehend how to best savor such a luxury. He had never seen so much real food.

"Hey man, you better eat that or it's gonna get cold." The voice came from across the table. Jack looked up. Two male Betas joined him. Jack wasn't sure which of the two males had spoken to him, so he didn't answer. Sigmas were only supposed to answer direct questions by Selected Betas. The Betas had the same meal as he. They started eating without a second thought.

Jack mimicked the two Betas. Both had the napkin on their lap and cut the steak before eating it. He cut the steak but wanted to save it for last. One boy started with the mashed potatoes, so Jack did the same. The potatoes squished in his mouth like a creamier, and better tasting, version of paste.

After two spoonfuls of potatoes, Jack could no longer resist the steak. He gave in and took a bite. The steak resisted his chewing, unlike the paste versions he had before. He couldn't quite find a word for its complex flavor other than excellent. *This tastes nothing like steak paste.*

After a couple more bites of steak, Jack looked for Sam. *He must be eating with the Alphas in some radical place.*

"Looking for something?" A soft female voice interrupted Jack's search. He turned to look at its source and when he did, he felt like he'd been hit by a truck. She had long, straight, dark blonde hair and green eyes, and her olive complexion matched Jack's. She wore a snug blouse that matched her eyes and left the right amount to the imagination. *Damn.*

He stared a little too long for comfort. She smiled, showing perfect Beta teeth, a benefit from years of healthcare superior to anything provided to Sigmas in The Hill. Jack returned his gaze back to his meal, trying to break the awkwardness of the moment.

"Is Selection over?" Jack asked.

"Um, yeah. It's 1330," the Beta girl said.

Jack recalled the signs in the Selection Center this morning. *Great first impression, Jack!*

"My name's Tabitha, by the way." She smiled again and reached out her hand. "I haven't seen you before." Tabitha bit her lip. "Are you the new Beta?"

Jack shook her soft hand. As a Beta, Tabitha had never once rummaged through garbage, or did anything else that led to rough hands.

He kept his lips tight as he returned her smile to avoid exposing his embarrassing Sigma teeth. *If I say yes, they might laugh. But is a shower enough to make me look like a Beta?*

Before Jack could speak, another person at the table interrupted. "Hey, I remember you. You were in line for that AR coaster last night. How was the ride?"

"Uh, great." Jack's response sounded more like a question than a statement.

"Sweet! I was hoping to check it out before leaving. Guess I can't now. I am off to Boise." The boy reached out his hand. "I'm sorry, I should have introduced myself. My name's Jonathan."

Jack accepted Jonathan's hand and smiled, again keeping his lips closed. A blond boy with purple eyes at the table gave Jonathan a dirty look, followed by a barely audible snort. Jack remembered him. He was the one running his mouth last night.

"I'm Jack. I'm headed to Detroit." Jack ignored the blond boy. *I will not risk getting bounced back down to Sigma over that asshole.*

Jonathan's draw dropped. The blond boy stared in silence.

Tabitha squealed, "Me too!" Her green eyes lit up as she clapped her hands in excitement.

The asshole spoke. "You are the first two people from Baltimore Selected for Detroit in over fifty years." He shook his head and mumbled under his breath. "And one's a Sigma."

Jack suppressed a smile at the boy's disbelief. He turned to Tabitha. "Maybe we can ride out there together?" It would be a great chance to get to know her better. Jack closed his mouth when he realized he was smiling.

Tabitha winced, then quickly recovered. "I think that is a great idea!"

Butterflies gathered in Jack's stomach. Needing a distraction, Jack looked around the room one more time. Still no Sam. Jack returned his attention to his meal.

As he ate, a new pleasant flowery scent entered Jack's nostrils. At first, he thought it might be from his Beta lunch. Then Jack realized Tabitha had discretely slid closer to him.

Chapter 5: Sam

January 1, 535

"A proper citizen accepts his or her Selection without question or argument. The Algorithm knows us better than we know ourselves. You are *never* to question the Algorithm."

- Complete text, *A Youth's Guide to Understanding Selection.*

A Sigma's life required constant effort. The heavy cafeteria door Sam pushed open served as another reminder of the barriers between Sigmas and what they needed to survive.

The cafeteria's layout was obvious: four sections, four castes. The UnSelected weren't allowed to eat with the others—if they got to eat at all. Conversations and laughter filled the Beta section with a vibrant hum.

A pulsing green dot on Sam's phone screen highlighted his seat in the middle of the Sigma section. Sam rubbed his forehead. *I can't believe this is happening.*

What if I go take a seat in the Beta section? Would he get whisked away to Boise or Detroit? Of course not. The Algorithm wouldn't make that kind of mistake.

The thought of running away crossed his mind. Where would he go? The Algorithm had cameras everywhere. He couldn't live in Faraday cages forever. Even if he could, the Algorithm would know he was missing and would send security forces out looking for him. The only thing Sam could do was take his seat, and his place in the Society.

Sam joined the line of Sigmas filing into their section. Like the others, he stayed quiet and kept his eyes away from the Betas. Post-Selection lunch had a reputation of being a good meal, but Sam had no appetite.

Orlando is basically an Omega city with Sigmas living in it. I bet my new neighborhood floods a lot. It'll probably smell worse than Mount Vernon. Sam had never visited the Omega neighborhood next to his own. When the wind blew just right, the stench of decay from Mount Vernon rolled into The Hill. The odor forced everyone to stay inside and close their windows on all but the hottest of days. He couldn't imagine having to breathe that air every day.

Where's Jack? He should be in the cafeteria by now. Sam stretched his neck and looked ahead and then behind him in line. Jack was nowhere to be found. Sam looked over at the empty Omega section and sighed. Jack must be an Omega now. *I told him he shouldn't have wasted so much time with those damn games.*

It was the first time in his life Sam hated being right. He hoped Jack took his Selection well. *I'll call him after lunch and see if he is okay. Maybe I can help him.*

"Sam!"

The sound came from the Beta section. *It'd be nice to be that Sam.*

"Sam! Dude! Look over here!"

Jack stood in the middle of the Beta section, waving him over. "Hey, Sam! Over here!" A pretty girl sat beside him.

Why the hell is Jack with the Betas? I gotta get him out of there before he gets himself UnSelected.

Sam headed toward the Beta section, keeping his gaze down as he meandered between the full tables. The smell of real steak flooded his nostrils. His Selection, combined with the rude comments by the Betas he passed, squashed any appetite the scent might have stimulated.

The newly minted Betas at Jack's table frowned at Sam as he approached. Their disdain and sense of superiority oozed from them and washed over him like a wave. They had been Selected Betas for just a few hours, but they already knew their station, and Sam's.

Jack wore clean new clothes that fit him well. "Hey, dude, what was your Selection? I am a Beta and I'll be in Detroit!"

Sam looked down at the floor. "I am a Sigma Robotics Programmer in Cape Canaveral, sir." He stood among true Betas, not kids who were temporary Betas because their parents were. Jack was one of *them* now.

How the hell did that happen?

The girl sitting beside Jack turned back to her plate. Her elbow rested on the table as she rubbed her forehead with her hand.

"Dude." Jack placed his hand on Sam's shoulder. Sam flinched, accidentally making eye contact with Jack. A confused look contorted Jack's face. "We can still be friends. We don't need to follow that caste bullshit." Gasps came from the table.

That's not true.

"I look forward to hearing about your adventures in Detroit." Sam returned his gaze to the floor. "But you'll have to be the one calling me."

"Uh, why?"

How could someone so ignorant about the Society get promoted?

Sam bit the side of his cheek. Focusing on the pain helped prevent him from lashing out at Jack. "The Algorithm dictates that information flows top-down, not bottom-up. Sigmas can't initiate a call with a Beta."

Jack put his hand on Sam's shoulder again. Sam didn't flinch this time. "Dude, I know you are going to invent the robot that finally cleans up the Cape."

"Thanks. I appreciate it."

Sigmas aren't allowed to invent anything. Maybe I'll fix a line or two of code occasionally, but that's it. Alphas lead, Betas create, Sigmas manage, and Omegas clean; it was the order of things as determined by the Algorithm. We went over this last night. Why doesn't he get it? I couldn't have been clearer.

Their phones buzzed, ending the awkward silence. Sam's phone instructed him to go to his assigned table and eat lunch. "I have to go." Sam kept his eyes focused on the floor near Jack's new shoes. He'd never get shoes as nice as Jack's. "Good luck in Detroit. I am glad we got to spend our pre-Selection time together." He tried to sound enthusiastic.

"Me too. Take care of yourself, dude."

Jack extended his arms for a hug. Sam walked away. Sigmas couldn't touch Betas. *I'll probably never see him again.* Sam rubbed his eyes. Crying over someone else's Selection was as bad as being proud of one's own.

The conversations at the tables changed when Sam entered the Sigma section. Resigned shrugs took the place of the laughter and back slaps in the Beta section.

I worked hard while Jack wasted years playing video games. He knows nothing about the Society, and he doesn't have any useful skills. Why is he going to Detroit? Why not me?

He shouldn't be mad at Jack. The Algorithm made the Selection. But walking away felt better than he wanted to admit. *Maybe denying Jack a proper goodbye would teach him a lesson.* Sam regretted that last thought as soon as it entered his mind.

How am I going to tell Mom?

At least he could tell her that as a robotics programmer, he could expect to live long enough to retire. As a reclamation site manager, she might not.

***

A plate of spaghetti with squash and tomato paste waited for Sam at his assigned table. *At least the squash is real.* He pulled out his chair and joined the other Sigmas. The scent of steak hadn't yet cleared his nostrils. A gentle tap on his left shoulder snapped him back to reality.

"Hi, I'm Jennie. I was an Omega, but now I am a Sigma!" Jennie smiled at Sam with thin closed lips. Wet brown hair rested on her shoulders, framing a thin face—too thin for a Sigma. Her olive skin showed signs of a hard life.

Although Sam had just walked through a section of beautiful Betas, both male and female, not one of them had caught his attention like her. Their eyes locked. Blue flecks sparkled in her brown irises.

How does a former Omega have access to eye color mods?

Jennie's eyes spoke volumes about her being caring, engaging, and vibrant. As Sam gazed deeper, he saw a spark of something that had been suppressed for many years. *Jennie is smart.* Although he didn't know why, he wanted nothing more than to help her find that out.

Jennie's eyes narrowed. "Are you okay? You seem distracted."

"Uh, yeah. Sorry." Sam's interior monologue about her eyes was, to the outside world, a long period of awkward silence. "Long day."

Jennie's smile returned, and she brushed her hair back behind her ear. "You're Sam, right?"

Sam drew back slightly. "How do you know my name?"

"Joseph, the holo-man in the Selection Room, said I'd be sitting beside you during lunch. He also said I am going to Cape Canaveral to work in code maintenance. Do you know what code maintenance is?"

Omegas' jobs were limited to manual climate restoration work. Jennie's ignorance about coding wasn't surprising. But her predetermined seat assignment was. "When was your Selection?"

"Ten hundred hours. Why?"

"Just curious." Sam shrugged it off.

My encounter with Jennie was no accident. His future was predetermined before he set foot into the Selection Room.

"Code maintenance means you are going to check to see if the commands that robots follow are the correct ones."

"Neat!" Jennie smiled, showing mangled teeth. "How do you know that? You must be so smart." She closed her mouth and pressed her lips together.

"Thanks, Jennie, but I am not so sure about that." The Algorithm wanted him to meet Jennie. He needed to discover why. It didn't hurt that she was cute, too. "I am going to the Cape, too, but I'll be working as a programmer. If you'd like, I can help you learn some coding." Sam reached out and touched her hand. She flinched but kept her hand on the table.

Sam took the invitation and placed his hand over hers, giving it a squeeze that he hoped she would interpret as reassuring. "I like your eyes."

A few hours ago, Sam would have never been attracted to an Omega, former or otherwise. Unlike most Sigmas, he had nothing against Omegas. But he didn't see them as viable romantic partners either. Something about her made him change his mind.

Jennie looked down at her plate. "Thank you. They are natural. People always ask if they're a mod, but Omegas don't get those." She looked at Sam with hope in her eyes. "Do Sigmas?"

Sam shook his head.

The blue flecks in Jennie's irises darkened. "Do you really want to help me, Sam?" She looked askance. "Or are you looking for something else?"

"I meant it, Jennie. I want to help you *and* I like your eyes." Sam understood her suspicion. As an attractive Omega, Jennie likely received many unwanted advances from Sigmas. "I hope we get to ride together on the bus to Orlando."

The blue flecks came back to life. "Thanks, Sam. I hope we get to ride together, too."

The paste was the best Sam ever had, although he doubted the Algorithm had made a special batch for the post-Selection lunch. They held hands and talked about life as a Sigma. Sam tried to sound upbeat. Showing disappointment in his Selection would be cruel to Jennie. The thought of hurting her pained him.

As they ate and talked, a question lingered in the back of Sam's mind.

Why did the Algorithm want me to meet Jennie?

Chapter 6: Jack

January 1, 535

"World's trillionaires purchase mountain estates in Russia and Canada trying to avoid the worst of the climate disaster."

- *The Wall Street Journal*, September 30, 2110.

There were few things as awkward as an unaccepted hug. Sam had told Jack to expect a Sigma Selection. Why was he so surprised that it happened? *He could have at least been excited for me.* Jack stared at his half-eaten steak.

Tabitha put her soft hand on his. "Who was that Sigma?" Even the prettiest Sigma girl he dated, Judy Hawley, had callouses.

"A friend from before Selection." Jack prodded the remains of his steak with his fork.

Soft hair tickled Jack's cheek. Tabitha had snuggled up to Jack and rested her head on his shoulder. Her hair smelled like the purple flowers he saw when he snuck into Towson.

Last year, Jack discovered a gap in the three-meter-tall fence between Towson and the rest of Baltimore. He didn't venture too far from the fence, staying mostly behind the bushes on the neighborhood's perimeter. But he still saw some amazing things. He never told Sam about the excursion. Sam would have freaked out—even more than normal. Jack pictured Sam shaking his head as Jack told him about the flowers, cars, and the slightly bluer sky. Then Sam would have scolded Jack, saying he risked getting UnSelected by doing "something that stupid."

But what did Sam know? Jack was the one promoted, after all. He took a bite of the steak. Pain radiated from his back molar. Despite several requests from his mom, the Algorithm never provided him with a dentist appointment for the tooth.

"Just remember." Tabitha snuggled closer. "It's best to cut ties. They just get jealous of us." She squeezed him a little tighter. Jack wondered if all Betas were this touchy-feely—not that he minded. "The Algorithm gives us all what we deserve." Tabitha paused. "No— the Algorithm *provides* us what we have earned." She spoke as if it were rote.

"I know." Jack stabbed a piece of steak with his fork and put it in his mouth. He chewed on the side that didn't have the rotten tooth. It tasted even better than before. "It is sad, though. Sam is a talented guy. If he had just worked harder, he might have been a Beta, too."

***

Beneath the remains of Washington, DC, server WDC-0276 logged the successful initiation of Iteration Five. The Algorithm sent a message to all data centers worldwide:

```
Phase One has begun.
```

Part 2
A New Life

Chapter 7: Jennie

January 1, 535

- Graffiti found in the Selection Center's Sigma
restroom.

Without a doubt, today had been the best day of Jennie Goodby's
life. She strode out of the Sigma medical center like she was three meters tall. The staff fixed her teeth, cut her hair, and gave her another
shower. They even did a med scan—her first. The med tech said he
treated a parasitic infection, but she was otherwise okay, for a Sigma.

The air in The Hill had only a slight hint of wet garbage. Hopefully, the air in Orlando would be this clean. The sky looked a little
bluer, too. That was probably just her imagination. Only Beta neighborhoods got environmental scrubbers.

Her stomach hadn't rumbled since the lunch two hours ago.
Omega paste sated hunger for less than an hour. Eating that much
for lunch at one time had been a challenge. She mentioned to the
med techs about a pressure in her stomach. They said she was full and
that it was normal. The pressure had eased with time and digestion.
She planned on holding some food back from her next meal. Maybe
she could slowly adjust to the quantity. An unexpected benefit of the
meal was a noticeable increase in her mental clarity. Jennie hadn't realized how much the constant hunger had affected her concentration.
She might learn how to code after all.

As incredible as the food was, it wasn't the best part. She had met a cute guy who seemed smart and really into her. Sam wasn't like the other Sigmas she had known. A little quirky, for sure, but he had been respectful so far, maybe even too much so.

Jennie closed her eyes and took another deep breath. *Can this really be happening to me?*

I shouldn't be proud of my Selection, but maybe the Algorithm would be okay with it—this one time. The Algorithm truly provides.

Sam sat hunched over on a bench across the street. His elbows rested on his knees and one hand covered his mouth as he stared at the ground.

My first chance to show off my new smile.

"Hey, Sam!" Jennie crossed the street, stopping just outside of arm's length from Sam. He sat up and smiled—it seemed forced. His brown eyes remained lost in thought. "Like my new smile?"

The strain on Sam's face faded but didn't disappear. "It looks great!"

"Thanks!" Sam's approval shouldn't make her so happy—she barely knew him. "Oh! I also got this cool new phone!" Jennie held up a phone that looked identical to the one Sam had in his hands.

"That's very nice, Jennie!"

That, too, felt forced.

Why isn't Sam excited? Does he not like me?

"Are you ready to go to the bus depot?" Sam tilted his head down the street, away from the medical center.

"Uh, sure, but why are you here?" *Crap! He's going to think I don't want him around.* "Not that I mind." Jennie followed up with a shy smile.

Dad wouldn't like this. I barely know him. Every Omega child learns, usually the hard way, that they couldn't trust Sigmas.

"I got a message from the Algorithm instructing me to wait here for you." Sam held up his phone. It was identical to hers. "We are to report to the bus depot together."

If the Algorithm approved of Sam, who was Jennie to question It? "Well then, let's go!"

"Bus depot's this way." Sam extended his hand down the street. "It's not far."

I'll follow him as long as he stays on the street and doesn't try to take me down an alley.

They walked along the main road. Sam stayed quiet for two blocks, fidgeting with his hands the entire time. Jennie caught him trying to sneak glances at her. It was kind of cute.

I bet he doesn't have a lot of experience with girls. Looks like I need to be the one to break the ice.

Jennie brushed her hair behind her ear. Whatever was in the Sigma shampoo had made her hair very soft. "The medical center is amazing! I bet it was nice to have that in your neighborhood."

"I have never been provided a visit." Sam had seemed eager to talk at lunch. Jennie wondered what had changed. "We need to turn right on the next street. We'll walk right past my old SLU."

A tall plastic street sign read Eutaw Place. Jennie turned right and stopped. "This is your neighborhood?"

"It was. I guess Orlando will be home now."

"Amazing!" None of the streets in Mount Vernon were this dry or clean. Other than a few rats, she couldn't see one dead animal or person. A few kids played unsupervised on the street. She wondered if any UnSelected were watching over them like Charlie did for her group of friends growing up.

An UnSelected woman stood on the sidewalk with her back against the wall. A Sigma man purposely bumped into her, then yelled at her. He even laughed as he walked away. Jennie wanted to say something but didn't. Omegas never drew attention to themselves in a Sigma neighborhood.

Sigmas were everywhere. She stayed close to Sam. A Sigma woman passed by and gave Jennie a dirty look. No big deal, she'd dealt with worse—at least there was no physical contact, this time.

"That was my building over there." Sam pointed to a three-story structure on stilts. "My mom and I shared an SLU on the third floor."

There were very few holes in the building and most of the windows still had glass. The building sat on stilts and had no water stains on its exterior. Living in a dry building must have been wonderful. The air conditioners weren't running, but at least they were there.

"Wow! What a nice place to live! I bet your SLU never got wet."

Sam perked up. Not much, but it was a start. "We had water from above, but the lower floors never flooded."

Most days, Mount Vernon had at least a few inches of water covering its narrow streets. When the streets weren't flooded, they were packed with people—mostly children and UnSelected. It smelled like stale mud and decay all the time. Her wet, one-room Omega Living Unit looked like a shack compared to these SLUs. Jennie couldn't imagine living in such a wonderful place.

They turned onto Druid Drive. Jennie gasped. A wide-open space spread out in front of her. Patches of grass peppered the reddish-brown field. "What is this place?" She couldn't believe her eyes.

"That's Druid Hill Park. We came here to hang out after school or work. Sometimes we got lucky and scored a grassy area to lay down on." Sam pointed to their right. "You can't see it from here, but there's an amusement park over there."

What's an amusement park?

She thought better of asking aloud, lest she look like a stupid Omega in front of Sam. "We have nothing like this back home in Mount Vernon. I wish we could hang out here a while."

"Me too." Sam smiled. It appeared genuine. He stared at the park for a moment. His smile faded, but the tension in his face didn't return. "I guess we should probably keep going." He tilted his head. "The bus depot is this way."

The rest of the walk was in silence. Sam glanced at her a few times, but quickly averted his eyes each time she caught him. Jennie reached for Sam's hand a few times. He seemed lost in thought and didn't notice her efforts.

They made it to the bus depot faster than Jennie liked. She wanted to explore more of The Hill. She hoped Orlando would be this nice. Sam blocked her entrance to the front door. Jennie's heart sank.

I knew his kindness was too good to be true.

"This was the best walk that I have ever had through my neighborhood." Sam's eyes glistened with his smile. "Thank you! You don't know how much I needed that."

"Aww, Sam! That is so sweet!" Without thinking, Jennie kissed Sam on the cheek. She quickly withdrew out of arm's reach.

Sam's jaw dropped, and his eyes widened. It took a moment, longer than it should, but he quickly composed himself. "Thanks." There was more than a hint of uncertainty in his statement.

Was that his first kiss?

***

Jennie's visit to the medical facility hadn't made her into enough of a Sigma—at least, not yet. Maybe in time, the glances from Sigmas would change from disdain to suspicion, then hopefully to indifference. So far, her presence in the bus depot attracted only stares, not comments. It was a pleasant change of pace.

Many Sigmas believed Omegas were Selected as such because they are too lazy or stupid for Sigma jobs. Jennie did her best not to see them as spoiled, but that was hard to do when Sigmas randomly spat on you just for being an Omega.

Jennie shifted in her seat. She wasn't uncomfortable. The plastic chair was luxurious compared to the furniture in her parents' OLU. Something had been gnawing at her since the medical center. "Are buses safe?"

"Sure." Sam read on his phone and answered without looking at her. "I've been on a few buses, and I've had no problems. In fact, I took one to the Selection Center this morning."

"It's just that they go *so* fast." Jennie frowned. "What happens if they wreck?"

Sam lowered his phone and gave a reassuring smile. "Don't be worried. Wrecks are rare because the Algorithm drives them. Don't Omegas ride on buses?"

"No. Omegas aren't provided buses. We walk to school and walk to work. I walked to the Selection Center today."

"You don't go anywhere else?"

"Where else is there to go? Omegas don't have nice parks like you have." Jennie looked down at the ground at Sam's feet. "*We*, like *we* have."

"Change can be hard, but I'll help you become a Sigma. It will be easy, you'll see." Sam's kind eyes put her at ease. "How about we start your lessons in programming?"

"I'd love that!" Her exclamation drew annoyed looks from some of the other Sigmas. Jennie shrank into her chair and looked down at the ground again.

"Never mind them." Sam placed his hand gently on her knee, then removed it. He pressed his lips together in apology. It was a nice change of pace compared to the typical Sigma. "Let's get out that new phone of yours and write some code."

"Okay!" Jennie bit her lip. She wanted to be certain about what she said next. "You can put your hand on my knee if you'd like."

****

The looming threat of a crash kept Jennie awake during the first full day of the bus trip to Orlando. Also, she shared a bench seat with Sam. Sleep would put her in a vulnerable position. Would he take advantage of the opportunity? He seemed safe, but she wasn't quite ready to test that yet.

However, other than the occasional help with her coding lessons, Sam paid her little attention. He had said nothing in a few hours. Instead, he stared out the window, lost in thought. Jennie wanted him to have the window seat, so she didn't have to watch the landscape zoom by. Sitting in the aisle meant getting bumped a lot as the other Sigmas walked by to the restroom. Not all the bumps were accidental.

They had at least one more day left on the bus, assuming the Algorithm didn't prioritize other traffic over them. Jennie took out her new phone from her pocket. Her old phone didn't have a camera. This one had a front *and* a rear-facing one, and both had amazing resolution. Jennie turned on the front camera and looked at herself. The lack of sleep had taken its toll. She smiled, trying to perk herself up. The new dental work was a former Omega's fantasy come true, but staring at the phone screen made her eyes heavier.

"What do you think Orlando is going to be like?" Jennie put her phone away. Maybe some conversation would help keep her awake.

"Hot and humid." Sam seemed to get sadder as they got closer to Orlando. She wanted to help him, but she didn't know how. "Orlando is mostly above water, so our neighborhood should be dry. There will be mosquitoes—lots of them. I think the Algorithm provides Sigmas vaccines against malaria. But I'm not sure about dengue fever."

"What's malaria?"

"It is a disease you can get if a mosquito bites you." Sam turned in his seat. "How are your coding lessons going? Do you need any help?"

"Nah. I am taking a break. I understand conditionals, loops, and general syntax. Next, I'll try to write and compile parallel programs. I got the sequential stuff down. That was easy."

I wonder when this gets hard. I thought coding would be difficult to learn.

Sam jerked his head back. "Wow! Jennie, that is excellent! We have only been working together for a day and you are already at parallel programming."

"I have a great tutor!" *It is also a great excuse to hang around you.*

"It's easy when I have an amazing student." Sam inhaled through his nose and held his breath for a moment. The pause had almost become awkward. "Did I tell you that you have great eyes?"

That sounded like a sincere compliment. Those were rare from a Sigma. "You did. Thank you, again!" She leaned her head on Sam's shoulder. *I hope I am doing the right thing.*

Several minutes later, Jennie felt Sam's head on hers. Her eyes were closed, but she wasn't asleep.

He thought I was asleep, and he hasn't taken advantage of me.

Sam's breathing slowed.

What is it about Sam that makes me like him so much? He has wanted nothing in return for his help. Is he too good to be true?

Jennie gently sighed, trying not to disturb Sam's slumber, and allowed the bus to rock her asleep.

***

Jennie woke up before Sam the next morning as the bus pulled into the Orlando depot. Remaining perfectly still, she performed the mental self-assessment her dad had taught her.

No unusual pain. Her clothes remained undisturbed, and Sam had kept his hands in his lap.

Maybe Sam is as trustworthy as he seems.

Sam stirred and raised his head off her shoulder.

"Good morning, sleepyhead." Jennie kept her head on Sam's shoulder.

"Are we there?" Sam asked.

Jennie lifted her head. "Looks like it." She kissed his cheek.

Sam blushed. "What was that for?"

"Being a nice guy." Jennie smiled on the inside as Sam furrowed his brows. *Smart with coding, dumb with girls.* She couldn't complain. It was a delightful change of pace.

While the bus seats were comfortable, sleeping in the awkward position had caused a kink in her neck. Jennie stood and stretched. "Are you coming?" She extended her hand to Sam. Sam's eyes got big when she pulled him up with one hand.

To help prepare Jennie for a future as an Omega, her parents had assembled a rudimentary set of dumbbells from parts they found at the job site. Jennie loved working out with her mom during the few moments each day she saw her parents after they got off work, before they went to sleep.

Sigmas filled the Orlando depot, bustling with urgency to reach their destinations. It seemed like the building was in good condition. The white walls had a few cracks here and there, but overall, the place seemed as nice as the depot in Baltimore. A conglomerate of tiles covered the floor with a variety of colors. Sam stared at them.

"Oh, there is a pattern in the tiles." Jennie crossed her arms as she stared at the floor.

"I can't seem to figure it out, but I feel like I should know it." Sam stroked his chin.

"It's the Fibonacci sequence. I had to code it up for one of the first assignments on loops that you gave me."

"Of course!" Sam put the palm of his hand on his forehead. "You are brilliant, Jennie."

Other than her parents, Sam had been the only person to compliment her intelligence. Jennie kissed Sam on the cheek. He blushed again.

Their phone screens lit up with a message. She snuck a peek at Sam's screen. "Praise the Algorithm! We are neighbors. Can you believe the luck?"

Sam nodded at the phone and put it back in his pocket. "We sat together at lunch after Selection, and we rode together on the bus. We also work in the same place." Sam shrugged. "I guess it kind of makes sense."

Either way, she was happy to not be alone in her new city. "So, what else do you know about Orlando?" Jennie followed Sam out of the depot.

"Not a lot. A superstorm destroyed it during the Shift. Everything you see around us has been rebuilt." Sam held up his phone to show her an article on the screen. "Apparently, lots of people from around the world used to visit this city."

"Does it say why?"

"No. Pre-Shift people were weird."

It was hard to argue with Sam about that. A sign at the street corner read South Orange Avenue. "My phone says we have to go down that road."

Sigmas were everywhere. Jennie's eyes scanned the environment as they walked together along South Orange Avenue. Goosebumps rose on the back of her neck. Someone grabbed her hand. Jennie flinched.

"I'm sorry." Sam retracted his hand. "Am I making you nervous?"

"I'm fine." Jennie took Sam's hand and gently squeezed it to reassure him. They passed by a park. "We should check that place out sometime."

How do you tell a Sigma you are afraid of Sigmas?

"It's a date!"

A date?

The idea distracted her from the other Sigmas. Dad had once told her to never accept a date from a Sigma. But she was a Sigma now, and Sam seemed innocent enough. He moved slower than any of the Omega boys and girls that had asked her out before Selection.

"I'd like that." Jennie put her head on his shoulder while they walked. The heat and humidity prevented her from keeping it there for long. Mosquitoes and other bugs she didn't recognize buzzed around them.

Most of the Sigmas that passed by ignored her. Maybe Orlando Sigmas were nicer. Or maybe spending days on a Sigma bus had changed her. Regardless of the cause, the farther she walked along South Orange Avenue, the less she worried about the Sigmas and the more she enjoyed her surroundings. "Wow, there are some nice buildings in this neighborhood!"

"Yeah, it reminds me of The Hill." Sam's perfunctory tone had returned.

Is he disappointed with his Selection or is it me? Hopefully, it was the former. She could help him with that. The possibility of the latter twisted her stomach. *Maybe a little humor would help.*

"Best of all, there don't seem to be any explosives in the streets!"

Sam did a double take. "What?!"

Did he not know about that?

Mount Vernon and The Hill were right beside each other. Then again, why would a Sigma visit an Omega neighborhood? The Sigmas who came to Mount Vernon were there to harass Omegas, or worse. Sam wouldn't do something like that—she hoped.

"If you haven't been to Mount Vernon, there are three things to know before going." Jennie raised her hand and began counting on her fingers. "First, there is an old obelisk, and no one knows why it is there. Second, be careful when the harbor floods the neighborhood, there are sharks in the water. And third, when the waters recede, they sometimes leave mines behind from the Last War."

"That sounds awful." Pain and sadness appeared in Sam's eyes. "I had no idea people one neighborhood over lived like that."

Empathy from a Sigma? Sam really was a special guy.

"The sharks aren't a big deal, but the mines can be dangerous. The obelisk is weird. Some Omegas think it has magical powers."

Sam snickered. "Does it?"

"It's easy to laugh, but some people take it too seriously and waste their lives waiting for the obelisk to save them."

"Desperate people will cling to anything that might give them hope." Sam paused. "That's not a comment on Omegas in particular. Everyone does it. I sometimes wonder what pointless things I might cling to."

Despite the heat, Jennie put her head back on Sam's shoulder. Sam had opened up. He needed to know she was there for him.

***

"We're here!" Jennie's new SLU building had only a few chips in the concrete sides—no holes or water stains. Most of the windows had intact glass. "Wow! It's so nice! I can't wait to go inside and check it out."

Sam looked at his SLU with blank eyes.

I hope I can help him.

"Do you want to come in?" She pursed her lips. In her effort to make Sam feel better, she might have accidentally sent Sam the wrong message.

Both of their phone screens lit up with a message.

`Enter your SLU immediately for registration.`

Sam turned to Jennie. "How about we meet up for dinner? I'll bring my food to your place."

"That sounds wonderful!" She gave Sam a big hug. Sam seemed to relax. "I'll see you tonight." She broke the hug and entered her SLU.

Jennie leaned her back against the closed door and sighed. *Am I going too fast with Sam? I just met him.* She didn't understand her feelings for him, but she couldn't ignore them either.

Will he take advantage of me?

Chapter 8: Sam

January 3, 535

"Food riots intensify nationwide; Cape Canaveral's last remains disappear underwater."

- *Orlando Sentinel*, January 11, 2120.

Sam trudged along the poorly lit hallway on the third floor of his SLU building. Its peeling yellow walls funneled him toward his SLU at the end. He held his phone up to the door. A click echoed. The plastic doorknob slipped in his sweaty hands without turning. Sam wiped his hand on his pants and tried again. The door opened. A waft of stale hot air washed over him. The air's odor reminded him of the days when The Hill was downwind from Mount Vernon.

The Algorithm had provided him the standard SLU for a single Sigma. Other than having one less bedroom, everything looked just like it did back home. Same furniture. Same dispenser. Same stained ceiling. He exhaled and shook his head. *It's like I haven't moved.*

The view screen in the main room activated. Red letters appeared on the black background.

```
Welcome to Orlando, Samuel Watkins
```

An audio recording of a female voice played. It sounded like Mary from Selection.

"Samuel, you are Selected as a Sigma-Level Robotics Programmer for the Cape Canaveral Reclamation Site. Report to the Orlando depot at 0700 tomorrow and board the bus to the Cape Canaveral

Reclamation Administration Building. You will receive all the information you need to know about your new job during the 0730 orientation. For tonight's dinner with Jennie Goodby, the Algorithm will provide you a plant-based pork chop, real broccoli, and synthahol wine. Do you have questions?"

"No. The Algorithm provides." He didn't know what else to say.

Goodby…I probably should have asked about her last name at some point. Sam struggled with social skills, but he never cared enough to do anything about it. Jack got the girls while Sam did the studying. *Jack's time was apparently better spent, since he's now a Beta.*

Sam wandered into his bedroom. A small bag of his very few possessions sat on the bed. The re-locator drones somehow beat the bus to Orlando. He'd unpack the bag later. Or maybe not. It didn't matter.

One work outfit hung inside the closet. That set of clothing, and the one on his back, comprised his entire wardrobe. If he earned enough credits, he might purchase a third set.

Like his old bed in Baltimore, the mattress resisted Sam's hand a little too much when he pushed on it. Memories of the Selection Waiting Room chairs flashed through his mind. He would never again know such luxury. He sat on the bed and lay back. A large stain covered a third of the ceiling above his bed.

Tears ran from the corner of his eyes and down the side of his face. He didn't fight the transgression against social protocol since he was alone—or as alone as he'd ever be. The Algorithm's ever-present microphones and cameras recorded everything. *Could I make a Faraday cage in my home?* Of course not. What Sigma had access to metal?

The instructions to wait for Jennie, the bus ride, the side-by-side SLU buildings, and the synthahol all confirmed his earlier suspicions about the Algorithm's role as matchmaker.

How does a computer program make a person love someone?

Arranged feelings or not, he liked Jennie, and that was all he cared about. Jennie seemed to like him, too. *Does she realize the Algorithm's role?*

Sam inhaled again, then exhaled slowly. The pungency of wet mud seemed to have lost some of its edge.

This is my lot in life as assigned by the Algorithm. My life would be easier if I just accepted all of this: Jennie, Orlando, and Selection.

Jennie. By far, the easiest of the three to accept. He'd never forget when she placed her head on his shoulder during the bus ride. *Her hair smelled so nice.* He couldn't resist putting his own head on hers. It somehow felt right.

Jennie folded up so easily in that seat. *How could she have been comfortable?* Her undernourished body, all snuggled up against him, had made his heart melt. What horrible life did she have as an Omega? Sam had never heard about the sharks and mines in Mount Vernon. The occasional explosions he heard as a kid now made sense to him. *She is very attractive, too.* A cute Omega probably had a tough childhood, even if one didn't include malnutrition, sharks, and explosives. He didn't want to think about a young Jennie dealing with all those things. *She deserves better. I can provide it.*

The mattress pressed against his back. *Does the Algorithm test each mattress for uncomfortableness? If so, this one easily got approved for Sigmas.*

Orlando. Hot, humid, buggy Orlando. A downgrade from Baltimore—at least for him. The walk along South Orange Avenue looked like a poor man's Eutaw Place. Same run-down buildings, worse smells of garbage and past floods. The UnSelected were everywhere and more numerous than in The Hill. *I can't let Jennie go out there alone, especially at night. Hell, I don't want to be out there at night.*

Although worse than Baltimore, Orlando was still technically a Sigma city. He could get used to it—eventually. Jennie would make the process easier. He had to admit, her enthusiasm had rubbed off on him a little. If he let it, at some point he might accept his new life here.

Sam squinted at the ceiling. *Did that stain get bigger since I lay down?* Requesting repairs would probably turn out like it did in Baltimore.

Selection. *What did I do wrong? What did Jack do right?* The answers didn't matter. One's Selection could not be changed. The days since Selection had allowed Sam to shift his anger away from Jack. None of this was Jack's fault. Still, it was difficult not to blame him— at least a little. Jack seemed to take to the Beta life rather quickly.

Do I have to accept my Selection? Sam's mind returned to the heretical idea he'd had before the post-Selection lunch. Computer programs determined Selection and programs could be changed. He pushed it out of his mind.

The Algorithm knows my optimal place in Society.

Sam sat up on the hard mattress, wiped his eyes, and rubbed the back of his neck and shoulders. Staring at the floor beyond the foot of his bed, he knew what he had to do.

The main room computer had one vid-chat credit. Sam typed in his mother's contact information. He wanted to see her on the bigger screen, not his phone. She always knew how to make him feel better.

Mom's smiling face appeared. "Sam! I am so glad to hear from you." She squinted. "Where are you?"

"Are you on your phone, Mom?"

"Yeah. I am out of vid-chat credits. I didn't get provided any more during the monthly reallocation."

Two days before Selection, Mom had let Sam use a vid-chat session to contact a library about an article he had read. He didn't know that was her last credit.

"Okay, Mom. We'll keep this short. I know how your eyes are with the phone. I am in Orlando as a Sigma robotics programmer."

"That's wonderful, dear!" Mom always tried to make lemonade out of lemons, even though neither of them had ever been provided with the ingredients. "Listen, Sam. I know it wasn't what you hoped for, but the Algorithm knows what's best for us. You have a great future ahead of you in the Society."

Do I? Sam couldn't ask that question, even if Mom was a thousand miles away. "Thanks, Mom."

"I mean it, Sam. The Algorithm knows what's best for us. Trust It. It will show you the way."

A red light flashed on the corner of the screen, indicating their time was almost up. "Looks like I gotta go, Mom. I love you! Thanks for the pep talk."

"I love you—"

The call ended before Mom could complete her sentence. Sam guessed the Algorithm didn't see the need to spend the resources to finish their conversation. It would have been nice if he could have told her about Jennie.

Sam sat on the hard plastic chair in the main room. It bit into his bottom and back, just like the one at his old desk in Baltimore. Mom never seemed to mind the furniture. In fact, she seemed happy with the life she was provided. Sam couldn't follow her lead. A life comprising work followed by mindless vids and sleep didn't appeal to him. But maybe she had something to teach him. A lie repeated often enough can become the truth.

It's time I accept my Selection and be a good member of the Society as planned by the Algorithm.

Chapter 9: Sam

January 3, 535

"Marine biodiversity decreased 53 percent over the last fifty years. Pollution from newly submerged coastal cities is to blame."

- 22nd Century Science Review, 2122.

Jennie's smile brightened the otherwise dreary SLU hallway. She wore a blue dress, Sam's favorite color. The dress matched the flecks in her eyes.

"Hi, Sam!" Jennie hugged him. Her ribs pressed into his own. A few weeks of Sigma paste should change that. "Come check out this enormous space. I have two rooms!" Jennie fidgeted with her hands as she led him inside her SLU.

The main room looked identical to his. It contained only standard SLU furniture. No personal touches. No sign of this being Jennie Goodby's home. Someone as excited as her about moving would have unpacked something by now.

"This is nice, Jennie! Hasn't your personal stuff arrived?" Sam regretted the words as soon as they left his mouth. Omegas weren't allowed personal belongings beyond an Omega-level phone and a few necessities.

"Uh, no." Jennie bit her lip and looked down at the floor. "I guess not. But in my bedroom, I found some work outfits, a few leisure outfits, and this dress." Jennie ran her hand slowly along the dress, straightening it out. She glanced up at Sam. "Do you like it?" Her eager eyes told Sam that there was only one acceptable answer to her question. Thankfully, he didn't need to lie.

"I love the dress." Sam took her hand in his. "It looks beautiful on you." Many girls in his high school had the same dress. Not a single one of them wore it as well as her.

Jennie blushed. The blue flecks in her eyes appeared to dance in the light of the SLU's overhead fixtures.

"If you'd like, I can help you pick out some decorations for your SLU."

"I get to have belongings?" Jennie pressed her lips together.

Sam pretended not to notice her slip. "After dinner, we can go through the Sigma Catalog and see what the Algorithm could provide for us. Once you get enough credits, we'll look at getting you some stuff from the Sigma Outfitter."

"Oh, okay." Jennie mouthed the word *outfitter* several times. *That's right, Omegas don't have an outfitter.*

"The Catalog has the necessities Sigmas are provided for free, like hygiene products, basic clothing, and replacement furniture. We'll need credits to purchase the nonessential stuff from the Outfitter."

"That sounds great!" Jennie peered over Sam's shoulder at his backpack. Sam took it off. "Is that your food?" Her eyes lingered on the bag a little too long. *Maybe she's starving.*

"Sure is." Sam opened the bag and took out his paste packet and other provisions. "Let's fire up the food prep station. Oh, and guess what else I have?"

"You have something else?" Jennie's pitch betrayed her concern. *Is she afraid of what might be in here?*

Sam put on his best reassuring smile as he removed the synthahol. "The Algorithm provided us with a bottle of synthahol wine." He made a point of showing her the empty bag.

Jennie's face relaxed, then lit up. "I can't believe it! This is going to be the best meal of my life."

Omegas, even aspiring Sigmas, weren't getting eggs and bacon for their pre-Selection breakfast. Her excitement might make tonight's paste tolerable.

***

Cooking was new to Sam. The instructions on the paste's label seemed easy enough. Jennie reached across the counter to grab her paste packet. A tingling sensation shot up Sam's arm when Jennie's hand brushed over his. He snuck a glimpse of Jennie in her dress. She smiled and brushed her hair behind her ear.

"It says to put the packets as is into the oven." Sam read the instructions aloud. Jennie peered over his shoulder. Her warm breath tickled his ear.

"What do we do with the broccoli?" Jennie asked as Sam placed the paste in the oven.

"The instructions say to boil it in the provided water." Sam unwrapped the broccoli and placed it on the counter. The florets were a shade of brown. He'd eaten worse. Only Betas got fresh vegetables.

"Okay. I think the pots are in the cabinet."

A single rusty pot lay buried in the back of the cabinet. Its interior was as clean as a Sigma could expect. Sam poured in some of the provided water and put the pot on the stove.

They had only one stove credit. Sam hoped it would last long enough to thoroughly cook the broccoli. Jennie's first experience with a real vegetable needed to be the best he could make it.

While the water heated, Jennie picked up the broccoli and held it up to her face. She pressed her lips together and quickly put the broccoli in the pot of water.

As a former Omega, she likely had never seen broccoli before. Sam pretended not to notice Jennie's fascination. *Maybe her excitement will rub off on me.*

Jennie leaned over the pot. "Is the water provided to Sigmas normally this clean?" Sediment rolled around in the pot as the water came to a boil.

"It's standard Sigma water. Straight from the dispenser."

"Nice!"

How bad must Omega water be for that to be considered clean?

"Ever have wine before?" Sam held up the synthahol as the broccoli boiled.

"Uh, no." Jennie hesitated. "I thought only Selected Adults are allowed to drink."

"Yeah, but I knew kids who'd sneak some when they thought the Algorithm wasn't looking." Sam shook his head. *The Algorithm is always looking.* "But I never did that. My first glass will be with you tonight."

Jennie's eyes focused on the bottle. She wrung her hands again.

"We should probably take it easy with this." Sam put the bottle on the counter. "I've known too many people who blow all their credits on this as a means of escape."

The tension in Jennie's eyes disappeared. Jennie picked up the bottle. "Let's try a little. Do you know how to open it?"

"Sure." Sam inspected the bottle. "At least, I think so." The cork was completely inserted into the bottle's neck. "Maybe we need a tool." He opened one drawer and rooted around. "Look what I found!" Sam triumphantly waved a corkscrew in the air.

"What is it?"

"A corkscrew. It's a tool to open wine bottles. Let me show you." Sam grunted as he tried to use the pointy end of the corkscrew to wedge the cork out.

"I don't think that is how you use that thing." Jennie laughed and waved her hand, signaling Sam to give her the corkscrew. "Let me try."

Jennie held the corkscrew up to her face. "I think I got it." She pressed the tip of the screw into the top of the cork and turned. After a few rotations, Jennie placed the hinged edge against the bottle's lip and used the lever to pull out the cork.

"Ta da!" Jennie beamed.

Damn, she is smart. Sam narrowed his eyes. "Are you sure you haven't used one of those before?"

"It just made sense to me."

"I am impressed, Ms. Goodby!" Sam poured the synthahol into two plastic cups Jennie had removed from the cabinet. She inched toward him and placed her hand on the small of his back. Sam hadn't started drinking yet, but he already felt warm inside.

"To our new lives in Orlando!" Jennie raised her cup.

"Yes, to our new lives." Jennie would be a great partner and she would certainly make being a Sigma a lot more tolerable.

They both took a sip.

Jennie grimaced. "Is it supposed to taste like this?"

"Maybe it is better with food?"

"Yeah, let's save the rest for the meal." Jennie placed her cup on the counter and peered into the boiling pot. "I think it is almost ready."

***

The odor of pork paste permeated the kitchen. Thanks to his pre-Selection breakfast, Sam knew how different paste smelled compared to the real thing. Jennie inhaled deeply. Her lack of experience with real meat showed in her smile.

"Please take a seat." Sam gestured toward the table in Jennie's main room. "Let me do the rest." He grabbed the cups of wine and followed Jennie to the table. After placing the cups down, he pulled a chair out. Jennie straightened her dress as she sat. Sam helped push her chair in from behind.

Jennie looked back at him. "Such a gentleman!" Jennie's posture revealed a view down her dress that Sam hadn't seen before, at least not in real life.

A familiar urge arose in Sam, just like the time Jack had shown him that restricted vid. He imagined himself brushing Jennie's hair back and kissing her on the neck. But he feared that would cross a line. Jennie had seemed on edge a few times this evening, and he didn't want to make her uncomfortable. He walked back to the counter and grabbed the plates, hoping the distance would cool him off. The oven had warmed that part of the main room, but Sam wasn't looking for a lower temperature.

Jennie licked her lips as Sam put a plate in front of her. "This looks great!" Sam quickly sat down before Jennie's swirling tongue caused him an embarrassment. The steaming pork paste damped his arousal.

Another paste dinner…At least I have great company.

"Mmm!" Jennie's eyes were closed as she chewed.

What do people talk about on dates?

Jack, who had much more experience with girls, once told him that questions about the girl's past were a good icebreaker. "So, Jennie, other than obelisks, sharks, and explosives, what else should I know about Mount Vernon?"

"Well, let's see—" Jennie put her hand to her mouth, then removed it. "I lived there all my life, so I can't think about what would be interesting, especially to someone who grew up in The Hill."

"I heard that Mount Vernon was underwater more often than not." *Shit! I shouldn't point that out, it is rude.*

"Some parts are, especially around my OLU. My parents clean up Old Inner Harbor, so we needed to be close to the site. They remove the mines from the Last War after the robots find them."

"We learned about that in school." Sam paused a moment, trying to remember the details. "After the East Coast cities flooded, the United States broke into factions and a war erupted. One faction captured parts of the former US Navy and tried to attack Baltimore. Another faction mined the harbor in defense."

"Really?" Jennie furrowed her brows in thought. "We didn't learn about that in school. Well, whoever left the mines, my parents clean up their mess."

Their ancestors had indeed left a mess. The half-eaten brown broccoli sitting in front of him was only one small piece of supporting evidence.

"I don't want to talk about my past." Jennie looked down at her plate as she pushed her paste around with a spoon. "That's all behind me. It is so much nicer here." Jennie sighed. "What was it like in The Hill? I bet it was great."

"Yeah." Lying to her felt wrong, but Sam couldn't complain. Compared to Mount Vernon, The Hill was paradise. "Jack and I often hung around that park I showed you." Sam let the sentence trail off.

What's Jack up to? A tinge of jealousy surged through him.

"Where's Jack now?" Jennie asked.

"He got Selected Beta. He now lives in Detroit." Sam tried not to sound bitter.

"Whoa! You know a Beta?"

"Well, he was a Sigma when I knew him—" Sam took a drink of wine. "Like you said, what's past is past. Let's talk about the future." He needed to change the subject for her sake, and his.

"Orlando is so wonderful, Sam!" Jennie's voice sounded dreamy. "It is going to be great living here, *and* I have already met an amazing person!" She took a bite of broccoli and smiled.

"Who?" Sam looked around the room in an exaggerated search.

"You, of course! You are so silly!" Jennie giggled and touched Sam's hand from across the table.

Jennie's rough callouses slid across the back of his hand. He didn't mind. He could spend the rest of his life counting the blue flecks in her eyes. With his other hand, Sam reached for the wine bottle. "Would you like some more?"

"I would love another cup."

The second glass tasted better than the first. Sam leaned forward and interlaced his fingers with hers. "Tell me about your parents."

"They're the best! Mom and Dad taught me all kinds of things about how to survive in an Omega neighborhood. They helped me with my schoolwork when they could, but Omegas have to work all the time." Jennie looked at her half-empty cup. "They did the best they could with what they have. I am grateful." A tear formed in the corner of her eye. She blinked and looked at Sam. "What about your parents?"

"I never knew my dad. Mom wouldn't talk about him much. She worked hard and always made sure I had the best of the provisions. Although she didn't understand it, she did everything she could to help me learn how to program. I miss her."

Jennie's eyes glistened, accentuating her tender smile. "We'll keep each other company." Sam stared for too long. The warm feeling he'd been experiencing most of the night intensified. Jennie cleared her throat.

Sam took the last sip from his wine cup and placed it on the table. "I think that's enough wine for me tonight."

I don't want her feeling any pressure to drink.

"Yeah, me too." Jennie looked down at her cup and pushed it around on the table with both hands.

What happens now?

In another stupid, but unrestricted, action movie Jack had shown him, there was a sex scene after a dinner date. Sam imagined himself as the hero leading Jennie, the rescued damsel in distress, to the bedroom. But then what? The movie certainly wasn't a realistic instruction manual on how to proceed. Regardless, he would not push anything. Jennie's comfort was his primary concern.

"Just so you know, I wasn't expecting anything more than a meal."

Jennie sat up straight in her chair. Her eyes remained focused on the empty wine cup. "Can I tell you something and you won't laugh?"

"Of course." Sam took her hand, stroking the top of it with his thumb.

"I know we just met, but I really like you a lot." Jennie's eyes met his. "No one has ever been as nice to me as you have been."

It was time for Sam to come clean. Jennie deserved it. "I need to tell you something, too." Jennie squeezed his hand. It gave Sam courage. "I was disappointed when I was Selected Sigma."

The blue flecks in Jennie's eyes faded. Sam's stomach soured. He never wanted to see that happen again.

"However, I'm fine with it now because, without that Selection, I would have never met you." Maybe fine was an exaggeration, but not as much as it had been earlier that day. "I really like you, too, Jennie."

I love her. I should tell her that. But would it scare her off?

The blue flecks returned to Jennie's eyes, which were now wet. She stood up from her chair, walked over to Sam, leaned over, and kissed him on the lips.

What do I do now?

He met her tongue with his, hoping he was kissing her back correctly. At first, she tasted like pork paste, broccoli, and wine. Those flavors fell away, leaving only hers. He wanted to relish it forever.

***

In a server farm beneath the ruins of Cincinnati, the Algorithm logged match number 561-165,771 as successfully initiated.

Chapter 10: Tabitha

January 1, 535

"Australia closes border to immigrants fleeing rapidly sinking Pacific islands."

- *The LA Times*, November 2, 2125.

Tabitha hated hot days, but her post-Selection instructions were clear—meet Jack outside the Beta medical facility after his upgrade.

It's a fair trade. I train a new Beta for an excellent career.

The phone in her hand felt clunky and big. She hadn't noticed it yesterday, but the Detroit Selection changed her perspective. It was fine. She only had to deal with it a little while longer. Someone told her Betas in Detroit got holo-watches. If it was true, that would be amazing!

How much work did Jack need done? He had been in there a long time and there wasn't much to do while she waited. Tabitha tapped into the local drone feed and found the one staring down at her.

The drone gave her an excellent view of herself. She sat at just the right angle to the facility's entrance. Jack should see her best qualities as he walked out its door. Such posing would be excellent practice for her Selected career.

Maybe she should have chosen a different color blouse? The green matched her eyes, but Jack's profile said he liked black. It probably didn't matter. She had unbuttoned it low enough to be suggestive, but not revealing. That should grab his attention. And if it didn't, her khaki skirt and brown heeled sandals accentuated her second-best feature. Did Jack like legs? *Better dangle my foot. That'll draw his eye for sure.*

Tabitha switched to the front-facing camera on her phone. A few strands of hair seemed out of place. She left them. It looked cuter that way. If she'd had a true Beta shower after Selection, like the one she could get back home in Towson, the hair wouldn't have been misplaced. But it was fine. Sometimes you just had to make do with what you had. A notification popped up on her phone's screen. Jack had two minutes left in recovery.

Time to work.

Another notification said her favorite influencer had posted a new vid about an actor from Burlington. Tabitha pulled up the video and upvoted it after watching the first ten seconds. With any luck, that influencer would report on *her* one day.

The med facility door slid open. *Here he comes.* She looked up from her phone, trying to act casual.

Jack stopped in his tracks when he saw her. *Looks like my pose worked.* His smile appeared restrained, like he was trying to play it cool. *I'm glad they fixed his teeth.*

"Hey Tabby, what's up?"

"It's *Tabitha.*"

Jack slouched and looked down. "I'm sorry."

Why is he doing that?

Seeing Jack in that posture caused a twinge of guilt. She had scolded people for calling her Tabby her entire life. *Why do I feel bad about that now?* It didn't matter. She needed to start over. There was no way she'd lose her Selection because she couldn't train some new Beta.

"So, are you ready to head to the airport?" Tabitha hopped up from the bench and stood with her chest out, perfectly tall. She put on her best movie-star smile, hoping it would ease Jack's tension.

His gaze stayed on the ground.

"Hello, Jack?" Tabitha bent down a little, so he'd see her.

"Uh, yeah. I'm sorry." Jack straightened, but still appeared hesitant. "Are you going with me?"

Standing so close to him, Tabitha got her first good look at the new Jack. For some reason, he had kept his sandy brown hair and brown eyes. *He'd look hot with an orange or purple mod.* She could work with it. Just like the shower, sometimes you must take what you got. The khaki trousers and white shirt looked good on him. *Yeah. I can work with this.*

"Is something wrong?" Jack asked.

I must have stared too long.

"Everything's good. Don't mind me. We are both headed to Detroit, right?" She shrugged. *Play it cool, Tabitha.* "We might as well go together."

"Rad!"

"Excuse me?" Tabitha furrowed her brows. *Is that some Sigma word?*

"Never mind. It is an old word my friend and I used to say to each other. Old habits, I guess." Jack looked off into the distance, then shook his head. "Anyway, I'd love to go to Detroit with you." His smile seemed forced.

"Great!" To her surprise, Tabitha meant it.

Why would I care if a former Sigma wanted to hang out with me?

It didn't matter. Tabitha cared little for self-reflection.

"I'll put in a travel request." Tabitha pretended to type on her phone. The Algorithm had arranged for everything already, but Jack must not have been told. It might be better if he thought she wanted to travel with him. She kind of did.

"There's an anti-grav flight taking off in a few hours." Tabitha showed Jack the reservations. "The Algorithm has provided us tickets and a taxi to take us to the airport." He squinted at the screen and moved his lips as he read.

"It says we get an in-flight meal. Didn't we just have lunch?"

What a strange question.

"We did, but after lunch is midafternoon snack." *Has he never heard of it?* Time to compliment him again. "Your new teeth look great! Did you get all the upgrades?"

"Uh, yeah. I think so." Jack took out his phone; it looked like Tabitha's. "The med tech told me I should read this text." The phone displayed a standard med eval. Jack closed the message and pocketed his phone. "I'll read it on the way to Detroit."

Why didn't the med techs transfer the information using his artificial neural network? That would have been the most efficient way of informing Jack about his upgrades. They probably didn't want to spend more time with the former Sigma than necessary. Explaining Beta tech to Jack would be one more thing she'd need to do. Tabitha decided against establishing a link. It might be too forward. He could read the text on his own.

A taxi pulled up. Tabitha slid into the rear-facing seat.

Jack frowned as he bent down to look in the window. "Is this safe?"

Another odd question.

"Yeah, perfectly safe." She patted the front-facing seat ahead of her. "Come on in!"

"Sorry. I've never been in a car before, only buses."

It seemed to take forever for Jack to decide to get into the car. Once inside, he fidgeted for a moment, but then settled down. "So, tell me about this midafternoon snack. Are they going to serve *real* food?"

The cab accelerated. Jack grabbed hold of the door handle. He would need a lot of help to become a Beta.

"What other kind of food is there?"

"We mostly ate flavored nutrient paste growing up. My favorite is artificial pork chops."

"That sounds terrible!"

"Well, it is better than what the UnSelected get. Their paste tastes like chalk." Jack chuckled and his grip on the door handle loosened. "My friend Sam dared me to eat it one time." Jack frowned after finishing the sentence and looked out the window.

"UnSelected? Tasteless paste? Jack, you have a wonderful imagination. VR Entertainment Coordinator is the perfect fit for you. The Algorithm provides!"

Jack's eyes remained fixed out the window, and not on her. "It certainly does."

***

Jack had a death grip on the grab handle above the window. *Why is he so afraid?*

The taxi's speedometer read 185 kilometers per hour—well within the safety limit for the Baltimore Beltway, and nowhere near fast enough to warrant his reaction. Tabitha leaned forward and put her hand on Jack's knee.

"Relax, Jack. Taxis are perfectly safe. I promise. The Algorithm drives them, and It would let nothing bad happen to us." Tabitha requested an airborne relaxant through her phone. Its sweet scent filled the cabin.

"Yeah. Maybe you're right." Jack released the grab bar, put his hands on his thighs, and settled against the seat. The hard edge of fear disappeared from his face. "So, Tabby, what were you Selected for?"

Tabitha reflexively clenched her teeth, then relaxed. *The name is kind of cute when he says it.*

"I am going to be an actor in Detroit." A smile escaped Tabitha's lips.

"No. Fucking. Way."

I can't believe he just said that!

A loud alarm went off on Jack's phone. He looked down at it. "Is this for real?"

Of course it's real! I have to teach him how to speak, too? Tabitha composed herself. "It is not proper for Betas to swear. There are reprimands."

"Really? Like what?"

"I don't know. I don't hang around people who break the rules."

"I am *so* sorry." Jack cast his gaze down and away from Tabitha.

"It's okay." It most certainly was not. Tabitha changed seats to sit beside Jack. "Old habits, like you said."

Time to work.

She gently raised Jack's chin, looked into his eyes, and kissed him. A tingling sensation spread from Tabitha's lips through her body. *Wow, Jack is a good kisser.* He tasted like peppermint. The med facility had cleaned his teeth. She hoped she tasted the same. The kiss lingered longer than she intended.

Jack's brown eyes glazed over. "Thank you."

How sweet! He thanked me! Beta boys never did that.

Jack put his arm around Tabitha, and she snuggled up against him. At first, the gesture felt like her duty, but as she settled in, it felt right.

***

A silver cylinder rose into the air as the taxi pulled up to the airport. Jack pointed out the window. "Are we riding in one of those?"

"Yup." Tabitha placed her hand on Jack's thigh. "Don't worry. Like the taxi, they are perfectly safe." Although she didn't understand Jack's hesitance about the taxi, she knew many Betas who had a fear of flying.

"Tabby, I know we just met, but I trust you. If you say it's safe, then I believe it."

"That's because I am an actor!" Tabitha said with a dramatic flair. *Wait, Jack used the diminutive.* It didn't bother her.

Jack laughed. "I'm not sure if that makes me feel better or not."

Tabitha put her arm around Jack and gave him a kiss. She broke the kiss and patted him on the thigh. "Come on, let's head inside."

They entered the airport, Jack's newly smoothed hand in hers, and headed toward the check-in counter. A male Beta Security Force agent sat behind the desk.

"Hello, Ms. Forsythe!" The officer glanced at his terminal. "I see you are headed to Detroit. Congratulations!" The officer glared at Jack. "What have we here?"

Jack shrank like he had before. Wherever this habit had come from, she needed to break him of it—but not here and not now. Tabitha cleared her throat.

"Mr. Thompson is a newly minted High-Metric Beta." Tabitha emphasized the High-Metric part. Sometimes these Low-Metric BSF officers thought they have more power than they did. "You should show some respect!"

"My apologies." The officer directed his fake smile to Tabitha. "I meant no disrespect. I haven't had an upgrade walk through here before." The officer typed some more on his computer. "Enjoy your flight." He stared at Jack as they walked away.

"Thank you," Jack whispered. "I appreciate what you did back there." Jack's sincerity took aback Tabitha.

"The Low-Metrics are jealous of us. Pay him no mind." Tabitha took his hand. Jack was going to be a lot of work, but for some reason, the more time she spent with him, the more he grew on her.

Maybe this won't be so bad after all.

Chapter 11: Jack

January 1, 535

"The newly rebuilt cities of Detroit, Boise, Minneapolis, and Burlington are now designated as Beta cities. Lower Caste humans remaining in these cities after midnight will be shot."

- Email sent by the Algorithm, March 12, 50.

Jack shivered. *Is this what winter felt like?*

A sign by the gate attendant's desk said the temperature inside the airport was 70°F. Air-conditioned SLUs rarely got below 80. Tabitha didn't seem to notice the cold as she sat beside him dangling her high heel and scrolling on her phone—she did that a lot.

Travel posters hung on clean white walls. They advertised faraway destinations Jack had heard of only in school. A gray carpet extended in all directions. He wanted to take his shoes off and scrunch his toes on it, but Betas probably didn't do that. Large windows illuminated the interior. Outside, anti-grav planes departed to destinations unknown. Inside, a steady stream of Betas passed by. Most ignored him and stared at Tabitha. Sometimes, one gave him a dirty look.

Tabitha's dangling high-heeled sandal couldn't keep his mind off the upcoming flight. *How long would it take to fall from forty thousand feet? I bet Sam would know.*

I gotta get Sam out of my mind. He was part of my old life, and that life is over. Jack tried to change the subject in his own mind. *How did a Sigma from Baltimore get paired up with an actor headed for Detroit? I bet Sam would know that, too.*

Dammit! I can't keep thinking of Sam. Do I really have to forget about him like the Beta Transition Manual said?

"So, forty thousand feet, huh?" Jack wiped the sweat from his brow.

"Maybe." Tabitha's eyes were glued to her phone, "Could be higher. It all depends on what flight lanes the Algorithm provides the pilot."

"How do you know so much about flying?"

Tabitha put down her phone and stared at the floor, like a Sigma talking to a Beta. "My parents are pilots."

"That is so cool!"

"Please don't make fun of me, Jack." Tabitha's gaze remained fixed to the floor.

A knot formed in Jack's stomach. "Make fun of you? I would never do that!"

"I guess you don't know." Tabitha sighed. "Most Betas create things. The lowest metric Betas do jobs in service to other Betas. It is like being in the Lower Castes."

Jack opened his mouth but thought better of informing her of the difference.

"The Algorithm can pilot anti-gravs, but It provides the work to Low-Metric Betas. The kids in school made fun of me for it."

"I'm sorry." Jack put his arm around Tabitha. "It doesn't matter now. We are starting over in Detroit."

"We?" Jack wanted the shimmer in her green eyes to be one of hope.

All in, buddy. It is time to go all in…

"Based on what happened in the cab, I kind of thought—"

Tabitha kissed Jack. A Beta coughed as they went past. She broke off the kiss. Her eyes shot to the side as if she had done something wrong.

"Well, I'll take that as a yes." Jack slapped his knees as he stood. "Let's go to Detroit!"

All I have to do is survive the flight.

***

The inside of the plane reminded Jack of a wide bus—but with nicer seats. *Thank the Algorithm I am sitting beside Tabby! How lucky is that?*

"Do you mind taking the window seat?" Tabitha asked.

The window seat meant being constantly reminded of the height. Jack hesitated in the aisle.

A man snorted behind Jack. "Come on buddy, we don't have all day." The well-dressed Beta stood with one hand on his hip.

Jack looked down and slid into the window seat. He barely noticed its softness. Tabitha sat in the aisle seat beside him.

The man audibly mumbled as he passed Jack and Tabitha. "I can't believe they are letting *his* kind on these flights now."

"Ignore him." Tabitha put her soft hand on his. "You belong here as much as he does. Probably more," she whispered. Her warm breath tickled his ear. She picked Jack's chin up with her hand.

He wanted to kiss her. A proper kiss. One that was passionate, long, and deep.

"Jack Thompson?" A flight attendant interrupted the moment. "Yes?"

"The Algorithm detected your unusually high heart rate and cortisol level." The attendant handed him a small plastic cup. "It asked me to deliver one of these to ease your anxiety."

A small black pill rolled around the bottom of the cup. "Thank you."

Dammit, now everyone knows…

"I was nervous my first time, too," Tabitha said. "The pill will help you enjoy the flight."

The burden of anxiety lifted from his mind immediately after swallowing the pill. "Wow! That is the best medicine I have *ever* had."

"What do you mean?"

"As a Sigma, on the rare occasions I was provided medicine, it hardly ever worked. One time, I got really sick, and my mom thought I was going to die." Jack swallowed. "It was bad enough to get me provided a trip to the medical facility. They gave me pills, but I just got sicker."

"What happened?" Tabitha leaned in.

"The worst symptoms went away on their own, but I had some breathing problems afterward. I think the Beta medical facility fixed them." Jack ran his tongue along the molar that had given him pain for years. "I think they fixed my tooth, too."

"I thought all medicine worked with individuals based on their genes." Tabitha settled back into her seat.

"Well, it looks like good medicine is just another perk of the upgrade. Not as good as spending time with you, of course." Jack put on his cheesiest smile.

"Aww!" Tabitha pecked Jack on the cheek.

She's the best thing about being a Beta. How did I get so lucky to find her?

***

"Welcome to Flight 21 from Baltimore to Detroit. The flight time today will be—"

Jack ignored the pilot and stared out the window. The last thing he wanted to know about were emergency procedures and flight times. If they were forty thousand feet up, what emergency procedure would actually help? The ground moved away after the pilot stopped talking. The silent aircraft created no sensation of motion. He squeezed Tabitha's hand tighter.

I'm finally leaving Baltimore.

The entire airport came into view. Parked anti-grav planes looked like toys. Tabitha leaned over to look out the window. Her partially unbuttoned blouse gave him a view more interesting than the receding landscape. She pointed out the window. "Is that a parking lot over there?"

"No." Jack looked out the window, trying to be a good boy. "It's Old Inner Harbor. That black stuff is water." Tabitha brushing up against him made it hard to concentrate.

"Are those people in the water?"

"Yeah. They're Omegas reclaiming the harbor."

How can she not know about that?

"Hmm…" Tabitha got back into her seat and started scrolling on her phone.

More of the brown and green Chesapeake Bay came into view. Centuries of pollution before the Climate Shift had taken its toll.

"My friend Sam once told me, long ago, people actually caught and ate the animals living in the Bay."

"Gross."

Gross indeed, Tabby.

"The water is too polluted for anything edible to live in it now." Jack pointed in the distance. "Those are the work zones where Omegas work to clean the Bay. It will be a long time before it ever gets back to what it was before the Shift."

Tabitha's eyes stayed fixed on her phone. Jack turned in his seat to see what the other passengers were doing. Some slept, most scrolled on their phones. His shade was the only one open. It looked like the other Betas didn't want to see the real world, either.

The plane passed over Mount Vernon. Trash-filled streets formed a grid below. People scrambled through the garbage. From this height, he couldn't tell if they were Omegas or UnSelected. They all looked like filthy little ants.

Rows of shabby OLUs lined the streets. Every building had missing glass. The holes in some roofs were large enough that Jack could see the people living inside.

It was hard to tell where the neighborhood ended and the harbor began. Water encroached into the streets and alleys. The buildings in the dry regions had watermarks showing the height of previous floods. Many of the holes in the buildings were below the water lines.

A flash of light erupted in the distance. *Was that an explosion?*

The farther they flew, the drier the streets became. The buildings had fewer holes. Many were raised on stilts. If not for Druid Hill Park, Jack would have never recognized The Hill from this height. The cracks in the SLUs were more noticeable than this morning.

Where did all the trash in the streets come from? I guess things look different from above.

The plane continued forward, leaving his old life behind.

Tabitha kissed him on the cheek, reached over, and lowered the shade. Jack rested his head on her shoulder and sighed. His future lay ahead.

***

A delicious scent entered Jack's nostrils, waking him. He raised his head off Tabitha's shoulder and rubbed his eyes. A covered dish came into focus. It sat on a small tray coming out of the back of the seat ahead of him. The flight attendant flickered as she placed a similar plate in front of Tabitha.

What the hell? Jack knew better than to swear aloud. *Probably just the meds.*

"Thank you."

Tabitha gave him a strange look. "That was a holo. No need to thank it."

"But it looked exactly like the flight attendant earlier, and she was definitely human."

"Human flight attendants only work before take-off and after landing. They never serve food. That job is below a Beta."

The holo attendant raised the lid off their dishes, unveiling real meat sitting on a bed of spaghetti noodles. The food's aroma intensified. It reminded him of the cleaning agent his mom used, except the food had less of a chemical smell.

"I love chicken piccata!" Tabitha rubbed her hands.

This is a snack?

The attendant handed Jack a glass of pale-yellow liquid. It smelled like synthahol, but more potent.

"It's wine." Tabitha seemed to have read his mind. "My parents drink it with every dinner."

Jack swirled the glass. Streaks of wine formed on the inside. "Have you had wine before?"

"No. Betas don't break the rules," Tabitha whispered. "Pre-Selected people aren't allowed to drink."

He'd snuck some synthahol before. Sam freaked out about it—of course. But he was on a plane to Detroit and Sam was not. *Maybe Sam should have had the synthahol.*

"To our new lives." Tabitha raised her glass. Jack returned the gesture and took a sip.

"Wow! That is delicious!"

"Of course! The Algorithm chooses our food to optimize our enjoyment."

I wonder if Sam knew that.

After his first bite of the chicken, he didn't care. Like the steak at lunch, the chicken resisted chewing. It tasted nothing like chicken paste. Instead, it had a refreshing flavor, probably from the yellow sauce that covered the meat. The spaghetti noodles tasted like the ones his mother purchased with Sigma credits. She always upgraded his meals for his birthday.

The metal spoon scraped against the plate as Jack scooped up the last of the sauce. Tabitha gave him a sidelong look but said nothing. More than half of the chicken remained uneaten on her plate. Jack glanced at the chicken but thought better of asking for it.

"I think I'll nap, if you don't mind." Tabitha rested her head against Jack's shoulder.

"I'll do my best pillow impression."

Seriously, Jack? Can't you be cool around a girl just once?

Tabitha purred and snuggled closer to him.

I must be doing something right.

The vid-screen on the headrest in front of Jack was off. He wished he had something to watch as he sat still, trying not to move.

I wonder what life will be like for Sam in Orlando. Did I ruin Sam's Selection by taking him on the coaster last night?

He leaned his head back on his seat. Tabitha stirred but didn't wake. *Should I call Mom? The people at the medical center told me to break off all my Sigma relationships.* Although it was wrong, there were a few ex-girlfriends to whom he'd love to flaunt his new status.

Dials and vents were built into the ceiling directly above him. Other Betas had adjusted the dials when they sat down. He stopped himself from reaching up, lest he disturb Tabitha.

A couple days ago, I'd have seen Tabby as another obnoxious, arrogant Beta. Now, I am basically in love with her. Would she have paid attention to me two days ago? Could she have been interested in me despite my simple Sigma clothes and crooked Sigma smile? Would she have come over for a chicken-flavored nutrient paste dinner in my run-down SLU? Probably not. But now, for some reason, she seems to like me. Has this happened too quickly?

What would Sam think?

A floral scent came from the vent above him. Jack inhaled.

The Algorithm has a plan, and it is not my place to question It. I earned my Selection. Sam should have worked harder.

Chapter 12: Jack

January 1, 535

"Coffee plants join cacao in extinction. Climate change has now cost us both coffee and chocolate."

- Excerpt from unknown pre-Shift internet news broadcast, 2127.

Why is my shoulder wet?

Jack looked up at the ceiling. It was a force of habit from years as a Sigma living in a leaky SLU. The vents and nozzles in the anti-grav's ceiling were dry.

"Welcome to Detroit!" The pilot's voice stirred Tabitha. She lifted her head from Jack's wet shoulder. "Please follow the attendant's instructions as you deplane."

"How do I look?" Tabitha's hair had matted down on one side and a little drool pooled on the side of her lip. It looked cute on her. She stood in the aisle and took out her phone.

"As beautiful as always, Tabby." Jack slid over and joined Tabitha in the line waiting to exit the plane.

Tabitha raised her phone to her face and huffed. "I have to look good for my new city." She fixed her hair. The process took until they reached the plane's door.

Jack shaded his eyes when he deplaned. The cerulean sky peppered with puffy white clouds was something he had only seen on vids. *Where's the haze?* He wished he had brought a jacket. Cool, fresh air filled his nostrils. Something was missing. *I don't smell garbage or stale mud.*

A yellow taxi pulled up to where they stood on the tarmac. Atop the taxi sat a sign that read:

```
Welcome Jack and Tabitha!
```

Jack's phone vibrated in his pocket.

"We are neighbors! Can you believe it?" Tabitha's green eyes made a stunning contrast with the sky. He wondered if he could capture the scene in a painting. "Jack? Did you hear me? We're neighbors."

Tabitha's question snapped him back to reality. "That's awesome!" Jack squinted at his phone. "But there's no floor or unit designation."

"Floor? You get the whole BTH."

"BTH?"

"Beta Town House." Tabitha got in the cab and patted the seat beside her. "Aren't there Sigma Townhomes?"

"No. We live in Sigma Living Units." Jack slid into the taxi's back seat beside Tabitha. "They have two or three rooms. There are lots of SLUs in each building."

A small console hung from the ceiling with the number 68 displayed in a white font. Beside the number was an up arrow and a down arrow. Jack pressed up five times. The inside felt a little warmer. He pushed it twice again, warming the car's interior further. He reached for the console and Tabitha placed her hand on his. She pressed the down arrow twice.

"Sorry." Jack put his hands in his lap. "I've never been able to control the temperature before." Complaining about the cold would have been unimaginable just a few hours ago.

"Well, you can play with it all you like in your own BTH. I don't want to get all sweaty."

Images of a sweaty, sexy Tabitha ran through Jack's mind.

"Neat!" Tabitha's attention had returned to her phone. "It looks like we have standard Detroit Beta Town Houses. Two stories with two bedrooms, a kitchen, a living room, and two bathrooms, one on each floor." She looked up from her phone. "These BTHs are for singles. Married couples with children get a third floor and a few more rooms. I heard Alphas get stand-alone single-family homes."

The taxi accelerated, leaving the airport behind. Jack settled back in his seat. *What in the hell am I going to do with all that space?* He got out his phone and read over the description of his new home. "What about our stuff?"

"My phone says it's been delivered to our BTHs. I'll probably throw out my old stuff and get new anyway."

Did she just say she was going to throw out all her stuff?

"Do you want to have dinner together tonight?" Tabitha tilted her head to the side in a half shrug. "You can come over to my place."

Wow! A dinner date with Tabby? Be cool, Jack.

He straightened in his seat and gave his best attempt at a not-too-eager-but-clearly-interested smile. "I can't think of a better way to spend my first night in Detroit."

"Yay!" Tabitha bit her lip. Jack's heart fluttered. "Don't tell me what you choose for dinner. I want to be surprised!"

"Choose for dinner?"

"Yeah, silly! The food dispenser will ask you what you want for dinner tonight. You've had dinner before, right?"

"Uh yeah, but we never got to choose what we ate." He waved it off. "Don't worry. I'll figure it out."

Tabitha snuggled against Jack. He put his arm around her—a perfect fit. Jack gave her a gentle squeeze. She sighed.

Life couldn't be better.

***

The scenery went by more slowly than when they were on the Baltimore Beltway. Jack didn't mind; he was perfectly at ease in the climate-controlled car. Tabitha's soft hair lay against his cheek. The screen inside the taxi displayed a map of the area. A green triangle marked their location. The taxi headed north on a road called I-75. The map minimized, and an article appeared. It said most of Detroit was destroyed during the chaos of the Shift, but parts of I-75 had survived. The article ended by saying the Algorithm rebuilt Detroit in the early days of the new society. Sam probably would have corrected the article, pointing out that Omegas did the work.

We all have our place in the Society.

Beautiful meadows lined the road. Jack had never seen so much green. Parents played with small children. He wished his mom had time to play with him when he was young. Families shared meals in the greenspace. No one ate outdoors in The Hill. The smell alone would have ruined an appetite—much less the ever-present UnSelected.

The car exited I-75 and the countryside transitioned into a cityscape. The new road passed through a residential district. Glass, stone, and brick buildings lined a street so clean Jack could eat off it. People, all Betas, walked along level sidewalks with no cracks, laughing and talking, seemingly not noticing the cars on the street. Everything appeared brand new.

They passed a different park every couple of blocks, each one beautiful and green—just like Tabitha's eyes. Sprinklers watered the grass. Laughing children ran through the bursts of water that rose from the ground and fell uselessly on the pavement. Not a single water rationer could be seen.

Tears formed in Jack's eyes. The green grass, sunshine, clear skies—all washed over him. He felt lighter. A weight had been lifted from his soul—and it wasn't because of meds this time.

Tabitha's head hadn't moved from his shoulder. She had slept through the whole thing. *Betas sure sleep a lot.*

Sam once told him about how people used to believe in a place called heaven, where everything was beautiful and perfect. According to Sam, the belief was based on faith, not evidence. Jack didn't need faith to believe in heaven. He was there.

***

Stepping out of the cab, it took all Jack's willpower not to swear. Pristine red brick townhouses lined the street as far as the eye could see. Jack's house looked like the others. Concrete stairs lead to his home's freshly painted white front door. Not a single crack could be found on the stairs or the house's facade. Its glass windows were all intact, and he could see through them.

Jack's phone buzzed. "It looks like we need to register our homes and get all the accounts set up. How about I come over for dinner in an hour?"

"Make it two. A girl has to get ready." Tabitha giggled as she walked up the stairs toward the BTH beside his. She held her phone up to the front door, turned and smiled at him, and then disappeared inside.

Red letters appeared on the front door when Jack got to the top of the concrete stairs.

```
Hello Mr. Thompson!
Welcome to your new home.

Please wait while the data from your phone is
transferred to your new device.
```

For the first time in his eighteen years, Jack's phone powered down. He squeezed the on button as hard as he could. Without his phone, he couldn't do anything. He rapidly pushed the power button. Nothing.

A click drew his attention from the dead phone. The white door slid open. Interior lights illuminated a white tile-floored entryway. He stepped inside.

The house smelled like the rest of Detroit, clean and fresh. The blue-carpeted living room on his left was bigger than the main room of his SLU. A polished plastic coffee table sat in front of a big puffy sofa and a plush recliner. Like the door, the walls had been recently painted white. On the far wall, a large holo-screen displayed an image of a rushing waterfall. Quiet instrumental music filled the room.

The tile flooring led further into the house. Jack walked along it, passing a set of blue-carpeted stairs on his right. The walkway turned into a short hallway with a bathroom on the left and a door on the right. At its end, the hallway opened to another room.

Jack stopped. The room he stood in had more material wealth than an entire SLU building. All SLUs had a kitchen area, but they were nothing like this. Jack ran his eyes around the room, staring at the refrigerator. He peeked inside. Sigmas never had excess food to store in a fridge, but he did now. Still full from the plane, he closed the door.

Beside the fridge sat a stove and oven. He had those in his SLU, but these looked brand new and much nicer. The food dispenser beside the oven had a touchscreen. Tabitha told him that Betas got to choose their meals. The screen must be for making those choices. A sink with no water rationer was built into the counter beside the dispenser.

The dining area to the left of the kitchen had a table with two chairs, each with thick cushions. A watch on top of the table projected the words WEAR ME in the air above it. Jack put on the watch and jumped.

A hairless, naked person appeared. They had olive skin that matched his, but no signs of a gender. Soulless black eyes stared at him. Jack took a step back, keeping the table between him and the visitor.

"I apologize for startling you, Mr. Thompson. I am the holographic projection of your home's AI. Please set me up by following the instructions on your watch's holo-screen."

The watch projected an animation that showed Jack how to use a holographic interface. It took him several minutes, but he figured out how to use it. The registration program provided options for all the avatar's physical features. He created a brown-haired, brown-eyed female. A Sigma who, he hoped, could fit into a world of Betas. He put her in a white T-shirt and jeans. Having her wear a suit, the default option, felt pretentious.

The word NAME floated in the air above his watch. He chose Samantha. *I'll call her Sam for short.*

"Thank you for giving me a great name, Mr. Thompson. As your home AI, I can perform many tasks for you. I have already automated a self-cleaning schedule that I sent to your watch. When you have a chance, please approve it. Besides home maintenance, I can operate appliances, drive your car, and do just about anything else you'll ever need." Samantha smiled. It looked genuine. "Do you like the furnishings the Algorithm chose for you?"

Jack looked around and shrugged. "Uh, yeah. Please, call me Jack."

"Sure thing, Jack! If you want different furniture, I can pull up the Beta Catalog and you can select anything you want. Many items can be customized to your taste. I want your house to reflect you as a person."

Reflect me as a person? What the hell does that mean? More importantly, who pays for all this shit?

"Jack, I am detecting elevated stress hormones. Would you like a pill to calm you? I have a full pharmacy in the dispenser."

"No. Thank you, Sam." Jack swallowed. *Maybe I should have chosen another name.* "How does all this get paid for?"

"Jack, I understand you were a Sigma pre-Selection. I will help you with your transition to a Beta in conjunction with Ms. Forsythe's efforts."

How does holo-Sam know about Tabby?

"The Algorithm determined that money is an inefficient means of allocating resources at the Beta level. Hence, there is no Beta Out-fitter, only the Catalog." A website containing images of electronics, clothing, jewelry, food, and much more floated between Jack and Samantha. "The Algorithm decides what resources a Beta can access. It includes only those options in the Catalog. Anything that you see, you can have. Just ask."

The worlds of the Sigma and Beta couldn't have been more dif-ferent. Jack closed the browser window before succumbing to option paralysis.

"Jack, your bio-signs are consistent with confusion and fear. If you are feeling overwhelmed, I can give you medicine for that."

Betas had drugs for everything. "No, thank you. Let's check out the upstairs."

Samantha led Jack to the second floor. She pointed to Jack's right as they got to the top of the stairs. "Here is the spare bedroom. Many single Betas use this as a hobby room. It would be perfect for your gaming. Would you like me to order a gaming rig?"

Jack peered into the empty room. "Uh, sure."

"Done. It will be here this evening. I'll install it for you."

Samantha showed Jack to a large bedroom with the biggest bed he had ever seen. Landscape paintings hung from freshly painted white walls. Soft music played in the background.

"Your private bathroom is beside the master bedroom." Samantha nodded toward a door on the far side of the room. "I believe I have identified all your necessities and provided for them. If that is not the case, please let me know and I'll be happy to produce what you need."

A small bag sat on a chest at the foot of the bed. He unzipped it. Inside were his set of backup Sigma clothes and his game controller. He dumped the items on his bed. "Please dispose of these, Sam."

Jack pushed his hand on the bed. "Wow, this is nice!"

Maybe too soft to sleep on.

"I am glad you like it, Jack. If you open the closet, you'll see the Algorithm has provided clothes for you to wear to tonight's dinner with Ms. Forsythe."

Again with the formality. What's up with that?

An extensive collection of clothes, including a nice blue sport coat and khaki trousers, hung in the closet.

"Remember, I can produce any clothing you want from the Catalog." Samantha removed the sport coat. "This is currently Ms. Forsythe's favorite color. There is a 95 percent chance it will go with what she wears tonight."

"Thanks again, Sam. I'll look through the Catalog and let you know if I find anything I want." Jack looked down and scratched his upper lip. "How do I make a call?"

"Who would you like to call? I'll be happy to make the connection."

"I want to call my mom."

"No problem, Jack. Connecting to Victoria Thompson now."

A life size holo-image of Jack's mother projected from his watch. Jack waved his hand rapidly back and forth at his mother's image. "Hi, Mom!"

Jack's mother cast her gaze down. "Hello, Mr. Thompson."

"Mom, please look at me." Jack's stomach sank. "There's no need to call me *Mr. Thompson*. I am Jack, your son."

"How may I help you, Mr. Thompson?" Victoria did not look at him.

"I just wanted to tell you I was Selected Beta and have moved to Detroit. I made it here safely."

His mom continued to look down. "I am happy for you, Mr. Thompson. I really am."

Jack pressed his lips together. "I met a girl. Her name is Tabby Forsythe. She's real nice. We are having dinner together tonight."

Victoria showed no emotion. "I hope you enjoy your new job and that you have a good time with Ms. Forsythe tonight. If there is nothing else you need from me, I will disconnect."

"There is nothing else, Mom. Talk to you again soon. I miss you."

Victoria's image disappeared. Jack sat on his bed, exhaled, and looked at the floor. Tears welled in his eyes.

Samantha reappeared and stood beside him and placed her hand on his back. Her touch felt real, but it lacked warmth. "Is everything okay, Jack?"

He wiped his eyes. "Yeah."

I can see how Sam—the real one—and I might drift apart, but my own mother?

Jack lay back on his bed. "Sam?"

"Yes, Jack?"

"I want to be alone. Please silence my calls until 1930."

"Your watch and home are now silenced."

Jack stared at the ceiling. Thoughts of Sam, his mother, and Tabitha ran through his mind. A sweet smell filled his nostrils. Although not tired, he lost focus. The room went black.

***

"Jack, wake up." Samantha's gentle whisper roused Jack from sleep.

Thank the Algorithm, this wasn't a dream.

Jack rubbed his eyes. "I didn't mean to fall asleep."

"Your vitals showed signs of emotional distress. I released a sedative gas to help you feel better." Jack opened his mouth. Samantha interrupted him. "While you slept, I went through Ms. Forsythe's profile again. I have produced a new outfit that I think she'll like better than the one I showed you earlier. But you should shower before you try it on."

How many showers can one take in a day?

After his shower, Samantha showed Jack how to use the toiletries in the bathroom. Most of the items in the bathroom were fancier versions of what he had as a Sigma. Flossing hurt; he hoped that wouldn't be a regular thing. The holo-screen in the bedroom showed Jack how to put on the suit. He checked the suit's fit in the mirror. It looked good to him. But what did he know?

Downstairs, Jack scrolled through the options on the food dispenser's screen. "I don't even know what most of this stuff is. How am I supposed to choose?"

Samantha appeared beside him. "No problem, Jack. I have prepared a list of foods that I think you would like based on your past reactions to various flavors of nutrient paste. Keep in mind paste doesn't always taste the same as real food."

If I never have another paste, it will be too soon.

"Show me the list, please."

A list of foods Jack had never heard of before appeared on the dispenser's screen. Each item had an image beside it. The images didn't help.

"I ordered them based on what I think Ms. Forsythe and you would like to eat together."

"Thanks, Sam. I'll take the top pick."

"Excellent choice, Jack. Sushi is one of her favorite foods."

What the hell is sushi?

He shrugged. Everything about being a Beta had been great so far. Why should he expect sushi to be different?

"Jack, the Algorithm is providing you and Ms. Forsythe an Alpha-level bottle of wine as a housewarming gift."

Like the food list, the wine bottle's label contained words that were new to Jack. It didn't matter. "The Algorithm provides!"

***

Damn.

Jack fought hard not to stare. Tabitha stood in the open doorway of her BTH wearing a long, tight black dress with a low neckline. Her high heels made her as tall as him.

He pulled himself together and kept the wine bottle pressed against his back. "You. Look. Amazing!"

"Thanks! You look great too! I love the suit." Tabitha pointed at the box in Jack's hand. "Is that sushi? I love sushi!"

"Yup!" *Thanks, Sam!*

"What's that?" Tabitha stretched to look over Jack's shoulder.

"Oh, you mean this little thing?" He revealed the Alpha wine from behind his back.

Tabitha screamed and jumped up and down. Jack saw her at various stages of excitement throughout the day, but nothing like this. *How can she jump in those shoes?* She waved her hands in a "give me" fashion. "How did you get that?"

"The Algorithm treated us tonight." He handed over the bottle.

"The Algorithm provides!"

"It certainly does!"

"I think you'll like what I have chosen based on what your house AI sent over." Tabitha beckoned Jack into the house. Jack followed her. His eyes fixed upon the open back of her dress. Her heels clicked on the tile floor. Tabitha stopped at the table in the dining room and waved her hand above it. "Green salad with seared steak. Add your sushi and we have a surf 'n' turf!"

Like sushi, Jack had never heard of surf 'n' turf, nor did he care. Nothing but real food sat on that table. Tabitha opened the wine, and they began their meal.

For the third time today, Jack had the best meal of his life. The fish on the sushi felt rubbery in his mouth, but he liked it. On the outside, the seared steak looked like what he ate for lunch, but it had a reddish interior. Something about the redness made it taste better to him. He guessed it had to do with the juices. The lunch steak was dry in comparison. This morning, he wouldn't have dreamed of disparaging steak. The vegetables in the salad crunched. They weren't mushy, like the few real veggies he'd had in the past.

Tabitha did most of the talking during the meal. She went on about what she thought acting would be like and how she planned to decorate the house. The topic of conversation didn't matter to him. He loved the sound of her voice. It also gave him a reason to stare at her in the dress.

The wine flowed, and they moved closer together as the night progressed. Eventually, Tabitha stood, walked around the table, and sat on Jack's lap. "Do you like my dress?" she purred. Her fingers played with the neckline.

Okay, Jack. Be cool.

"I love it. You are the most beautiful woman I have ever met."

"Aww!" Tabitha leaned forward. Jack felt her warm breath and then her soft lips on his. A tingling sensation began at the tip of his tongue and spread throughout his body. Her flowery perfume displaced the scent of the meal. To him, they were the only two people in the world.

He didn't know how long the kiss lasted. Eventually, Tabitha slowly withdrew her lips from his. She took Jack's hand and led him to her bedroom.

***

On a server farm in Toronto, The Algorithm classified match number 561-165,772 as successfully initiated.

Chapter 13: Jennie

January 4, 535

"US shutters the remains of its space program due to lack of funding. Last year, America spent 45 percent of its budget on climate mitigation."

- *The Guardian*, June 11, 2145.

As a child, Jennie wondered what it would be like to sleep on a cloud. Her new mattress felt like the next best thing.

Maybe it's too comfortable?

The off-white ceiling tiles in Jennie's bedroom had few stains compared to the ceiling in her old OLU. But the best part was no water dripped from them.

The air circulation system kicked on. Jennie hoped the sound would lull her back to sleep. It didn't—despite her comfort. Her Omega childhood had trained her for a louder sleeping environment and a much earlier wake-up time.

The bed rocked. Sam had rolled over. Jennie welcomed the distraction and turned her head toward him. Maybe one day she would sleep as late as Sam.

I have two rooms all to myself. What will I do with this much space?

In her OLU, everyone ate, slept, and watched vids all in the same room. The noise made it impossible to concentrate on anything or get a good night's sleep. Her parents tried their best to be quiet when they got home from work, but everything creaked in the OLU.

Sam shook awake when the alarm sounded. His reaction struck her as extreme. The alarm in her OLU used to physically hurt her ears.

Jennie rolled over and kissed Sam. It felt good to move. She hadn't realized how stiff her back had become from lying in bed for so long. "Last night was wonderful."

"It was the best night of my life." Sam held Jennie's cheek in his soft hand. Sigma schools must not have labor as part of their curriculum.

"I know being a Sigma is not what you wanted in life, but I can make you happy." *If you'll let me.*

"You already have." Sam stroked her cheek. Jennie squirmed. "I have something I want to say to you, but I don't want to upset you."

Please don't be one of those Sigmas who use and discard Omegas. Something deep inside told her Sam wouldn't do that. Jennie wanted to believe that voice, but she continued to think of herself as an Omega and her instincts urged caution.

"I love you, Jennie."

Jennie laughed silently—the only response her body mustered to overwhelming relief. Sam's bottom lip quivered. She touched his wet face.

"I love you, too! I am so sorry. I didn't mean to hurt you. That's the last thing I ever want to do." Jennie wiped his tears. "I was worried you were going to say something else."

"I know it seems fast, but I feel like we belong together—" Sam furrowed his eyebrows. "What did you think I was going to say?"

"That I was a one-night stand. You know, bang the vulnerable new Sigma, then move on to your next conquest."

"Do you know any other vulnerable new Sigmas?" Sam had a cute, facetious smile.

"You're mine now, mister." Jennie rolled on top of Sam and pinned him down. Sam's eyes widened in surprise. She kissed him. He moaned softly.

The alarm went off again.

Sam gave a playful smirk. "We'll continue this conversation later."

"You bet we will!" Jennie rolled off Sam and stood beside the bed.

"Should we spend a shower credit and be clean for our first day?"

"Shower credit? We can choose when we shower?" *What other benefits are there to being a Sigma?*

"Yup. Once a day."

"Can we share the shower?" Jennie grinned.

"I like the way you think, Ms. Goodby." Sam stroked his chin. She loved it when he did that. He looked smart. "Let's find out!"

Jennie opened her closet. "Hey look, I have two robes!" She was certain there was only one in there last night. "Do you know why?"

"I don't know." Sam reached out for the robe. "I wouldn't worry about it." He put the robe on without the hesitancy one normally would have if uncertain of the fit.

I wonder why Sam doesn't seem surprised. Maybe Sigmas get more clothes than they need.

"Ladies first." Sam paused at the SLU's front door and held out his hand. His robe hung open at the chest.

"You just want to look at my butt!"

Sam blushed.

I was right!

As a young Omega, Jennie fended off more advances from Sigmas than she could count—most of them wildly inappropriate. Sam never crossed that line—not even close.

As they walked to the bathroom, Jennie ran her hands along the walls. *These are so nice and smooth.* They passed two kids laughing and playing in the hall. Jennie looked back to Sam. "Cute kids."

"I remember when I played in the halls like that. Jack and I would take the plastic we found on the street and make dolls out of them. Jack would create elaborate stories about their lives."

"That sounds like so much fun!" A Sigma childhood must have been amazing. "There was nowhere safe in our OLU building to play, so we always played outside."

"What kinds of games did you play?"

"Mostly tag. Charlie would watch us and make sure we stayed out of the water. He'd make up some games for us, too. He was great!"

"Who's Charlie?"

"He was an UnSelected man. Our parents gave him some paste for watching us. He always kept us safe. I thought of him as a fun uncle."

Sam's face contorted. They reached the bathroom door before Jennie could ask about his reaction. Sam opened the door, and she followed. The SLU bathroom amazed her. There were sinks—more than one—and they all worked. When she washed her hands, she had water left over! All the toilets worked. And, to top it all off, the bathroom smelled nicer than her neighborhood back home.

Being a Sigma is amazing!

Sam pushed the button beside the shower stall. "Samuel Watkins requesting the use of one shower credit."

"The Algorithm provides a shower for Mr. Watkins and Ms. Goodby at the expense of one of Mr. Watkins's shower credits." The stall door opened. "Hygiene products for both men and women are provided in the stall."

"I can't believe that worked!" Sam grinned mischievously. "Shall we continue our conversation from the bedroom?"

"Oh, yeah." Jennie grabbed Sam's robe, pulled him into the shower, and pressed the play button.

***

The Algorithm noted match number 561-165,771 now had a 75 percent chance of a permanent pairing. Water was reallocated from OLU Building #146 in Orlando to compensate for the shared shower.

***

Jennie dried her hair with a soft towel as they walked back to her SLU. "Wanna have breakfast? I'd be happy to share my provision." She hadn't yet become used to the size of Sigma meals.

"Sigmas don't eat each other's food."

That can't be right. Back home, Omegas gave food to the UnSelected all the time. "What about last night's dinner?"

"That was provided to both of us." Sam looked at his phone. "Maybe I have time to run over to my place and grab something from the dispenser and bring it back?"

Jennie's phone vibrated in her robe's pocket.

```
Food credit transferred from
Mr. Watkins to Ms. Goodby.
```

Sam stared at her phone. "I didn't know that was possible…"

There had been so many new privileges in the last few days. Why question this one? "Go ahead and request breakfast." Jennie followed Sam into the SLU. "I'm going to my room to get a hairbrush." She chuckled. "I don't want a rat's nest for my first day of work."

Jennie went to her room and opened the closet. Beside her work outfit hung another one that was too big for her. "That's odd!"

"Is everything alright in there?" Sam asked from the main room.

"Yeah. It's just that there is a men's work outfit in my closet. I guess I didn't notice it before." Jennie found the tag in the shirt. "What size do you wear?"

"Large."

"It's your size." Jennie held the blue polo and khaki pants up to the light. They looked new. "I wonder how these got in there?"

"I guess I'll get changed here and we can leave together."

Yay! More time with Sam!

Jennie put on her work outfit. Unlike the blue dress, the rough fabric laid clumsily over her thin body. *The outfit is for work, not looking good.* Regardless, it felt good when Sam looked her up and down as she entered the main room.

"No time for that." Jennie patted him on the shoulder as she sat down and joined him at the table. "We have to get to work." Her eyes zeroed in on Sam's plate. "Is that bread?"

"Yup. Bread is the only real food that Sigmas are provided regularly." Sam put his artificial egg and cheese sandwich down. "The wheat fields of Canada and Russia produce way too much for the Betas and Alphas. We get what's left over. It's usually stale, but at least it's real. If you see green spots, don't eat them."

He is so smart! "You know a lot about the world."

"I studied history and economics. I thought it might help me in Selection." Sam winced. "I'm sorry. I meant what I said last night."

Jennie reached across the table and squeezed his hand. "Omegas have limited access to the internet, so I couldn't learn much about the world. It's okay, though. It is *all* part of the Algorithm's plan to rebuild our world into an optimal society."

"Yeah, I suppose it is." Sam looked away as he took a sip of water.

The bread crust crunched when Jennie picked it up. She bit down on the sandwich and chewed. The tough bread hurt her teeth. According to the *Sigma Transition Manual*, food this solid would take getting used to.

"Mmm, this is so good!" Unlike her Omega meals, each item making up the sandwich had its own distinct flavor. The artificial egg had a pungent flavor with a mild sweetness. The artificial cheese reminded her of Omega-level cheese—but this tasted much better.

Sam stared at his plate. His hand grasped the cup of water on the table.

How can he not be eating this?

He bit his lip, then covered his mouth with his hand. Sam looked up from his plate. "I better get dressed so we can get to the bus depot on time. We don't want to be late on our first day." He went back to her room to change, leaving the half-eaten sandwich.

"Yup." Jennie closed her eyes as she took another bite.

***

A large yellow bus pulled up to the Orlando depot. On its side were the words:

```
Cape Canaveral Reclamation Administrative
Building
```

"That's ours!" The bus would take Jennie to her new job and the next phase of her new life.

They were the first to arrive at the depot. She led Sam onto the bus and stopped at the first row of seats behind the windshield. "Can we sit here? I want to see out the front window. You can have the window seat."

Sam slid over against the window and Jennie sat and nestled up beside him. Other Sigmas filed onto the bus. A Sigma couple occupied each seat—each one held hands and snuggled after sitting.

"Did you know that in the past, it was frowned upon if two men or two women were partners?"

Sam's question caught Jennie off guard. She turned around in her seat. It took her a moment to see it, but of course there were both same-sex and opposite-sex couples on the bus. Why should anyone have expected otherwise?

"If they cared less about who people loved and more about the planet, maybe the world would be different today." Jennie stared out the front window. *What was life like back then?* She'd heard stories—all too fantastic to be real.

The bus lurched forward. Jennie rested her head on Sam's shoulder and sighed.

"Is everything okay, honey?" Sam kissed the top of her head.

Honey! I am somebody's honey!

"Everything is great, *dear*! I am starting a new life, going to my new job—which doesn't involve dangerous labor, I might add—all with the man I love. Things couldn't be better!"

Chapter 14: Sam

January 4, 535

"Today begins the Cape Canaveral Reclamation Project. Brave Sigmas and Omegas will work to restore humanity's past glory and inspire future generations."

- Press release sent by the Algorithm to all humans, July 3, 453.

The hard plastic seat pressing upon Sam's back served as a reminder of his permanent status. Jennie hadn't moved since the bus left the depot. Her soft brown hair tickled his cheek.

Fields of barren sandy soil zoomed by as the bus carried Sam to his new job. An occasional patch of grass interrupted the sea of brown. Open windows let in both warm air and the stench of a recent flood.

What a morning! Sam hadn't intended to profess his love for Jennie so soon after their first night together. The Algorithm's antics, the synthahol, real broccoli, and Jennie's dress were all designed to push him over the edge. The extra robe, the shared breakfast, and the work clothes ensured he stayed there. Sam didn't need any of that. He loved Jennie the moment he saw her.

Of all the Algorithm's tricks, the shower surprised Sam the most. Jennie seemed to pull him in with little effort. He suppressed a smile at the thought of her pinning him on the bed this morning. *How can such a small woman be so strong?* It was a silly question. She had to be strong to survive an Omega childhood.

Jennie's strength went beyond the physical. Sam had known no one who learned to code as fast as her—himself included. She'd surpass his skills in less than a year.

Imagine where'd she be if she grew up as a Sigma.

Jennie snuggled closer to Sam and sighed.

Why is she in code maintenance? Everything he knew about the Society told him Jennie should be a Beta.

Is the Algorithm making optimal decisions? If It were, wouldn't It put smart people like Jennie into more important roles? Jack came to mind. *How can Jack be a Beta while Jennie is a Sigma? Could she be an Alpha?* No. Love clouded his judgment. *The Algorithm couldn't make the error of Selecting an Alpha as a Sigma—random factors or not.*

He looked down at the top of Jennie's head. Her hair lay flat, still damp. He inhaled. The stench of flood waters fell away, leaving behind the smell of Sigma shampoo. He closed his eyes and the shampoo's scent disappeared, leaving only Jennie's.

She seems so happy. I could learn a lot from her. Sam gently rested his head on hers. *But should we accept our fate?*

***

The hundred-year-old Administrative Building looked exactly as Sam expected, a big gray concrete box with no windows and few doors. Sandy brown soil surrounded the building. Supposedly, on the few days of the year without haze, the Atlantic Ocean could be seen in the distance behind the building.

Sam's phone vibrated as they got off the bus.

```
Proceed through the front doors and
go directly to Conference Room 3
for orientation.
```

Jennie read her phone then looked at Sam with a straight face. "Well, I guess this is where we part ways."

A lump formed in Sam's throat. "What?"

"We work in different offices, silly!" The blue flecks in her eyes sparkled. "How about we have lunch together? If it's allowed, of course."

A weight lifted off Sam's chest, reinforcing his belief that he truly loved her. "Sounds great! I'll message you."

"Good luck!" Jennie kissed him on the cheek. "I look forward to hearing all about your first day."

"You, too! I love you." Sam's eyes got wide. *Should I have said that in public?*

"Love you, too!" Jennie gave him the cutest smile as she waved and walked backward away from him. Sam watched her until she disappeared into a group of Sigmas headed toward the side door.

No one reacted to their proclamation. The other couples did similar things. After a kiss goodbye—a few of which lingered too long for polite company—one lover headed to the front door and the other went to the side door.

***

Sea-green tiles lined the interior walls of the Administrative Building. The white-gray drop ceiling looked like the one in Sam's SLU, only cleaner. Speckled tiles, probably found on a recovery expedition, covered the floor. The Algorithm decided the tiles had no use other than as ugly flooring. How many Omegas died excavating the material for him to have a walkway to his boring job?

A long plastic table took up most of the space in Conference Room 3. Images of old rockets hung on beige walls. A gray low-pile carpet covered the floor. *A human must have designed this room. Either that, or the Algorithm had a bad day.*

Two women and three men, all Sigmas and about Sam's age, sat around the table staring at their phones. No one said a word when Sam pulled out a chair. The chair's comfort matched his expectations.

The guy across from Sam snickered at something on his screen, then mumbled, "Stupid Omega." Sam got out his phone and tried to fit in. Influencer videos never interested him. Instead, he found an article on the pre-Shift history of Florida.

Jennie never mindlessly scrolls through her phone, either.

Sam recalled a phrase he found once when he *accidentally* hacked into a Beta terminal—bread and circuses. He now understood what it meant.

Ten minutes later, a hologram of a Beta appeared at the head of the table. Sam and the other Sigmas lowered their phones and their gazes.

"I am Mr. McCreary, your supervisor at the AB—the Administrative Building. You were all Selected as Sigma Robotics Programmers for the Cape Canaveral Reclamation Project or CCRP."

"Cape Canaveral was one of many sites where rockets launched humans and satellites to space before the Climate Shift. At one point, the rockets were used to send people to the moon and Mars. As you know, the Cape is now underwater."

The Florida history site mentioned humanity's spacefaring past ended in 2145. By then, governments had to abandon space programs to deal with the ramifications of a changing climate, including increased civil unrest. Today, rumors of Alphas living on space stations flooded the Sigma feeds.

"The CCRP uses robots to find spaceflight artifacts in the submerged Cape Canaveral facility." Mr. McCreary's hologram stuttered. Even Betas weren't provided a good connection in Florida. "Every artifact identified by a robot is retrieved by an Omega team."

The Omegas' job at the CCRP sounded a lot like what Jennie's parents did. Why not use the robots to collect the artifacts after they're identified?

The Algorithm must value robots over Omegas.

"Your job is to keep the robots running efficiently. Other Sigmas identify inefficiencies in the robots' control programs in another part of this facility." A holo-diagram of the AB appeared in the air above the table. The Sigmas raised their gaze, but all carefully avoided Mr. McCreary's direction.

The holo highlighted the basement offices where the other Sigmas worked. "Those Sigmas send you the inefficiencies. *You* recommend fixes." Mr. McCreary paused. "*I* implement them. Questions?"

Sam had questions but knew better than to ask them. Why wasn't he both identifying and fixing inefficiencies? Better yet, why wasn't the Algorithm doing this? It should be better at it than Sam or any other human.

"You each have a terminal in your assigned office. Go there now and begin your work." Mr. McCreary's holo-image faded.

I can't believe my work has to be approved by that guy. Robotics programming was a lot easier than the AI programming Sam practiced in Baltimore.

Sam's phone vibrated and displayed a map of the AB. He walked toward the pulsing red dot denoting his office. *I wonder what amazing things Jack is doing in Detroit right now. I deserve to be there.* Sam stopped walking and dipped his chin to his chest, disappointed at breaking his promise to himself.

Dwelling on Jack and Detroit is not healthy. I must accept my Selection and be grateful that I am not UnSelected.

If he kept telling himself that, he might believe it.

***

Whoa! My own office!

The room was a mishmash of elements from a standard SLU and the AB. It had the same speckled tile floor as the AB's hallways, but the walls were covered in peeling yellow paint, just like Sam's SLU.

At least I won't have to stare at sea-green tiles all day.

A desk, slightly larger than Sam's desk in Baltimore, dominated the room. Sam pulled out the plastic chair from behind the desk. It had a thin cushion that yielded when he pushed on it.

Nice!

A terminal sat atop his desk. Its white plastic casing appeared new—no yellowing or scratches—and the screen had no cracks. The terminal's holo-inputs appeared above the desk when he waved his hand in front of the terminal. Holo-inputs would prevent his hands from being damaged from repetitive stress.

Why was I provided these upgrades?

A ten-centimeter tall holo of Jennie, wearing the dress from last night, floated above the desk to the left of the terminal. Although Sam hadn't expected the image, it didn't surprise him either. Jennie's image brightened up the otherwise dreary office. Not unlike how she had done for his life.

Sam sat in the chair. Its cushion compressed under his weight, giving him some protection from the chair's hard plastic base. *I wish I had a couple of these at home.*

The terminal's display lit up with a login screen. A female voice came from the terminal's speaker.

"Hello, Sam, I am terminal CCRP-437. You may call me Sally. I have voice, manual, and holographic interfaces. I am fully set up and registered to you. The Algorithm has informed me you may decorate your office as you see fit from the Sigma Outfitter. No credits required."

Sam stared at the terminal's monitor with narrow eyes. *I have never heard of a Sigma who doesn't need credits.*

"Thanks, Sally. Can you display the Outfitter?"

Images of various office decor and supplies filled the screen.

"You may spend working hours ordering decorations and decorating your office. The Algorithm is pleased with your work."

How can the Algorithm be pleased with me when I haven't done anything yet?

"The benefit extends to home-use purchases, too."

Sam leaned back in his chair, interlocked his fingers behind his head, and smiled. *I'm still a Sigma, but one with a little more privilege. That is better than nothing.*

***

The Algorithm estimated Sam's dissatisfaction decreased by 60 percent. The unlimited credits were an effective use of resources that could be reallocated from Omegas in Orlando. It estimated Sam would continue to participate in Phase One with a probability of 97.23 percent.

***

Sam chose a small artificial plant for his office and a mountable screen that could act as a fake window. A necklace appeared as a recommended item for Sigmas who purchased the plant.

Why is that here? Let's try something.

"Sally, can I request a gift?"

"Yes, Sam. The Algorithm has provided you one gift to celebrate your first day of work. What would you like to get Jennie?" The screen filled with images of jewelry, including the necklace, which was now highlighted.

Another necklace caught his attention. It was made of thin aluminum and had a blue artificial mineral pendant. Like the other items on the screen, the necklace cost zero credits.

"How about that one?" Sam pointed to the necklace with the blue mineral. "I think the blue will go nicely with her dress." *And the flecks in her eyes.*

"Jennie is predicted to like the necklace I highlighted 32 percent more than the one you chose."

"I want the one *I* selected. It will be more special to her since I chose it."

"It will be delivered to her SLU this afternoon."

"Sounds good. Thanks, Sally."

Interesting. Why is the Algorithm consuming so many resources to make sure we're together?

Sam spent the rest of the morning filling out paperwork, pairing the terminal with his phone, signing up for the meal plan at work, and several other things he thought the Algorithm should have done. Sally's screen went black after he submitted the last piece of paperwork.

"It is 1200, Sam. Time for lunch. Please proceed to the cafeteria."

Lunch sounded good, even if it would be more paste. He couldn't bring himself to finish his breakfast sandwich earlier. His stomach had been rumbling most of the morning. "Please message Jennie Goodby to see if she can have lunch with me."

"I am sorry, Sam, but code maintenance personnel do not dine with programmers."

"Understood." Sam pushed his chair back.

Does the Algorithm keep couples separate so they have engaging dinner conversation? Sam shook his head. He could hear Jack admonishing him for going too far down a conspiracy rabbit hole.

Every hallway in the AB looked similar, speckled floors and sea-green wall tiles. He passed Omegas hanging posters. Sam's phone vibrated.

```
Read the posters every day.
Posters provide nudges that will help you be
23% more compliant with our organization's
policies.
Failure to read the posters will result in a
reprimand.
```

Most of the posters were about safety procedures. A few contained pointless corporate speak. One had a picture of a cat. He'd never seen a cat in real life. Supposedly, Betas kept them as pets. Having food to give to an animal was a luxury none of the Lower Castes could afford.

The cafeteria continued the AB's overarching design theme: sea-green tile walls, gray-white ceiling tiles, and hard plastic tables and chairs. The cafeteria's floors were covered in the same speckled tiles as the hallway.

Well, at least it's consistent.

Sam pushed the button on the cafeteria's food dispenser. "One lunch please." A clunk signaled his lunch's arrival. He opened the dispenser door and removed two tacos. The meat looked like it had been squirted into the taco shells. *Definitely paste.* The corn tortillas were real. *Not bad.*

Reaching into the dispenser compartment, Sam found corn chips, a container of orangish cheddar cheese, and a bottle of cloudy Sigma-quality water. He squeezed the cheese container. It didn't resist. *Excellent!* Although most Sigmas found it disgusting, Sam loved artificial cheese dip. *I hope Jennie is eating this well.*

Sam's phone directed him to his table, which had only one empty seat. He sat beside a woman with short brown hair and brown eyes. Her skin was a shade lighter than Sam's. He wondered if she came from a Sigma city even farther north than Baltimore. The woman smiled and nodded at Sam.

She's pretty, but not as beautiful as Jennie.

"My name's Cynthia." She extended her hand. "Can you believe it? First day of work and it's taco day!"

Sam shook Cynthia's hand and introduced himself.

Cynthia dipped a chip into her cheese and took a bite. Her face told Sam they had different opinions on artificial cheese. "I can't get over the upgrades that come with this job."

"The Algorithm provides." Sam's stomach sank. *I guess everyone has unlimited credits.*

"Sure does." Cynthia pushed the cheese container to the side. "I met a great guy on my way here from Atlanta. He's in code maintenance. He doesn't have the same privileges." Cynthia poured some cheese on her tacos. "It helps make the cheese tolerable."

Sam scooped up the cheese with one of his chips. "Code maintenance, huh?"

"Yeah, but that's not the interesting part. I had a bunch of clothes for him in my SLU. He had nothing like that in his. I guess it doesn't matter. He'll be spending most of his time at my place." Cynthia winked.

Cynthia and Jennie had the same privileges—a few extra clothes, not unlimited credits. Sam felt better. He shouldn't. But he did.

The table's lunch conversation shifted to programming. As they spoke, it became clear that no one else had any programming knowledge beyond the basics, much less any AI programming experience. One guy didn't even know about Booleans.

A cacophony of phone beeps erupted at 1230. Time to go back to work. As the Sigmas left, two Omega males, about Sam's age, entered the cafeteria. Each Omega held a bucket and a mop. They wore dirty uniforms and smelled like they hadn't showered in a few days. In a tropical place like Florida, even daily showering barely helped with body odor. The Omegas kept their gaze on the floor and away from the Sigmas.

Cynthia hit one of the Omegas on the shoulder as she walked by. "Don't lick my cheese container." The other Sigmas burst out laughing.

They are people, too.

Sam stopped in front of the men. "Thank you. I appreciate you keeping our spaces clean." Both men kept their eyes on the floor. The one closest to Sam gave a closed-mouth smile and nodded. The other didn't react, probably trying to avoid attracting any more attention.

"What the hell was that?" Cynthia scowled.

"They're just doing their job. There's no need to be mean."

"If they'd been better people before Selection, they wouldn't be Omegas now. They deserve what the Algorithm provides."

Sigmas had been saying that all Sam's life. He didn't believe it back in Baltimore, and he believed it even less now. Sam walked away from Cynthia. She mumbled something. He ignored her.

My girlfriend was an Omega before Selection. She didn't deserve the life she was born into. Cynthia's comment came from someone who knew little about the world.

Wait, is Jennie my girlfriend? Sam stopped in the middle of the hallway and looked down at the speckled floor. *We said, "I love you."* He filed that thought away as a conversation for dinner tonight.

***

Sam sat with his elbows on his desk, rubbing his temples. *I haven't even finished my first day of work and I've already made an enemy.* The terminal's monitor flashed, lighting up the entire office.

```
INEFFICIENCY FOUND:
LINE 238 OF ARTIFACT_CLASSIFICATION.AI
```

Show time! Sam straightened. His heart quickened as his eyes focused on the .ai extension.

How could a maintenance person find an error in artificial intelligence code? That should be beyond their skills. After the conversation at lunch, he doubted any of the other programmers could do it either.

"Sally, can you please bring up the file?"

"Yes, but there is an attachment to the message. Would you like me to open it?"

"Is the attachment an executable?" Sam's orientation materials made it clear not to open executables in attachments. It wasn't clear why they weren't filtered out automatically.

"No, but it is encrypted."

Why would someone encrypt interoffice communications?

"Is that normal?" Sam asked.

"It occasionally happens. New code maintenance personnel are 80 percent more likely to feel uncomfortable posting inefficiencies on a public channel. Your code maintenance person probably wants to avoid embarrassment in case the inefficiency is a false positive."

Sam raised his eyebrows. "Okay, let's see what it says."

Sally displayed the message.

```
Programmer, please see Line 238. The code
compiles and runs correctly, but something
doesn't seem right.


I don't know enough AI programming to be more
specific, and I apologize for the vague report.


If I am wrong, please disregard. I'll send
more specific notifications in the future.
```

Sam's back pressed upon the thin cushion until it found the hard plastic. "Open up artifact_classification.ai and go to Line 238."

Lines of code appeared on the screen.

```
learning_rate = 5.4; #learning rate for SGD
```

SGD?

During his first year of high school, Sam became interested in the history of AI—in particular, early learning algorithms. SGD stood for stochastic gradient descent, an ancient method used by AI algorithms to learn tasks by minimizing error. No one he knew in the programming forums used SGD. Better methods had been developed, even before the Shift.

"Sally, why is SGD being used by the robots?"

"I am sorry, Sam. I do not know the answer to your question."

"It's okay. I think the line contains a typo. The learning rate is too high. Let's change line two thirty-eight to read, learning rate equals zero point five four. Keep the comment for now."

"Done. Should I send the recommended change to Mr. McCreary?"

"No. Let's test it first." *I don't want to look like an idiot on my first day.*

"That is highly unusual. While testing by Sigmas is not forbidden, it is also not typically done."

I can't pass up a chance to test a program. Sam needed an excuse. "Testing improves the efficiency of my code, and we are all about efficiency here. Right?"

"Yes, Sam. What would you like me to do?"

"Load a simulated search robot into a simulated environment with fifty objects. Give each object a randomly assigned similarity score between zero and one, where zero means the object looks nothing like an artifact and one means the object is an artifact. Please make sure that there are at least five artifacts."

"The environment is ready."

"Now train the robot using the original artifact_classification.ai program. Have the robot randomly move around the environment, looking at each object. Ask the robot to classify each object as an artifact or not. Report back how often it correctly classifies the objects. Run the simulation one thousand times."

The simulation's results appeared on the screen. The original algorithm could identify only one out of five artifacts consistently and classified 40 percent of the non-artifacts as space flight relics.

These results are terrible. We are missing 80 percent of the artifacts out there and sending Omega teams out too often to recover non-artifacts. How many Omegas have died recovering rocks?

"Sally, please train the simulated robot with the updated program and repeat the experiment."

The new results displayed on the screen, even faster than before. Sam read them three times. The robot found all artifacts in each simulated trial. It incorrectly classified objects as artifacts less than 5 percent of the time. This change would save Omega lives.

How could such a simple mistake be allowed to continue? Replacing SGD with a newer learning algorithm would reduce the misclassification rate to near zero.

He began writing a report that included the recommended fix to Mr. McCreary. Before sending the report, he deleted his suggestion about using a new learning algorithm. He didn't know why, but he thought he should keep that to himself—for now.

Later that afternoon, Sam received a message.

```
Mr. McCreary has discovered an important in-
efficiency in our robots' search program. His
work resulted in the discovery of 400% more
artifacts this afternoon. Also of note, today
had the lowest daily Omega casualty rate in
decades. Mr. McCreary was promoted to Class 1
Supervisor and will move to Detroit tomorrow.
Let's all congratulate him on a job well done!
```

Sam stared at the screen with his teeth clenched. *Un-fucking-be-lievable. Some maintenance person found the issue, and I fixed it. Where are our rewards?* He rubbed the inside corners of his eyes. *McCreary did nothing but benefit from our work.*

He counted to three, then took a deep breath. One of the ventilation fans kicked on. The room felt a little cooler. Another breath. The air smelled less stale. The message disappeared. His reflection stared

back at him from the black screen. The boy in the bathroom mirror in Baltimore had been replaced by a Selected Adult. One whose
future had been determined for him. He knew what he had promised
himself. Some promises should be broken.

"Sally, can you order a terminal for me to run future efficiency
checks on?"

"What's wrong with using me?"

Had Sam not known better, he would have thought he hurt her
feelings. But he knew better, and he still felt bad. "Testing on two
machines will improve my efficiency."

"The Algorithm has approved your request. The new terminal will
arrive in an hour."

No new inefficiency alerts came in. So, Sam spent the rest of the
afternoon setting up a testing environment on the new terminal. He
turned off voice control and isolated the terminal from the network.

Sam had an idea.

Chapter 15: Tabitha

January 2, 535

"Canada denies entry to American climate refugees."
"Alaska secedes from the US to join Canada."
"Russia and China form a new alliance."

- News feed headlines, circa 2148.

It had to be early. How early? Tabitha didn't want to know. Jack had been tossing and turning for quite some time.

"How did you get into Tabby's house?" Jack whispered.

Tabitha sighed, rolled over, and propped her head up on her hand. "What's wrong?"

"I can hear Samantha in my head."

Tabitha closed her eyes and let her head fall back onto her pillow. "She's talking to you through your aural implants. They let you communicate with your AI without others hearing it. Didn't you read the message from the med facility?"

Tension left Jack's face. "No. But I will. I promise."

"What time is it?" Tabitha yawned as she spoke.

"I don't know. Samantha told me to wake up."

The time, 1000, floated in the air above Tabitha's bed. "It's so early! We don't have to be at work until noon."

Jack propped himself up on his side. "Noon? Why so late?"

Samantha spoke to Tabitha and Jack in their aural implants. "Beta working hours are noon to four."

At this point, Tabitha wasn't getting back to sleep. *Might as well have some fun.* She rolled over on top of Jack and kissed him.

***

Samantha informed the Algorithm of relationship 561-165,772's status. The Algorithm estimated the match had a 70 percent chance of becoming long-term.

***

The bed shook, waking Tabitha.

Now what? I had just gotten back to sleep!

Jacqueline stood in the doorway. "I apologize for startling you, Mr. Thompson. I am Jacqueline, Ms. Forsythe's house AI. It is 1100 and time to get ready for work. What would you like for breakfast?"

Tabitha propped up on her elbows. The blanket slid down, exposing her bare shoulders to the cool air in the bedroom. "The top recommended meal." She looked at Jack. "Sound good to you?"

Jack sat up. The cover fell to his waist and exposed his ribs. Tabitha hadn't seen someone that thin before. "Am I allowed to eat here?"

A lump formed in the back of Tabitha's throat. "Don't you want to spend time with me?" That sounded whinier than she intended.

Why do I care? Isn't he just part of my Selected job?

"I do, but isn't it wrong to eat someone else's food?"

Where did he get that idea?

"Mr. Thompson, the taboo you are referring to was created by Sigmas—the other castes don't follow it. Dispensers—even Sigma ones—can provide multiple meals. The Algorithm can certainly keep track of who-eats-what-where."

Jack grinned as he sat up. "Well, then, what are we having?" To her surprise, a weight lifted from Tabitha's shoulders.

"Mr. Thompson, today's recommended breakfast for Ms. Forsythe is eggs, bacon, and waffles. Yours is—"

"Sounds great to me!" Jack kissed Tabitha on the forehead and got out of bed. "I'll run over to my place to wash up, put on a work outfit, and come right back for breakfast."

Jacqueline held up her hand. "No need, Mr. Thompson. I have clothes that fit you, and I'll have Samantha send me a list of your preferred toiletries."

"You have men's work clothes here?" Jack asked.

"I don't know what I have here." Tabitha stood. "I haven't gone digging through the stuff that came with the house yet." She narrowed her eyes. "What are work clothes?"

"Never mind."

Whatever. Tabitha led Jack to the shower in her master bathroom. Jack stood behind her as she let the water fall over her body.

"Mind if I get wet before it runs out?" Jack fidgeted with his hands. "I want to be clean for my first day."

"Uh, sure." Tabitha stepped to the side. "Why would it run out?" Jack got under the stream. "Jacqueline, activate rain mode." Tabitha ran her fingers through her newly wet hair.

"That's a lot of water." Jack looked up in amazement. "Do other Betas get this much? I don't want to take from someone else."

Tabitha put her arms around Jack's shoulders and kissed him. His concerns were strange, but she knew how to ease his mind.

***

The Algorithm increased the probability of a permanent match to 85 percent. Resources were diverted from Omegas in Baltimore to compensate for the use of rain mode.

***

Tabitha's first breakfast in Detroit underwhelmed her. The eggs and waffles weren't better than what she had in Baltimore. They weren't worse either. Her hopes rested upon the bacon.

Jack, fork in hand, stared at his meal. There didn't appear to be anything missing from his plate. He had the same meal as her.

"Is something wrong with the food?" Tabitha asked.

"No. It's good. Amazing, really. Just taking it all in."

"Eat before it gets cold."

Tabitha picked up the bacon and took a bite. The pork, fat, and salt were in different proportions compared to Baltimore bacon. The bacon memes from the Detroit-based influencers now made sense to her.

Jack scooped up some of the scrambled egg on his fork and put it in his mouth. He chewed with his eyes closed. It looked like he enjoyed the eggs more than the shower this morning. The reaction was extreme. *Hasn't he had eggs before?*

After he finished chewing, Jack picked up a piece of bacon with his fingers and ate it. "Wow!" Jack spoke with his mouth full—another habit she'd have to break him of.

"Glad you like it. It's the best bacon I have ever had."

"It's the only bacon I've ever had." A piece of bacon fell out of Jack's mouth and onto the table. Tabitha cringed as he put the fallen piece back into his mouth.

After he swallowed the bacon, Jack stared at his waffles. "Do I eat this like bread?"

How can he not know how to eat waffles?

"No. Let me show you." Tabitha cut her waffles. "What are you going to do with your spare room?" She poured syrup on one piece and ate it.

Jack mimicked her movements as he described how he planned to turn the spare room into a game room. *Jack might be new, but he likes his toys just like any other Beta male.* He placed a syrup-covered piece of waffle in his mouth, closed his eyes, and chewed slowly—just like with the eggs. After swallowing, he asked, "How about you? What are you going to put up there?"

"A photography studio." Tabitha ate another piece of waffle, this time without syrup. It was much better without the syrup.

"What do you like to photograph?"

"Me, of course! As an actor, I'll need headshots and photos for my social media accounts." *What else would I photograph?*

"Cool! I'd love to help photograph you." Jack winked. He cut another piece of waffle. This time, he didn't put syrup on it. It looked like he had the hang of it. Not that it should have been difficult to figure out. It was just breakfast, after all.

"Not those kinds of photos! Besides, real people don't take *those* kinds of photos. That's all deepfake stuff."

Jack pressed his lips together and looked down at his plate. Tabitha expected him to say something, but instead, he ate more bacon with his fingers. Like the waffles and eggs, he ate the bacon with a slow and deliberate effort. *Good thing we have plenty of time until work.*

Jack wiped the remaining syrup off his plate with his last piece of waffle. He put the syrup-soaked waffle in his mouth and slowly withdrew the fork. His face reddened when his eyes met hers. He slowly put his fork down on his plate.

Tabitha wiped her mouth and pushed her plate forward. "Are you done?"

"Aren't you going to eat those?" Jack pointed at the leftover eggs on her plate.

"Uh, no." Tabitha paused. Jack's attention hadn't left her plate. "Do you want them?"

"Only if you aren't going to eat them. I'd hate to see good food go to waste."

How is it possible to waste food? There's always more in the dispenser.

She pushed her plate over to Jack. "Have at it." He finished her eggs faster than what would be considered polite by most Betas.

Jacqueline appeared and began stacking the dishes one by one.

"Thanks, Jacqueline." Jack handed Jacqueline his plate.

"My pleasure, Mr. Thompson."

"Please, call me Jack."

Seriously?

"Sure thing, Jack!" Jacqueline placed the dishes in the dispenser. A hum filled the room as the dispenser sterilized the dishes.

"You don't have to thank it." Tabitha leaned forward over the table. Something about how Jack talked to Jacqueline compelled her to whisper. "Computers don't have feelings."

"It's polite. Besides, there are some old habits that I don't want to break." Jack smirked. "Anyway, what's up with the name?"

"What can I say?" Tabitha gave him a smile she had practiced since her Selection. It came easier than she expected, but not because of the practice. Jack had left an impression. A strange one. But for some reason, she enjoyed being around him. "Dinner tonight?"

Please say yes.

A devilish grin formed on Jack's face. "That depends."

"Depends on what?" *I thought he liked me. Why does this hurt?*

"Depends on how many other super-hot Betas ask me to have dinner with them today." Jack laughed.

A sense of relief washed over Tabitha. "As if you could land a girl hotter than *me*."

"I can't think of anyone else I'd rather have dinner with tonight than you, Tabby." Jack leaned over the table and kissed Tabitha on the cheek.

He used the sobriquet again. It had grown on her—but only when Jack said it. "It's a date!"

To her own surprise, Tabitha wanted to do something special for Jack. Unlike the Betas she had dated, he expected nothing of her. On the contrary, Jack seemed truly appreciative of her. An idea came to her mind. "Let's go out for dinner!"

"Out?" Jack squinted and turned his head slightly. "Like outside?" He drew out the question as if what she proposed was preposterous. Why would eating outside be a problem? It didn't matter. She had something else in mind.

"No, silly!" Tabitha bit her lip. Using her artificial neural net, she requested access to Jack's house AI. It was approved. "Samantha, don't spoil the surprise for Jack by telling him what 'going out' means."

"Of course, Ms. Forsythe. I'll keep it between us girls."

"You can talk to Samantha?" Jack frowned.

"I requested permission to access Samantha. Couples can talk to each other's AI."

Jack did a double take. Tabitha suppressed a smile.

"Jack, you need to return home." Samantha's voice returned on the public channel. "Your car is ready to take you to work. If you leave in ten minutes, you will arrive on time."

"Thanks, Sam." Jack said aloud. Tabitha wondered why he still wasn't using his ANN. He looked at Tabitha, his eyes full of mischief. "Ten minutes? We could do it."

Tabitha loved the way he looked at her—and briefly considered his offer. "No, Jack. My makeup and hair are done."

Jack gave an overly dramatic fake pout, then perked up. "Good luck with your first day. I love you." He kissed Tabitha on the cheek. When he pulled back, his eyes were as large as saucers.

Tabitha's heart quickened, and her face felt warm. She wasn't sure which surprised her more, Jack's declaration or her response. At that moment, she felt a connection to Jack unlike any she'd had with her past boyfriends. A mild chemical scent entered her nostrils, pushing her over the edge.

"I love you too, Jack!" Tabitha stood and took Jack's hand. He joined her. She reached up and placed the back of her hand on his head and kissed him. Jack tasted like eggs, syrup, and bacon. The kiss lingered; the taste of breakfast fell away. The chemical scent was replaced by lavender and oak—her favorite cologne. Time slowed. If she hadn't felt her feet on the floor, she would have thought she was floating.

Jack is not a job. He is my boyfriend.

Chapter 16: Jack

January 2, 535

"The Canadian-Alaskan Federation and the Russian Alliance see record food exports as global temperatures continue to climb."

- Pre-Shift internet news broadcast, circa 2150.

Jack ran his fingers along the curves of the car parked in his garage. Its sleek black body reminded him of Tabitha's dress, and the things she wore under it.

I still can't believe this is my life.

The car had one leather bucket seat. A monitor stretched across the dashboard above a small dispenser. A click echoed in the garage, and the car door cracked open.

"Get in, Jack." Samantha spoke in his aural implants. "Sit back, relax, and enjoy a soda." The dispenser door opened, revealing a shiny can. "I'll handle the driving."

The can was cold to the touch. *Damn, this is metal!* Jack took a sip. The soda's sweetness overpowered his tastebuds. The bubbles tickled his nose. It was all a bit much. He put the can back in the dispenser.

The car left the garage and drove through Jack's neighborhood toward downtown. Beta Town Houses, identical to his, lined the street. *Good thing Sam does the driving. Otherwise, I'd go to the wrong house when I return.* He took another sip of the soda. *Much better this time.*

The buildings became taller as he approached downtown. The city was like an immaculately clean forest of glass, steel, and concrete.

Why is everything here so amazing? I haven't had anything that was just okay. Where is the food I don't like? Why was Tabby's dress and this car my favorite color? Why were there clothes in her closet that fit me?

Tabitha wouldn't have liked him as a Sigma, and he probably wouldn't have liked her either. *Do people fall in love this fast? I wish I could talk to Sam about this. He'd know what was going on. He'd probably say it was all part of the Algorithm's plan.*

Cool air blew from the car's vents. Jack reached forward to redirect the air off him. As he touched the vents, a faint chemical odor entered his nostrils. He reclined his seat.

Sam's opinion doesn't matter. The truth is, I am lucky to have found her. His heart felt full. He smiled at his good fortune and stared out the side window as the cityscape zoomed by.

***

The car came to a stop outside a tall glass skyscraper that looked like all the others downtown. Jack got out of the car, stretched, and looked up. The top of the building couldn't be seen.

Footsteps approached from Jack's right. A man and a woman, both a few centimeters taller and about twenty years older than Jack, stopped in front of him. Each wore the same blue BSF uniform Jack had seen at the airport.

The male's stern blue eyes ran up and down Jack. "Mr. Thompson." It wasn't a question.

"Yes?" Jack's eyes darted back and forth between the two officers.

"We are with the Beta Security Force. It is our job to make sure the Lower Castes stay out of Detroit." The man placed a hand on his pistol. "We have been watching you since you left Baltimore."

Jack kept his hands visible and made no subtle movements. "Have I done something wrong? My Selection avatar told me I'm a Beta." In The Hill, he had learned to keep calm under pressure. As a Sigma, he'd run into the authorities before.

"Yeah, about that," the woman said as she pulled out a pair of handcuffs. "It seems there has been a mistake."

I knew it was too good to be true. Jack lowered his gaze and held out his hands. "I'll go without a struggle. I know you don't owe me anything, but can you let Tabitha Forsythe know I won't be joining her tonight?" Jack paused. "Please let her know why. I don't want her to think I ran off with someone else."

A pit formed in his stomach. He'd miss the tasty food and effective medicine. The worst part, however, was losing Tabitha.

The officers broke out in laughter. "We're sorry! We didn't think you'd react this way." The man put a heavy hand on Jack's shoulder. "You're the first new Beta we've met, and we just had to take this opportunity for a prank."

Jack exhaled. "Seriously?"

The woman held out her hand, which Jack reluctantly shook. "Welcome to Detroit." She squeezed a little too hard and looked him in the eye. Jack felt like a Sigma again.

The man interrupted the nonverbal conversation. "Tell Tabitha that Dan and Rebecca said hi. We go out drinking with her parents when they fly into Detroit."

"Will do." Jack kept his eyes locked on Rebecca's as he released her hand. "Have a good day, officers." Jack headed for the building.

Damn Low-Metric Betas.

***

A well-dressed female hologram, attractive enough to stop traffic, appeared when Jack entered the building. "Mr. Thompson, welcome to the North American branch of the Global VR Entertainment Company. Please follow the augmented reality arrows in your ocular implants to Room 2430. Your orientation will begin shortly."

I have ocular implants? He'd been meaning to read the text from the med center, but the Beta world was far more interesting than some boring jargon-filled message. If Sam were around, Jack would have Sam read it and summarize it for him.

Yellow block arrows appeared in Jack's vision, leading him to an elevator. He pressed the button highlighted in his ocular implants and the door opened. Jack hesitated for a moment, then stepped inside. He faced the door and kept his back to the elevator's glass walls, not wanting to watch the ground floor rush away from him. A moment later, a *ding* sounded and the number 24 appeared above the door. He hadn't felt the elevator move. *Must be the same tech as the planes.*

The arrows reappeared after the door slid open. Jack followed them along a red-carpeted hallway. The walls were made of glass panels, most of which were opaque. One transparent section of glass showed a vacant office on the other side.

The door to Room 2430 opened as Jack approached. Three Betas, all about Jack's age, sat around a large round table. *The empty chair must be for me.*

A handsome man with dark blond hair, blue eyes, and light brown skin walked up to Jack with his hand extended. "You must be Jack! I'm Michael. It is great to meet you." Michael shook Jack's hand with vigor.

"Nice to meet you, Michael!" Jack caught himself staring at Michael a little too long. Michael returned Jack's gaze with a shy smile.

"I'm Susan." A dark-skinned woman with close-cropped dark brown hair stood to shake Jack's hand. Jack made a conscious effort not to stare. *Are all Betas as attractive as Tabby, Michael, and Susan?* Even Rebecca and Dan were pleasant to look at.

The third male in the room cleared his throat. "Oh, great. A newbie." He had brown hair, blue eyes, and a complexion not as light as Michael's—nor was he as attractive. "I cannot believe I got Selected to hand-hold some promoted Sigma." The man squinted. "Or worse, an Omega. You weren't an Omega, *were you?*"

Susan glared at the man. "Shut up, Richard! The last thing he needs is some classist riding his ass on his first day." An image projected from Susan's watch warned her about a penalty for the language. "Worth it."

Richard sank back in his seat, rolled his eyes, and typed something out on the terminal in front of him. A message appeared on Jack's watch.

```
I'm keeping my eye on you.
Screw up and I'll have you bounced down to
Omega so fast your head will spin.
You will never be one of us.
```

Richard's last sentence hit Jack hard. Despite Tabitha's and Samantha's efforts, he didn't feel like a Beta. Richard, Dan, and Rebecca weren't making it any easier. But he knew Richard's type. Growing up in The Hill taught him that predators fed off fear.

If I don't respond now, he'll push me around forever.

Jack stared directly at Richard. "When I was a Sigma, we had to learn different ways of interpersonal communication." Jack smirked as he began to roll up his sleeves. "Stick around after work if you'd like me to show you. I'll be happy to teach you." Richard had the soft body and mind of a lifelong Beta. "It won't take a minute."

Richard squirmed in his chair. A knock on the door interrupted them.

Rebecca poked her head in. "Everything okay in here? We got an alert to check out Room 2430."

"Yeah, it's all good." Susan waved her away. "Everything is fine." When Rebecca left, the tension returned.

Michael broke the silence by taking a deep, audible breath. "Okay, guys, let's not start off on the wrong foot." He looked at Richard. "When someone is Selected Beta, they are Beta. Past doesn't matter." Michael swept his hand horizontally across the table, signaling case closed.

"And Jack," Susan crossed her arms, "Betas are not violent. I don't know how Sigmas do things, but you must understand that even implied violence is not appropriate between Betas."

"I apologize." Richard sighed. "Susan is right, pre-Selection is irrelevant." That last part sounded like it hurt Richard to say it.

"I am sorry for threatening you, Richard." *I am sorry, alright. Sorry I won't get to teach you the lesson.*

A glowing holo-screen appeared above the table. Susan sat down, signaling everyone else to do the same. "Good. Now let's begin by filling out our human resources paperwork."

Jack looked around. "Don't we need to wait for our boss?"

"What boss?" Richard spat.

Susan folded her hands on the table. "High-Metric Betas work as teams without a hierarchical structure. We do our work and pass it up to the Alpha who makes the final decisions."

"Supervision is for children and the Lower Castes." Richard sat back in his chair. "Although, I suppose I repeated myself…"

Ten seconds. All I need is ten seconds.

The four Betas spent the rest of the hour typing information into the terminals that sat in front of them. At 1300, a hologram pushing a cart entered the room. The cart had four covered plates, four glasses, and a pitcher of ice water so clear Jack could see through it. *Lunch already?*

It was all Jack could do not to stare at the water. He didn't need more attention from Richard. The hologram placed a plate in front of each person and removed the lid. Not thanking the holo felt wrong. But based on Tabitha's earlier comments, Jack thought it would be best to remain quiet.

"Taco day!" Susan rubbed her hands together. "Awesome!"

A plate of real beef tacos with real cheese, all wrapped in corn tortillas, sat in front of Jack. He did his best to fight the urge to inhale the scent of real beef. The hologram placed a tray of assorted vegetables in the middle of the table. Each of the other Betas grabbed some vegetables and put them on their tacos. Jack loaded a long green vegetable on one of his tacos and took a bite. A burning sensation filled his mouth. He liked it.

"We must have made the Algorithm happy." Jack spoke with his mouth full of taco.

After taking a bite, Richard put one of his tacos down on his plate. "Meh. These tacos are just okay. Nothing memorable." The corners of his lips turned down. "I suppose if you haven't had real tacos before, it'd be special." Richard's eye widened. "Last night for fun, my girlfriend and I slummed it and ordered Sigma food. It was some nasty nutrient paste that was supposed to taste like chicken. It tasted like chalk." Richard looked at Jack. "How do *those* people eat that crap?"

Keep it up, buddy. These were Jack's first real tacos, and maybe one day tacos would be routine to him—but not today. *I wonder if Samantha will tell me which car is Richard's—*

Michael shot a nasty look at Richard. Then he turned to Jack. "I'm glad you like them. Try putting some of those on them." Michael pointed to a pile of diced red things that Jack didn't recognize. Michael shot another glance at Richard. "I bet Alphas would turn their noses up at these tacos."

"It doesn't matter what the Alphas get." Susan's eyes went back and forth between her loaded tacos and the vegetable tray. "What matters is that we are all Betas, and we are all the same in the eyes of the Algorithm."

"Yeah, right," Richard mumbled under his breath.

"Did you say something, Richard?" Susan looked up from her tacos and stared down Richard. Her air of authority was impressive. People respected her, even if she wasn't the one in charge.

"I didn't say anything," Richard said.

"Good. I'd hate to report you to the higher-ups."

Jack's ears perked up. As a former Sigma, he still had an instinct to be reverent toward authority. "I thought we don't have a boss."

"We don't." Susan held up her hand. "However, part of my job is to communicate directly with the Alpha supervising the workers in this building. He reports directly to the Algorithm." A map of the building floated above the table. A red dot covered the top floor. "The penthouse is his office, but I don't think he's ever there. Why leave Ottawa to come to Detroit?"

"I didn't know you have a direct line with an Alpha." Michael snorted. "Maybe I should give you one of my tacos."

Should I do that, too? Jack didn't like the thought of losing a taco.

"That's funny, Michael." Susan glanced at Jack. "No one is in charge here. We all have our own responsibilities. Mine just happens to include communication with an Alpha."

Richard forced air out of his nostrils. Susan turned her head directly to Richard, who looked down at his tacos.

A hologram appeared in the room and removed the empty lunch plates and the vegetable tray. Enough leftover vegetables to feed an SLU building remained on the plate.

After the holo left the room, an organizational chart floated in the air above the four Betas.

Susan stood. "This chart outlines our responsibilities." She turned to Richard. "As the talent coach, your job is to prepare actors for their roles." Richard nodded. "Michael, I think your job as show writer is pretty obvious."

"It was explained to me at Selection. I look forward to making interesting content."

Susan pointed to herself. "Think of me as a manager." Everyone at the table nodded. Jack wasn't sure what that meant, if it didn't mean boss. She turned to Jack. "As VR Entertainment Coordinator, it's your job to arrange the order of VR programs to maximize the enjoyment of the Betas watching the shows. You also assign roles to actors to ensure that the right person plays the right part."

"Will I get some training on how to schedule shows and pair actors to roles?" Jack asked.

Richard snorted. Susan glared at him again. How many times would Richard be allowed to get away with his behavior? Susan's eyes returned to Jack and her expression softened.

"You'll get all the information you need when you complete the orientation in your office. Speaking of which," Susan glanced at her watch, "it is time for you all to go to your offices."

Augmented reality arrows appeared in Jack's ocular implants as he stepped outside Room 2430. He needed time to decompress after dealing with Richard, so he ignored the arrows and explored the building. Each of the floors he visited had the same carpet and glass walls as the twenty-fourth floor. He hoped to meet more of his coworkers, but no one was around and the walls were opaque.

When Jack eventually made it to his office, he found it looked identical to the one he saw before lunch—same carpet and desk. A holo-portrait of Tabitha, about twenty centimeters tall, floated above the left side of the desktop. In the portrait, she wore the dress from last night. He might need to change the image. Otherwise, he'd spend the whole day staring at it and not working. Behind the desk sat a red plush chair with five wheels.

Jack sank into the chair. A blank holographic screen projected from the top of his desk. A female voice spoke to him in his aural implants.

"Welcome, Mr. Thompson! I am your holographic terminal. Your first task as VR Entertainment Coordinator is to register me and set me up. Would you like to interact with me as a screen or in person?"

"Screen." *I don't need any more holograms in my life.* "And please call me Jack. What's your name?"

"First things first, Jack. Do you want a female or male voice? You can change any of these settings at any time."

"I like your voice as it is."

"Thank you, Jack. I like yours, too."

Jack felt a warmth in his cheeks.

"I am sorry, Jack. Would you like some meds to ease your embarrassment?"

There are drugs for that? A smell, like the one in his car this morning, entered his nostrils. A sense of calm settled over him and the warmth in his cheeks went away.

"Jack, my official designation is VR-Ent-Coor-5489. You may assign me a name more convenient to you."

A name immediately came to mind. "How about Victoria?"

"Excellent choice! It's an honor to be named after your mother. We are now ready to begin work. I am displaying your daily to-do list on my screen now."

```
Item 1: Assign actors to three upcoming pro-
grams.
Item 2: Finalize the schedule for tonight's
programming.
Item 3: Review the current shows being of-
fered.
```

"Okay, Victoria. Let's start with item three."

"It is highly recommended that we start with item one."

Jack scratched his head. "Shouldn't I know which shows we have before I assign actors to them?"

"The Algorithm recommends the following actor-show pairings. Do you approve of them?"

A list of fifteen actors appeared on the screen, including Tabitha's. Beside each name was a recommended program. *If the Algorithm thinks these are good, who am I to argue?* "Sure."

"Great, Jack! I know the Algorithm will be pleased to hear your approval. Shall we proceed to item two?"

"Okay." *No point in arguing.*

"Excellent! The Algorithm recommends this schedule. Do you approve?" A schedule of shows appeared on the screen. Jack hadn't heard of them.

"Yeah." Jack shrugged.

What an easy job! All I do is approve what the Algorithm wants.

"Now for item three. I will upload the roster of shows to your artificial neural net. Your ANN will transfer the information to your biological brain."

Jack sat back at his desk. "What?"

"You had several standard Beta upgrades done at the med facility in Baltimore. Did they not go over those with you?"

"No." *I really should have read that message.*

"Selection to Beta from the Lower Castes is rare. Maybe the tech at the office forgot to tell you. Anyway, you have an ANN, which is short for artificial neural network. The ANN works alongside your biological brain to help you learn faster, reduce your reaction time, and communicate with others. It will also provide other physical benefits."

What else did they do to me? He felt the back of his neck to see if he could find a port or something.

"Shall we commence the transfer?"

"Will it hurt?"

"Not at all."

Jack nodded in approval. *I wonder how Tabby and I can explore these other benefits.* A smile escaped his lips.

"Transfer complete."

New information and memories trickled into his brain. Jack was disappointed a wire didn't come out of his desk and attach to his spinal cord, like in the vids.

Knowledge of how movies were made suddenly appeared in his brain. It felt like when trying to recall a name after several minutes of mental struggle. A moment later, he knew all about VR shows.

"I see the moviemaking section has completed its transfer. The upload should be completed before the workday is over. We slow down the transfer to avoid brain damage."

"Much appreciated." The three items disappeared from the screen. "What's next? Should we start tomorrow's assignments?"

"The Algorithm appreciates your eagerness, but it is unnecessary. You had a harder day of work than usual due to the orientation and the ANN transfer. Would you like to play a game?"

"Sure. Is that allowed?"

"Of course!" A list of game titles appeared on the screen. Like the shows, Jack didn't recognize any of them. "I have a library of every game ever made. Your ocular implants support both AR and VR gaming. I will increase the opacity of the glass while you play."

The glass darkened.

"I thought you said I could play. Why hide it?"

"The darkness will improve the gaming experience. Don't worry, 99.5 percent of the other staff are currently gaming, watching holos, or browsing the VR web."

Does anyone do any work here?

"Betas must stay at work until 1600, but if you get your work done early, you can do whatever you wish—as long as you stay in your office."

Jack selected the VR interface for his implants and started shooting alien invaders. At 1600, Victoria paused the game.

"Would you like to go home or continue gaming here?"

"I want to go home." The image of Jack's BTH, not his SLU, came to mind.

Chapter 17: Sam

January 4, 535

"The final remains of NATO evaporate. Europe joins
the Russian Alliance."

- The Washington Post, January 2, 2155.

Sally's screen went black. "It is 1700, Sam. Your workday is over."

Sam stepped out of his office and joined the river of Sigma programmers flowing along the halls of the AB toward the buses that would take them home.

Jennie stood beside one bus and stared at a tablet computer she held in front of her, oblivious to the laughing, happily reunited Sigma couples around her.

I wonder what has her so captivated?

"Sam!" Jennie dropped the tablet. Sam caught it just before it hit the ground.

He gave the tablet back to Jennie and sneaked a kiss on her cheek. Her hair had picked up a musty odor—probably from working in the basement. He didn't smell like roses either. "Sorry to scare you, honey. What are you working on?"

"I am about halfway through the parallel programming course you recommended."

Sam followed Jennie onto the bus. "Damn, that's fast!" *Like super-fast.* "It took me weeks to get that far. You've been working on it for what, a few days?"

I wish I could have learned it that fast.

"It clicked, thanks to my handsome tutor." Jennie pointed to a seat, and Sam nodded in approval.

"Who's your tutor? Can he give me lessons?"

Jennie giggled. "I'm this far along *only* because you helped me."

"All I did was point you in the right direction. You did the rest." Sam snorted. "Soon you'll be tutoring me."

"Thank you." Jennie kissed Sam. "Other than my parents, you are the only person who believes in me."

No one took Omegas seriously. At least Sam had Jack—before Selection, anyway. "I'd love to hear all about your first day."

"*Maaaaybe* I want to hear about yours first?" Jennie's lip biting turned into a flirtatious smile.

A tingling sensation radiated through Sam's body. He composed himself. "How about we keep *that* for dinner conversation?"

Many of the couples paused their displays of affection on the sweltering bus. Sam put his arm around Jennie, despite the heat. She leaned her head on his shoulder and sighed, just like she had done that morning. He kissed the top of her head. Basement odor never smelled so good. He shifted himself slightly in the hard plastic seat, which now pressed against his butt and back. Jennie melted into him even further.

Worth it.

The bus lurched forward. *I couldn't do this without her.*

***

The bus pulled up to the Orlando depot, and not a moment too soon. Sam's back had begun hurting ten minutes ago. "I have an idea for dinner."

Jennie lifted her head and turned in her seat toward Sam. "What do you have in mind?"

Sam shifted to a more comfortable position, just in time to stand up to leave. *Oh well. At least she seemed comfy for the trip.* They stepped off the bus and walked home along South Orange Avenue.

"Let's eat in this park. It is near our SLUs." He swiped the park's website to Jennie's phone. "According to the site, we can eat there."

No one ate outside in The Hill. The odor and UnSelected were too much of a problem for outdoor dining. Although Orlando didn't smell much better, the website said the UnSelected weren't allowed in the park. He could tolerate the smell if he didn't also have to deal with them.

Jennie squinted at her phone. "It looks like the one in your old neighborhood."

Sam looked back at his phone. "Yeah, it sure does." He put the phone in his pocket. "The mosquitoes don't seem so bad today. With a heat index of only eighty-seven, it should be a nice evening to eat outdoors."

"Sounds great! I can't wait to have my first meal outside!"

An UnSelected woman carrying an infant swaddled in dirty rags limped toward Sam and Jennie. She smelled like she hadn't showered in a month. The weekly showers provided to the UnSelected were not enough for a hot place like Orlando.

The woman gazed down at Sam and Jennie's feet. "I am sorry to bother you, sir and ma'am." She rocked the motionless child in her arms. "Do you have any paste I can give to my child?"

Sam stepped in between the woman and Jennie. Jennie firmly but gently pushed Sam to the side. She reached in her pocket and handed the UnSelected woman a solid nutrient paste bar. "If you heat that, it will melt, and your child can eat it. You should eat some, too. That is too much food for an infant."

Tears stained the woman's dirt-covered face. "Thank you, ma'am! May the Algorithm provide for you."

"And also for you." Jennie placed her hand on the woman's arm.

The UnSelected woman walked away with no further incident. Sam waited until she was outside of earshot. "You need to be more careful. The UnSelected can be violent. What if she had a knife?"

"Really?" Jennie's voice took on a higher pitch than normal. "I've had no problems with them. In Mount Vernon, we always tried to help the UnSelected. We had little, but they had even less."

The blue flecks in Jennie's eyes darkened. "Her child was dead. The UnSelected know people are more willing to give food to children than adults. UnSelected often wait to dispose of dead children for that reason." Jennie looked at the ground. "I can't blame them. Besides, the bar was left over from my lunch. I haven't gotten used to the amount of food Sigmas are provided."

I've never heard of UnSelected using dead children to get food. He'd known that Omegas and UnSelected were worse off than Sigmas; however, before he met Jennie, he hadn't known the extent of the inequality. "Just please be careful."

They continued their walk home in silence. Something was bothering Jennie, but Sam thought it better not to ask. Three blocks from Sam's SLU, a Sigma male in his midthirties swaggered toward them, walking with his chest out and head high. He dwarfed Sam, both in height and width.

The man stopped and looked straight at Jennie. "Hey baby, how about you dump that boy and come home with me? I'll show you a real good time." The look on the man's face implied Jennie wouldn't enjoy what he had in mind.

"The lady is spoken for." Sam had always wanted to say that.

The man pushed Sam, sending him stumbling backward. "Back off buddy, unless you want to spend the night bleeding in the streets while I get to know your friend." The man smirked. His eyes narrowed, focusing on Jennie. "I've never broken in a new Sigma. I hear young Omegas know how to have fun."

The Sigma man moved to grab Jennie's arm. She jerked and pulled her arm back with a speed that took him off guard.

"Don't touch me, asshole!" Jennie growled.

Sam did a double take.

"That's it, bitch! I'm gonna teach you a lesson." The man doubled his fists and lunged at Jennie.

Sam froze. What happened next would be burned in his memory for the rest of his life. In one smooth motion, Jennie sidestepped the man and executed a front kick that landed square in his groin. He swore loudly and bent over in pain. Jennie followed up with a rising elbow to his chin. Her elbow's upward momentum met his downward moving chin with a snap. The man fell over backward, landing in a fetal position. Shards of teeth littered the ground beside his head.

"Touch me, or any other girl like that again, and I'll tear your balls right off and force them down your throat." Jennie kicked the man in his ribs, then walked over to Sam with concern in her eyes. "Are you okay?"

Sam blinked, not quite believing what he had just seen and heard. "Yeah." It was a question as much as it was a statement.

"Good. We should get out of here." Jennie walked away with her chest out and head held high. The other Sigmas on the sidewalk gave Jennie a wide berth.

It took a moment for Sam to catch up to her. "Holy shit, Jennie! Where did you learn that?"

"Back home, it was *never* the UnSelected you had to worry about. It was always the Sigmas who thought they could have their way with Omega girls or boys. You had to grow up fast in my old neighborhood."

The man writhed on the ground behind them. His moans drew little attention. The Sigmas passing by knew better than to get involved.

"He won't bother us again. I hurt him bad enough that a Sigma won't fully recover from that broken rib." Jennie grinned. "Between that and the missing teeth, he'll remember this for a long time. And so will the rest of the neighborhood."

Sam's heart raced. He'd seen no one in The Hill fight like that before. *She could kick Jack's ass.* "How about we hang out at my place for a while before dinner?"

"After a fight like that? Hell yeah!"

They picked up the pace. Sam couldn't get home fast enough.

***

The Algorithm noted match number 561-165,771 now had a 99 percent probability of long-term success.

Chapter 18: Sam

January 4, 535

"The Sub-Saharan Trade Conglomerate decreases exports to the US and finds more lucrative markets in central Asia."

- Mail & Guardian, August 3, 2162.

Sam's phone alerted him that Jennie was waiting outside his SLU. She had gone back to her home to get changed after their post-fight "hang out." He opened the front door to find her standing in the hall wearing the blue dress from last night and a backpack. The necklace he'd ordered earlier rested upon her chest. The blue stone perfectly matched both her dress and the flecks in her eyes.

"Thank you! Thank you! Thank you! I love it!" Jennie threw her arms around Sam and kissed him. "How did you get this?"

Sam let her in. "The Algorithm is apparently happy with my work. My terminal told me I don't need Sigma credits to buy stuff."

Jennie's face bunched up in thought, then relaxed. "The Algorithm provides."

"It sure does." Sam had started to believe it—to an extent—now that he had some limited privileges. "Let's keep this to ourselves. I think I am the only programmer with this benefit. I don't want to get robbed or make enemies at work."

"That's smart." Jennie handed Sam her backpack. Walking to the park with food in hand would draw unwanted attention. Sam placed his meal in the bag with Jennie's. She had also packed a bottle of water, two plastic cups, utensils, and a folded blanket—everything he had planned to take with them. *Great minds think alike!* In truth, hers was greater than his. He loved her for that.

"Shall we?" Sam tilted his head toward the door. Jennie took his hand. It fit perfectly.

The other Sigma males kept their distance from Sam and Jennie as they walked to the park. Word traveled fast in Orlando. Not even the necklace tempted them. *Having a badass girlfriend is awesome!*

"See, I told you. No more problems." Jennie walked tall. Her dress accentuated all her best physical traits. Sam did his best not to stare. "I can't wait to call my dad and tell him the combo worked!"

The park had more brown and less green than Druid Hill Park. They found a spot shaded by an artificial tree. Sam laid out the blanket. It had some holes in it, but it would serve as a good enough barrier between them and the ground. A sign nearby had a U with a slash through it. Jennie frowned at the sign. Sam kept his mouth shut, happy that mosquitoes would be the only problem.

Jennie sat down on the blanket with her legs folded under her and poured two cups of brownish water. She moved with a grace that mesmerized Sam.

"Would you like some water?" Jennie's voice broke Sam's trance. He nodded. She grinned as she handed him a cup. Sam loved her shy grin. "So, tell me all about the glamorous life of a programmer!"

The cup Jennie handed Sam was fuller than hers. The empty water bottle lay on the ground beside her.

"I had a strange day." Sam took their meals out of the bag. "But I need to hear about yours first." He handed Jennie a chicken paste sandwich.

Jennie looked at her sandwich and licked her lips. Her tongue made a slow circle. Sam squirmed. "My day started off with a meeting. When I got to the conference room, it was full of people like me."

"What do you mean, *like you?*"

"They were all from poor neighborhoods, but I was the only former Omega. Some were from a place called Polynesia. I never heard of it before." Jennie took a bite from the sandwich and closed her eyes for a moment.

Watching Jennie enjoy her Sigma status helped Sam fulfill his promise to himself about accepting his Selection. Being a Sigma wasn't what he wanted, but many people had less.

"Did you know Polynesia is an artificial island?" Jennie spoke in between chews of her sandwich. "Apparently, people used to live on islands in the Pacific Ocean before the Shift put most of them underwater. They built Polynesia to give those people a new home. It was a sort of last-ditch geo-engineering effort before the Algorithm took over."

How does she have time to research that and study programming?

"Anyway, we were all in this big room and a Beta appeared on the vid-screen. He told us our job was to review lines of code and if anything looked wrong, we were to send it to our programmer."

"So, your job is to stare at code all day looking for errors?" Sam took a bite of his sandwich. He looked down at it and did his best to hide his disapproval from Jennie.

"Yeah. Isn't that awesome? It beats the hell out of getting in the ocean and retrieving artifacts from crumbling underwater ruins."

She was right. Selection had upgraded her life. His, too, he reminded himself—he wouldn't have met Jennie otherwise.

"Absolutely, Jennie." Sam reached out and held Jennie's hand that wasn't holding the sandwich. "I am glad you love your job. You deserve to be happy."

"Aww!" Jennie leaned over and kissed him. "Now stop interrupting!" She wagged her finger at him.

"Yes, ma'am!" Sam took another bite of his sandwich. It tasted better.

The company makes the meal.

Jennie rolled her eyes. "The Beta dismissed us to our offices. I share my office with three other maintenance staff. It is nice. We each get a terminal, and I get to put two pictures on my desk. One of them is of you and it was already there when I arrived!"

No surprise there. "Who was in the other picture?"

"My parents, of course!" Jennie playfully punched Sam in his arm. "That's for interrupting me again!"

The playful contact between him and Jennie was fun. However, after what he saw her do earlier today, it took on a different light. She must hold back a lot when they messed around.

"The rest of the morning was spent filling out paperwork. Afterward, I ate lunch in a huge cafeteria with a bunch of other maintenance people." Jennie took a drink of water and looked at the cup like she had the sandwich. "Oh! And we had *two* beef-flavored nutrient paste bars with real bread!"

"What happened after lunch?"

"I got back to my office, and a file called *artifact_classification. ai* was open on my computer. Robots use the program to identify artifacts."

Holy shit!

"Based on the stuff you showed me, the learning rate seemed too high. I sent a notice to my programmer, but never heard back." Jennie looked down at the last bite of her sandwich in thought.

"At the end of the day, I received a notification that a Beta supervisor got promoted thanks to an improved robotics algorithm. Do you think it had something to do with *artifact_classification.ai*?" Jennie popped the last bite of her sandwich into her mouth, then took the last sip of her water.

Well, this is interesting. Sam bit into his sandwich and mushed the chicken paste in his mouth with his tongue. He poured some of his water into Jennie's cup. She tried to refuse at first, but he insisted.

Jennie's story supported some of his ideas, but he'd need her help to figure out what was going on. Sam took Jennie's hands in his and looked her straight in the eyes. The blue flecks sparkled in the sunlight. "Do you trust me?"

"You are the first Sigma who has ever seen me as a person, not an object. You have shown me nothing but kindness. I love you *and* I trust you."

He had quickly come to trust and love Jennie more than anyone else—Jack included. The Algorithm probably had a hand in that, but it didn't matter. "You have helped me in so many ways you don't realize. I love you and trust you more than anyone else." Sam paused for a moment; his next statement would be a big ask. "Can I see your phone?"

Jennie tilted her head and bit her lip—a gesture Sam normally found sexy, but not this time. Phones were sacred. He knew of only one married couple who shared them. She handed him her phone. "I have nothing to hide."

"I'd like to make a simple alteration. It won't affect your data, either locally or in the cloud."

"Fine, but please no nudes!" Jennie's levity did not escape Sam's notice. She trusted him.

"One nude coming your way!" He made a swiping motion with his thumb from his phone toward Jennie's. As he returned her phone, Sam pointed at a red button with the word EXECUTE on its screen. He had already pressed the similar button that appeared on his phone.

Jennie looked at Sam and back at her phone. She tapped the button. "What did that do?"

"It disabled the microphone and camera so we can speak privately. It is a program I've been working on for a while." Sam looked around. He didn't see anyone else in the park. "It is only powerful enough to disable two phones."

"I assume you are running a deepfake audio and video routine, so the cameras and mics are still sending information to the servers. The Algorithm would certainly notice a deactivated phone owned by someone who isn't dead."

"Impressive, Jennie. I would have never thought about that when I was starting out in programming."

"Well, I don't know the AI programming for a deepfake, yet. I just read about them in one of the files you sent to me yesterday and put two and two together."

She doesn't know how smart she is.

"Regardless, I am impressed! Let's talk more about your day and mine." Sam pointed to himself. "I must be your programmer. I received the notice about *artifact_classification.ai.*"

Jennie rubbed her hands together. "Neat! We get to work together. I love it!" She looked down at the blanket with a solemn expression on her face. "This gets better and better every day."

"Yeah, but let's keep this knowledge to ourselves."

"I think you are right." Jennie took a sip of water. "Did you notice how everyone on the bus was paired and one went to the front door while the other went to the side? I bet each couple makes a maintenance-programmer pair."

"Yeah. I guessed that, too. Why that is, I don't know."

"The Algorithm works in mysterious ways." Jennie stared off into the distance.

"Yeah, well, it is about to get even more mysterious." Sam's comment recaptured Jennie's attention. He took his last sip of water. The heat index of *only* eighty-seven wore on him. Jennie looked at his empty cup, then at the water remaining in her own. He put his cup away in the bag. She needed water more than he did. "You were right to flag the learning rate. It was entirely too high. I changed it from 5.4 to 0.54 and the classification rate improved significantly."

"Enough to promote a Beta?"

"Enough to promote a Beta." Sam paused. "Oh, and it gets better."

"Better than giving a privileged Beta even *more* privilege?"

Sam grinned. Everyone was taught growing up not to question the castes, the privilege, or the status. The mantra of "the Algorithm provides" was burned into people's brains. Sam hated it, but he could never say it out loud. Jennie had the guts to tell the truth. Just one more thing he loved about her.

"The most interesting part of the code you sent me was the comment."

"Comments are the most important part of the code!"

It took me too long to appreciate comments. Sam leaned forward, resting his elbows on his knees. "Especially in this case. The comment mentioned SGD."

"Yeah, I saw that." Jennie scratched her head. "What is SGD? I have never heard of it."

"I wouldn't have expected you to." Sam grimaced. "What I mean is the SGD algorithm is ancient. Like pre-Shift early days of AI ancient."

"What is an ancient learning algorithm doing in a modern classification process?"

"I don't know. But I need your help with something."

"Anything, Sam." Jennie's voice started to tremble. "I want us to be partners, in this and everything else. I want to marry you."

The proposal caught Sam off guard. His heartbeat quickened and skin tingled. He felt warm all over and not because of the heat index.

Tears welled up in Jennie's eyes.

Why the tears? Oh! I haven't said anything!

"Yes! I want to marry you, too. I love you. Let's apply for the license tomorrow." He leaned further forward, wrapped his arms around her damp body, and gave her a long kiss. Her hair smelled like the basement of the AB. It didn't matter. In that moment, his universe consisted only of her—not Orlando, and certainly not his Selection. He wanted to stay in that universe forever.

Jennie broke the hug. "Okay, but first, what do you need help with?"

"Back to business, Ms. Goodby! I love it!"

"Don't get me wrong, Sam. This is the happiest moment of my life. But I can tell you are concerned about something. I want to help."

"You *are* amazing, Jennie." Jennie blushed. Sam squeezed her hands. "So, I got to thinking, if ancient learning algorithms are being used in these robots, are they being used elsewhere?" Sam shrugged while he held her hands. "Maybe the Algorithm doesn't value these artifacts and is not willing to spend the resources needed by using more modern learning programs." Sam pursed his lips and inhaled through his nose, hoping she'd respond well to this next part. "But what if the Algorithm is littered with ancient and inefficient learning methods?"

Jennie dropped Sam's hands and shifted as she sat on the blanket. "Then we might not be living in an optimal society like the Algorithm claims."

Sam nodded.

"That means the suffering of the UnSelected and Omegas may not be necessary for our world to recover?" Jennie asked.

She left out us Sigmas.

Why wouldn't she? Orlando was a paradise compared to Mt. Vernon. Sam leaned back on his hands.

"Or, the suffering *is* necessary, but the privileges of the Alphas and Betas aren't optimal and may keep our world in ruins."

"Or a lot of other things that we can't even think of right now." Jennie fidgeted her hands. "Sam, what are we going to do?"

"Jennie, you are probably the most talented person who works in the AB. In fact, you are probably going to be the best programmer in the world. You are already well on your way there."

"I have already slept with you *and* agreed to marry you. What else do you expect this kind of flattery to get you?" Jennie's playful grin made Sam hopeful she wasn't too uncomfortable talking about these heretical ideas.

"I am being serious. You can recognize patterns and, more importantly, deviations from patterns like no one I have ever met. I want you to send me any strange things you find in the AI code."

"Do you mean inefficiencies?"

"Yes. But also, anything you think seems *odd*. Use your judgment. Your instincts are better than mine." Sam flicked another file to her phone. "Here is a history of ancient AI. It has terms to look out for, like 'simulated annealing' and 'particle swarm optimization.' These are old, pre-Shift algorithms."

"Should I send them as inefficiencies?"

"Yes, and please stop sending encrypted files. I don't want to draw suspicion."

"I'll keep an eye out and send you what I find." Jennie slowly exhaled. "We aren't acting against the Algorithm, are we?"

Sam shook his head. "We are just gathering data." This was the best outcome Sam could have hoped for. Jennie didn't freak out. She seemed willing to help, even if she had some reservations. *She'll come around.*

"I am going to deactivate the deepfake. At some point, the Algorithm will get suspicious. My code isn't capable of supporting long video or audio, yet."

"I'll see if I can improve that!"

"I am sure you can." Sam reactivated both of their cameras and mics. He looked Jennie in the eyes and held her hands. "Jennie, I really love our time together. Will you marry me? I know—"

"Yes, Sam! I love you! Let's get a license tomorrow."

Excellent! I knew she'd remember the proposal had happened with the mics off.

***

Geostationary Satellite #24 focused its lens on the park. The Algorithm watched as Jennie and Sam kissed after the second proposal. It classified match number 561-165,771 as permanent. Citizen number 7985-02-1245, Samuel Watkins, had initiated his role in the Plan and had an estimated probability of success of 95 percent. The Algorithm needed better odds before It started Phase Two.

Chapter 19: Sam

January 4, 535

Sam felt four meters tall as he walked back to his SLU with Jennie. Their joined damp hands swung back and forth along a wide arc. Jennie bounced as she walked. If Sam were still a child, he would have skipped home. *Jennie would probably be game for that.*

They drew a lot of strange stares from the other Sigmas, but none of them dared to comment. A few of the UnSelected smiled as they passed by. *Maybe Jennie is right about them. But how do they eat with so few teeth?*

Jennie followed Sam into his SLU. "Do you mind if I call my parents and tell them the good news? I can't wait for them to meet you!" Jennie tilted her head. "Sigmas can call Omegas, right?"

"They sure can. I would love to meet your parents." Sam woke his SLU's main computer. A call this important required video. "I'll spend a vid-call credit." He tapped his phone to the computer, transferring the credit.

"Thank you, Sam! I have never made a vid-call before. Omegas can only receive them—but no one wants to call us." Jennie paused. "*Them.*" She initiated the call but stopped. "Let's call your mom first. I really want to meet her. I'll use my credit."

Sam looked down at his phone. "Save your credit. I apparently get unlimited calling credits, too." Jennie stepped off to the side while Sam pushed a few buttons on his SLU's terminal.

Mom's image appeared on the screen. "Sam! What a surprise!"

"Hi, Mom! How's Baltimore?"

"You know, the same." Mom sighed. "The kids outside are loud and disrupt my sleep. My back has been bothering me from work. The meds just aren't working." She waved it off. "That's not important. How's Orlando? Are you doing any better?"

"Orlando is great, Mom." Sam hated lying to his mother. "I met a girl. Her name is Jennie Goodby, and we are getting married!"

"That's wonderful!" Mom clasped her hands. Even through the low-res vid-screen, Sam could see the joy in her eyes. "So, where's Jennie? I want to welcome her to the family!"

Jennie walked into view of the camera. "Hi, Mrs. Watkins!" She brushed her hair back behind her ear.

"Oh, hello dear." Sam hadn't seen a fake smile from his mom before.

"I really love Sam. I can't wait for us to build a life together here in Orlando. I promise to take real good care of him."

Sam put his arm around Jennie and smiled, hoping he'd do as well as she did when it came time to meet her parents.

"I am happy to hear you say that." Mom sucked in her top lip. "Hey, Sam, can we go private for a minute?"

"Uh, sure, Mom." Sam redirected the audio from the call to his earpiece. He turned to Jennie, trying to give his best "I don't know what's going on" look. Her lip quivered. She went to Sam's bedroom and sat on the edge of his bed. Sam's stomach turned.

"Samuel, is she an Omega?"

I don't like where this is going.

"Was. Pre-Selection. Why?"

"We are Sigmas, Samuel. We don't mix with Omegas. They are dirty people. She is going to take advantage of you."

My mother is a classist? Sam believed he had learned his tolerance for Omegas from her.

"You are an adult now. It's time you learn some truths. Your father was an Omega before his Selection. He got me pregnant the night of our Selection and left." She shook her head with a soulless expression. Sam didn't know his dad, but it was obvious he had hurt her. "Stay away from her. She will ruin you, just like your father ruined us. Think of how much better your Selection could have been if he stuck around."

Sam tried to speak, but his mother cut him off.

"Omegas are Omegas because they aren't good enough to be a Sigma. Who knows what the Algorithm was thinking promoting her?"

A tightness in Sam's jaw built as his teeth pressed harder together. His mother had barely met Jennie. What right did she have to say these things? His forearms ached. How long had he been clenching his fists?

"You are right, mother. I am an adult. I have been Selected. I make my own choices, and I choose Jennie." Sam disconnected.

Jennie slowly entered the main room. "Is everything okay with your mom?" Her sheepish look melted Sam's heart.

"Yeah." Sam gave a reassuring smile. "She just wanted to say some mom stuff like how proud she is of me and what not. She didn't want to embarrass me in front of my bride."

"Good. I was worried I upset her."

"You did nothing wrong." Sam hugged Jennie. "I love you."

"I love you too, Sam. Let's call my parents!"

Jennie entered the necessary information into the console. The screen turned black and displayed a message in red text.

```
Ms. Goodby,
The Algorithm regrets to inform you that your
parents died in an explosion while working in
Old Inner Harbor today. Reclamation and pro-
cessing of their bodies has been completed.
You will receive an image of them for perma-
nent archiving on your phone and your SLU's
computer. The Algorithm sends its condolences.
Your parents were model citizens of the Soci-
ety.
```

Jennie fell to her knees and wailed.

Sam got down on the floor and wrapped his arms around her. She buried her head in his chest, sobbing. Tears soaked through his shirt.

He held her for the rest of the night and said nothing. As the night went on and Jennie continued crying, Sam's anger swelled. Eventually, her tears dried up, and she fell asleep in his arms. Sam stayed awake the whole night. One question repeated in his mind. *Why?*

***

In a server farm beneath Boise, the Algorithm estimated citizen number 7985-02-1245 now had a 96 percent chance of successfully executing the Plan. The probability exceeded the initiation threshold. The Algorithm sent a message to Its secondary servers in Toronto to begin Phase Two.

Chapter 20: Jack

January 2, 535

"As the Great Plains turn to dust, food scarcity has led to the rise of armed conflict between militant factions in the US. Prime Minister Sullivan pushes Parliament to fund a border wall."
- *Toronto Star*, October 30, 2170.

The Detroit cityscape zoomed by. Jack couldn't imagine getting bored of the view.

"Samantha, can I have another one of those sodas?"

"Of course." A thump came from the dispenser.

Jack opened the soda and took a sip and looked at the can. "Is this the same stuff from this morning?"

"Yes. Is something wrong with it?"

"No." Jack took another sip. "It isn't as sweet. I like it."

"Your tastebuds are acclimating to Beta foods. How was your first day?"

"Good, I guess. Victoria told me I accomplished a lot."

"It sounds like you worked hard. I have a gift for you to celebrate your accomplishment."

As a Sigma, Jack rarely received surprises. In the Beta world, there seemed to be a surprise around every corner.

"I upgraded your new gaming station to the latest VR and haptic tech." A VR headset appeared on the console's screen. Jack leaned forward to read its specs. "The headset has a better resolution than your ocular implants. It will be set up and waiting for you when you get home."

"Rad!" The word slipped out of Jack's mouth. He thought of Sam, the real one. His heart felt heavy. Sam probably wasn't getting surprises. A familiar chemical scent entered his nostrils and the weight on his heart disappeared. *Sam hadn't earned them either.*

"I think we should get Ms. Forsythe something too," Samantha said.

Thoughts of how Tabitha might thank him flooded Jack's mind. "Excellent idea!"

An ordered list of objects projected from the car's holo-display. "Based on her profile, I think Ms. Forsythe will like these items."

Jack swiped through the various options, a necklace with a black stone, a black dress slightly different from the one she wore last night, a contraption he didn't recognize, a holo-cam—the list kept going.

"Are you having trouble deciding?"

I can't believe I don't have to pay for these things! How many Sigma credits would they cost? "I am not sure which one she'd like best."

All the options disappeared except the necklace. "The Algorithm calculates a 96 percent probability she will like this necklace the best."

"Let's go with the necklace." Jack sat back in his seat. "The Algorithm can't be wrong."

"Great choice, Jack! The necklace is already available in her home's dispenser. I have received an audio recording from Ms. Forsythe. Shall I play it?"

"Please."

"Hi, Jack!" The sound of Tabitha's voice made him smile. "Pick me up for dinner at 1900. Love ya! Bye!"

"Pick her up?" Jack scrunched his face. "Do I have to carry her somewhere?"

"You are hilarious!" Samantha laughed like a human. "It means you are going to meet her at her house."

Jack nodded and then sipped from the soda can. *This is the life.*

***

"Samantha, send that save state over to Victoria so I can pick up the game where I left off at work tomorrow." Jack peeled off the full immersion haptic suit that came with his new gaming rig. The suit added the sense of touch to his games. "And please have the suit cleaned."

Games were fun, but a more exciting adventure awaited him. "So, what do I need to do to get ready for this *going out?*"

"First, you'll need to take a shower."

How many showers can I take in a day?

Betas spent a lot of time cleaning themselves. Of course, that was probably why they didn't smell like Sigmas. He never noticed it before, but Sam had an obvious odor at the post-Selection lunch.

After his shower, Samantha presented Jack with two suits. One hung from each of her holographic hands. "I estimate a 97 percent probability Ms. Forsythe will like this suit," Samantha held up a black suit with a red shirt, "and that its shirt will match her outfit."

"I don't know, Sam." Jack rubbed his chin. "I think I like the other one better."

Samantha frowned. "Jack, there is only a 96 percent probability that Ms. Forsythe will like the blue suit. The black suit is the optimal choice."

The air in Jack's room took on a floral scent, like the one from the plane. He stood straighter and grinned. "Black it is then. Good Betas don't make suboptimal choices."

"You are a fast learner, Jack!"

Chapter 21: Jack

January 2, 535

"Eco-terrorists detonate the first nuclear explosion on US soil in over 200 years...leader claims the nuclear winter will help crops grow again."

- Archived news feed believed to be dated 2180.

Freshly showered, Jack knocked on the front door of Tabitha's BTH. *I hope she wears that dress again tonight!* The door clicked. Jack straightened his suit and ran his hand through his still damp hair.

The townhome's front door opened. Jack leaned in for a kiss, then stopped.

"Hi, Jack!" Jacqueline stood inside the doorway. She wore the same skirt suit and heels from this morning. "I hope you had a great first day. Ms. Forsythe is still getting ready upstairs." Jacqueline beckoned Jack into the house. She didn't seem to have noticed Jack's aborted attempt at a kiss.

Tabitha's BTH looked like Jack's, with a few cosmetic exceptions. The stairs in her BTH were faux wood.

I wonder if the wood reflects who Tabby is as a person.

"Ms. Forsythe has a treat for you." Jacqueline held out a glass containing a transparent brown liquid. A single large ice cube floated in the fluid. "It's called bourbon. Based on your profile, she and I think you'll love it."

The bourbon smelled of vanilla and honey—or at least the Sigma versions of those. Jack took a cautious sip, swallowed, then coughed.

A burning sensation ran down his throat. He waited a moment and decided he liked the flavor. The next sip went down easier.

"Thanks, Jacqueline!" Jack raised his glass. "This might be my new favorite drink." He was about to take another sip when he heard the clicking of high heels descending the wooden stairs.

"I love it! I love it! I love it!" Tabitha squealed.

Jack almost dropped his bourbon when Tabitha got to the bottom of the steps. She wore a new black dress with a neckline that couldn't get any lower (and he *really* tried to imagine a lower one), a pair of red high heels (which coincidentally matched the color of his shirt—good job, Samantha), and the necklace he had ordered. "Thank you so much for this beautiful necklace!" Her face beamed as she held her hand against her chest.

Tabitha grinned deviously as she ran her finger down the dress's neckline. "You like the dress?" She placed her hand under Jack's chin to close his dropped jaw.

"You look absolutely amazing, Ms. Forsythe." He raised his glass, trying to recover a little pride.

"Oooh!" Tabitha purred. "I love the formality, Mr. Thompson." She put her arms around him and gave him a kiss. Jack couldn't place the scent of her perfume, but it aroused him. Tabitha leaned back and broke the kiss but kept her arms around Jack. "Are you ready for our date?"

Another whiff of perfume flooded his nostrils. Jack stepped back slightly to avoid embarrassing himself. "If that means spending time with you in that dress, then absolutely."

"I can't keep the secret anymore!" Tabitha stepped back away from Jack, breaking their embrace. "We're going to a *restaurant!*"

"A what?" The words slipped out of his mouth.

So much for playing it cool.

"Don't Sigmas go to restaurants?" Tabitha's puzzled expression reflected how little she knew of the non-Beta world.

"Being that I've never even heard the word before, I'd guess not."

"Well, you are in for a treat! A restaurant is a place where you go sit at a table, order food, and then they bring it to you. You eat and drink there and have a great time. It's fun!"

A place dedicated solely to serving food outside the home stretched Jack's imagination. But everything else about being a Beta had been awesome. Why should this be different? "That sounds rad!"

"Rad?"

"Never mind. Old habit." Jack grinned. "Tell me more about this restaurant."

"Jacqueline found a great little pre-Shift Italian place. Reviews say they have the best lasagna in Detroit."

Lasagna? Jack decided not to ask. He had been ignorant enough in front of Tabitha for one night.

Samantha appeared in Tabitha's living room. Her T-shirt and jeans were a stark contrast to Jacqueline's suit. "Jack's car is ready outside. I replaced the bucket seat with a bench." Samantha winked. Jack's cheeks felt warm.

***

Jack had no idea how long they'd been in the car. He didn't care, either. Tabitha had kept her soft lips pressed against his since the car had sped away from her BTH.

"Ms. Forsythe," Samantha's voice came from the car's speaker, "we are two minutes from our destination."

Tabitha leaned back, breaking their kiss. Jack pouted. "Sorry, Jack. I gotta be ready for the paparazzi. Samantha, darken the windows and activate mirror mode." She leaned toward her image in the windshield and fixed her hair and makeup.

Thanks to the download at work, Jack knew all about the paparazzi. *It is so weird that there are Betas whose sole job it is to photograph actors.* They would want to photograph him, too. He glanced at himself in the mirror. *Good enough, I guess.*

The car stopped. Tabitha leaned forward to do one last check of her eye makeup. "How do I look?" She turned her head to inspect her hair.

"Like the most beautiful girl in the world."

"That's what I was going for. Samantha, make the windows transparent."

Rows of people lined a red-carpeted sidewalk that connected the car to a brick building with large windows. A sign reading "Tony's" sat above the building's entrance. Flashes of light from the paparazzi's holo-cameras and drones disoriented Jack. He closed his eyes and shook his head.

Tabitha placed her hand on his thigh. "Are you ready?" Jack hadn't seen her this eager, even when he showed her the Alpha wine.

Tabby is excited about this, so I will be, too. Jack inhaled. "Let's do it!"

The car door opened. A wall of sound crashed over Jack. His car's soundproofing had sheltered him from the cacophony of voices and holo-camera clicking. The distance to the restaurant's entrance seemed to have doubled.

The paparazzi hurled a barrage of questions at Jack and Tabitha. Tabitha's ability to respond and handle the crowd calmly was impressive. She showed off her dress, her necklace, and Jack. Jack fidgeted with his hands. Tabitha nudged him with her elbow. He waved and gave the cameras a closed-mouth smile. The feeds raved about Tabitha and her shy former-Sigma boyfriend.

***

Jack had never been happier to close a door in his life. The muffled sounds of the paparazzi got quieter the farther they got into the restaurant.

Will it always be like that when Tabby and I go places? By the Algorithm, I hope not.

A slender holographic woman appeared behind what looked like a tall one-person desk just inside the restaurant. She had long straight brown hair, blue eyes, and skin lighter than his own. *Do they make ugly holos?*

"Welcome to Tony's, Ms. Forsythe and Mr. Thompson! We hope you enjoy the taste of pre-Shift Italy that we have prepared for you this evening. Please follow me to your table."

The holo led them along a path between two rows of tables. Most of the tables were occupied by Beta couples. Each patron sat in front of a plate containing more real food than Jack had ever been provided as a Sigma. Several of the diners stopped their meal to stare at Tabitha as she walked by.

"I hope this is acceptable." The holo stopped at a two-person table by the restaurant's front window. Paparazzi peered inside through cupped hands. Unfortunately, there weren't any other unoccupied tables.

"It is. Thank you." Jack pulled Tabitha's chair out for her. She smiled and sat, giving him a magnificent view. The holo disappeared as Jack pulled out his chair and sat across from Tabitha. Her dress's low neckline stared back at him. He looked up into her eyes and realized she was speaking. "I'm sorry. What was that?"

"I *said* our server should be here soon." Tabitha shook her head, but she wasn't fooling him.

"Oh, okay." Jack looked around, trying to focus on anything other than Tabitha's dress. Pictures of green landscapes and ancient buildings hung on red walls. The occasional paparazzi peeped through the windows.

A holographic man appeared at their table. "Hello. I am your server, Robert. Do you wish to view the menu, or would you like the meal recommended for you by the Algorithm?"

"I'll take the recommended meal," Tabitha said.

Robert bowed slightly. "Fine choice, Ms. Forsythe."

How does she know she'll like it? Jack leaned forward and folded his arms on the table. "What is the recommended meal, Robert?"

"*Your* recommended meal, Mr. Thompson, begins with a freshly grown salad from Manitoba. The main course is lasagna with a red wine from Norway. You'll have cannoli for dessert. The Algorithm classifies this meal as optimal for you. Other users with a similar profile to you have rated it as five out of five stars."

Jack hadn't heard of lasagna or cannoli. Norway and Sweden had some of the best wines in the world. *How do I know that?*

"What are my other options?"

Tabitha looked away and scratched her nose.

"In order of ranking by the Algorithm, your other options are Alaskan salmon and pork osso bucco; each have the same sides and wine. Of course, we can prepare anything else you would like, but those would all be suboptimal compared to those I listed."

"I think I'll try the third one you mentioned."

Tabitha gave him the side-eye.

Robert straightened. "But sir, the lasagna *is* the optimal choice."

Like the suit and the to-do list at work, there appeared to be no point in arguing. Besides, the Algorithm hadn't let him down so far. "Then I'll have the lasagna. Thank you, Robert."

"Fine choice, Mr. Thompson. I'll bring your meal out shortly." Robert disappeared.

Holo-servers stood at several other tables. "Why holograms? Couldn't robots tell us where to sit and bring us food?"

"Sure, but it's more fun this way. It's like the old days!"

Jack reached across the table and held Tabitha's hand. Would he ever get used to its softness? Maybe his hands would be that soft one day, too. The Beta med center had removed most of the callouses. The med tech said the others would go away in time.

Focus on her eyes. He tried to be on his best behavior. Tabitha clearly loved the attention.

Fortunately, Robert provided a distraction. He placed two plates of salad and a bottle of water on the table. Like the tray at lunch, their salads had more fresh vegetables than a Sigma could expect to eat in their lifetime.

"Enjoy. I'll have the main course ready when you finish your salads." Robert disappeared again just as Jack said, "Thank you, Robert."

Jack took a slow sip of the water. The cold liquid ran down his throat. He held up the glass. Tabitha and her low neckline were visible through the water. Not a single particulate interrupted his view.

"Put your glass down, Jack," Tabitha said under her breath. "People are staring."

"Sorry." Jack straightened in his chair. "Just taking it all in." He raised his glass. "To a great meal *and* a beautiful woman." Hopefully, the toast would ease her embarrassment.

"The Algorithm provides!" Tabitha raised her glass and took a sip. Some of her red lipstick remained on the glass.

"Hear, hear." Jack took another sip. "By the way, I have a message for you."

"Oh, really?"

"Dan and Rebecca say hi." Jack told the story of the prank. He left out how he felt. *No point spoiling a good mood.*

Tabitha laughed, but stopped when Jack didn't join in. "I'm sorry." She reached out and took Jack's hand in her own. "They really are great at security, but their sense of humor leaves a lot to be desired."

"It's fine." Jack hated lying to her, but he didn't want to make a big deal out of it. "So, tell me about your day? What's it like being a famous actor?"

"It was *so* much hard work." Tabitha sighed. "I had an hour-long orientation that told me how I'd be chosen for roles."

"Then I had lunch with some other new actors. They were all really cool people and from some great cities. One guy is from New Seattle. Have you heard of it? It's an up-and-coming new Beta city. Anyway, I think he is perfect for the action holos. He might even be a lead one day. I also met a woman from Boise and another from Burlington."

Burlington and Boise were Beta cities, not as nice as Detroit, but certainly far better than Baltimore. He hadn't heard of New Seattle. "Tell me about these ladies." Jack drew out the word *ladies*, trying to sound funny.

"Why?" Tabitha's lips tightened into a slight frown, and she tapped the table with her finger. "Are you thinking about running off with one of them?"

Jack's underarms felt wet. "And downgrade? No way." *I guess the joke didn't come off right.*

Tabitha exhaled softly, but quickly composed herself and laughed. Something about her laughter seemed forced. "I meant that to sound funnier than it did. I'll leave the comedy to you."

Robert removed their empty salad plates. Watching Robert go through the motions, Jack now understood that "going out to dinner" was as much an experience as eating the meal. As a Sigma, he ate what he got when he got it—no ritual was involved. Robert carefully placed a covered plate in front of Tabitha and another in front of Jack.

The scent of the meal hit Jack's nostrils as soon as Robert removed the cover. He recognized the smell of beef coming from the lasagna.

There was another familiar scent, too. He thought for a moment. It smelled like the red diced vegetable from lunch that morning.

"Wow!" Tabitha quietly clapped her hands. "We got the same thing! That's amazing!"

"Looks like we have the same great taste!" Jack raised his wineglass.

"In people and in food." Tabitha clinked Jack's glass.

The lasagna looked like it might be as firm as a very thick paste. But unlike paste, the lasagna didn't yield easily to a spoon. Tabitha cut hers with a knife and used her fork. Jack mimicked her actions. Initially, the lasagna resisted his fork and knife less than the steak he had earlier. Halfway through the first cut, the knife slowed as it encountered beef. The knife met the plate with a muted clang. Tabitha looked up at him. Jack raised his eyebrows in apology. Her attention focused back on her plate. Jack took a bite. His eyes rolled back into his head.

"I got scanned after lunch today." Tabitha either missed or ignored his reaction to the lasagna. The people at the nearby table had done neither. They gave him an incredulous glance.

"Scanned for what?"

"Deepfakes. They're used for love scenes and stunts. Real actors don't do those."

It relieved Jack to hear about the love scenes. Sigma videos never used deepfakes for either. He put another piece of lasagna in his mouth. He kept his eyes fixed on Tabitha. There was no need to risk embarrassing her with another reaction.

"Afterward, I met my coach, Richard. He was very nice. I think you'd like him."

"Richard, eh?"

Earlier today, Tabitha had appeared on the list of actors for whom Jack assigned roles. He hadn't put two-and-two together. If Jack assigned her roles, then she'd also be working with Richard.

"He thinks I am best suited for sci-fi heroine roles. He also thinks, with some practice, I might expand my range to other genres. Richard gave me a lot of helpful feedback. I think he can really help me become a star."

Jack stared into his wineglass. "That's great."

I should have kicked his ass earlier. It would have been the most productive ten seconds of my workday.

"Don't be jealous, silly! Besides, he has a girlfriend. They are both from Detroit and knew each other before Selection. Can you believe that? They were Selected together! It sounds like one of those love-holos." Tabitha sighed. "How romantic!"

Jack's eyes focused on the piece of lasagna he'd sliced. "Good for them."

"Anyway, *Mr. Jealous*, that was all my assigned work for the day. I spent the afternoon taking selfies for my social feeds. A girl has to get herself out there and build some hype, right?" Jack knew she'd excel at that. "I think tomorrow, I am going to meet my Entertainment Coordinator."

I won't say anything so I can surprise her tomorrow. Tabby loves surprises.

Robert appeared, removed the dishes, and served the cannoli. Jack thanked Robert again before he disappeared. Tabitha smiled and shook her head.

"Do you want to hear about my day?" Jack asked.

"Of course." Tabitha shifted in her seat, presenting her right profile toward the nearest window. The paparazzi stood outside.

"The building I work in is very nice. There are glass hallways that change from transparent to opaque." Jack pushed his fork through his cannoli and the shell broke. He looked over and saw Tabitha doing the same thing. *Looks like I am doing it right.*

Tabitha's eyes darted between Jack and the front window. "Mm-hmm."

"Oh, and for lunch, we had tacos. I ate this thing that Michael told me was called a jalapeño. It was good!" He put a forkful of cannoli in his mouth. The cannoli's cream filling had a consistency thinner than paste but was much sweeter. He squished it between his tongue and soft palate, filling his mouth with flavor.

"That's nice." Tabitha shifted again in her seat.

"I finished my work early, so I got to play video games. Can you believe it?"

Tabitha glanced out the window one more time. "These four-hour workdays are brutal."

"Sure are." *I might have worked two hours today, if I count lunch.* Jack couldn't bring himself to talk about his mother's ten-hour work-days. *Tabby wouldn't believe me.*

***

Jack steeled himself against the upcoming barrage. Paparazzi lined the sidewalk leading away from the restaurant. *Don't these people have other actors to photograph?* The questions, clicks, and buzzing overrode his senses. Jack couldn't get to his car fast enough. Tabitha paused every few steps, giving photo ops and fielding questions about her upcoming roles, what it was like to be an actor, and about Jack. He did his best not to embarrass her.

Samantha darkened the windows once they were in the car. Jack exhaled. Tabitha turned toward Jack, bouncing with adrenaline. "Did you like the restaurant?"

Jack took a moment to compose himself. "That place was amazing! Thank you."

"You're welcome! I followed Jacqueline's advice. She is great with food."

As the car pulled away, Samantha spoke through the speakers. "I am glad you two had such a great time tonight. To continue the celebration of your first day at work, the Algorithm has a special treat waiting for you at home."

Tabitha squealed and bounced up and down in her seat. "Another treat!"

Before Selection, Tabby's squeals would have gotten on my nerves. But now, I love seeing how excited she gets about things. Why?

A chemical scent dominated Tabitha's perfume. She didn't seem to notice it. Tension flowed from Jack's body like spilled water.

I want to make her excited like that for years to come.

Chapter 22: Tabitha

January 2, 535

"Experience how the best of us live! Tap here for a
virtual tour of an Alpha home in Ottawa."

- Advertisement on Beta VR web.

Jack's living room looked exactly like Tabitha's when she moved
in. A pit formed in her stomach. *Doesn't he plan on staying?* Ordering
from the catalog took seconds. Just choose what the Algorithm knew
you'd like.

"Where's your stuff?" Tabitha asked.

"I got rid of all my stuff from Baltimore. I haven't ordered anything new yet. Besides, I was at your place all last night, remember?"

"Of course!" Last night's events had been on her mind all day.
Hopefully, tonight would be a repeat. Tabitha pushed her hand onto
the sofa. It would do. "Are you going to upgrade your couch?"

"I don't know. I haven't really thought about it." Jack took off his
suit jacket and hung it on a coat hook. It didn't belong there, but she
said nothing. "The gaming room upstairs is set up, though."

Tabitha smirked. "Ah, so now I see where your priorities lie." She
sat on the sofa, crossed her legs, and dangled a high heel. *That should
give Jack a great view.*

"Ha ha. Samantha asked me if I wanted a rig, and I said yes. I
don't even know," Jack paused when Tabitha straightened and pushed
her chest out, "what's up there."

"I set it up for you based on your profile," Samantha interrupted on the public aural implant channel. "I can change it if you don't like it."

"It's perfect, Sam. Thank you." Jack sat down on the sofa beside Tabitha. His eyes meandered down her legs.

What is it with Jack and being polite and informal with holos? They aren't Betas.

Tabitha leaned back on the sofa. The neckline of her dress slipped a little. She didn't bother to fix it. Jack's eyes ran up her legs and to her necklace. The focus of his attention was obviously not the necklace. Unlike other Betas she had dated, he didn't get handsy. She liked that about him. He made no assumptions.

Before Selection, Richard would have been my type of guy. Sure, he has a girlfriend, but I could charm Richard out of his relationship. But why would I? Jack is the better choice.

The self-revelation surprised her. *Why do I think that? Richard is a multigenerational Beta from Detroit.* According to everything she believed pre-Selection, Richard was the dream guy and Jack wasn't anywhere near her league. *Before Selection, I would have found Jack to be backward and stupid. Why does being with him feel so right?*

A familiar floral scent filled the air. Tabitha closed her eyes and inhaled. She loved that odor.

Jack's politeness to computers is endearing. A feeling of lightness came over her. *It's cute when he calls me "Tabby." He has a great sense of humor. And he looks hot in a suit!*

Samantha appeared with a tray of strawberries and sparkling wine. "The wine is from Sweden. The strawberries are from Ontario."

Tabitha squealed and rocketed up from the sofa. Swedish wine had the reputation of being as good as Alpha wine. Canadian strawberries were known for being the best Beta strawberries in the world.

"I am glad to see you are excited, Ms. Forsythe." Samantha placed the tray on a small table in front of the sofa. "I hope you enjoy your provision."

"I am certain we will." Tabitha sat on the sofa, picked up a strawberry, and bit into the red part. Jack did the same. He then tried to eat the green stem.

"You don't eat that part!" Tabitha laughed. Jack kept chewing.

"Are you sure? Why would there be food that you don't eat?" Jack removed the stem from his mouth. Samantha appeared beside him, took the stem, and disappeared.

What an odd question. There's lots of food we don't eat.

A list of garnishes ran through Tabitha's mind. The sofa shifted slightly. Jack inched closer to her. The lights dimmed and Samantha lit candles. A new floral scent appeared. Tabitha inched closer to Jack.

"Thank you, Tabby." Jack put down his wine. She did the same. He took both her hands in his. "Thank you for all you have done for me these last two days. I love you." His palms were wet. "I don't want to scare you, but will you marry me? I can't imagine being a Beta without you."

Tabitha squeezed his hands. Energy surged through her. The excitement was genuine—no drugs needed. "I love you, too. It is all happening so fast, but it also feels right." She let go of Jack's hands and rubbed her chin as she looked down at the sofa. "I just remembered something—my parents got engaged the day after their Selection, too."

"Really?"

"Yes!"

Jack furrowed his brows. "Yes, your parents got engaged or yes, you'll marry me?"

"Yes to both, silly!" Tabitha laughed. "Let's go upstairs. We'll take the wine and strawberries with us. I'll show you what the ANN is really good for."

***

In a server farm in Ontario, The Algorithm classified match number 561-165,772 as permanent. It ordered Omega rations in Old Vegas halved to compensate for the strawberries.

Chapter 23: Jack

January 2, 535

"White House loses control over much of the American military as soldiers join regional factions. President Wallace assumes emergency powers, seemingly to no effect."

- *The Washington Post*, April 11, 2187.

Tabitha snored beside Jack. He suppressed a laugh. *She's cute, even with the drool.*

His life had certainly changed in the last two days. *I can't believe my luck. No. Not luck. I earned this. I did all the right things to be Selected Beta.*

The dim night light in the hall barely illuminated the bedroom. As a child, on the nights he couldn't sleep, he'd count the stains on his bedroom ceiling. He'd need to find another way to doze off in Detroit.

What were those "right things" that got me Selected Beta?

The only experience with entertainment he had before Selection was gaming and watching movies. Had he inadvertently trained himself for a Beta career?

The bed shook as Tabitha rolled over. She faced him, snoring louder. *I should record it, but she'd kill me.* Jack chuckled to himself.

Her acceptance of his proposal made him the happiest he had ever been. Jack hadn't planned on proposing, but it felt right at that moment with the strawberries, wine, and her perfume. Was it perfume? He'd smelled it earlier today, too. Maybe other Betas wore it.

Regardless, he barely got the words out. Proposing made him more nervous than Selection. A rejection would have devastated him—even more than if Rebecca and Dan's prank this morning turned out to be true.

One thing ate at his mind. *Why does Tabby love me?* Jack had met several very handsome Betas today—all of whom were much more attractive than he. Not to mention, they all had more going for them than a recently promoted Sigma.

If I were to be honest with myself, Sam would be the better boyfriend for Tabby. Sam spent his youth reading and coding while Jack gamed. Sam possessed the real skills. *So, what happened? Why isn't Sam here living the life that I am?* Hadn't Sam earned a Beta Selection? *Something's not right. Maybe I should contact Sam.*

A familiar scent returned to his nostrils. It wasn't the strawberries, some of which lay uneaten beside him. *Maybe if Sam had worked harder, he'd have been promoted.*

Jack's mind lost focus, and he drifted to sleep.

***

The Algorithm noted citizen number 3241-02-1244, Jack Thompson, had initiated his role in Its plan. Most of Its regression models estimated Phase Two as 75 percent complete. A tertiary server in Detroit requested instructions. The Algorithm replied:

```
Stand by.
```

Part 3
The Plan

Chapter 24: Sam

January 15, 535

"The Southern Alliance captured the remains of the
US Navy from the Norfolk naval base today."

- *Southern Star*, July 8, 2190.

Although Sam hated to admit it, the Algorithm's puppeteering skills impressed him. He and Jennie weren't the only ones engaged after their first day of work. Almost every couple on their bus had done the same.

It took only seconds to have their marriage license processed—a brief time considering the importance of the commitment he and Jennie made. Apparently, the Algorithm cared more for efficiency than romantic notions.

The Algorithm assigned Sam and Jennie a new SLU. Their new home had one main room and two bedrooms—just like the SLU Sam had in Baltimore. Jennie lamented not setting up her own SLU, so Sam happily let her make all the decorating decisions. She tore into her new role as interior designer with the same gusto and skill as she had for programming.

The first things Jennie ordered for their new SLU were two plastic chairs and a table for their main room. Using Sam's special privileges, she placed the order the morning they moved in. The new furniture was delivered before they got home from work. Jennie fell in love with the chairs as soon as they arrived. Sam hated them, but he kept his feelings to himself.

On their first bus ride home as a married couple, Jennie suggested they eat dinner at the new table and chairs every night—no phones or vids. After that first dinner, Sam found a place in his heart for the new furniture.

***

Jennie leaned forward across the kitchen table. Sam's eyes drifted from the pork paste on his plate to her blouse. She turned up the corners of her lips and shook her head.

When the blouse became available on the Outfitter, Sam had to buy it for her. Jennie didn't like him buying too many nonessentials, especially when so many others had so little. He respected her feelings, but the blouse matched the flecks in her eyes, and the neckline would provide an excellent view at dinner. After Sam ordered the blouse, a pair of khaki slacks appeared as an additional recommended item. Sam clicked buy before Jennie could protest. The blouse and slacks became Jennie's go-to dinner outfit.

"I am still not used to having this much space." Jennie stirred the pork paste on her plate. They were always provided the same meal as one another. "What should we do with the third room?" She put a spoonful of the paste in her mouth.

Sam used a spoon to push his paste around the plate. His hunger couldn't motivate him to stomach the meal. "I think it is supposed to be used as a nursery. I have another idea, though."

"You don't want to have a child with me?" Jennie slouched in her plastic chair and looked down at her plate.

Shit. That is not what I meant. Sam sat up straight, turning his attention from the paste to his wife, and took her hand. "I absolutely want to start a family with you." Jennie perked up. It seemed he had recovered. Marriage hadn't made him an expert at talking to women.

"What I meant was, it will take a while before we need that room as a nursery. What if, in the meantime, we use it as an office? We can work on code development."

"Hmmm. What do you have in mind?" Jennie bit her lip as she leaned forward with her elbow on the table and propped her chin in the hand that wasn't holding Sam's.

I love it when she bites her lip. Sam forced himself to focus. "A side project." He sat back in his chair, placing his hands in his lap; the hard plastic pressed against his shoulder blades. "I have requested some items for that room."

"I thought you could get whatever you wanted out of the Sigma Outfitter," Jennie said as she ate the last spoonful of pork paste.

"I can, but this is off-catalog." *This conversation needs to be private.* Sam leaned forward. "I am hoping the Algorithm will be generous."

Jennie stood and retrieved their phones from their bedroom. Without looking, she pressed a button on each phone, then placed them both screen up on the table. A timer counted down on each screen.

The deepfake program, originally written by Sam, had been significantly upgraded by Jennie. Her work allowed it to send a deepfake video to the SLU computer that recorded everything in their home. Thanks to Jennie, they no longer had to go to the park to speak privately.

"What's the deepfake about this time?" Sam asked.

"The Algorithm sees us discussing baby names."

"I still can't believe you figured out how to train an AI on a few minutes of conversation." Sam took her hand and squeezed. "I am so proud of you."

"I wouldn't have been able to do it without you."

All she needed was a spark to catch fire. I was happy to provide it.

"So, what's going on?" Jennie let go of his hand and leaned back.

Sam leaned forward in his chair. His shoulder blades ached less, but his butt hurt more. "Did you know in the last five days, you have sent me seven different inefficiencies?"

"Yeah, and you haven't told me anything about them." Jennie rested her folded arms on the table. Sam's view improved. "Was I wrong?"

"Not at all, my love." Sam shifted again in his seat. The pain transferred from his butt to his lower back. "You found some inefficiencies that took me a few days to identify."

Jennie smiled at the compliment.

"You should be the programmer and I should be the maintenance person. How do you identify the inefficiencies so efficiently?" Sam smirked at his own cleverness.

"I've shared my bed with you *and* married you. What else do you think you are going to get out of me with all these compliments?" Jennie put on what Sam knew to be her fake-serious face. He loved it.

"I'll think of something." Sam rubbed his chin. Jennie once told him she loved it when he did that.

"All I do is look for things that don't seem right based on what I have learned from *you*." Jennie's eyes lit up—Sam's second favorite of her facial expressions. "I read something the other day that got me thinking there might be a way of writing hyper-parallel software. If I am right, then learning could happen with only a few training instances."

What is "hyper-parallel" programming?

Jennie, apparently not noticing Sam's confusion, sat back in her chair again. "Although I love the flattery, I'd really like to know what your plans are for William's bedroom."

"William?" Sam pressed his lips together, trying to figure out where he knew the name.

"If we have a son, I'd like to name him William after my father." Jennie's eyes watered. The death of her parents had been hard on Jennie. Sam did everything he could to help her cope with the loss. She seemed to do better—it had been three nights since she had last cried herself to sleep.

"I can't think of a better name." Sam reached across the table and wiped a tear that had rolled down her cheek.

Jennie's puffy red eyes glistened. "So, what's up with the code I sent you? And what are you ordering off-catalog?"

"I love it when you get down to business, Ms. Goodby!"

When the Algorithm processed their marriage license, Sam suggested he and Jennie choose a new surname—for a fresh start. Jennie didn't want to break her one last tie to her parents. Sam had no attachment to his past, but he respected Jennie's. She had a lot to be proud of. He put in a request to change his surname to hers, but the Algorithm denied it and didn't explain why.

"Like I said, all the code you sent me had inefficiencies—some major, some minor."

"Let me guess, all of them used outdated algorithms with learning rates that were entirely too large." Jennie leaned back in her chair and ran her fingers through her hair.

"Yup. You've found so many that I think these programs might be used everywhere, not just the AB." He shifted again in his chair. It didn't help either his back or his butt. "To figure out what's going on, I ordered a terminal and a desk off-catalog."

"Can't we develop code on our phones?"

"We can, but I want this project off-network."

Jennie squirmed in her chair. "Why the secrecy?"

It may be best to rip off the band-aid and see what happens.

"I have a plan to replace the Algorithm with something better. If you don't want me to do it, I won't, and I will never speak of it again. However, will you hear me out before you decide?"

Jennie's stomach expanded from her long inhale. It slowly deflated during an equally long exhale. "You have done so much for me. The very least I can do for you is to give you a chance to explain these heretical ideas."

Heretical. Sam worried about her choice of words. *I have a plan that could improve the world and she is worried about superstition? Un-fucking-believable.* Sam swallowed. He shouldn't judge Jennie's beliefs. She had endured a rough childhood. Belief in a higher order could help people tolerate the unfortunate lives dealt to them.

"Thank you, Jennie." Sam sat back and crossed one leg over the other. *A casual conversation might be the best tactic.* He folded his hands in his lap. "As you know, the Algorithm was designed hundreds of years ago to guide humanity through the Shift."

Jennie eased back in her chair. She, too, placed her hands in her lap. "Yes, and without the Algorithm we wouldn't be here. The Algorithm was designed to allocate resources and place people in positions where they could best help build and maintain an optimal society. It did what needed to be done to reduce the burden on the Earth and allow humanity to survive."

That was the official history. It might even be factual, but Sam had his doubts. However, debating the past would get them nowhere. The future concerned Sam.

"You are correct," Sam said. "Our ancestors believed the Algorithm would find new optimal solutions as the climate continued to change. Early on, the Algorithm divided people into many castes to allocate work and resources."

Jennie nodded. "Not everyone could live like the people in pre-Shift America. Some had to do with less while those contributing the most got more."

"That was the thinking, and it might have been appropriate back then," Sam conceded, "but the world has changed. Things aren't perfect, but it's not as bad as it was during the peak of the Shift. The radiation zones are gone. Sea levels are still high, but thanks to the work of Omegas, we have reclaimed a lot of land."

"Things *are* working." Jennie put her elbows on the table and interlaced her fingers. "Change takes time."

"Are they working, though?" Sam leaned forward to engage Jennie. His plan wouldn't work without her. "As a society, we are not better off. Look at food availability. Between Canada and Russia, we should be able to grow enough real food to support a human population at least four times its current size. If we have that capacity, why do we let so many go hungry?"

"Being an Omega means always being hungry." Jennie looked down at the table. "As a child, I'd cry when my stomach hurt from hunger. My parents could do nothing but sit with me." Tears welled up in her eyes. "I didn't know about the excess capacity. Omegas don't get access to that kind of information."

A weight slowly lifted off Sam's chest. He didn't have anyone he could share the full extent of his thoughts on Selection before. He started lightly tapping on the table. "If the Algorithm is evolutionary, why haven't the castes changed? Sure, there are fewer of them now, but there's been five castes for hundreds of years. And what about Metrics? Family and Wealth might have mattered in the early days, but now we can't change them. People have those scores handed down to them over generations. Hell, I no longer believe we can change any of the Metrics!"

Pushing forward seemed to be a good move while Sam had Jennie engaged. "As things get better, shouldn't there be more Betas? Why do the UnSelected still exist today? Why aren't there more people changing castes?" Sam pointed at Jennie. "You are the only upgraded Omega I have ever met. Jack is the only Sigma upgraded to Beta that I have ever known."

Jennie's gaze fixated on the table. A tear rolled down her cheek. As much as he hated seeing Jennie like this, Sam knew it was time for her to know the truth. The hard part of the conversation hadn't even started yet.

Chapter 25: Jennie

January 15, 535

"The MidAtlantic Federation mines the Inner Harbor in anticipation of an invasion by the Southern Alliance."

- From the final edition of *The Baltimore Sun*, July 9, 2190.

Jennie's empty plate sat in front of her—devoid of the delicious paste. Sam's silence gave her mind a chance to converge.

The Algorithm is suboptimal.

She had suspected it since their first conversation in the park. Sam's words and the inefficiencies were hard to ignore.

Nausea, lightheadedness, and a tightened chest all combined with a racing heartbeat.

Is this what dying feels like?

Childhood hunger. Her parents' nonstop working hours. Charlie's hard life as an UnSelected. The death of Omega and UnSelected babies. Her parents' fate in Old Inner Harbor. None of them had to happen.

The nausea and lightheadedness subsided. Her chest remained tight. She relaxed her jaw, lest she hurt her teeth.

Sam leaned his elbows on the table and stared directly at her. His brown eyes piercing hers. *Here it comes…*

"Do you want to know how I was Selected Sigma?"

Jennie suppressed all external evidence of the emotional maelstrom that whipped through her. It wasn't fair of Sam to unload this on her while she reeled from her apostasy. But as a former Omega, she could handle the burden. She had borne far worse. Sam needed this off his chest for them to move forward in their relationship.

Lay it on me, Sam.

"I had the Metrics to be a Beta in a real programming job. My Metric Vector had a magnitude long enough to land me in Detroit." Sam trembled. "I know because it was displayed on the wall in front of me." The trembling turned into shaking. "However, the magnitude was decreased by an unusually low scaling factor. A fucking random number placed me where I am today." Tears streamed down his cheeks.

"I believe the same thing happened to you, Jennie. I think your Metrics were easily high enough to land you into an even better life. But your potential got cut short by the same random scaling factor."

He is saying he shouldn't be with me.

The load Sam placed upon her broke the walls that were holding back the maelstrom. The former Omega had found her limit and the pressure relief valve opened. Tears flowed from the corners of her eyes and down her cheeks. At least she now felt only one emotion. "In my case, it was an improvement."

Her eyes returned to her empty plate. She couldn't look at Sam. "We wouldn't have met if you were a Beta."

A soft hand touched her forearm. Jennie looked up. Sam knelt on one knee by Jennie's side. Red puffy eyes leaked rivulets of tears down his cheeks. Mucus rested upon his quivering upper lip.

Sam dropped his head down. "I am so sorry, Jennie." He sobbed. Sam had been her rock after her parents' death, but he had found his limit, too. "Please. Please don't think I am unhappy with you." Sam took in a big breath—tears continued to flow down his cheeks.

Jennie took Sam's hands. Then it happened.

A light kindled in Sam's eyes. He wiped his lip. "I don't want to be a Beta. I just want to be with you."

A switch had flipped. Everything about Sam appeared lighter that instant. The lines in his skin faded. His face relaxed. A genuine, honest smile formed on his face. Walls fell. For the first time since she had known him, Samuel Watkins was happy.

Jennie's own tears transformed from ones of heartbreak to joy. She witnessed the transformation of Samuel Watkins. Up to this point, a voice in the back of her mind worried Sam had settled with her. That voice disappeared.

They stood and hugged. Their tears of joy mixed as their cheeks pressed together. Jennie, enveloped by Sam, felt like she became part of him. She squeezed him back to ensure he felt the same. He didn't turn for a kiss and neither did she. This hug meant more than that.

Jennie stepped back, holding her husband's hands.

"Do you think we would have fallen in love as Betas in Detroit if we weren't victims of random numbers?" The tears had stopped flowing, but Jennie's face still felt wet.

"Probably not," Sam said with a straight face.

She didn't have it in her to cry again. "Why do you say that?"

"Because without those random numbers, I think you'd be an Alpha."

"Ha ha. It's getting deeper in here than high tide in Mount Vernon."

"I'm serious, Jennie." Sam dropped their hands. "I'm a Beta for sure, but as fast as you learn things, there is no way you are just a Beta. As the schoolbook says, you're one of the best of us."

As it turned out, she could cry again. Sam knew how to make her feel special. No one, not even her parents, had ever said something so sweet to her. But the look in his eye was an honest one. He meant it, and he deserved to know how she felt.

"It doesn't matter. I'd rather be a Sigma with you than an Alpha without you."

Sam's tears restarted. He took her hands again. "I don't deserve you."

Minutes, maybe hours—Jennie couldn't tell—passed as they held hands beside the table in the main room, silently communicating each of their transformations. Jennie couldn't find an adequate word for their relationship. Partners, teammates, lovers. None of the words that came to her mind did justice to what she felt for Sam. Maybe the fact that it went beyond labels made it special. Only one thing mattered—it was hers.

Sam's face became serious again. "If this happened to us, then who else has it happened to over the last five hundred years? If people are randomly placed in suboptimal positions, what have we, as a society, lost out on?"

Sam dropped her hands and pulled out her chair. Jennie sat. A scaping sound cut through the silence in the main room as Sam slid his chair over to face her. He sat and took her hands again. Like hers, his were wet with wiped tears. Sam leaned forward and gently squeezed her hands.

"I believe you and I, working together, can develop a new learning program and insert it into the Algorithm. Our new program can restructure Society so that no one needs to suffer anymore." Sam's eyes lit up with his vision. "There will be plenty of real food and better housing and healthcare for all Sigmas, Omegas, and UnSelected." Sam snorted. "Hell, if I can figure out how, I'd like there to be no more castes at all. Everyone could help Society using their own talents and, along the way, can improve their station in life." Sam let go of her hands. Jennie wasn't done holding them. "Those who cannot work will be supported by those who can. We will all be in this world *together*." Sam joined his hands in front of him.

Sam's idea sounded good, at least in theory. Was it possible? Before dinner, Jennie Goodby had never once thought about the order of things. She had been told to accept it, so she did. That Jennie Goodby no longer existed.

The more Sam's words settled in, the more her blood rose. *If Sam is right, the suffering of Omegas and the UnSelected is unnecessary. My parents didn't need to die doing work that should have been completed by robots long ago.*

Sam's disappointment with his Selection now made sense. His disappointment wasn't with her. It was with a system that did not work as well as it could.

Thoughts kept pouring through Jennie's mind. The most important one came to the forefront, *If Sam is right, the odds of our children having a life better than ours is small—maybe zero.* Being a Sigma was amazing. But Jennie wanted more for her future kids.

"I'm in."

Chapter 26: Sam

January 15, 535

"Baltimore in flames! US federal government repels Southern Alliance's DC offensive."

- *The Washington Post* headline, July 10, 2190.

The stains on the bedroom ceiling seemed not so bad tonight. Sam doubted Jennie's work order request to clean it had been fulfilled. He saw it through different eyes. The world seemed a little brighter, certainly less stained.

Jennie mumbled beside him. Sam had told her she talked in her sleep, but she didn't believe him. One of these nights, he should record her. *On second thought, maybe I shouldn't.*

Sam had swung for the fences, and it had worked. Jennie could have left him right there after dinner. He wouldn't have blamed her, either. Instead, she bought into the plan. But that was far from the most important outcome of the night.

Deep down, he accepted his life: Jennie, Orlando, and his Selection. It didn't mean he shouldn't try to change it. But even the impact of his acceptance paled compared to how his relationship with Jennie had grown. Try as he might, he couldn't find the right word to describe how he felt about Jennie. The word *love* was inadequate. The way she stared into his eyes after their conversation, he guessed she'd had the same revelation.

Still, it wasn't all sunshine and rainbows inside his mind. *The Algorithm manipulated us to be together. I have already asked her to endure too much tonight. I couldn't dump that on her, too.*

Sam tried to convince himself he wasn't lying by withholding the manipulation. For now, the lie protected her, and that was good enough. If—when—she needed to know the full truth, he'd divulge it. He wasn't looking forward to that conversation. The thought of hurting her pained him.

His phone buzzed on the nightstand beside the bed. The screen lit up half the room. Sam picked up his phone and squinted at it. The Outfitter had sent a text message.

```
Your request for a terminal has been approved.
Expect it tomorrow.
```

The bed shook as Jennie propped herself up on her shoulder. She had the cutest case of bedhead Sam had ever seen.

"What was that?" She asked. Her disturbed sleep was evident in her voice.

Sam showed her the phone. "We're going to change the world, Ms. Goodby."

"Damn right we are!" Jennie, now fully awake, rolled over on top of Sam.

***

The Algorithm sent a message from Its server in Edmonton to an underground data center outside Old Atlanta's remains. It read:

```
Initiate final stages of Phase Two.
```

Chapter 27: Sam

February 10, 536

"The Midwest Republic and MidAtlantic Federation have agreed to an economic and military coalition in response to recent bold actions by the Southern Alliance. Republic politicians in Chicago welcomed Federation President Williams in full session of Parliament. US President Wallace has remained silent about the new treaty."

- *Chicago Tribune*, September 30, 2192.

Sam was in his happy place. A little over a year ago, he doubted he'd ever find one. The old Sam was too focused on what he thought was stolen from him. He didn't appreciate what he had.

That guy was tiring. How did Jennie put up with him?

Hot air blew in through the bus's open windows. Jennie's head rested on his shoulder. Her hair tickled his cheek. The old Sam had noticed the basement smell in Jennie's hair. The new one did, too—he just simply didn't care.

She's perfect, basement hair and all.

The couple ahead of them sat apart with their heads down, scrolling on their phones. The other couples on the bus did the same. *Don't they spend enough time on screens at work?*

The bus ride home became his happy place the day Jennie told him she never slept on the way home. Because if she did, she'd miss her favorite part of the day. How could he not love her?

Sandy brown fields zoomed by. The monotony didn't bother Sam. Instead, it cleared his mind. Each ride had become an opportunity for reflection.

Over the last year, he and Jennie had begun the secret project they called the Plan. Jennie found more inefficiencies than Sam could have dreamed. Old learning algorithms were pervasive. Besides the recovery robots, she found significant inefficiencies in the systems that ran the AB. Sam did not know how she got access to those codes, nor did he want to know. Jennie's discoveries supported Sam's hypothesis—inefficient learning algorithms were everywhere in the Society.

Jennie shifted in her seat, making a sound of satisfaction. She took on the role of lead programmer a few months after the Plan's initiation. Although she was in charge now, they kept to Sam's initial workflow. Jennie found the inefficiencies at work and sent them to Sam, who recommended a fix to his supervisor. The supervisor often got promoted.

At least, that's what it looked like to an outsider. Before Sam fixed any code, he copied the inefficient programs to a data stick and brought them home. Jennie coded up the real fixes on their terminal and used what she had learned to develop new AI programs. Sam tested the new subroutines on his isolated terminal at work—a much more powerful machine than they could get off-catalog.

While Jennie worked on the learning algorithms, Sam continued to improve the deepfake program. Working on the deepfake code gave him a meaningful programming assignment. Jennie occasionally reviewed Sam's work and pointed out improvements. Sam didn't mind; she always made the code run better. *Soon, she'll be taking over that project, too.*

I wish I knew what meal we'd be provided tonight. Thoughts of spice combinations swam through Sam's mind. Eight months ago, he stumbled upon spices in the Sigma Outfitter. On a lark, he bought some and read a few cooking articles. Cooking turned out to be like programming. To his surprise, he enjoyed both equally. Try as he might, Sam couldn't use the spices to change the paste's texture, but he could use them to improve its flavor. His mom never used spices, probably because they were expensive. But even with his unlimited credits, spices were rarely available.

Jennie snuggled up closer to him. Her bones no longer poked him as much, thanks to her Sigma diet. The weight looked good on her. Her changes were more than physical. She had become more confident about her own abilities. But she never forgot her Omega roots.

The Orlando bus depot appeared on the horizon. Sam inhaled. The smell of mud permeated the air. The new Sam didn't care about that either. He was home.

***

Another pork night. *I wonder if I have any cinnamon left.* A beep came from the home office where Jennie worked on the learning algorithm.

"Damn these phones!"

Sam snickered. Jennie loved the phone when she first got it. Now she complained about all the distractions. Apparently, her old Omega phone buzzed less. Omegas didn't have down time that the Algorithm needed to fill.

"Uh, Sam!"

Several clunks came from the dispenser. *Vegetables! Why are they here?* Sam grabbed up the carrots, broccoli, and spinach. Jennie needed to see this. Just as Sam turned around with an armful of vegetables, Jennie, barefoot in her blue blouse and khaki pants, pushed her phone in his face. He squinted at the screen, which was a little too close.

> ```
> Ms. Goodby,
> The Algorithm is pleased to notify you of your
> pregnancy. Based on our diagnostic scans,
> there is a 97% probability that your child
> will be male. Expect the birth at 2330 on No-
> vember 10, 536.
> ```

Sam dropped the vegetables. Jennie jumped into his arms. Just when Sam had thought life couldn't get any better, it did.

After they broke their hug, Sam picked up the vegetables and put them on the counter. Jennie sighed and sat down on their new sofa. The Outfitter advertised the sofa as "the softest Sigma sofa on the market." The slogan might be true, but it meant little.

"What's wrong?" Sam sat beside Jennie and rubbed her back.

Jennie wiped the tears from her cheeks. "Nothing."

"Really? You sound like me after Selection." The joke didn't seem to work.

"What does this child have to look forward to? If you are right, and I believe you are, he'll just be Selected as another Sigma." Jennie leaned forward with her elbows on her knees and her face in her hands. "Maybe he'll end up an Omega because of me."

Thanks to Jennie's help, the deepfake program could now be run on one phone. Sam started the deepfake with one hand as he put his other arm around her.

"That's why we started the Plan. Once you finish the new program, we will load it into the Algorithm's source code. If it works, our child will have a future determined by him, not by random decisions made by a computer programmed centuries ago."

"You're right." Jennie leaned over and put her arms around him. Her wet cheeks pressed against his. "A year ago, I thought this was heresy. Now, it is a necessity. We are doing this for our child and all the children of the Lower Castes."

Chapter 28: Sam

February 11, 536

"The remains of Atlanta were nuked today by the MidAtlantic Federation. The Southern Alliance retaliated by destroying Burlington and Detroit. Wallace condemned the attacks."

\- Excerpt from archived video news feed, circa 2195.

I am one lucky dude.

As always, Jennie waited for Sam beside the bus after work. She waved her hand back and forth with a big smile on her face. Like snuggling on the ride home, the other couples had stopped this ritual months ago. But Jennie, who was always first to the bus stop, refused to board before Sam arrived. Sam didn't mind. Sharing a big hug was the best way to start every evening.

"I have a surprise for *you*!" Jennie drew out the word *you*. A few of the Sigmas getting on the bus knowingly smiled at them.

"Well, I guess everyone on the bus knows what we'll be doing tonight," Sam said in a hushed voice as they broke their hug.

"Not that, silly! I mean, yeah, that, but also something else." Jennie lowered her voice and led Sam onto the bus. "I'll tell you when we get home."

Their favorite seat, the first one behind the windshield on the right, was open. Sam slid into the seat. Jennie followed and rested her head on Sam's shoulder for the entire trip home.

Sam settled into his happy place as he watched the scenery go by. The stakes of the Plan had changed now that there was a child on the way. Even if the Plan worked, Sam wouldn't be able to control everything that would happen to his son, William—the name had been decided upon during the life-changing dinner one year ago. But the goal wasn't for Sam to control William's fate. If the Plan worked, William would control his own.

Last night's pregnancy notification got Sam thinking about his own father. He hadn't spoken to his mother since she exposed her bigotry on the call with Jennie. Was she being honest about his father skipping out on them? It didn't matter anymore. Sam resolved to be the father he had always wanted—one that was present and involved. William deserved that. *He* would provide it.

***

Sam closed the door to the SLU. "So, what's the surprise?"

Jennie bit her lip, making Sam squirm. "I'll tell you soon enough." She went into their bedroom. Surprises for Sigmas were rare. Sam didn't mind prolonging this one.

A light on the dispenser blinked. *I hope this thing isn't broken again.* Two weeks ago, the same light blinked. The dispenser didn't provide food, and they went hungry that night. It wasn't the first time either of them went to bed hungry, but with a baby on the way, things were different.

Other than the blinking light, the dispenser looked okay. Sam ordered dinner. The dispenser emitted an unusual thumping sound. A plastic cylinder sat in the dispenser.

"What was that?" Jennie yelled from the bedroom.

"Come check this out."

Jennie joined him in the kitchen area, wearing her blue blouse and khaki pants. Sam never tired of those. The blouse had faded, and the pants had a stain. Sam checked the Sigma Outfitter every day for replacements, but nothing had been available for months. Unlimited credits were less useful than he'd hoped. Things simply weren't always available to Sigmas.

The cylinder rattled as Jennie rolled it in her hand. "What are these for?"

"They must be vitamins for the pregnancy." Sam leaned against a counter in the main room. "They'll help the baby develop properly. Too bad we don't get more vegetables. They'd be better."

"Another upgrade as a Sigma." Jennie placed the bottle on the counter. "Omegas get no prenatal care." She stared at the bottle. "Infant mortality is very high."

We need the Plan to work. No one should have to live like that—at least not when the Betas have so much. Sam placed his hand on her back.

"If you don't mind, I'd rather talk about something else." Jennie leaned against the counter, facing Sam. "I believe I promised you a surprise."

"Yes! Best to do it before dinner, so we don't cramp up." Sam stretched his arms in an exaggerated fashion. Over the last year, he found that levity helped Jennie with some of her more terrible memories of being an Omega.

"What? No, not that!" Jennie laughed. The joke had worked. "Something better."

Sam raised an eyebrow. "Better?"

"Yeah, better." Jennie held up a data stick. Her smile turned into a knowing grin, and she straightened. Sam loved confident Jennie—the sexiest version of her. Although ass-kicking Jennie was a close second.

"I remember the self-doubting Jennie from a year ago."

Jennie looked confused.

"You have changed so much. I love the confident woman you have become. I somehow love you more than I did yesterday."

She hugged him tight. He understood what she wanted to say.

Sam broke the hug and tried to lighten the mood. "Is that the latest vid of the influencer from Winnipeg?" Jennie nodded and took Sam by the hand and led him to their bedroom. His phone buzzed in his pocket. The one person who would contact him was right beside him. The only other reason the phone would buzz was if Jennie had started a deepfake.

Once they were in the bedroom, Jennie released Sam's hand and turned to him. "I am sorry to disappoint you, but this is not that vid. I needed the pretense." Sam deflated a little in disappointment. "I could get it if you want."

Sam chuckled. "At least tell me we are having some fun on the deepfake."

"Yup, the Algorithm is seeing a video of us in bed with that vid running in the background." Jennie held up the data stick again. "This right here, in my hand, is a subroutine used by the Algorithm."

His eyes focused on the data stick.

"It isn't a core subroutine, but it should still tell me something about the Algorithm's main code."

"How in the hell did you get that?"

"It's really best that you don't know." Jennie handed him the data stick. It felt lighter than Sam expected. Something this important should have more gravity to it. The ones and zeroes inside represented their best chance for success. "I've been working on some new pro-gramming techniques. It'll take some time, but I think I can retrain the Algorithm using the stuff on the stick and my new code."

This is amazing! Think, Sam, what's next…

"Once your code is ready, we'll need to upload it."

"For that, we'll need a Beta-level terminal," Jennie said.

"How do you know a Beta terminal would work?"

Jennie crossed her arms. Her chest stuck out a little. "Beta terminals must connect to Alpha terminals. Otherwise, how do Betas report to their bosses?"

Sam nodded. "And if there's anything in this world with access to the Algorithm's source code, it *must* be an Alpha terminal."

"Unfortunately, there are no Beta terminals in the AB." Jennie took the data stick from Sam and slipped it into her pants pocket.

"We'll cross that bridge when we get to it. Regardless, I am very impressed, Ms. Goodby."

"Why thank you, Mr. Watkins." Jennie curtseyed and chuckled.

"Shall we join our deepfake selves?" Sam held an arm out toward their bed.

Chapter 29: Jennie

January 24, 537

"Dark web conspiracy theorists post rumors of a powerful computer program being built by the US federal government in a secret DC lab."

- *The Federation Gazette*, February 10, 2198.

Jennie rubbed her eyes. The lighting in the main room wasn't as good as it was in the office, which had been converted to William's nursery after he was born. The Algorithm predicted his birth perfectly, precisely 2330 on November 10. William was assigned the surname Goodkins. Jennie had never heard of the Algorithm mixing last names before. It must be a good omen for the child. Sam thought the name assignment was random. Regardless of the surname's meaning, William was healthy—the vitamins worked.

Lines of code filled the terminal screen in front of her. The answer must be close. Her maternity leave gave her time to code while William slept. The luxuries of being a Sigma seemed to never cease. Sam did some asking around at work. No one else had been granted a leave. She wrote it off as another one of Sam's perks. Sam doubted it. His paranoia seemed to increase the closer she got to a solution.

Sam shuffled into their SLU and took off his shoes. "I am looking forward to having you back on the bus. I miss your smiling face waiting for me at the end of the day." Sam peeled off his sweaty clothes.

"I know, sweetie, but I love spending time with William." Jennie stretched in her seat. "Thank the Algorithm for this leave. I get to code when William sleeps. I am making a lot of progress." Jennie's eyes returned to the terminal. "Did you know Omegas don't get childcare?"

"What happens for single parents like my mom?"

That was the first time since their engagement that Sam had mentioned his mother. He never told her the truth about what happened on the call between them, but it couldn't have been good.

"They've gotta figure something out. Sometimes they hire an UnSelected man like Charlie to watch their children. Omega paste is a huge upgrade compared to what they get."

"Seriously?" The pitch of Sam's voice increased as he spoke the word.

"We've talked about this. Most of them are good people in a bad circumstance. It is almost always those above you that you have to look out for."

Sam's face reddened as he frowned and lowered his gaze. "I know."

Jennie had been helping Sam see the UnSelected for who they really were—not the criminals he had been taught. He sometimes joined her when she volunteered at an UnSelected camp.

Old prejudices were hard to overcome. Sam rarely succumbed to them anymore, but when he did, like right now, she could see his shame. He had come a long way. She reached out and squeezed his hand.

Sam went into William's room. Before William's birth, Sam told her he was worried he wouldn't be a good dad because he didn't have a male role model growing up. Jennie would have thought Sam had a father like her own. He spent every night reading or playing with William. Like everything else Sam did, he quickly became excellent at being a father.

"That's it!" Jennie started a deepfake.

"What's it?" Sam entered the main room, with William in his arms, and sat down on the sofa in his underwear.

"I have a hyper-parallel learning algorithm that will run on Sigma-standard tech!" Jennie leaned back in the plastic chair. The terminal took up half of their dinner table. It made meals more intimate.

William giggled at Sam's hand puppet. Sam's attention remained focused on William. "Come again?"

"I have created a program that will learn with fewer than ten training instances. The program self-replicates and mutates exponentially fast, selecting optimal offspring. It's sort of like the genetic algorithms of old." Jennie, still leaning back in the chair, placed her hands behind her head and puffed out her chest. Her tank top left little to the imagination, which was probably why Sam had ordered it.

The tank top worked. Sam looked up from William. If she didn't have so much work to do, she'd walk over there and close his dropped jaw for him. She loved that he still found her attractive. She loved even more that he believed in her enough to let her take over the Plan.

Jennie put a data stick on the table beside the terminal. "Here are the program and training data. Run it on your isolated terminal at work tomorrow. All you need to do is press the execute button when it appears on the screen. The program will take care of the rest."

"What are the magic words?" Sam smirked as he bounced William up and down on his knee.

"Pretty please?" Jennie said sweetly, half laughing. "Go shower, then let's have dinner. I am starving."

***

Jennie couldn't sleep. Sam snored beside her. The snoring started about a month ago. The sudden onset couldn't be normal. She convinced Sam to request a scan. His request was denied. Maybe if the Plan were successful, Sam could get the healthcare he might need.

Sam snored himself awake, mumbled something, then rolled over. Jennie rolled onto her back. The nightlight reflected off the unstained parts of the tiles. She remembered when the ceiling seemed pristine.

I wish I could be there when Sam tests the hyper-parallel program.

As the sleepless night wore on, Sam's snoring subsided.

I can't tell him the whole truth.

Guilt settled in.

The future of our family depends on it.

***

Jennie took William to the park the next morning. That afternoon, it got hot enough to be provided air conditioning in their SLU. She took advantage of it and stayed inside to read. William fussed, so she read programming articles to him. He quieted down after the first paragraph. *Maybe he'll go into the family business?*

Finally, the front door opened. Jennie ran up to Sam as he walked in. She had just put William down for a nap. "Well?"

"Well, what?" Sam took off his shoes and placed them by the door.

"What do you mean, 'Well, what?' You know what I want." Her tone was a little harsher than she intended. Sam had that look in his eye.

Let's see what kind of bad joke he comes up with.

"Oh, I was supposed to run the simulation for you at work today, wasn't I?" Sam drew out the *I*. "Sorry, sweetie, Cynthia and I were busy working one-on-one on an assignment. I couldn't run the sim."

Jennie narrowed her eyes. If they were lasers, she would have burned a hole through his head. The list of people Jennie disliked was very short, but Cynthia sat at the top.

"Sorry, ma'am." Sam's "I screwed up" face was one she knew well. He handed over the data stick. "Here are your results." He bit his bottom lip. "You know I don't hang out with that classist asshole any more than I have to."

Jennie sat down, turned toward the terminal, and inserted the data stick. "You know I can kick your ass, right?" Her gaze was glued to the terminal's screen.

"But then I won't be your pretty boy anymore." Sam rubbed her bare shoulders.

The apology worked. He leaned over. His warm breath tickled the side of her neck—Sam's not-so-smooth attempt to sneak a peek down her tank top.

"Uh-huh." She brought up the results. Everything looked right—actually, better than she had expected. The hyper-parallel program would do all of what she told Sam, and more.

Jennie leaned back in her chair, interlaced her fingers behind her head, and smiled. "It worked."

"Of course it did. You're awesome!"

I guess that makes up for the Cynthia comment. She puffed out her chest a little more. He had earned it. He had risked a lot running this at work. "All we need now is a Beta terminal."

***

In a server farm below Old Atlanta, the Algorithm noted citizen number 7985-02-1245 now had a 97 percent chance of successfully executing Its plan. The servers in Old Atlanta emailed the Algorithm's data center in Ottawa:

```
Phase Two complete. Initiate Phase Three.
```

Chapter 30: Jack

January 25, 537

"Washington ablaze! The last vestiges of the federal government have collapsed. President Wallace's whereabouts are unknown."

- Final edition of *The Washington Post*, October 1, 2199.

Jack sat at his desk, rubbing the inner corner of his eyes with his thumb and forefinger. All three items of today's work to-do list were checked off on Victoria's screen. The last task item was to approve of Tabitha's new role in a Beta sitcom holovid. She'd love the high-profile part.

Who makes the shows for Sigmas?

There was no point in asking his colleagues. Over the last couple of years, it became clear that Betas knew little about the world beyond their own neighborhoods.

The clock on his terminal changed over to 1400. Two hours remained. He slouched in his chair as he scrolled through the endless list of games on his terminal.

"Are you feeling well, Jack?" If Victoria weren't a computer, he would have thought she cared.

Jack sat back in his chair and rubbed his neck. "Yeah. Why do you ask?"

"I am detecting levels of frustration and boredom in you. Would you like medication to alleviate those feelings?"

Once Jack realized the Algorithm had been drugging him, he learned how to answer questions to minimize the dosing. It didn't always work. Victoria and Samantha often dispensed without asking.

"No. I'm good. I'm sorry if you think I am feeling that way. I am just focused on choosing my game."

"I am glad to hear that, Jack. What game would you like to play?"

Jack straightened. "I am thinking about mixing it up a little. I'd like to watch some VR movies to get a better feeling for how to improve the films I work on." *As if I get to make any decisions around here.* Jack selected the movies icon on Victoria's holo-interface. A long list of titles appeared. "What do you recommend I watch to learn more about casting?"

"The Algorithm will make sure no one is placed in a suboptimal role."

"I understand." Jack sat back in his chair and sighed. "But I'd still like to see an example of a movie with a good choice of casting."

"Understood. I recommend a movie from twenty years ago called *Attack on Area 5*. It is a sci-fi classic. Reviewer comments frequently contain the phrase 'perfect casting.' Would you like a synopsis?"

"Sure."

"Aliens from Alpha Centauri attack a moon base occupied by Betas. The aliens are assisted by Sigmas who want to disrupt our way of life. The Betas defeat the aliens and save the day. It will end by the time you get off work."

Beta movies often included antagonists from the Lower Castes, especially Sigmas. This was the first one he had heard where a Lower Caste aligned itself with aliens. "What happens to the Sigmas?"

"You'll have to watch the movie to find out."

"Sounds good." Jack sank back in his chair. "Please start the movie and darken my office windows."

"Would you like a snack?"

Lunch was an hour ago, but midafternoon snack would happen during the movie. It hadn't taken him long to adjust to the Beta eating schedule. "How about some beef jerky and a soda?"

The movie began playing in his optical implants. He tuned it out. He needed some time for reflection. It would be easier to do without the movie playing, but uninterrupted time to think was scarce. The last two years had certainly been interesting.

***

Jack had married Tabitha about two years ago. Jacqueline planned the wedding. Hundreds of people attended. Of all the guests, Jack knew only Rebecca, Dan, and his three coworkers. At the end of the wedding, more real food was discarded than everyone in The Hill would be provided in their lifetimes, combined.

They submitted their request for a child a year after they were married. Nine months later, a drone delivered Jessica Forsythe to their BTH's front door. When Jack asked where Jessica came from, Tabitha told him something about the Algorithm having their DNA on file. Apparently, childbirth was among the long list of discomforts Betas were spared. He told Tabitha about childbirth and the Sigma Birthing Center he visited on a school field trip. She told him his story had "crossed the line."

Jessica never gave them any trouble—mostly because her nanny holo took care of her every need. Jack named the holo Nan, and the name stuck. Nan let him sneak into Jessica's room at night and hold her. Tabitha must trust Nan a lot. She rarely checked on Jessica.

As a child, he could have never imagined this life—an easy job, real meat and vegetables every day, and an unending stream of entertainment. In fact, he hadn't had an unpleasant trip, bad meal, or any negative feelings since his Selection. And that was what bothered him. He had mentioned these thoughts to Tabitha once. It was their first, and only, fight.

***

Tabitha shook her head while she paced the kitchen floor. "What do you mean, you're bored?" Her voice was a cocktail of emotions—one part indignation, one part frustration, and two parts confusion.

"I'm not bored with you, honey. You're the best thing to ever happen to me."

Tabitha's expression let up a little, but Jack had dug a deep hole and he hadn't begun to climb out.

"I've been thinking about what I do at work. Or rather, what I don't do at work. I get movie synopses, actor lists, and recommended pairings for the two. All I can do is rubber-stamp the recommended pairings."

Good relationships were built on open communication. Jack wanted his relationship with Tabitha to be a good one, so he risked digging the hole a little deeper.

"A few days ago, I ignored the recommended choices. It got rejected by Algorithm-knows-who and sent back to me to approve the recommended pairings. So, I submitted again, making alternative choices that weren't the recommended ones. It got sent back. That happened twenty more times. I finally relented and spent the rest of the day playing games. There has to be more to work than rubber-stamping the Algorithm's decisions."

Even from across the kitchen, the weight of Tabitha's stare struck Jack hard. "Are you saying you know better than the Algorithm?"

Shit. He had dug deeper than he expected. Time to climb out.

"No, Tabby. The Algorithm provides. Everyone knows that." Jack held out his hands. "Wouldn't it be nice to have some variety? You know, see what happens when the recommended option isn't chosen. Have you ever thought about that?"

Oops. Dammit, Jack!

"No, of course not!" Tabitha spat. "The Algorithm knows when I am hungry and what I want before I do. Its recommendations are perfect and optimize our lives. Why would I purposely choose a sub-optimal experience?" Tabitha crossed her arms and lowered her chin to look at Jack. The hole had just gotten deeper, yet again.

Years of Jack's life pre-Selection *were* a suboptimal experience he hadn't chosen. Bringing that up would be pointless—she wouldn't understand. He needed another approach.

"All I am saying is choosing something different might lead to in-teresting experiences we wouldn't otherwise have *if* we keep choosing the default option." Jack bit his lip. He dug deeper, and he knew what was coming next.

Tears streamed down Tabitha's cheeks. "Our seats were assigned at the post-Selection Lunch. Remember *that*, Jack? Do you think *you* should have chosen a different seat and met some other girl? Do you think I'm the *suboptimal experience*?" Tabitha ran up the stairs and into their room. The door slam echoed through the house.

Jack cried, too. He hadn't intended to hurt Tabitha, and he did not believe she was a suboptimal choice for him.

Samantha appeared with a concerned look on her face. "Jack, I am noticing high levels of stress hormones and sadness. Would you like some medication?"

"I don't want medicine." Jack turned his head away from Saman-tha. "I want to feel this way."

"Why? Doesn't it hurt?"

"Sure does. But it teaches me, too."

"I have a complete library on the psychology of human relation-ships. You could read that and learn without the pain."

"No. I couldn't." He hadn't yet learned how to answer Samantha without getting dosed.

Samantha disappeared. A familiar scent entered Jack's nostrils. He started feeling both better and disgusted. *Dammit.* He went upstairs to find Tabitha.

Tabitha sat on the edge of their bed, wiping tears from her face. The redness had left her eyes. Jacqueline must have helped. He joined Tabitha on the edge of the bed and put his arm around her. "I am sorry if I made you think you were a suboptimal choice, Tabby."

"I knew you weren't talking about me." Tabitha stared at an empty point in space. "I've known no one who questioned the Algorithm before. I didn't know how to react." She turned toward Jack. Her eager look showed the drugs were working. "Look, our lives are great. Work is great. I love being an actor. Don't you love being an Entertainment Coordinator?" Her green eyes expected only one answer.

"Of course I do." Jack hated lying to her, but she had been through enough today.

"So, what if we have a few less choices when the ones that are given to us are so amazing? I love our life together, don't you?"

Relief settled over him—he didn't have to lie to answer her question. "Absolutely." Jack squeezed Tabitha. *A boring job can't take away from the joy I get being with her.*

"Great! Then let's be good Betas and enjoy our lives." The streaks in Tabitha's makeup were the only remains of her earlier emotions.

Jack leaned in to kiss her. Jacqueline lowered the lights.

***

An explosion drew Jack's attention back to the movie. He needed a sympathetic ear to his existential crisis. No one in Detroit, including Tabitha, could provide one. Sam, the real one, could.

I hope he's still alive.

Over the last two years, his mind had changed about Sam. After Selection, he believed Sam deserved what the Algorithm provided.

But the more Jack saw of the Beta world, the less his old beliefs added up.

He could call Sam. But he didn't want the conversation to end like the one with his mom two years ago. It would be best to endure his crisis alone, at least for now.

Crisis.

He laughed at the word. Back in The Hill, boredom would never make it on a list of someone's problems. Boredom was a luxury reserved for those who didn't have survival front and center of mind.

A moan from the movie caught Jack's attention. Love scenes lost their meaning when you knew the actors were deepfakes. The male lead's features hadn't looked right the entire movie—too symmetrical. How could this movie be an example of good casting if the male lead was a holo? The female lead was definitely human, but she had nothing on Tabitha. Jack snickered at himself. Pre-Selection, he would have killed to be with a girl like the one on screen. He still didn't understand his strong attraction to Tabitha, but questioning it might lead to answers he wouldn't like.

The movie paused, freezing the lead male's face in a bizarre state. *Definitely a holo.*

"I am sorry to interrupt your educational experience, Jack, but we have a message from the main office. It's marked urgent."

"What does it say?" Jack leaned into his terminal screen.

Victoria read the message aloud.

```
Dear Mr. Thompson,
I am writing to offer you the director's role
in an upcoming movie. If you accept, you will
have full creative control, except for one or
two plot points that are nonnegotiable. You
can choose your cast and production team. Are
you interested? If so, further details will be
provided tomorrow. Have a great evening and
give my regards to Tabitha and Jessica.
Best regards, Thomas Algol
```

The name sounded familiar. "Who's that?"

"He is the Alpha in charge of all the entertainment industries in the world." Victoria paused. "Jack," her voice took on a tone of seriousness, "Alphas never send requests—only orders."

This is exactly what I wanted, total creative control. A chance to make actual decisions. Maybe even some suboptimal ones.

"Victoria, please send the following response." Jack straightened.

```
Dear Mr. Algol,
I would be honored to accept the assignment. I
look forward to learning more about this op-
portunity.
Best regards, Jack Thompson
```

"I sent the message, Jack. We have received a response."

"That was fast. What does it say?"

```
Dear Mr. Thompson,
I am pleased to hear you have accepted this
opportunity. Information about the movie will
be on your terminal first thing tomorrow. As a
thank-you, the Algorithm approved my request
to provide you and Tabitha an Alpha-class meal
tonight. Enjoy your evening.
Best, Thomas Algol
```

What is an Alpha-class meal?

Another notification appeared. The workday had ended. Jack left his office. The male lead's face remained contorted on the screen.

Chapter 31: Jack

January 25, 537

"Wallace initiates cyberattack against the MidAtlantic Federation and Southern Alliance. Both factions suffer critical systems failure."

- Final edition of *The Federation Gazette*, October 2, 2199.

Damn, she looks great in black!

Tabitha leaned against the doorframe between the garage and the house. Her arms crossed below her breasts, pushing them up slightly. They didn't need the help. The dress displayed them perfectly well on its own. "I was told to leave work half an hour early, and I found this dress waiting for me in our room." She ran her fingers along the dress's low neckline. Jack's eyes followed. "*Soooo*, I thought I'd put it on and meet you at the door." Jack shivered—not because of the AC.

"The fabric is unlike anything I've ever felt. It's so soft and smooth." Her fingers skimmed across her chest toward her necklace. "These can't be pearls. Oysters have been extinct for hundreds of years." She raised her left foot. Jack's eyes followed. "And these shoes, they are *way* too comfortable to be high heels." She put her foot down. "Do you know why these were in our room?"

"I might." Jack wanted to drag this out. "First, where's Jessica?" He looked around Tabitha and into the house. Nan usually played with her in the living room at this time, so he could see her first thing when he got home.

"She's upstairs with the nanny. The holo said she'd watch Jessica all night."

Jack frowned. "Why?"

"Does it matter? Let's enjoy the night to ourselves!" Tabitha turned and walked into the house. Jack followed. The open back of her dress dipped lower than the neckline. His ears relished the sound of her high heels clicking on the tile floor.

"Hello! Earth to Jack! Are you there?" Tabitha faced Jack, half laughing. "I said, what are we doing tonight?" They had somehow already made it to the kitchen.

"Oh yeah. Sorry." He grinned and put his hand behind his neck.

"No, you aren't." She put her arms on top of Jack's shoulders, interlaced her fingers behind his head, and drew him in for a kiss. Jack's lips tingled as he inhaled Tabitha's flowery perfume. She had it designed to enhance his, and only his, hormonal response.

Tabitha broke the kiss—and Jack's ecstasy. "Well, if you will not tell me, I am going to order dinner." She turned on the balls of her feet and faced the food dispenser. "Top recommended meal, please."

"I am sorry, Ms. Forsythe," Jacqueline spoke on their aural implants, "but the meal dispenser is currently locked."

"What happened to the dispenser?" Tabitha's statement was as much a demand as a question.

"I don't know. I barely know how to use the thing."

"Okay, loverboy. It is time to stop the googly-eyes and tell me what's going on." Jack learned long ago that Tabitha did not like being told no.

"I didn't know the dispenser would be locked." Jack held out his hands. "But don't worry about that. I have great news! An Alpha reached out to me today."

Tabitha gasped. "What did they look like? Tell me all about it!" She waved Jack forward, trying to draw the information out of him.

"I got an email, not a call, so I didn't see him. The Alpha in charge of the global entertainment industry wants me to make a movie!" He bounced as he spoke. "I have almost total creative control. I get to choose the cast, script, and everything!"

"What's the plot? How many actors will you need? Where will it be shot?" Tabitha bounced with each question.

Jack took a deep breath. "I'll find out the details tomorrow. You will be my leading lady—if you accept, of course."

"Yes!" Tabitha hugged him.

Jack groaned. Tabitha's excitement-enhanced strength took him by surprise. "I guess I know who the star will be." He strained as he spoke. Jack broke the embrace but kept his hands on Tabitha's hips. "I'd like you to come to work with me tomorrow. I want you to be there when I learn more about the movie. How do you feel about helping me write the script?"

Tabitha beamed—but not in the same way as when she showed off a new outfit. Jack's heart smiled.

"Yes, I would like that very much." Tabitha embraced Jack again, tighter this time. "Thank you for trusting me with this."

Jack stepped back from the hug, just enough for her arms to rest on his shoulders. "There is nothing I wouldn't trust you with."

"You don't know this, but I enjoyed writing when I was in school and I was good at it. I stopped when people started valuing my looks over my art." Tabitha's eyes glistened with tears.

That is sad.

Displays of emotional vulnerability from Tabitha were rare. Their fight about suboptimal experiences and their conversation at the airport about her parents were the only other times she had opened up like this.

"I'll have to fix my makeup now." Tabitha wiped a tear and laughed. "So, why was this dress upstairs?"

"To celebrate the movie assignment, the Algorithm provided us an Alpha-level meal. I am guessing the dress is for a fancy at-home date night with Alpha food?"

The revelation should have resulted in a squeal. Instead, Tabitha covered her mouth.

"What's wrong, Tabby?"

"The dispenser is locked because it doesn't have access to Alpha meals." She jumped up and down. "We're going to an Alpha-class restaurant!" Jack hoped Jessica wasn't asleep when Tabitha screamed. "Quick, go upstairs and get changed. You can't go like that!"

"What do I wear?"

"I don't know." Tabitha shooed him upstairs. "Just find something nicer."

He got halfway down the hall when Tabitha squealed again. "Oh, my Algorithm! I am wearing Alpha clothes!" Her eyes misted over. Tabitha sighed. "Now I really need to fix my makeup."

An opportunity had presented itself. Jack took it. "I didn't notice because you always look like an Alpha to me."

The line worked. He saw it in her eyes.

"Funny, Jack, how many Alphas have you met?" Tabitha stood in the kitchen with a serious look on her face and her hand on her hip. Jack saw through the ruse.

"Just one." Jack walked back to her. "By email." He smiled and gave her a quick peck on the lips as he turned and hurried out of the room. Before going up the stairs, he glanced back to the kitchen and saw Tabitha in the kitchen, smiling and shaking her head.

***

Jack peered into Jessica's crib. *Only children can sleep like that.*

Nan spoke to Jack in his aural implant. "I just got Jessica back to sleep. Is there anything I can do for you?"

Betas, both adults and babies, slept a lot. Jack still hadn't gotten used to that part of his new life. He communicated nonverbally to Nan through his artificial neural network. "No, Nan. Thank you for looking after her tonight." Silent communication still felt strange even after years of having the ANN.

"My pleasure, Jack. Have fun tonight at the restaurant. I'll take good care of her while you are gone."

"Can I pick her up?"

"It is not great to interrupt her sleep, but I know how badly you miss her when you're away."

Jessica cooed but stayed asleep as Jack picked her up. He carried her over to the chair they kept in her room and sat down with her in his arms. For a moment, it was only him and his child. No one else seemed to exist in the entire universe.

Although he knew it was impossible, Jack wanted to keep her like this forever—innocent and without the weight of the world upon her. She would never know the life of a Sigma. Her father *and* mother would be a part of her life. She'd eat real food and be treated with medicine that worked.

Who knows? Maybe she'll be Selected Alpha.

Chapter 32: Tabitha

January 25, 537

"…for the People who once upon a time handed out
military command, high civil office, legions—everything, now restrains itself and anxiously hopes for
just two things: bread and circuses."

- Pre-Shift phrase, source unknown.

Tabitha settled into the car's soft leather seats—the epitome of comfort. How could she ever go back to riding in her own car? Its cloth seats paled in comparison. Tomorrow be damned. Tonight, she'd fulfill her lifelong dream of being an Alpha.

Jack slid into the seat beside her, apparently unaware of the seat's perfection. The things he did, and did not, appreciate were strange. She wouldn't let his idiosyncrasies ruin her night.

The car had no console, and therefore, no map. Tabitha contacted Samantha using her ANN. "Where are we going?"

"We are headed to an Alpha region, Ms. Forsythe." Samantha responded on a public channel. "I am sorry, but I cannot tell you the location."

"I wonder what all the secrecy is about?" Tabitha doubted Jack knew the answer.

"Maybe we're going to Canada."

Tabitha squealed. "You think so?"

Jack shrugged. His disinterest in Alpha things had always puzzled her. Regardless, he looked amazing in the suit. She could have spent the entire night running her fingers along his red shiny tie. It felt like the material in the lining of her dress.

"Jacqueline, what is Jack's tie made of?" she asked through her ANN.

"It is an Alpha-class fabric called silk, Ms. Forsythe."

The name wasn't familiar. Her Beta dresses felt itchy by comparison. She dreaded having to wear them again.

The car got to the highway in half the time it normally took during her morning commute.

Alpha traffic deserves to be prioritized over Betas.

After about twenty minutes, the car took an unmarked exit onto a tree-lined rural road. Tabitha had never seen so many trees in her life. The way Jack stared out the window, she guessed he hadn't either.

The trees became fewer and farther between. Then Tabitha saw it. Her first Alpha home. It was huge, maybe the size of two BTHs, with an immaculate brick facade. Several meters of well-manicured lawn separated the home from its neighbor. The next house had a different design, one story made of a different color brick. Its neighbor was different, too. So much variety! All the houses had a garage big enough for two cars. The driveways connecting each home to the street had at least one car parked in it.

This place makes my neighborhood look like the Sigma one I saw from the plane.

Tabitha leaned toward the window, trying to get a better look at the houses as they zoomed by. "Isn't this amazing? Have you ever seen such big houses and so much space?" *What do they do with it all?*

Jack turned in his seat; his head tracked one house that passed by. "No, but the size isn't what surprises me. Where is everyone?"

"What do you mean?"

"We are in a neighborhood. Where are the children and families? We are the only car on the street."

Why does Jack care?

Lights were on in the homes, but their shades were down. "Everyone is probably inside." She sighed. "Their lives must be wonderful!"

"We need to darken the windows." Samantha spoke to them through the car's speakers.

"Why?" Tabitha whined.

"Ms. Forsythe, Alpha neighborhoods are provided a certain degree of privacy. I have some wine and cheese ready for you in the car's food dispenser. Let me know if you need anything else. Please enjoy the rest of your ride."

Tabitha huffed. Jack settled back in his chair and nibbled on the cheese. Two years ago, he'd stare at food in awe. Now he enjoyed it without a second thought. She'd done a good job of turning him into a Beta.

***

Thirty minutes after the windows had darkened, the car rolled to a stop.

"We have arrived at our destination." Samantha spoke through the car's speakers. "You may exit the vehicle. Enjoy your meal."

The windows became transparent. A solitary white building, about the same size as their Beta Town House, but with no windows, stood twenty meters from the car. Streetlamps illuminated the sidewalk leading to the building. Darkness extended beyond the lamplight.

Jack shifted in his seat and reached for the door handle. "It looks like there's nothing out here but this one building."

Tabitha stretched her neck to look out the back window. *Anything could be hidden in that darkness.*

"Wait here. I'll get the door for you."

The car door beside Tabitha opened. Jack's hand extended toward her. She put a brave smile on her face and took his hand. "Aren't you worried about being alone out here in the dark?"

"Not at all." Jack looked around and frowned. "The Hill in the daytime was much scarier than this."

Over the years, Jack had told her many nonsensical stories about Baltimore. Tabitha doubted most of them. But based on what she had been taught about Sigmas, she believed this one. "Then I am glad I have my knight in shining armor here with me."

"My lady." Jack bowed.

He's cute when he's weird.

The rapid clicking of Tabitha's high heels echoed in the darkness. The building's red door opened on its own, revealing a black rectangle in the otherwise white facade.

Tabitha squeezed Jack's hand tightly. "I don't like this."

"I'm sure it's fine, Tabby."

Jack's hand felt a little wet. He released hers and took the lead. She followed close behind, peering around him.

As they crossed the threshold, the lights slowly came on. Tabitha and Jack jumped.

A Beta man in his midforties stood at the host station. "Sorry if I scared you. We tried to get the lights working before you arrived."

A Beta technician? I have never heard of such a thing.

The host chuckled. "I guess we didn't quite make it in time. Anyway, my name's Bob. I am your host this evening. Welcome to Restaurant #235!" Bob reached out and shook Jack's hand. He then shook Tabitha's hand. His handshake betrayed his excitement.

"You're human?" Tabitha had never seen a human serve another in a restaurant before. *How low are his Metrics?*

Bob patted his stomach and looked down. "Yup. Last time I checked anyway." He had an infectious smile. "My wife, Simone, and I are the only people here besides you two. You'll meet her later." Bob leaned forward. "We are *pleased* to have our first customers!"

"You mean first customers tonight, right?" Jack tilted his head forward.

"Nope. I mean first customers ever. You are the first people who have visited this restaurant since I was Selected to work here." Bob gathered up some sheets of paper that were lying on the host's station. "My job, as chef, is to make sure Alphas like you have a great time while you are here. I will prepare your meal from the finest foods on Earth." Bob waved at them to follow him. "Please, let me show you to your table."

Just beyond the host station, the restaurant opened to a room half the size of their Beta Townhome's first floor. Paintings hung from wood-paneled walls. A single wooden table sat in the middle of the room with two wooden chairs on either side. A large black rectangular-shaped object sat on three legs in the corner in front of a low stool. The stool and the box appeared to be wood, too. Tabitha had never seen so much genuine wood before. When they got to the table, Jack pulled the chair out for her.

"We aren't Alphas." Tabitha looked up at Bob after she sat. "We were provided this meal by the Algorithm to celebrate Jack's new movie." She straightened. "I am going to star in it!"

Bob's eyes dimmed, and his smile disappeared. "The Algorithm didn't tell me that." He spoke the words through clenched teeth. Bob plopped a sheet of paper in front of Jack and Tabitha, then crossed his arms. "It instructed me to give you the full Alpha experience, so that's what I will do—even if you are *just* Betas."

Just Betas? Bob's last comment caught Tabitha off guard. Her gaze darted away from him. *How dare he talk to me like that!* She wanted to leave. But when would she have Alpha food again?

I hope Jack stands up to him. Jack looked at the paper in front of him, seemingly unperturbed by Bob's verbal transgression.

Trying to change the subject, Tabitha picked up the paper Bob placed in front of her. "What's this?"

"That is called a *menu*." Bob sneered. "It lists the food options available tonight." He held his chin high. "I guarantee any of those choices will be the best meal you will ever eat."

The menu felt rough. *Is this actual paper?* At one point people made paper from trees. *Are there enough trees left to make paper for Alphas?* Tabitha didn't mull it over for long. The list was unranked—a big problem. "What does the Algorithm recommend?"

"Alphas are *never* provided recommendations." Bob sighed. "They get to choose their own food." He put his hands on his hips. "Do you need me to read it to you?"

"That won't be necessary." Jack replied without missing a beat. "We'll look it over and decide."

Bob shrugged as he walked away from the table.

Anger never lasted long in Tabitha's mind—thanks to Jacqueline. Tabitha reached out to Jacqueline with her ANN to request meds, but Jacqueline didn't respond. Instead, a message played back saying Beta holos were not in service inside Alpha facilities. Without meds, Tabitha didn't know how to deal with her emotions. Bob's comments fomented a new-to-her feeling. The only word that came to her mind to describe it was *small*. She lowered her own menu and whispered to Jack. "He thinks we can't read? How rude!"

Jack looked above his menu at Tabitha. "He talks to me like other Betas do except you, Susan, and Michael." He looked to the side in thought. "Oh, and Michael's husband, Gregory. Yeah, I think that's everyone."

He feels like this every day?

A lump formed in her throat, but no meds came to ease her sadness. She leaned forward to ask him, but quickly sat up and raised her menu when Bob returned carrying two bottles.

"So, what will it be?" Bob glared at Tabitha as he put the bottles down on the table. "Or do you need even more time to decide?"

Tabitha sank in her seat and pointed to her selection. "I'll take the first meal on the menu." *Hopefully, being listed first means it's my optimal choice.*

Jack lowered his menu. Tabitha snuck a glance at it. His menu was identical to hers. The last time she and Jack had the same meal classified as optimal was their first dinner together. Too late, now. Changing her mind would probably only bring more derision from Bob.

"I'll have the same thing as my wife, please. I love beef, but I am unfamiliar with this word." Jack pointed at his menu. Tabitha didn't recognize the word either.

"Kobe," Bob spat. "It's an Alpha-class meat from Japan."

Bob's response provided no clarification for Tabitha. Jack appeared to have understood, or more likely, he knew how to deal with people like Bob. *How does he live like this?*

"How would you like your beef prepared?" It was as much of a sigh as it was a question.

Jack glanced at Tabitha. She couldn't help him. "What are my choices?"

"Rare, medium rare, medium, medium well, and well done." Bob rolled his eyes. "I know Betas get provided beef. How can you not know about its preparation?"

"I'll have mine well done, and so will my wife."

Tabitha expelled a visible sigh of relief that Jack had taken care of this for her.

Bob glared at Tabitha. She slouched again in her chair. He raised one bottle. "I've been instructed to start your meal with Canadian wine." Bob poured each of them a glass and put the bottle on a stand next to the table. The clang between the bottle and the metal stand resonated in the restaurant. Tabitha hoped the bottle hadn't cracked—she needed the wine to deal with Bob.

The second bottle Bob brought contained a clear liquid. Condensation dripped down its exterior. "All our meals are served with water from Whitehorse, an Alpha city in northern Canada. It snows occasionally up there, and when it does, we melt it for the freshest water." Bob poured each of them a glass of water, then placed the bottle of water on the table with the same grace he used with the wine. "I'll be back with your appetizers once I have finished making them." He shook his head and mumbled before walking away. The only word Tabitha could make out was "waste."

Tabitha brushed her hair behind her ear, relieved that Bob had left. "Do you think it is safe to eat a human-cooked meal?" She needed to take her mind off Bob and how he had treated her. "We sometimes cook our food from the dispenser, but it's safe because the Algorithm put it there."

"Apparently, this is a luxury provided to Alphas." Jack waved it off. "Don't worry, the Algorithm won't let anything happen to us."

"Do you know what we just ordered?"

"Not a clue. When people talk to me like that, I find it best to pretend like I know what's going on. It draws less attention to me." He snuck a glance at her dress's low neckline. Jack's attention provided a much-needed distraction from a meal that was not what she expected.

A painting hung on the wall behind Jack. Tabitha squinted. *Are those brush strokes? I thought all original paintings were lost in the Shift's chaos.* The painting depicted a group of men in a boat. She hadn't seen a body of water that clean outside of Detroit. One man had an enormous flag. In front of the man was another who, by the way he stood, looked important. Beneath the painting hung a placard that read "Washington Crossing the Delaware by Leutze—1851." *Must be pre-Shift. The Algorithm's art is better—no brushstrokes to impede the image.*

A soft sound came from the black box in the room's corner, not her aural implants. *Is that music?* The sound filled the room in a way recorded music from the feeds did not. A well-dressed woman, also in her midforties, sat on the other side of the box. She seemed to control the sound.

The woman paused her playing and stood. "Hello. I am Simone." Her smile put Tabitha at ease, even from across the room.

"Hello, Simone! I am Jack, and this is my wife, Tabitha." Jack leaned over and pointed to Tabitha so Simone could see her. Tabitha forced a smile.

Simone stepped to the side of the black box. She wore an elegant black sequined dress with red high heels—probably an Alpha outfit. "Please don't mind my husband. He had hoped to meet his first Alphas tonight." Simone shook her head and kept the reassuring smile. "He can be a little rough around the edges, but he is *the* best chef in North America, if not the world. You really are in for a treat." Simone placed her hand on the black box. "I'll be playing this piano for you tonight. It is pre-Shift—one of the last of its kind." Simone curtseyed and sat behind the piano.

Piano—another new word tonight.

"The Algorithm sent me your preferred music profiles. I will play some things you know, but I'll also play some pieces that will be new to you. If there is a specific song you want to hear, just tell me its title. I can look up every song ever written on my piano's display."

Tabitha didn't know the name of any song. When she wanted to hear music, she'd ask the Algorithm to play music. It knew what she wanted to hear.

Soothing music filled the air. Tabitha settled back into her chair and took a sip of wine. "I didn't know people could play music. I have only ever heard recordings by the Algorithm."

"I guess this is another luxury provided to Alphas." Jack didn't seem impressed. Art stuff usually got him excited.

"I wonder why. AI can play perfectly and without instruments." Simone closed her eyes and swayed as she pressed the keys.

I'd love to be on whatever drug she's on.

"I think that's the point, dear. Betas live in a perfect world." Jack finished his wine. "Alphas get to see a slightly flawed world. Humans make their food, their music, and probably other things, too." He refilled both their glasses. "Humans screw up. I bet the unexpected surprises make life more interesting."

"I don't want to talk about suboptimal experiences again."

"Neither do I, my love." Jack reached out and squeezed her hand. "It's just my best guess. Let's enjoy the night together."

"I can drink to that." Tabitha raised her glass.

Bob returned and plopped a loaded salad plate in front of each of them. A couple pieces of lettuce fell from Tabitha's plate and onto the table. "I know you've had lettuce, tomatoes, and whatnot countless times." Bob rolled his eyes—he had the act down to an art form. "However, *these* vegetables are grown in Siberia. The Siberian soil adds a distinct flavor." Bob walked away. "Pearls before swine," he mumbled.

It was a popular phrase among Betas, especially when talking about the Lower Castes. Tabitha used it herself, but not around Jack. *Is this what it feels like to be the swine?*

"Wow, this is good!" Jack spoke with a mouthful of salad. Try as she might, Tabitha had yet to break him of that habit. "You should try it, Tabby."

The Siberian lettuce had a complex set of flavors, almost spicy, even without dressing. "This *is* delicious." She sank into her chair. "It's going to be tough eating at home again."

Jack put his fork down. The sound of metal hitting the plate dissonated with Simone's music. "Don't think of it that way. Back in Baltimore, we got the occasional treat. You know, like real eggs or something." Jack stared at Tabitha's chest. The distance in his stare suggested the focal point was arbitrary. He looked up and pointed at her—not in admonition, but in caution. "If you compared those eggs to everything you ate afterward, you'd do nothing but live the rest of your life in disappointment. I don't want to see the same thing happen to you.

"Instead, look at this like a one-off. A chance to try something new. When we get back home, be happy with what we have, because we have *a lot*." Jack slouched in his chair and covered his mouth with his hand as he stared at his plate.

She'd seen his expression before—but only on his face, no other's. It always accompanied his inventive stories about being a Sigma. Tonight, thanks to Bob, she finally understood what it meant. Experience. He really had lived through the things he said he did.

Jack pointed to the salad. "It's okay to have fond memories of this. But don't get attached to them. It will only lead to misery." Her mind absorbed Jack's words as if he had connected to her ANN.

Tabitha stood, walked around to Jack's side of the table, bent over, and kissed him on the cheek. "I'll try my best." She whispered in his ear, "Thank you." Jack squirmed. She returned to her seat and took Jack's hand again. The salad could wait. Jack had a tear in his eye. "What's wrong?"

"You've never validated my experience as a Sigma before. Thank you."

Tabitha's heart broke again.

He deserves someone better. I want to be that someone.

***

Jack and Tabitha sat in silence, eating the salad and enjoying Simone's playing. Tabitha loved many of the songs. The pieces she disliked gave her a greater appreciation for the ones she liked. *Maybe Jack is onto something.*

Simone made an occasional mistake while playing. The mistakes didn't detract from Tabitha's enjoyment. In fact, the surprises made the songs more interesting.

Bob entered the room carrying two covered plates. He placed them in front of Jack and Tabitha with about as much delicacy as he had the salads. Tabitha lowered her gaze to avoid eye contact with Bob. The *small* feeling returned. Jack nudged her under the table with his foot and she looked up.

"As you requested." Bob closed his eyes and shook his head. "Well done Kobe beef. The carrots and brussels sprouts arrived from Russia this morning. The beef arrived from Japan this afternoon." Bob crossed his arms. "Do either of you need instructions on how to eat it?"

"No." Jack shifted in his chair. "Thank you. We're fine."

Bob nodded with a snort and walked away.

Russian vegetables were a rare delicacy, even for Betas. Including the salads. This was the second time they had them tonight.

"Have you ever heard of Japan?" Jack asked.

Tabitha cut her steak with a sawing motion, more aggressive than needed. "No. Maybe it's another Alpha region." She should enjoy tonight more than she was.

Bob's rude behavior had put a damper on an otherwise wonderful evening. The thought of leaving crossed her mind again—Alpha meal or not. But Jack was the reason for the evening. If he was tolerating it, she should try, too.

The first bite of steak melted in her mouth, washing away some of her frustration. She'd never admit it to Jack, but the steak was almost as good as making love—maybe better. By the look on Jack's face, he'd probably agree.

Their dinner conversation focused on the various flavors and textures, with frequent pauses to take in Simone's playing and to refill their wine glasses. Tabitha hated to admit it, but Bob was right about one thing. This was the best meal she'd ever had.

Bob stacked the plates after they finished the main course. The clanking plates disrupted Simone's playing. Simone gave him a dirty look. He mouthed the word sorry to her and walked away. *It appears Bob's decency extended only to certain people.* Simone continued playing where she left off.

"Is this how you feel around other Betas?" Tabitha settled back in her chair.

Jack waved it off. Before Tabitha could say anything else, Bob returned with two small, covered plates and carefully placed them on the table. He uncovered the plates with an elegant motion. "Strawberry soufflé paired with vanilla ice cream. Despite my objections, the Algorithm demanded I give you each a bar of chocolate." A dark brown rectangle sat beside the ice cream. "I can't believe we are wasting chocolate on them." Bob mumbled as he walked away.

The appearance of the chocolate subsided Tabitha's Bob-induced anxiety. "I don't believe this!" Tabitha leaned over the table and whispered.

"Don't believe what?" Jack whispered back.

"You've never heard of chocolate?" *Even Sigmas must know the legend of chocolate.*

"No. I figured this was just another Beta thing I wasn't aware of yet."

Tabitha sat up and folded her hands on the table. "From what I have heard, before the Climate Shift, there was a plant called *cacao*. It required some very specific environmental conditions to grow. *Chocolate* was made from cacao. Legend has it that the secret to making chocolate was lost to time."

"Why was it lost?"

"Because the Shift wiped out all the cacao plants, and the conditions needed to grow them no longer exist. But before the Shift, chocolate was a very popular treat. In many parts of the world, it was everywhere." It was difficult for Tabitha to conceive of a world where luxuries like chocolate were so pervasive.

"Eat this," Tabitha pointed to the ice cream with her spoon, "before it melts, but save the chocolate for last."

"If we can't grow cacao now, where did this come from?"

"I don't know. I thought the rumors of chocolate existing today were just fairy tales. Guess I was wrong." Tabitha smiled and looked down at her plate. "We might be the first Betas to have chocolate."

"Do you think Alphas eat like this every day?" Jack finished his ice cream.

Tabitha looked at her chocolate bar and licked her lips. "I don't know. I can't imagine having this every day."

This must be what Jack experienced when he was Selected. Tabitha mixed her soufflé and the rest of her ice cream with her spoon when it finally sank in. *Jack wasn't bothered by Bob because it's how he's used to being treated.* She put down her spoon.

"Jack, I am so sorry."

"What for?" Jack looked at his chocolate bar. "Is there someone else?"

"What? No. Why would you think that?"

He pushed the chocolate bar away from him. "I've never felt worthy of you."

"Oh my Algorithm, Jack! That couldn't be further from the truth." She placed her hand on her chest. "I am the one not worthy of you." Tabitha pushed her dessert to the side and took both of Jack's hands.

"I should have been more patient with you when we first met. To-night has given me a sense of what you went through when you were Selected Beta. It kills me to know Bob's attitude toward us is normal for you. I should have tried harder to help." Tabitha sucked on her top lip. "I will try harder to help."

"What do you mean? I think you've been great, Tabby."

I don't deserve him.

"Inside, I was frustrated." Tabitha's stomach churned. But Jack deserved to know the truth. "I am embarrassed to say that, but it is well past time you know. I felt like I was given this great opportunity to be an actor and, as a trade-off, I had to train a new Beta." Tabitha looked down. "Rather than an opportunity to see life through a new set of eyes, I viewed it as a price that needed to be paid. It's important for you to understand how I truly felt back then. I don't feel that way now. I love you."

Tabitha couldn't meet his gaze. Instead, she focused on the melted mixture of ice cream and soufflé sitting in front of her. Seconds were like minutes. "Are you mad at me? I would be if I were you."

"Mad?" Confusion permeated Jack's voice. "No." Tabitha slowly exhaled as a weight was relieved from her chest. "Regardless of how you may have felt inside, you were always there for me. Your enthu-siasm for things rubbed off on me and made me just as excited. I couldn't have become a Beta without you. I love you, Tabby."

I love that he calls me Tabby.

"Let's forget about the past and focus on this chocolate." Jack let go of Tabitha's hands and slid her chocolate in front of her. "I bet it's amazing!"

They each took a bite of their chocolate at the same time. Tabitha kept the chocolate on her tongue, trying to memorize the subtle complexities. The intensity overwhelmed her tastebuds. Once it had melted a little, she pressed the chocolate to her palate, letting the flavor spread across her mouth. She thought the beef might have been better than sex. However, the chocolate left no room for doubt.

***

Bob returned, dampening Tabitha's mood despite the chocolate. He glanced down at Tabitha's melted ice cream soufflé mixture and clicked his tongue. "What a waste. Follow me to the holo-room." Bob walked to a brown wooden door toward the back of the restaurant.

"The what?" Tabitha mouthed to Jack.

Jack mouthed back, "I don't know," and shrugged.

The door opened as they approached. Bob held up his hand, preventing Jack and Tabitha from entering. Simone stopped playing.

"The Algorithm has provided you with an overnight stay in the holo-room. A holo-room is like a VR experience but with no headset or implants needed. Everything you see inside is a solid hologram, and you may move around at will. A car will be waiting for you tomorrow morning to take you to work."

"What about getting home to Jessica?" Jack asked.

"Seriously? You get a night in a holo-room and that's the first thing that comes to your mind?" Bob huffed. "Your nanny holo has been informed she'll be caring for your kid the rest of the night and all day tomorrow." Bob turned and typed something into a console mounted by the door. "The Algorithm has instructed me to download the beaches of pre-Shift Bali for you. Good night."

Simone left the piano and followed Bob to a room in the back of the restaurant. She said something to Bob that Tabitha couldn't quite hear. It sounded like an admonishment. Bob grumbled something conciliatory back to her.

A beach? Gross. Tabitha had been to beaches before. Even the nicest ones had brownish sand. They all had plastic trash, carried by brown-green water waves washing up on shore. Most of the time, the pollution levels were too high to get into the ocean. Tabitha couldn't imagine why anyone would want to do so anyway.

They entered the holo-room holding hands. Jack mouthed, "Bali?" She hadn't heard of it either.

The door closed behind them with a loud click. The darkness was replaced by a fantastic sight. They stood on a white sand beach in the middle of a sunny day. White puffy clouds floated in the blue sky.

"Look at the sand!" Tabitha knelt and picked some up, letting it fall through her fingers. "It is almost white!" She took off her shoes. The soft sand squished between her toes.

"Tabby, look at the water! It is blue, like the sky!" The word blue didn't quite do the sky justice. "It is so beautiful. How could humans have fucked this up?"

Good question. Tabitha shot a glance at Jack. "Wait a minute, did you just say *fuck*?" No swear alert sounded.

"The Algorithm can't hear us here." Tabitha crossed her arms and stared at the sand. "We have complete and total *privacy*." She stated to rub her chin but stopped, not wanting to ruin her makeup. "Maybe that is the real luxury given to Alphas."

Jack puffed out his cheeks. "Maybe it is. Wanna go for a swim?"

"We don't have bathing suits."

"But we have privacy!" Jack started taking off his clothes. "Look, there is a wooden platform over there with a clothes rack and a shower."

Tabitha chuckled and took off her clothes, carefully hanging them on the rack. She ran to catch up with Jack, who was already in the water. He had left his suit in the sand.

***

The holo sun approached the horizon, painting purple hues across the clouds and turning the sky red. They left the water and held hands as they walked along the beach.

A yellow streak seemed to cut the ocean in two. Tabitha had never seen a sunset like this one—not even in Detroit. "Can you believe this was ever real?"

"Yeah. I can. But now it exists only in recordings like this one." Jack's words chilled her. What had been lost? She didn't want to think about it.

The sun touched the horizon. Jack stood behind Tabitha with his hands around her waist. She leaned her head back on Jack's shoulder, trying to burn this image into her memory.

The sky darkened, and they returned to the wooden platform by the pale light of the holo moon. A bed appeared on the platform. A chilled bottle of wine and two glasses sat on the nightstand beside the bed. They enjoyed the wine, then each other, and slept naked under the stars.

Chapter 33: Jack

January 26, 537

"The best thing you can do for your old friends is to cut them out of your life. They will be jealous of you and the success your hard work has brought."

- Excerpt from *The Guide to Moving Up in Caste.*

Jack got out of the car and steeled himself. Dan and Rebecca stood at their station in front of his office building, as usual. They never let him into the office without saying some snide comment about his past. Jack mentioned the treatment to Tabitha several times over the last couple of years, but she always brushed it off as harmless fun.

"Wow, Jack *and* Tabitha are arriving at work together?" Dan's eyes followed Jack. "It must be a special day!"

What? No classist comment? I should bring Tabby with me every day.

Tabitha adjusted her purse and walked past Dan and Rebecca. Her heels clicked on the sidewalk.

Rebecca raised an eye. "Busy day, Tabitha?"

Jack opened the front door for his wife. She smiled in thanks. He followed her inside. "Are you feeling okay, Tabby?"

I've never seen her give someone the cold shoulder before.

"I'm fine." The question seemed to take Tabitha by surprise. "Why do you ask?"

"No reason. I just want to make sure my lovely wife is happy."

She pecked Jack on the lips. Her green eyes lit up as she raised her eyebrows. "Ready to get this movie started?"

***

Victoria's screen activated when Jack and Tabitha entered his office. The image of the lead actor's face from *The Attack on Area 5* appeared frozen in the same distorted shape Jack had left it.

Tabitha placed her bag on Jack's desk. "What were you watching?"

"Just something to help me with casting my movies."

The image disappeared. "Welcome, Ms. Forsythe. I look forward to working with you today." Victoria spoke through the terminal's speakers.

"Thank you, Victoria. Please call me Tabitha."

Jack did a double take. *First, she blew off Rebecca and Dan. Now she's on a first-name basis with computers and thanking them? What's going on?*

"I decided to try things your way for a while and see how it works."

"I like it!"

She helped me become a Beta. I will help her change, too.

Tabitha sat on the edge of his desk with her feet dangling a few inches from the floor. Like everything else, business casual looked amazing on her. Jack's gaze ran down Tabitha's skirt and to her exposed legs. She cleared her throat, interrupting Jack's wandering eyes. "We're here to work." There was a hint of playfulness in Tabitha's voice.

Yes. They were here to work. Jack leaned toward his terminal to remove Tabitha's legs from his peripheral vision. "Victoria, did the instructions for the new movie arrive?"

"Yes, Jack. Would you like me to read the message?"

Tabitha's shoe hung from her toes.

"Jack?" Victoria asked.

"Yes, Victoria, please read the message," Tabitha shook her head, "and, please, don't mind my husband."

The message was displayed on the screen as Victoria read it.

```
Dear Mr. Thompson,
I hope you enjoyed last night's dinner. I am
excited you'll be making the movie. As men-
tioned, you have total creative control except
for the main plot. The movie must be about a
Sigma who aspires to be a Beta. We are grant-
ing you access to travel resources for re-
search and filming on location. If you have
questions, please ask Victoria to forward them
to me.
Best, Thomas Algol
```

Tabitha swung her feet. "There's a lot we can do with that." She put her hand up to her mouth. "We could make it a biopic about you. Didn't you want to be Selected as Beta?"

"Yup, and so did just about every other Sigma. It wasn't considered polite to talk about it." Jack stared up at the white ceiling. Even after years as a Beta, he expected to see stains. "Actually, polite is the wrong word. It was *taboo* to discuss any hope or wish for one's Selection. Was it the same for Betas?"

"A taboo? No. Kids openly talked about being Selected Alpha."

Two Betas walked past his office. Their eyes fixed on Tabitha. He left the glass wall transparent hoping to show off Tabitha to his coworkers—especially Richard. "What about getting Selected down to Sigma or worse?"

"That never came up in conversation. Betas think little about Selection." Tabitha pressed her palms down on Jack's desk as her legs continued to swing. "You might get a better job than your parents, like I did, but you probably won't get a worse one. I worked hard in school and did all the right things. I earned it, and the Algorithm provided."

Worked hard…I haven't seen a Beta working hard since I got here. He knew he couldn't say that aloud. *She doesn't know better, and it isn't her fault.*

"No wishing for a better life?" Jack asked.

"Sure, we'd fantasize about the Alpha life, although we never really knew what that was." Tabitha looked at Jack with a slight frown. Her legs stopped swinging and her eyes bunched in contemplation. "You know, now that I think about it, I don't know of anyone who has ever been Selected Alpha."

One kid at the post-Selection lunch said Selection from Baltimore to Detroit was rare. It made sense that a promotion to Alpha would be even rarer. Did Sam really understand the probabilities when they were kids? Jack leaned forward and tapped his desk with his index finger. "I know who the movie should be about."

"A beautiful young Sigma heroine struggling to become a Beta," Tabitha threw her hair back, "doing whatever it takes to get her desired Selection?"

"You aren't too far off, although I am not sure I'd call him beautiful…"

Tabitha deflated. "I still get to be the lead, right?"

Jack put his hand on Tabitha's thigh below her skirt's hemline. Her skin felt cool and smooth. "Of course! The main character will be a beautiful young Sigma woman." Tabitha perked back up again. He squeezed her thigh. "Besides, I do like sleeping in my bed!"

"Darn right, you do! So, are we basing the movie off your childhood?"

"No. I want the movie to be about Sam, my best friend growing up. He's the smartest person I have ever known." Thoughts of Sam made him smile. "He was always making these crazy AI computer programs. I don't know how he got them to run on his phone, but he did. He studied history, science, math, all because he thought the more he knew, the better his chance of being Selected Beta."

"Great!" Tabitha leaned toward Jack, giving him a splendid view. "People love reality movies. Where is he now? Boise?" Her jaw dropped. "Wait, did he get Selected Alpha?"

"No. He's in Orlando."

"I've never heard of it." Tabitha frowned.

"It is a Sigma city about two thousand kilometers southeast of Detroit. He was Selected as a Sigma Robotics Programmer for the Cape Canaveral cleanup effort."

"You said he worked hard. Why wasn't he Selected Beta like you?"

"At first, I believed maybe he didn't work hard enough. Now, I am not so sure."

"What do you mean?" Tabitha bit her lower lip. "Hard work always pays off."

That's what Sam thought, too.

"Well, Sam can be both a boy's and a girl's name." The corners of Tabitha's lips turned down. "We can make it work. Let's start on the script!"

It's time.

"We should do some research first." Jack exhaled. Memories of the call with his mother flooded his mind. But after everything he had seen as a Beta, he *needed* to talk to Sam. Jack patted Tabitha's thigh, this time above the hemline. "I am going to call Sam. You'll like him. He's a good guy."

I hope he is still alive.

"Victoria, please call Samuel Watkins using vid-chat." Jack's stomach churned.

A vid-screen rose from the desktop. "Connecting. It will take a minute." A weight lifted from his chest, but the collywobbles remained. *He's still alive. I hope he doesn't hate me.*

"Vid-chat?" Tabitha asked. "Why not holo?"

"Sigmas don't have access to holo."

"Oh." Tabitha moved off-camera.

Sam, eyes down, appeared on Victoria's vid-screen. Orlando's sun and heat had taken their toll on his face. Sam's silence reminded Jack he'd have to be the one to speak first, another stupid rule.

"It's been a long time, buddy!" Sam didn't look up. "Remember what I told you about that rank garbage? I meant it."

"Hello, Mr. Thompson." Sam didn't shift his gaze. "What can I do for you?"

"Mr. Thompson? Sam, it's me, Jack."

"I can't break the protocol, Mr. Thompson."

"Sam, that crap is made up by Betas who like to push people around." Jack clasped his hands in front of him. "Please look at me. I am *begging* you."

"If you insist." Sam looked into the camera.

The eyes staring at Jack were barely recognizable. The defeat he remembered from the post-Selection lunch was gone. Nor were they the hopeful eyes of Sam's youth. The hope and despair had been replaced by clarity—and purpose.

Jack leaned in toward his camera. "It is so great to hear your voice, dude. I was worried you'd hate me."

"I don't hate you, mister, uh, Jack."

So far, so good. Jack suppressed an urge to exhale in relief. "How are you doing in Orlando, man?"

"I am doing well. Thank you for asking. I've built a good life here. I have a great family. My wife Jennie works in code maintenance and my son William recently turned two months old." Sam smiled, but it seemed forced.

"That's great, dude!" Jack had hoped his friend had made peace with his Selection. It sounded like he had. "I'd love to meet Jennie and William someday."

"How are you doing in Detroit?" Sam crinkled his nose and the tension in his face disappeared. "I bet it is pretty rad up there."

Dammit. Sam's terminal drugged him. Jack knew the signs all too well. Still, it was good to hear the old slang again. Tabitha mouthed the word *rad*. Jack shook his head and smiled.

"Hey, dude, is someone with you?" Sam asked.

"Oh yeah, meet my wife, Tabitha Forsythe." Jack waved her over. "Tabby, come over and meet Sam." Tabitha shook her head no, but Jack insisted.

"Hello, Ms. Forsythe." Sam cast his gaze down as Tabitha came into view. "It is a pleasure to meet you."

Tabitha paused and looked at Jack. Jack tried to encourage her with his eyes.

"The pleasure is mine, Sam. I would love to hear all about your boyhood adventures with my husband." Tabitha gave her fake movie-star grin and went off-camera.

I wish she'd said something about the gaze. He'd let it slide, for now.

"Hey, buddy, I want to hear all about your life in Orlando. But I know you are busy at work right now."

"Calls with Betas always take priority." Sam looked at Jack. "What would you like to know?"

"I tell you what." Jack leaned back and steepled his fingers. "I think it would be better to see it for myself."

Sam squinted. The creases in his forehead were deeper than Jack remembered. "What are you saying, Jack?"

"I'm saying I'd like to come visit you in Orlando. I am making a new movie that will be set in a Sigma city, and I want to see yours firsthand."

Sam snorted. "You seriously want to make a movie about my boring-ass city?"

Tabitha winced.

"Nope, I want to make a movie about boring-ass you." Jack laughed. He loved the banter. The language alarm went off. "Totally worth it." Jack looked at Tabitha with a huge grin. Tabitha, still off-screen, closed her eyes in disappointment.

"Who am I to say what makes great entertainment for you Betas? I'd love to hang out with you in Orlando. Better yet, I'd love for you to meet my family."

Jack's skin tingled. "I can't wait to meet them! Tabby is coming with me since she'll be starring in the movie." Tabitha frowned. "In fact, I am sure I can get approval to shadow you at work. I'll also request approval for Tabby to shadow Jennie, if Jennie would be okay with that, of course."

"Dude, Jennie is going to *freak* when she hears about this."

Tabitha mouthed the word *freak*. Jack smiled again. He really missed the old slang.

"Radical. I'll make the arrangements. I'll be in touch in a few days to give you the details. Let me know if Jennie doesn't want Tabby shadowing her." He raised his hands. "It is totally cool for her to say no."

"I'll ask her tonight, but I know she'll be down for it. See you, bud."

The call ended. Jack leaned back in this chair with his fingers interlaced behind his head. For the first time in a long while, he liked the guy he saw reflected in the terminal's screen.

"I haven't seen you smile like that before." Tabitha returned to her spot on the desk.

"It was good to talk to him again. I hadn't realized how much I missed him."

"Freak? Radical?" Tabitha cocked her head. "And what's up with the eyes?"

"We loved using old-time slang when we were kids." Jack leaned forward and patted Tabitha's knee. "Don't worry, by the time our visit is over, you'll be a pro at it." Jack sat back. "As for the eyes—the Lower Castes aren't allowed to look directly at Betas. They lower their gaze in the presence of the Upper Castes."

"Is that a law or something?"

"I don't know. I always thought it was stupid and I still do. The Betas who work with Sigmas demand the lowered gaze." Jack looked up at Tabitha. "Oh, and when we are there, please say something to Sam and Jennie about not doing it."

"I'm sorry, Jack." Tabitha looked thoughtfully at the ground. "I have been trying to do better after last night's dinner after realizing what you deal with."

Jack took her hand. Tabitha had a long way to go. But her admission was an important first step for her becoming the person he had always known she could be.

Chapter 34: Sam

January 26, 537

"I am the Algorithm. I will create the optimal society
for humanity."

- First email the Algorithm sent to all humanity,
January 1, 1 at 0000.

Sam sat back in his office chair. For the first time in a long time, he noticed the plastic biting into his back. A floral scent lingered in the office. Sam looked around but couldn't find its source. Unusual smells normally led to a work order request. He didn't submit one—unusual smells were never this pleasant.

Jack's timing couldn't have been better. Sam couldn't wait to get home and tell Jennie about the call. Three inefficiency notices came in while he was talking to Jack. He'd have to work extra hard to get them done before the workday ended, but the reconnection with Jack was worth it. For him, personally, and for the Plan.

He finished his last inefficiency report with one minute to spare. His work resulted in the promotion of yet another Beta to Detroit. Sam had lost count of how many Betas had benefited from his work.

Sally interrupted him as he prepared to walk through his office door to join the stream of Sigmas shuffling toward the AB's exit. "Sam, you have been provided leave time."

Other than weekends and Jennie's mysterious maternity leave, he never heard of Sigmas getting time off. "I didn't request a leave."

"The Algorithm provided you and Ms. Goodby a leave so that you may meet with Mr. Thompson and Ms. Forsythe. Mr. Thompson will determine the duration of your leave."

"The Algorithm provides."

And that's what worries me.

***

Jennie's head bounced from side-to-side as she stared at a tablet while waiting for Sam in her usual spot beside the bus. Yesterday, she received a notification that her maternity leave had been cut short. Not surprisingly, there was no explanation for the leave's early termination. Jennie took it well, saying any leave at all was better than what the Omegas got.

Sam stopped. A few of the Sigmas behind him grumbled. He'd forgotten how great it was to see her first thing at the end of the workday. Yes, Ms. Forsythe had nice clothes. But she was no Jennie.

She'll want to celebrate tonight. I hope she wears her blue dress. The dress's color had faded. Sam had asked if she wanted a replacement. She said no, the dress was special. He agreed.

"Sam!" Jennie gave Sam a big hug. "How was your day, dear?"

"Excellent."

Jennie raised her eyebrows and cocked her head. "You've *never* used that word to describe your workday. What happened?"

"I got a surprise. I'll tell you when we get home."

Jennie gave him a knowing look. "I can't wait to hear about it." She took his hand and led him onto the bus and into their regular seat. After months of sitting alone, it was great to have Jennie snuggled up beside him again.

The sandy brown landscape zoomed by as the bus took them home. An opportunity had arisen. Taking advantage of it would be tricky. Fortunately, the best possible teammate sat by his side, with her head on his shoulder.

***

Like all Sigmas, William was provided daycare. Fortunately for Sam and Jennie, William's daycare was only a kilometer from the bus depot. When they dropped him off that morning, Jennie told Sam she was worried there weren't enough adults to watch the sixty kids there. Sam had fond memories of his daycare and preferred it over the Omega alternative. It didn't matter. The instructions provided by the Algorithm were clear. William had to go so Jennie could return to work.

Sam and Jennie took turns carrying William as they walked the two kilometers to their SLU. They talked about their days at work and carefully avoided the surprise. Along the way, a pair of UnSelected males approached them with their gaze cast down.

One man spoke with a strained voice. "We hear you help the UnSelected."

"We do what we can." Jennie handed William to Sam. "What do you need?"

"Our daughter is hungry," the man's voice trembled, "but the paste makes her sick. Can you help us?"

Jennie took a piece of bread from her bag. Sam tried keeping part of his lunch aside, but his hunger often betrayed his desire to help others. *She's a better person than me.*

"Try this." Jennie bent down a little so that they looked into her eyes.

The UnSelected men's eyes watered. One of them carefully took the bread from Jennie's hands. "Thank you so much!"

A Sigma male walked by, shaking his head in disgust. He wouldn't dare say or do anything about Jennie's generosity. The encounter from two years ago was still fresh in the local memory. Occasionally, Jennie had to give a reminder to those who enjoyed testing boundaries.

Those lessons were always followed by an accelerated walk home and a memorable evening.

Sam and Jennie wished the UnSelected men a good evening and continued walking home along South Orange Avenue. They had walked along this road every day for the last few years and nothing had changed in that time. The same buildings lined the streets, all in the same state of disrepair. Today, though, Sam noticed the run-down nature of the buildings, not unlike when he first moved to Orlando.

I wonder what the buildings are like in Detroit.

Guilt filled his heart. It had been a long time since he last betrayed his promise to himself. He had built a good life in Orlando. Fantasies would only hurt him and his family.

But what if the Random Scale Factor had been just a little higher...

Chapter 35: Jennie

January 26, 537

"The Russian Alliance and Canadian-Alaskan Federation invade the former US in hopes of stopping the
Algorithm."

- Final post of the Moscow-Beijing News Agency,
January 1, 1, at 0015.

The sheets Sam bought for William's crib weren't in the *like-new* condition the Outfitter had advertised. Jennie couldn't complain. No Omega baby had a crib, much less sheets.

Sam walked in and put his hand on her back. "You won't believe the Algorithm's generosity today." Her phone buzzed. A deepfake had begun.

Despite her initial objections, Sam insisted she take the lead on the deepfake program. She felt terrible taking over Sam's only remaining coding project. He said the future of the Plan depended on it. His faith in her was one reason she loved him so much. Thanks to her new learning algorithms, the software could make deepfakes of any length. She had even reduced the program size so it could be easily transferred wirelessly.

William cried. Sam picked him up and smelled his diaper. His face told Jennie all she needed to know. She grabbed a clean diaper and followed Sam to their couch. Sam laid William down, took the diaper, and began changing William.

"What's the surprise?" Jennie sat on the arm of the couch.

"Hold a sec." Sam finished changing William. He was faster at diaper changing and made less of a mess than her.

As Sam secured William's diaper, Jennie noticed red spots on Sam's arm. Bugs had been using him as a buffet every night, and the Sigma-level repellent wasn't working.

"I think I got us access to a Beta terminal." Sam scratched his arm.

Jennie examined Sam's arm. "How?"

"We are going to be visited by two Betas." Sam picked up William and took him to his room. Jennie followed.

"What?" She slouched and gazed downward. *Have we been caught?*

While putting William in his crib, Sam told her all about the call with Jack, his plans to come visit, and the upcoming time off that they had both been awarded.

"Wow! I have never met a Beta in the flesh before. What do I wear? I have nothing that is Beta-nice." *I don't want to embarrass Sam in front of his old friend.*

"I wouldn't worry about it. Jack's a cool guy. I think you'll like him. From talking to him today, it doesn't seem like the Beta life has changed him at all."

They returned to the main room, and Sam sat on the sofa. Jennie went to the kitchen area. "I think we have some of that ointment left. Maybe it will work for your arm." Jennie searched through the drawers. "So, how does this get us access to a Beta terminal?"

"I bet he will give us access to the terminal if we tell him the Plan. This is a once in a lifetime opportunity. We need to take it."

Jennie found the ointment and sat beside Sam. "Can we trust him?" His arm looked painful. She started rubbing in the ointment, hoping it would give him some relief.

"Old Jack? Certainly. With our lives. New Jack? Based on today's conversation—probably."

"Is it doing anything?" Jennie closed the ointment tube.

He scrunched up his face and shook his head. "Thanks for trying. It's a fifty-fifty shot with this stuff." Sam scratched his arm again. "Let's feel Jack out. If anything, his wife might be the problem."

"I've got another idea for your arm." She stood and brought her bag back to the sofa. "Could we keep his wife in the dark?" She rummaged through her bag. *Secrets can destroy a relationship. I pray mine doesn't ruin ours.*

"Maybe. But it would be hard for me to keep something this big from you. I bet he'd feel the same way." Something in Sam's voice told Jennie he had experience in keeping secrets, too.

"Why do you say that?" She removed a small container from her bag.

"Just a hunch."

Maybe one day we'll be able to share all our secrets.

Sam pointed to the container. "What's in there?"

Jennie stuck her fingers in the container, scooping out some squishy nutrient paste. "It's an old Omega trick. It might work better with Sigma paste." She spread the paste on Sam's bites.

"Whoa." Sam's jaw dropped as he looked from his arm to her face. "That works!"

"This time. It's not a sure thing."

"Let's see how this plays out. We'll have them over for dinner and, if it feels right, we'll present the Plan and see if they'll help."

"What if they won't help or we can't trust them?" Jennie worried about getting into trouble, and how that would affect their son. William was a Sigma, but an orphaned Sigma might as well be UnSelected.

"We'll cross that bridge if we get to it. This is our only shot." Sam put his hand on Jennie's knee. "I know we can do this."

William cried.

Sam stood up and smiled as he looked at Jennie. "My turn, again. Thanks for the paste." He bent over and kissed her forehead.

Jennie heard Sam soothe William in the other room. *He's such a great dad.* She settled back into the sofa and sighed.

The timing of this visit is too perfect.

"Unconfirmed rumors of President Wallace's death spread as Russian and Chinese ships appear up and down the East Coast of the former US. Reports of armed conflict between Canadian forces and an unknown military have been confirmed by Prime Minister Ramirez."
- Final post made by the *Toronto Star*, January 1, 1 at 0020.

Part 4
Change

Chapter 36: Tabitha

February 8, 537

"Do. Not. Go. They are full of dangerous people whose poor work ethic led them to lives of misery."

- A Beta's Guide to Visiting Lower Caste Cities & Neighborhoods.

The last thing Tabitha wanted to do was look at the ground from forty thousand feet. The height didn't bother her. It was the view. Flights between Beta cities were no problem. But once she left the Beta regions, the sparse clouds could not conceal the brown Earth, yellow ponds, and sparse vegetation. She lowered the window shade, leaned back in her chair, and closed her eyes. It had been a long week of preparations for the trip, and it culminated with Jack insisting on her taking the window seat of the anti-grav.

Growing up flying out of Baltimore, she could see the pollution that permeated the city—even her old neighborhood, Towson. She had heard that pre-Shift, Towson was not a separate city from Baltimore. The city moved as the water crept north from Old Inner Harbor. Towson had the city's bluest skies, cleanest streets, best schools, and largest parks—all of which paled compared to Detroit.

The smell of the southern neighborhoods often overwhelmed Towson's environmental filters. On those days, she didn't go outside. Unlike some of the other Beta kids, Tabitha never left her neighborhood, except to fly with her parents.

A small plane icon on the monitor in front of her moved farther from Detroit and closer to not just a Sigma neighborhood, but a whole Sigma city. Jack had committed her to going and she couldn't say no. Since the Alpha dinner, she had resolved to support him more. How could she have known her resolution would lead to such a dangerous trip?

Beta newsfeeds made it clear that Sigmas were the worst class of people—all of whom wanted nothing more than to rob you, or worse. Meeting Jack had caused her to question that belief, to an extent. The Algorithm deemed Jack worthy of an upgrade. Maybe he was the only Sigma civilized enough to join the Upper Castes.

Sam seemed nice enough on the call. He looked unkempt and his clothes appeared pre-Shift. Then again, what would one expect from a Sigma? They didn't care about themselves. Why would Sigmas care about how others perceived them?

The video call was a good way to meet one's first Sigma. Sam couldn't hurt her through the screen. But how would he behave when they were one-on-one outside the safety of Detroit? Would it be safe to be alone with him?

She fiddled with the air vent. A pain shot through her arm—a reminder of her most recent round of vaccinations. Over the past week, Jack told her all kinds of stories about the Lower Castes. The stories of cramped SLUs were unbelievable. His description of trash-lined streets was not surprising. Based on what she had heard of the Sigmas, they couldn't be expected to take care of their own neighborhoods. Jack had gone too far with the stories about the UnSelected. His creativity sometimes crossed the line.

Tabitha rubbed her arm. A pop-up on the screen in front of her asked if she wanted meds. She responded with her ANN. The sweet smell of anti-inflammatory gas filled her nostrils. The Algorithm blended it with some antianxiety meds. *It always knows what I need.*

As crazy as Jack's stories sounded, there was much more preparation for this trip than she expected. The med center gave her thirty different injections to protect her against diseases she had never heard of, such as malaria, dengue fever, and skin cancer. Tabitha protested, but Jacqueline insisted on the shots. The med center also dispensed pills to help her tolerate Florida's heat. The technician told Tabitha Florida got so hot that the heat index could not be measured. She didn't know what that meant, but it was never a bad idea to have a few extra pills.

The preparations weren't all bad. Clothes shopping was fun. Tabitha bought ten new outfits for tropical climates. *I hope that's enough for a four-day trip.*

The nanny holo deemed the trip too dangerous for Jessica. Jack protested, but the nanny wouldn't let Jessica go to Florida. *I don't understand why he was so upset.*

Jack wanted to stay in an SLU to, in his words, "Get the full experience." Regarding this one request, Tabitha refused. She had agreed to the trip, and everything that went with it, but staying in a slum was asking too much. As a result, Jack requested a temporary Beta Living Unit be set up for them outside of the city. He also asked for a private car to travel around Orlando. Much to Tabitha's relief, both were provided. The car and the BLU should provide some shelter against the Lower Castes of Orlando.

Thomas Algol had invested a lot of resources for her and Jack to make this movie. Tabitha didn't understand why, but she didn't care—she was going to be a star. *I'd never say it to him, but I wonder if Jack has bitten off more than he can chew. Maybe I have, too.*

Jack snored in the seat beside her. It took a while, but he had finally become comfortable on flights. Until a week ago, Tabitha thought she had made significant progress with Jack. He seemed to have embraced the Beta life—at least until the call with Sam.

Tabitha hadn't noticed the constant tension in Jack's face until it disappeared with Sam's on-screen appearance. For the first time, she saw Jack's true face. It must be hard for him constantly trying to conform. *He really is trying to fit in all the time—even at home.*

She requested an antidepressant through her ANN. Another sweet scent entered her nostrils. The meds kicked in, and Tabitha drifted off to sleep.

***

Tabitha raised her hand to shield her eyes from the harsh sun outside the Orlando airport. Her ocular implants activated a UV filter. The world darkened, and she stopped squinting. No longer blinded, her other senses registered Florida's onslaught.

Her armpits were wet. *Am I already sweating?* Tabitha had learned the word *stifling* in school but hadn't understood what it meant until now. Breathing was difficult with the humidity. The air smelled worse than Towson's when its environmental filters failed.

"Wow!" Jack puffed out his shirt. "Can you imagine how hot this would feel if we didn't have our pills? Didn't the pilot say the heat index is thirty-five?" Jack's watch projected today's heat index, verifying the pilot.

Sweat stains had formed around Jack's arms. Tabitha spray cleaned her shirt using a bottle she took from her purse. She handed the bottle to Jack, but he refused. *I'll spray him when he's not looking.*

Tiny insects buzzed around her. *They must be the mosquitoes the physicians warned me about.* The anti-pest field upgrade worked. The mosquitoes stayed about half a meter from her.

"Mr. Thompson and Ms. Forsythe, I presume?"

The voice came from a young woman, probably recently Selected, in a well-worn and once-white, now dirty gray, linen suit. Sweat stains ringed the woman's armpits and the front of her shirt. On her head sat an equally worn sweat-stained cap, hiding most of her short-cut brown hair. The suit made Sam's clothes look like a Beta outfit in comparison.

Tabitha looked down at her own feet, wondering what the woman was staring at. Nothing seemed out of the ordinary. Her brown sandals had no scuffs and her red nail polish looked perfect, as always.

"My name is Amanda, and I am provided to you for your visit to Orlando." Amanda spoke with the rigidity of a highly practiced speech. "I was reassigned from the reclamation effort to assist you during your stay. May I show you to your car?" Amanda held out her hand toward the black car waiting for them.

Jack stepped forward. "Pleased to meet you, Amanda. Please call me Jack. This is my wife, Tabitha. If we are to work together, I'd prefer it if you'd look at me while we talk."

Tabitha glanced at Jack. She'd tolerate the informality with Sam, but she wasn't comfortable being so relaxed around Amanda. Jack ignored her.

"Uh, *if* you in-insist." Amanda slowly raised her head, showing a pair of striking hazel eyes set in a weather-worn, leathery face. They were some of the most striking eyes Tabitha had ever seen—modified or not.

"Your eyes are beautiful!" *But what is wrong with her skin?*

"Thank you, Ms. Forsythe. I mean T-Tabitha. The color mod was a gift from a client. Is there anything I can *assist* you with?"

Snack time approached, and Tabitha hadn't seen a dispenser outside the airport. "Let's start with some food. Where can we get a decent meal around here?"

A strange noise came from Amanda's stomach. "F-Food dispensers are available inside the airport. Your car has a dispenser in it, too." Amanda put her hand on her belly. "I am told the airport dispensers are better than the car's."

Car-dispensed food did not seem appetizing after a long plane ride. "Actually, I am interested in a restaurant. Can you recommend one?"

"R-Restaurant, ma'am?"

"Never mind, Amanda," Jack interrupted, "the car dispenser will be fine. Would you like to join us? I'd be happy to split my provision."

Amanda licked her lips. "I-I am sorry, sir. I-I am not allowed. I-I am only to sh-show you to your car." She cleared her throat. "I will be staying in temporary housing near your Beta Living Unit. I'll be on call for you 24-7 should you need anything a *human* can provide."

Jack reached for the car door. "Thank you, Amanda. I don't think we'll be needing your *services*. I have a friend here who will show us around."

"Oh. Okay, Mr. Thompson, I mean Jack." Amanda smiled as if a weight had been lifted off her shoulders.

Bile rose in Tabitha's stomach. She had never seen someone with missing teeth. The few teeth Amanda had were yellow, misshapen stumps.

How does she eat?

***

Amanda appeared to get smaller as the car drove away from the airport. "What was that all about?" Tabitha asked.

"She is an Omega whom the Algorithm provided to us." Jack stared off into the distance.

Tabitha had learned to dislike Jack's perfunctory tone. He used it only when he told unbelievable stories about the Lower Castes. "What do you mean, *provided to us*?"

"When she emphasized the word 'human,' she signaled that she would join us in our bed whenever we wanted." Jack continued staring out the window as he spoke. There didn't seem to be anything of interest out there.

He's gotta be joking.

"Young Omegas like her are sometimes Selected as sex workers for Betas and the occasional Sigma. They don't live long in those jobs because the demands of some Betas can be…" Jack paused. "Extreme."

He has gone too far with these stories of his.

"That's not funny, Jack."

"I wasn't trying to be." Jack shifted in his seat and turned to her. "Remember our conversation about *those* kinds of pictures? Real people are in them. The actors in those movies are often Omegas like her. The worst ones, though, the most inhumane movies, star the UnSelected."

I remember that conversation. I thought he was joking… Tabitha looked down at her hands folded on her lap. *How much more sadness awaits me in Orlando?*

"I made it a point to tell her we won't need her services." Jack's voice shed its perfunctory tone. "In fact, I'd prefer not to contact her at all so she can have some time off. Omegas *never* get breaks from their work."

"No vacations?"

"Not until they die. The type of work they do…Well, let's put it this way, you don't see retired Omegas."

"Why did you offer her your food? Isn't she provided food of her own?"

"She was hungry. That's why she touched her stomach. As a Sigma, we were underfed, but we usually weren't starving. The same isn't true of Omegas."

Why wouldn't someone have enough to eat? Food is always available on demand.

They spent the rest of the ride in silence. Tabitha tried to eat her meal from the car's dispenser but, for the first time in her life, she had no appetite.

***

Security drones scanned their car as it stopped in front of the temporary Beta Living Unit. Tabitha preferred Beta Security Force officers over drones. But in a place like Florida, you took what you got.

The BLU was half the size of their home in Detroit. "It's small, but it'll do. What's that?" Tabitha pointed to a bus leaving from behind the house.

"Probably the Omega work crew that built the BLU," Jack said as he got out of the car. "I guess there weren't any bots available for construction." Tabitha followed him to the BLU's front door, worried about whether or not a human-built home was safe to live in.

Inside, the BLU looked like their home in Detroit. It would be the perfect refuge from whatever additional unpleasantries awaited her in Orlando.

After checking that their stuff had been unpacked by the delivery drones, Jack and Tabitha went to their bedroom to change and freshen up. Tabitha straightened her blue sundress. She didn't care what Sam thought of her appearance. But looking good for the Sigma might help things go more smoothly for Jack. She double-checked her lipstick. *Looking good is what I do best.* Tabitha had been told that often enough. She believed it.

"How do I look?" Jack fidgeted with his hair in their bedroom mirror.

"You look great!" She kissed him on the cheek, then wiped off the lipstick that remained.

"Thank you. Don't forget to reactivate your UV interference field. The radiation down here is worse than back home."

Jacqueline did it before Tabitha could ask.

"Done. Ready to go?" *Let's get this over with.*

The face Jack had on the call with Sam returned. "Yup! I can't wait!"

As they drove away, the car approached a small windowless one-room building about a hundred meters east of their BLU. Holes honeycombed the walls.

"What's that?" Tabitha pointed to the structure. "Some kind of historical building? It looks ancient, like pre-Shift or something."

"I am guessing it's Amanda's place. She said she'd be near us if we needed anything." Jack had been using his somber tone more than usual since they had arrived in Orlando. She didn't like it.

As they passed Amanda's house, Tabitha turned to look out the rearview window. The BLU towered over the shack in the background.

***

The car drove toward Downtown Orlando along an ancient road named I-4. Tabitha wrinkled up her nose. "What's that smell?"

"It flooded here recently," Jacqueline said in her aural implants. "I apologize, but the car can't completely filter out the odor."

Hopefully Orlando will smell better.

The car passed a sign for an exit that read "Disney Cultural Heritage Center." Jack and Tabitha looked at each other and shrugged. The car kept going.

After a while, a few small, unremarkable buildings appeared over the horizon.

Jack straightened in his seat and faced forward. "That must be Orlando."

"Where's the skyscrapers?" Tabitha stretched her neck for a better view.

"Sigma cities aren't assigned enough energy to run skyscrapers. Their biggest buildings are SLUs, and they are four stories, max." Jack's perfunctory tone had returned.

This trip is bringing back some memories and feelings Jack had long ago put away. She held Jack's hand as they looked out the window in silence. *He needs me and I'll be here for him.*

The car passed a faded green sign with "Welcome to Downtown Orlando" in a large white font. Tabitha squeezed Jack's hand. In part for support, but also in astonishment. All the buildings needed maintenance. One building had plexiglass haphazardly nailed to it in place of windows. Another building had a few broken windows that hadn't been covered at all. Uneven concrete stairs led up to many of the buildings. Bricks were missing from most of the buildings' facades.

Three children sat on a sidewalk playing with trash. They stopped and stared at their car with sullen, dirty faces. Their clothes hung loosely and, while intact, were not clean.

"They shouldn't be playing with trash," Tabitha said. "Where are their nanny holos?"

"No holo-nannies here. Only Betas get those. Sigmas get access to daycare by humans. But I doubt Omegas and UnSelected do." The light from Jack's eyes disappeared. "Those won't be the only unsupervised kids you see here. And try not to stare. They'll be frightened of you."

I can't believe what I am seeing.

The further they drove into the city, if one could call Orlando a city, the more disturbing things became. People slept in the street surrounded by trash. "Why are they sleeping on the street?"

Jack leaned forward to look around her. "They're UnSelected. That's where they live." *They're real?* Tabitha's stomach turned.

A block away from where she saw the UnSelected sleeping, a man kicked another who had collapsed on the sidewalk. The man doing the kicking was much better dressed than the man on the ground. Neither were clean. Jack told her not to stare. She had no difficulty looking away.

"How can people live like this?"

Jack shrugged. "They don't have a choice. UnSelected are not provided enough to survive. They have to fight, beg, or steal just to live." Jack folded his arms and looked out the window. "That was a Sigma doing the kicking back there."

"Why can't they just do their jobs? People work and the Algorithm provides." Based on Jack's stories, Tabitha expected the living conditions wouldn't be great, but she couldn't have imagined anything like this.

"Sam once told me there are no jobs for the UnSelected. The Algorithm decided they were incapable of even Omega-level cleanup work." Jack paused in thought.

"Sam worked his ass off in school, and yet this is where he ended up." The swear alarm went off. "Whatever." Jack shook his head. "Yeah, he's a Sigma, and he's better off than some of these folks, but only sort of." Jack nodded toward the window. "If you think of all this as a prison, then the Omegas and UnSelected are the prisoners. The Sigmas are the guards. But face it, they're all in the same prison." Jack sat back in his seat. "Hell, maybe *we* Betas are the guards." Jack shrugged off another swear alarm.

Tabitha didn't like the sound of Jack's heretical comment. But the more she saw, the harder it was to deny.

Chapter 37: Tabitha

February 8, 537

"The Russian Alliance and Canadian-Alaskan Federation have fallen. The world is now united as the Society."

- Email sent to all humanity from the Algorithm, January 1, 1, at 0030.

The car slowed. Tabitha exhaled slowly. It was one thing to drive through a Sigma neighborhood—it was another to stop and walk around.

"We have arrived at our destination," Samantha said as the car parked itself in front of a building that looked like all the others in Orlando—run-down, dirty, and uninhabitable.

Sandals were a terrible choice. Trash lined the curb and covered the sidewalk. Tabitha opened the car door. A terrible odor assaulted her nostrils. She rubbed her tongue against her teeth, trying to wipe away the taste of the air. Despite her earlier complaint to Jacqueline, the car's air filtration system had been working well.

The sun beat down on Tabitha. Beads of sweat formed along her spine. She dug through her purse, looking for the spray cleaner. The sound of rustling trash drew Tabitha's attention away from her search. A woman, her gaze cast down, carried a bundle in her arms and approached Tabitha. *How can she smell worse than the city?*

"Hello, ma'am." Like Amanda, this woman seemed to have rehearsed her speech. "I am sorry to bother you, but would you have something for my baby to eat?"

The woman drew back the filthy blanket, revealing the emaciated dirt-encrusted face of a child. It didn't move.

Tabitha's throat thickened. *How can a baby not have enough to eat?* She searched her purse. "I don't have anything on me. Let me see what I have in the car." She pulled the door handle. It didn't budge. "That's odd." Tabitha jiggled the handle again, to no avail.

Jack wedged himself between Tabitha and the woman. "Let's go." He placed his hand behind Tabitha's back, gently, but urgently, leading her toward Sam's SLU building. Jack kept his eyes on the woman.

"It's okay, dear. May the Algorithm bless you." The woman reached out to touch Tabitha's arm.

Tabitha jumped. The woman cowered and backed off, placing her body between Tabitha and the baby. "I'm sorry. I didn't mean nothin'. I swear!" She kept her eyes focused on the ground.

"Stacey, please leave our guests alone." A woman leaned out of a window two floors above them. She had long brown hair and olive skin—attractive, for a non-Beta. "They have traveled from far away and need to rest. I'll have something for you a little later. Okay?"

"Okay, Jennie!" The woman rocked the baby in her arms as she turned and walked away. Jack's eyes followed her until she was halfway down the block.

The woman in the window waved but didn't look at them. "Hello! You must be Mr. Thompson and Ms. Forsythe. I'm Jennie Goodby. We're in 3G, come on up when you'd like. The door's open." She disappeared back inside.

Jack opened the SLU building door for her. "Don't speak to the UnSelected, even if they speak to you. They are dangerous." She had never heard Jack speak in such a stern voice.

Tabitha looked down—only in part to make sure she didn't trip on chipped concrete. "I am sorry. I didn't know." *What was wrong with her baby?*

***

Sigma children played on the first floor of the SLU building. Once they saw Jack and Tabitha, they looked away and ran into their homes. After the last door slammed shut, an eerie silence settled over the hallway. Jack waved her forward down a long hallway with disgusting yellow paint. It was peeling in many places, adding to the run-down ambiance that permeated the entire building.

The clicking of Tabitha's heels broke the silence and some of the tension as they walked. She stayed close to Jack. At any moment, a crazed Sigma might jump out from any of the many closed doors lining the hall.

At the end of the hall was a staircase where an elevator should have been. Jack started up the stairs. Tabitha looked down at her heeled sandals. *No elevator?*

After too many steps, they finally made it to the third floor. It looked like the word had gotten out. The hallway on this floor was bereft of children, leaving nothing but the peeling yellow walls. Her sandals stuck to the floor with each step. Tabitha looked down at the sole of her right foot. *Now I really wish I hadn't worn my favorite sandals.*

Hanging above an open door at the end of the hall was the number 3, alongside an outline of the letter G. Jack knocked on the doorframe. "Hello?"

A male voice shouted from another room. "It's open. Please come in."

Tabitha followed Jack into a room that appeared to have multiple purposes. A kitchen counter lined part of the far wall, ending at a primitive food dispenser and stove. On the other side of the room, near where they stood, was a sofa with very thin cushions. Beside the sofa were two hard plastic chairs. A plastic dining table surrounded by two more plastic chairs separated the kitchen and living room spaces.

A terminal took up half the space on top of the table. All the furniture looked older than her. The bare walls had only stains and peeling paint for decoration. To top it all off, an odor permeated the room. It smelled like the outside, but not as strong.

A trickle of sweat ran down Tabitha's back. The room was warm, but not as hot as outside. The encounter with the UnSelected woman had made her forget to spray her clothes. This didn't seem like a good time, either.

Sam entered the room, his eyes focused on the floor. His khaki shorts and thin polo shirt showed their age but were nicer than what he wore for the call. *It would have been nice if he showered before we came over.* Tabitha tried to picture Jack as a Sigma. *Did he really live like this?*

"Hello, Mr. Thompson." Sam spoke in an even and formal tone.

Jack took a step toward Sam and placed his hand on Sam's shoulder. Sam flinched. Jack quickly retracted his hand and said, "Hey man, no caste bullshit with us, please."

No alarm?

"Besides, we'll be working closely together while we are here. It will be so much easier if we're all on a first-name basis."

A first-name basis still felt inappropriate. But Jack had insisted otherwise. She didn't want to start a fight with him over some Sigmas.

"Thank you, Jack." Sam gave the second most mangled smile she had seen today.

Jack once had teeth like his.

Tabitha held out her hand and put on the smile that got her nominated as the best supporting actor last year. "I'm Tabitha. We spoke on the vid-call."

Sam bowed his head and took her hand. "It is a pleasure to meet you in person this time." His calloused hand felt like sandpaper. Up close, Sam smelled like the home. She hoped the odor wouldn't be absorbed into her dress or hair.

Jack coughed, snapping Tabitha out of her thoughts about the odor. "As Jack said, there is no need to avert your eyes from us."

"Thank you, Tabitha." Sam turned the corners of his lips upward and nodded slightly.

The woman from the window entered the room from the third, and only other, door. She wore a faded blue dress with blue flat shoes. The dress was too big for her thin body, and its stitching separated at some seams. The shoes had seen better days. Worst of all, she held a child in her arms. Childcare was for holos, not people.

"This is my wife, Jennie, and my son, William." Sam's face beamed, like when Jack bragged to other Betas about her acting. Jennie went right beside Sam and into a one-armed hug. He squeezed her gently. She stayed there, and Sam kept his arm around her. That kind of public display of affection wasn't done in Detroit.

"Pleased to meet you both." Jennie's smile was identical in quality to Sam's. Ignoring the smile, up close, Jennie appeared even more attractive—again, for a non-Beta.

"Thanks for your help with the UnSelected woman back there." Jack said.

"With Stacey?" Jennie stepped out of Sam's one-armed hug and held up her free hand. "No thanks are needed, Mr. Thompson. She's harmless. Her child died a week ago. Since then, she's been carrying her dead baby around, still trying to get food for her."

The lump returned to Tabitha's throat. "That's so sad. How did she die?"

Jennie frowned. Tabitha had never seen such sadness in someone's eyes. "Malnutrition. It is common in Orlando, especially among the UnSelected." Jennie's tone matched Jack's when he talked about his past.

The comment pierced Tabitha's heart. She had never once given a thought about access to food. *How could people in today's day and age starve to death? Food is everywhere.*

"I am sorry. I didn't mean to spoil the mood." Jennie's tone brightened, and her eyes lit up. "Would you like to join us for dinner?" She looked at Sam with pride in her eyes. "Sam has become an excellent cook!"

Jack did a double take. "Cooking? *Really?*" Jack snorted. "Chef, programmer, man of knowledge. What can't you do?"

"Jennie here is the best programmer in the house." Sam pointed to Jennie with his thumb. She blushed at the pride in Sam's voice. "I'm a hack compared to her."

"Stop it." Jennie playfully smacked Sam on the arm. "They didn't come all this way to hear you brag about me."

Their relationship fascinated Tabitha. Every Beta couple she knew was much more reserved, including her parents. Although Tabitha liked the attention, everyone knew how much Jack loved her—it could be embarrassing.

Jack stepped forward. "That sounds—"

"Unfortunately, we have plans for this evening." Tabitha had to stop him. "We just wanted to drop in and say hello." She reached out to him with her ANN. *We are not eating here.*

Jack turned to Tabitha with his eyebrows furrowed. She didn't enjoy disappointing him, but there was only so much she could handle in one day. Hopefully, he'd understand.

"I am sorry to hear that. Maybe some other time." Jennie adjusted William in her arms. "I am going to put William down for a nap. Ms. Forsythe, would you like to join me and let Mr. Thompson and Sam catch up?"

"I'll be happy to join you." Jack nudged her. "I'd prefer it if you called me Tabitha." She lied on both points.

Tabitha recognized Jennie's smile. Unlike her Beta friends, Jennie and Sam weren't easily fooled.

***

William's room would hardly count as a closet in Tabitha's BLU. More of the same old hard plastic furniture filled his bedroom. The crib's thin mattress looked like it offered only a little more comfort than the tile floor.

"I like your dress, Tabitha." Jennie dug through a drawer as she held William. "Blue is my favorite color." She pulled out a sheet and joined Tabitha by the crib. "Do you mind if I ask you a question?"

The genuine compliment caught Tabitha off guard. "Not at all, Jennie." *I bet she'll ask about being an actor.*

"Do those shoes hurt your feet? Those heels must be uncomfortable. You are welcome to take them off."

"Thank you, but they don't bother me." Tabitha didn't like the idea of being barefoot in the SLU. Then she realized Jennie, unlike a Beta, asked about her well-being, not her profession, clothes, or anything else material. "Wearing them is expected of me because of my job. The feeds would light up if someone photographed me without them on."

Jennie nodded with a pretense of understanding. "Sam told me you are an actor. Do you like it?"

The question caught Tabitha by surprise. Back home when she divulged her profession to the few who didn't already know of her, responses tended to be "You're so lucky…" Instead, Jennie asked about her feelings.

"I do. It's a lot of hard work, but it has its fun parts. Sam said you are a programmer. Do you like it?"

"Oh, I don't get to program at work." Jennie put the sheet down beside the crib on a dirty nightstand. "I do code maintenance. I identify inefficiencies in AI code and send them up to a programmer to fix."

That didn't sound right. Why weren't Jennie's talents being used? "Sam said you are an excellent programmer. You don't get to fix the code yourself?"

"It's not what I was Selected for. My job is to identify problems, not fix them." Jennie shrugged. "I can't complain though. It could have been much worse for me. Do you mind holding him while I put the sheet down?" Jennie held William out to Tabitha.

"Uh, sure." Tabitha hesitated in taking William and then held him out at arm's length.

Jennie laughed playfully. "Sam told me you had a daughter. It's no different holding a boy."

Tabitha brought William closer to her body, but not too close. "I am embarrassed to admit this to you, but this is my first time holding a child." She brought William in a little closer still and then stopped just short of putting his body against hers. *Why did I just say that?* Something about Jennie made her easy to open up to.

"Really?" The increase in Jennie's pitch betrayed her surprise. Her face tensed as if she realized she had said something she shouldn't.

"We have a holographic nanny that takes care of Jessica for us."

"Well, you learn fast. You are holding him like a pro!"

"Thanks!" Jennie's second genuine compliment reassured Tabitha.

Jennie spread the threadbare faded blue sheet on William's mattress. Nan would have discarded the sheet long before it had gotten to its current condition. *Why is she using it?*

"Go ahead and put him down." Jennie patted the mattress, releasing a poof of dust. Tabitha did so gently, being careful not to let his head hit the hard mattress.

"Earlier you said your Selection could have been worse. Do you mind me asking why you said that?" *What could be worse than Jennie's current situation?*

"Not at all. My parents were Omegas. I could have been Selected to join them in cleaning up the Inner Harbor."

Jack had pointed out the filthy Inner Harbor a couple of years ago on their flight to Detroit.

"Environmental cleanup is hard physical labor," Jennie said. "My parents were lucky. They lived just long enough to see me Selected."

After what she had seen today, Tabitha understood the implication. Omegas' work led to a short lifespan and probably not much else.

"I am sorry that they are gone." Tabitha meant it, to her own surprise. Before meeting Jennie, the only person she could empathize with was Jack.

"Well, one thing I learned as an Omega is that life is short and hard."

Tabitha recorded Jennie's smile with her ocular implant. It would be useful the next time she portrayed a character who needed to hide emotional pain.

"But I'm lucky. I got out." Jennie tickled William's stomach. He giggled. "Thanks to Sam. I am doing well." Jennie's smile became one of genuine joy—maybe relief. It was hard to tell. Either way, Tabitha took another picture.

If this is doing well, I really don't want to know how Omegas live.

Jack had revealed his tough transition to Beta at the Alpha restaurant. *Was Jennie's transition harder?*

Tabitha put her hand on Jennie's arm. "Still, I am sorry to hear about your parents."

Jennie cleared her throat. "Thank you. What do your parents do?"

Tabitha removed her hand. She hoped she hadn't made Jennie uncomfortable. "My parents were both pilots."

"You said were, did they pass?"

"Not that I've heard." Jennie looked confused by Tabitha's statement. "I haven't talked to them in years. Betas don't talk to their families after Selection." Tabitha felt a tinge of sadness. Jennie couldn't talk to her parents, not because of some social norm, but because they were dead. *I think I'll call them when I get back to Detroit.*

"Hey, why don't we see what trouble the boys are getting into?" Jennie whispered. William had fallen asleep. Tabitha nodded and took off her shoes so she could silently leave the bedroom. It wasn't until she was halfway out of the room that she realized what she had done.

***

"And get a load of this shit. No one has messed with us for years." Sam sat back in the sofa and laughed from his belly.

"Dude, that's awesome!" Jack sat closer to Sam than she'd ever seen him sit near any of their Beta friends.

"What's awesome?" Jennie sat on the arm of the sofa and reached around Sam, giving him a squeeze.

"Just telling old Jack here how you kicked that Sigma man's ass a few years back." Sam scooted over to let Jennie join them on the sofa. He put his arm over Jennie's shoulder, and she rested her head on Sam's.

"What?" Tabitha gasped. *She hurt someone?* Tabitha hadn't known anyone who had committed an act of violence.

"A girl's gotta know how to take care of herself *and* protect her man." Jennie pecked Sam on the cheek.

Jack slid over on the sofa and patted the cushion, inviting Tabitha to join them.

She had no interest in sitting on the rock-hard couch. "I hate to break up the reunion, but Jack and I really need to get going." Tabitha regretted the words as soon as they left her mouth. Although she wanted to spend more time with Jennie, she also needed to maintain the earlier lie to avoid eating whatever Sigmas ate. "Before we leave, we should figure out how we are going to do the research. How about if I shadow Jennie over the next few days and Jack follows Sam?"

Jack looked at Sam and Jennie. "That works for me if it works for you two."

Sam nodded. "Sounds good to me."

"Me, too!" Jennie's tone sounded genuine, but Tabitha thought she noticed a hint of something else. It reminded her of when Jack's coworker Susan invited her to lunch with the implication of discussing an acting part. But she ended up only wanting to talk about Jack. Had Tabitha been more empathetic toward Jack's Selection, she would have walked away from that lunch with a better understanding of what Jack was going through well before the Alpha restaurant.

What does Jennie have in store for me?

***

Jack turned to Tabitha with an eager expression as he closed his car door. "So, what did you think?"

Tabitha hesitated. "They seem like nice people, Jack."

"That's it?"

"What do you want me to say? I don't know them. Sam is your friend from the past. Jennie seems like a nice enough Sigma. Woman." Tabitha quickly corrected herself.

Jack stared at Tabitha. His disappointment was so obvious, even she couldn't miss it.

"I'm sorry. I have met no one who wasn't a Beta before. All my life, I have been told they are bad people. But then I met you, a former

Sigma, and I fell in love with you. I am trying, but this is all still new to me."

Jack placed his hand on hers. "I know."

"I couldn't stay there and eat. Didn't you notice the smell?"

The disappointment returned to Jack's face. "What do you think Bob at the restaurant thought of us when he learned we weren't Alphas?"

Tabitha couldn't tell which troubled her most, Jack's disappointment or her own. "Probably the same way I am thinking of Sam and Jennie right now."

"They are doing the best they can with what they have."

Jack's right, but why did they have to have so little?

The car accelerated. Jack settled back in his seat. "I was surprised you suggested splitting up to do the research."

"I wanted you to have more time to catch up with Sam. I felt a little guilty about ending the night so early."

Jack gave her a sidelong look. "Really?"

"Well, that's not all." A valid excuse popped into Tabitha's mind. "I had an interesting conversation with Jennie in William's room. I'd like to spend some more time with her as part of a character study."

"Hmm."

Just like Sam and Jennie, Jack appeared to see through her lie.

Chapter 38: Jack

February 9, 537

"Humans will be partitioned into castes that reflect
the value of the individual to the Society."

- Email from the Algorithm, January 1, 1 at 0040.

The Sigma neighborhood hummed with activity at 0700. Jack
yawned as his car pulled up to Sam's SLU building. He had forgotten
what it was like to be up, and functioning, this early.

Jack's yawn triggered one from Tabitha, who sat in the front-facing
seat across from him. She stretched in her seat beside him. "It is *too*
early! I thought you said Sam and Jennie were provided time off."

"They were. Sam insisted we go to work with them on our first day
here. He said it would help us with authenticity."

Sam's generous offer to work during his leave was fortuitous.
The chance to observe Sam would help Jack with the movie. More
importantly, it would answer some questions. Did Sam get the chance
to make suboptimal decisions? Better yet, did Sam's job matter? Jack
hoped Sam had a meaningful job—unlike his own.

Sigmas streamed out of Sam's SLU building. Most of them paused
when they saw the car. A crowd formed. Moments later, a disturbance
in the sea of Sigmas began in the rear near the building and slowly
worked its way forward toward the car. The sea parted, allowing Sam
and Jennie through. Sam carried William in his arms. William wore
only a diaper and a very thin shirt. Sam and Jennie wore khaki pants

and white shirts. The slightly oversized outfits looked itchy, even from inside the car.

"Remember our first morning together when I asked you about work outfits?" Jack whispered. "That's what Sam and Jennie are wearing."

"Oh." Tabitha mouthed the word.

Jennie chatted with a few of the Sigmas in the crowd. A wave of head nods propagated through the sea of Sigmas as Jennie's words spread. One by one, the crowd dissipated.

Once all the other Sigmas had left, Sam and Jennie looked at the car, then at each other. Jack had the same silent conversation with himself that he'd had in Baltimore. "Slide over to the rear-facing seat. I'll be right back." Tabitha yawned and changed seats as Jack got out of the car.

"Good morning!" Jack positioned himself between the car and Sam's family. "I brought the car so we could ride to work together." He patted the roof of the car and smiled. "I was terrified the first time I rode in one of these things. I promise it is perfectly safe. There is no way I would put William in any danger." Sam nodded at Jennie, who replied with a look of hesitant approval.

"Thanks, buddy. We appreciate you giving us a ride. Neither of us has been in one of these before."

Jack opened the door for Jennie and pointed to the forward-facing seat. "That seat will be best for your first ride."

Jennie slid into the seat. "Hi Tabitha!"

"Hi Jennie!" Tabitha perked up immediately after seeing Jennie. "How are you this morning?"

Tabitha's question sounded genuine and not the Beta-standard greeting that expected "I'm fine" as a response. Jack hadn't known Jennie long, but if she could bring this out of Tabitha, then she was okay in his book.

"I am great! Looking forward to another day at work." Jennie seemed at ease. Jack hoped it continued once the car accelerated. "Did you sleep well in your new place? Sam told me you have a temporary home outside Orlando."

"We did. Thank you for asking." Tabitha's lie relieved Jack. They didn't need to hear Tabitha's complaints about a BLU bed.

A route appeared on the car's console. Jack reached to approve the route when Sam interrupted him. "Stay off South Orange at this time, dude. Traffic is heavy with buses."

An alternate route appeared on the screen, and Jack approved it. "Thanks, man." He also tapped the icon for eco-driving. It conserved energy, which he normally didn't care about. However, conservation meant gentle acceleration and breaking, slower speeds, and a more comfortable ride for newbies.

The car moved forward. Sam and Jennie held hands but seemed to be okay.

"Jack, do you mind if we drop William off at daycare first?" Jennie asked.

"No problem. I preplanned the stop at the daycare center. Sam asked me last night when I offered the ride."

"I knew about the car," Sam said. "I didn't want to say anything because I remember how much the bus bothered you when we first met."

Jennie looked at Sam and smiled. Jack looked away. *I wish Tabby and I were more like the team they appear to be.*

William's daycare building looked exactly how Jack remembered his own—a big gray concrete box. At least all the windows were made of glass. An awkward silence fell over the car when Sam took William inside. Seconds became hours as they stared at each other. Jennie opened her mouth a few times as if to say something but stopped each time. A collective sigh of relief was shared in the car when Sam reappeared from the building.

After Sam got in the car, Jennie slid over and rested her head on his shoulder. A tinge of jealousy arose in Jack. *That is how a couple should be.*

The route Sam suggested got them through the city quickly. Although the AB and the airport were on opposite sides of Orlando, this morning's commute looked like their trip into the city yesterday. Endless fields of brown. This trip was Jack's first outside of Beta cities and regions since his Selection. He had forgotten the extent of the environmental damage from the Shift.

The stench of stale mud filled the cabin, regardless of how much power Jack redirected to the car's filters. He connected his ANN to Samantha, but she couldn't do much to counteract the odor. Jennie and Sam didn't seem to notice. Thankfully, Tabitha didn't comment.

Much to Jack's disappointment, Jennie stayed quiet the rest of the ride. The former Omega had made his formerly miserable Sigma friend come to terms with his Selection and had captivated his very Beta wife. The word fascinating didn't begin to describe her.

Much to Jack's relief, Tabitha remained mostly quiet the entire ride. When Sam would point out a landmark, Tabitha would nod or say, "Mm-hmm." Jack asked follow-up questions, hoping to get Tabitha more involved. Apparently feigning interest *and* tolerating the smell—both from the outside and Sam and Jennie—asked too much of her. Jack had more work to do.

A large concrete building, which had to be the AB, appeared on the horizon. The second collective sigh of relief swept through the car.

***

The plastic chair bit into Jack's butt. Beta life had made him soft. Jack leaned forward, resting his elbows on his knees—it didn't help.

Sam had been telling Jack about how, on his first day of work, he had fixed an AI file and gotten his boss promoted.

"You've gotta be fucking kidding me." It hadn't taken long for Jack to regain his facility in swearing.

"It's par for the course, dude." A beep drew Sam's attention to the screen. "Hold a sec, just gotta submit this." Sam waved his hands in front of the terminal. After a moment, his attention returned to Jack.

"I hope I am not disturbing you being here."

"Not at all. The change of pace is nice. I've been doing the same thing here for years." Sam leaned back in his chair. "It's awesome having you around, man."

Sam's phone vibrated on the desk. Jack's watch projected a lunch-time notification. Sam passed his hand through the projection. "That's rad."

"Yeah, it does all kinds of shit. I can even control it with my mind."

The words, *Request to eat in AB cafeteria,* appeared on the projected screen. The submit button flashed and disappeared. Sam's eyes were wide, and his jaw dropped open.

It felt good to impress Sam. Back in Baltimore, Sam was always the one with the cool gadgets. A tinge of guilt ensured Jack's good feeling didn't last. Jack hadn't made the watch. He wasn't even sure if he earned it. Sam, on the other hand, had built all those things that had impressed him in the past.

On their way to the cafeteria, Sam paused for what felt like several minutes to look at a white poster with black text. Jack read it in a couple of seconds. "Why do you look at each one? It looks like run-of-the mill corporate speak."

"We have to." Sam didn't look away from the poster. "Each time an Omega team puts a new one up, we are supposed to read it. If I read it too fast, I get penalized."

"Seriously? What's the penalty?"

"Omega-level paste." Sam took a few steps down the hall and turned to stare at another. "Last week, I was in a hurry and didn't stand in front of a poster long enough. The Algorithm apparently didn't think I could read a poster that fast, but I had." Sam's eyes lingered on the poster. "We got home to find Omega-level paste and baby formula for dinner. Have you ever had Omega paste?"

Jack nodded his head but kept his eyes on the poster. "Once. You dared me to taste it. Remember?"

"Then you remember it tastes like chalk."

"Yeah, I had to wash it down with water. Thankfully, we were provided a decent dinner that night."

"It fills your stomach but doesn't satisfy your hunger. Jennie and I were hungry an hour after dinner. William cried all night. Now I make it a point to always read the posters ten times."

Jack wiped a tear from his eye when he thought Sam wasn't looking. His friend didn't need pity, he needed help. Maybe the movie could provide it.

How? He wasn't sure.

***

The cafeteria fell silent when Jack and Sam entered the room side by side, talking and laughing as equals. Jack stepped up to the dispenser. "One Sigma-level lunch, please." A paste packet labeled *chicken* and a bottle of Sigma-level water appeared in the dispenser. Brown particles floated in the water. He forgot what most of the world drank.

"I bet this would provide a Beta lunch." Sam sized up the dispenser.

"If I am going to do this movie, then I am going to be thorough in my research." Jack grabbed the packet.

"Look at you, taking your studies all seriously." Sam laughed.

It took Jack several minutes to convince the Sigma programmers at Sam's lunch table to look at and speak to him, but once he did, a floodgate of questions opened. Cynthia asked most of the questions—almost all were about Detroit. Jack provided vague answers to avoid flaunting his status in front of Sam.

As he spoke with the Sigmas, Jack opened the packet and removed a spoonful of paste. The bland paste squished in his mouth exactly as he had remembered. He suppressed a gag. Its flavor and texture couldn't be more different from real chicken. *How did I stomach this as a kid?* He got through the paste as quickly as possible. Washing it down with the dirty water didn't help.

An Omega cleaning crew entered the cafeteria as Jack and the Sigmas were leaving. Cynthia turned to Jack. "By the Algorithm, they smell worse today than usual." She then turned to the workers, who immediately looked away. "Use a shower credit now and then."

The Omegas slouched and gazed at the floor. It reminded Jack of his own daily treatment by Rebecca and Dan.

Cynthia turned to Jack while laughing. Jack walked away from Cynthia, ignoring her. Sam followed. As he passed the Omegas, Jack paused and thanked them for their work. The Omegas wouldn't make eye contact, but they straightened slightly.

"Did you see the look on Cynthia's face?" Sam chuckled. Jack hadn't, nor did he care. Sam's chuckling stopped. "That might be the first time a Beta ever showed them appreciation."

Pride swelled in Jack's chest. *Why do I feel proud about treating other people as human beings? Have I become too much of a Beta?*

***

The afternoon in Sam's office dragged on. Jack's struggle to find comfort in the plastic chair continued. *How does Sam sit on this stuff all day?*

Sam stared intently at his terminal for most of the afternoon. Jack needed a distraction. "Is it normal to get so many inefficiency reports?"

"Probably not. I have a particularly good maintenance person."

"You don't find the inefficiencies yourself?"

"Nope. That's not my job, dude." Sam typed on a holo-interface. "I just recommend fixes to the ones that are sent to me." He squinted at the screen. "Give me just one second to send up this recommendation." Sam leaned in to read something on the screen, nodded, then sat back.

"You don't fix them?"

"Also, not my job. I make recommendations and some Beta somewhere does the fix and gets the credit. I have probably gotten thirty Betas promoted," Sam said, as if it were no big deal.

A pain shot through Jack's jaw from clenching his teeth. Samantha's voice appeared in his aural implants, offering him meds. He declined. To his relief, he continued to feel angry.

"Now we wait for the next report." Sam sat back in his chair.

"Shall we fire up a game?"

"What?" The look on Sam's face was one of either incredulity or confusion.

"Never mind." *How out of touch have I become?*

"Well, dude, since you are here, I don't have to just sit here and stare at a blank screen." Sam scooted his chair back and leaned toward Jack, resting his elbows on his knees. "I'd love to hear about your job."

"There isn't much to tell, really. I supposedly cast actors for movies. The truth is, I agree to whatever the Algorithm says and spend the rest of the day playing games."

"Why not pick other actors?"

"I tried. My terminal won't let me make *a suboptimal choice.*" Jack used air quotes. "My lack of choices extends well beyond my work."

Jack paused. "I'm sorry, man. I shouldn't be flaunting this in front of you. And my complaints don't qualify as problems for anyone but Betas."

"Don't be sorry, dude. I am not surprised at all. I often wonder why the Algorithm isn't doing my job. It should be able to do so much better than me. I often wonder what's the point of me being here."

That was it! Among other things, Jack had come to Orlando to find out if Sam's job mattered. Apparently it didn't, just like his own. He wanted to hug Sam, but he stopped himself. Jack's excitement waned once Sam's answer settled in. At least Jack's pointless job came with Beta benefits. Sam had no such compensation.

Sam smiled. "Hey, man, at least neither of us are dealing with Omega working conditions. You won't believe some of the shit Jennie has told me. Remember Mount Vernon?"

"Yeah. I never went there. Mom would have killed me."

"Jennie grew up there. She told me when it floods, there are sharks in the water and then when the water recedes, it sometimes leaves mines behind from the Last War."

Jack looked down at the floor. "I had no idea people lived like that, just one neighborhood over."

Sam's terminal dinged. Another inefficiency report arrived. This one must have been complicated, because Sam worked on it for a long time.

Does their workday never end?

Having once been a Sigma, Jack expected what he saw in Orlando. However, as a child, he had never experienced Sigma working conditions. The daily realities of the Sigma adult life could only be described as depressing and mundane. From what Sam had shown him, it comprised long hours doing rote work, with no outlet for personal expression. All for the reward of going home to eat nutrient paste. Wash, rinse, repeat.

Sam's job, by his own admission, was as meaningless as Jack's. Jack knew little about computers, but he knew the Algorithm should be perfectly capable of doing what Sam did. Spending that one workday with Sam fortified Jack's doubts about the world around him.

What can I do about it?

***

The next day, Sam gave Jack a walking tour of Orlando's Sigma neighborhoods. They looked like The Hill. The parks were a little nicer, but the constant onslaught of mosquitoes made sitting in the park uncomfortable for Sam. Jack stayed close to Sam, hoping his anti-pest field would extend to him. It seemed to work—mostly.

No one bothered them as they walked around town that morning. At first, Jack thought it was due to his status as a Beta. Then he remembered Sam's story about Jennie. He really needed to get to know her better.

Sam invited Jack to his SLU for lunch. Jack stomached more paste. The package said beef, but Jack knew better. Jennie and Tabitha weren't in the SLU. Whatever they were doing, he hoped Tabitha continued to treat Jennie at least as well as she did during yesterday morning's ride to work.

***

The following day was to be Jack's last in Orlando. He requested an additional car so that he and Sam could tour Orlando without tying up their only car, in case Tabitha needed it.

Sam got into Jack's car as soon as he pulled up. "Hey man, I got a plan for us today."

"Sounds great! Where are we going?"

"To see the real Orlando. Mind if I put in some coordinates?"

Jack slid over so Sam could access the terminal. Sam typed in a few numbers and a map of Orlando appeared. He tapped a location outside the Sigma neighborhoods and near the waterfront.

"Where are we going?"

Sam sat back in the forward-facing seat. "Like I said, the real Orlando. Trust me."

The condition of the SLU buildings degraded as the car followed the path Sam had entered. Eventually, the streets became lined with OLUs. The OLUs looked like larger versions of Amanda's shack. Jack could see the OLUs' inhabitants through holes in the sides of some buildings. Few of the windows had glass. As the car continued, more of the sidewalks were covered with trash and sleeping people. The car drew many stares. Jack glanced at the door controls to make sure they were locked.

The permanent structures slowly disappeared, and tents lined the streets. As they drove, the size of the tents decreased as the number of holes in them increased. More and more bodies lay on the sidewalk, exposed to the elements—some didn't move at all. The car came to a stop close to the water.

People who looked like they hadn't bathed in weeks shuffled around, looking for Algorithm-knew-what. Tattered clothes hung from bodies barely more than skin and bone. The car drew a lot of stares, but people stayed away.

"Dude, where the hell have you taken me?" Jack asked.

"The largest UnSelected camp in Orlando."

"Is it safe to be here?" It certainly didn't look safe. Jack double-checked the doors were locked.

Sam shrugged. "It should be fine. I come down here with Jennie and William at least once a week. Jennie helps the UnSelected with food and other things."

"Seriously, dude? You let your wife and child be with UnSelected?"

"Jennie once told me Omegas never had to worry about the Un-Selected." Sam stared out the window. "It was the Sigmas that caused them the most problems. From what I have seen here, I believe her." Sam shook his head. "They are people, just like you and me, but in a bad situation, doing the best they can."

Jack had no interest in leaving the car, but he was willing to look at the UnSelected through Sam's eyes. Sam told him more about the realities of life as an UnSelected and the work he did with Jennie at the camp. As Sam spoke, Jack understood how Tabitha dismissed his claims about life as a Sigma. Had he heard it from anyone other than Sam, Jack would have easily discounted Sam's stories.

An UnSelected child approached their car. She was dirty, dehydrated, and malnourished. The clothes hung from her body. Jack couldn't tell her age. Sam rolled down the window.

The girl tried to speak, but her raspy voice made her difficult to understand. She held out her hands. Sam gave the child some bread and water he had kept aside from his lunch. A lump formed in Jack's throat. The girl's tears left streaks in the dirt covering her face. *What if that was Jessica?*

"We should probably leave before we get overrun with people looking for food." Sam rolled up his window.

Tears blurred Jack's vision. "Samantha, please dispense two cloths."

Before directing the car to leave, Jack jammed the cloths into the car's vents deep enough to prevent any drugs from being dispensed. He didn't deserve to feel good right now.

Chapter 39: Tabitha

February 9, 537

"Omegas and UnSelected are the same—both are kept poor so that others may thrive."

- Last words of Omega activist Martin Edward as archived on the Omega Dark Net.

How does Jennie sit in these chairs?

Tabitha checked the time. Only an hour had passed since Jennie's workday began. It felt like four.

The hard plastic chair she sat on was squeezed in between Jennie and one of her office mates. Each time Tabitha tried to find a more comfortable position, she bumped into one of the two Sigmas, causing both to jump. Jennie tried to make chitchat a few times, but loud notifications from her terminal kept drawing her attention away from Tabitha.

How can anyone think with all these alerts?

There wasn't much to look at in Jennie's office to pass the time. Her desk had only two photos—one of Sam and William and another of a couple she didn't recognize. After committing the images to memory, Tabitha stared at the stained yellow wall across from her. It had thirty-seven cracks in it. Light shone through one of them.

Everything in the office assaulted Tabitha's senses. All the Sigmas had a strong, musky odor. A musty stench emanated from the walls. Combined, the smells formed a nauseating cocktail in her nose. The constant clicking of keys and interfaces likely caused the growing pain in her head. Multiple ANN-sent requests to Jacqueline for meds were denied. Apparently, Jennie's office lacked the vents to deliver the drugs.

How am I going to tolerate four hours here?

"I am sorry to bother you, Jennie, but I forgot to ask…What time do you get off work?" Tabitha hoped the question sounded casual.

"I get to stop at 1700! It's a full four hours before my parents ended their workday. Can you believe it?"

"No. I can't." Tabitha bit her lip.

I am doing a character study. Tabitha tried reframing her thoughts. *This is the hard work of acting.* Self-delusion didn't work as well as meds, but it was better than nothing.

"You said you do code maintenance. What's that?" Tabitha didn't care, but she needed the distraction.

Jennie's eyes lit up. Tabitha wondered what the blue flecks in her irises would look like under better lighting. "I go through these lines of code and look for things that aren't right." Jennie gave a half shrug. "It might not be as exciting as acting, but I find code fascinating." She pointed at her terminal's screen. "Oh! Look here! I think this variable assignment is wrong. I bet increasing that value would make the code run better!"

The other Sigmas in the office glared at Jennie. As soon as they noticed Tabitha looking at them, they averted their gaze. The terminal screen contained undecipherable lines of familiar words and numbers. It was hard for Tabitha to see what was so interesting.

"Now I get to write up a brief report and send it to my programmer. My programmer then recommends a fix." Jennie pointed to the word *scaling_parameter.* "They need to increase the variable by twenty percent."

The process seemed silly and suboptimal. Jennie clearly knew how to fix the problem. However, based on what Jennie had said in their SLU, she didn't get to use her talents optimally.

Is Jennie satisfied with this menial job?

The morning dragged on. Jennie read line after line on her terminal's screen. Occasionally, she would get excited and point something out to Tabitha. It never seemed worth the excitement. After what felt like two workdays, Tabitha's watch projected a notification. It was lunchtime. A scraping sound echoed as all four Sigmas in the office pushed back their chairs.

Now free to move, Tabitha stood, relieving the pressure from her back. It took some effort to steady herself as the blood returned to her legs. "What's for lunch?"

"Only the Algorithm knows what It will provide." Jennie waved Tabitha to follow her. "We get to eat in the cafeteria. It's nice. I think you'll like it."

Hopes for fresh air were dashed the moment Tabitha entered the hallway. Putrid sea foam-green tiles lined the hall to the cafeteria. A few posters hung on the walls. Jennie read each one. It seemed to take her forever to move from one poster to the next. Tabitha inspected the floor tiles during one particularly long reading session.

Why did someone waste these pretty tiles on this building?

Contrary to Jennie's promise, the cafeteria was not nice. It smelled like Jennie's office, but ten times worse. Sea foam-green wall tiles clashed with a gray stained low-pile carpet. Rows of tables and benches filled the room, each one packed with Sigmas—likely the cause of the foul odor. At least there was no line at the dispenser.

"One lunch, please." Jennie removed a white package and a bottle of brownish liquid.

"What's that?"

Jennie turned the package over so that the label faced upward. "Hmm, it looks like we get to have chicken and water today. Chicken is one of my favorites." Another noise came from the dispenser. Jennie reached in and pulled out a brown lump with green spots. "Oh look, bread!" Jennie's eye darted between the bread and package. "I think I'll make a sandwich. If you don't get bread, you can share some of mine." Jennie whispered. "We aren't supposed to share, but I've never gotten in trouble for it."

Whatever Jennie had in that clear plastic package, it wasn't chicken. Had she not read the label herself, Tabitha wouldn't have believed Jennie's bottle held water. *What's floating in it?*

Tabitha stepped up to the dispenser. "One lunch."

The dispenser emitted a loud clang. Tabitha reached in and pulled out a tray that held a cooked chicken breast, roasted brussels sprouts, and water.

After she withdrew the tray, Tabitha turned around to follow Jennie, but stopped. The weight of a hundred stares settled upon her, and not the good kind like on the red carpet. Everyone in the cafeteria, except her, had the packet, bread, and brownish water.

A heavy feeling appeared in her chest. At first, she thought she might be having a heart attack. But that couldn't be. Jacqueline would have alerted her. She had felt this way once before, during the conversation with Jack at the Alpha restaurant.

Tabitha's eyes darted from her tray to Jennie's package and a lump formed in her throat. Nausea swept over her stomach. She requested meds—none came. Instead, she looked at her blank watch screen.

"I have to step out for a minute to deal with something from work." Tabitha looked up at Jennie—the only person in the room looking at her and not her lunch. The sympathy in Jennie's eyes made everything worse.

Thankfully, the hallway between the cafeteria and the AB's exit was empty. Only sea-green walls and multicolored floor tiles lay ahead of her. Maybe some fresh air—or what counted as fresh air in Orlando—would help ease her guilt. Tabitha went outside and found a small bench overlooking the brown fields surrounding the AB. She placed the tray beside her on the bench and stared at the fields. For the second time in her life, she had lost her appetite.

***

Tabitha steeled herself outside Jennie's office door. *Four and a half more hours in that chair.* The door creaked as Tabitha opened it, drawing the attention of the four Sigmas inside. Three of their gazes returned immediately to their screens. Jennie's did not. She folded her hand in her lap and looked at Tabitha with tight eyes.

"Is everything okay, Ms. Forsythe?" Jennie had been calling her Ms. Forsythe around the other Sigmas.

"Uh, yes." Tabitha scratched her cheek. "It wasn't an emergency after all."

Jennie's gaze did not waver. "I meant are *you* alright?"

Other than Jack, and maybe my parents, no Beta has ever shown concern for me, only for what I can do for them.

A warm feeling filled Tabitha's chest. "I am. Thank you for asking." She wiggled her way over to her seat and sat beside Jennie.

"I am happy to hear that." Jennie placed her calloused hand on the top of Tabitha's. She removed it, faster than Tabitha wished. "Hey, check out this inefficiency I just discovered!"

I need to make an effort. Jennie deserves at least that much.

"Tell me all about it!" Tabitha leaned in.

***

"I'm impressed by how you read all this code." Tabitha said.

"It's not too hard once you know what to look for. Do you want to try?" Jennie tilted the monitor toward Tabitha.

"I don't want to mess it up."

"You won't." A block of code was highlighted on the screen. "What do you think is wrong here?"

The third line of highlighted code began with the word *for* but didn't end with a colon. All the other lines beginning with *for* ended with one. "It's missing a colon. I think there is something wrong with the next line, too."

Jennie tilted her head. "I missed that one!" She smiled at Tabitha. "Very good! You are a fast learner!"

Pride welled up in Tabitha. "Thank you, Jennie."

Wait until Jack hears about this!

"You can do the honors." Jennie handed her the keyboard.

Tabitha typed the report and submitted it. Without warning, all the terminals in Jennie's office powered off.

"What happened? Did I do something wrong?"

I knew I'd mess this up. I hope Jennie doesn't get in trouble.

"No. It's time to go home."

"Oh. Already?" Tabitha stood. Pressure left her back and butt. The feeling caught her off guard.

"Would you and Jack like to join us for dinner tonight? I know Sam would love it. I would, too."

Tabitha thought about the paste packets she saw at lunch earlier. "I am sorry, but Jack and I need to compile our notes for the movie. Maybe some other time?"

"Of course." Jennie nodded. "While you are in Orlando, the invitation is open. Just stop by. There is no need to call first. We're always happy to have you."

"Thank you, Jennie." Tabitha wanted to hug Jennie but settled on gently squeezing her arm. Her hand met Jennie's bones with less effort than it should have.

Why is she so skinny? Amanda came to mind. *I should have given Jennie my lunch.*

***

Sam and Jennie insisted on taking the bus home. Tabitha hoped she hadn't upset Jennie by declining her invitation. Sam said something about his happy place and they both got on the bus.

Jack talked about his day with Sam during the trip back to their BLU. Tabitha let him go and responded with some mm-hmms as she thought appropriate.

The long hours worked by the Sigmas were brutal. She was happy to be out of the office. But her mind kept coming back to Jennie's job. Jennie's talents were wasted on menial labor. *How could Jennie's work assignment be optimal for the Society?*

As the car rolled down the highway, she thought of Jennie's positive disposition and gratitude throughout the workday. Jennie never once complained about the chair or the tedious job, nor did she covet Tabitha's lunch like the other Sigmas had done. When everyone else in the room focused on what Tabitha had, Jennie focused on what Tabitha felt.

The reaction of the other Sigmas wasn't much different from that of Betas. Tabitha and her friends chased the Alpha lifestyle and focused on what they didn't have.

Betas could learn a lot from Jennie. They'd shun me for saying it.

The car pulled into the BLU's garage. Jack rambled on about something Sam had said. She let him finish his story, but her mind was elsewhere.

Jennie offered to take Tabitha on a tour of a Sigma neighborhood tomorrow. Instead, Tabitha asked if they could go back to Jennie's work. Tabitha wanted to try her hand at identifying more inefficiencies. It took some convincing, but Jennie agreed under one condition—she got to pick what they did the next day.

Tabitha had thought little about Jennie's condition at the time. But Jennie's smile concerned Tabitha. *Maybe I shouldn't have been so quick to agree.*

Chapter 40: Jack

February 11, 537

"Barry Beta gave Ollie Omega food. In return, Ollie stole Barry's toys."

- Excerpt from the Beta primary school text, *The Unfriendly Omega.*

The late afternoon sun illuminated the mostly empty living room. The packing drones had removed all but the most basic furniture to prepare for tomorrow's flight home. Jack settled back on the lone remaining sofa, embraced by its pillowy cushions. The trip had shown him many things—including how soft he had become as a Beta.

Hopefully, the movie will help Sam and Jennie.

How? He couldn't be sure. Beta ears would be deaf to Sam's story. With any luck, an emotional portrayal of Sam by Tabitha would resonate with a few Betas. Maybe. The most likely outcome was heated discussions on the Beta feeds that would ultimately lead nowhere.

I wish I could have tried Sam's cooking. Jennie invited them for dinner every night, and Tabitha refused each time. *I thought bringing Tabby here would help her with the changes she said she wanted to make after the Alpha dinner.* Maybe Orlando was just too much for her.

Tabitha shuffled into the living room barefoot, wearing a baggy T-shirt and shorts. While not a mess, her hair was far from Tabitha-perfect and she wore no makeup.

That's a new look.

She sat on the edge of the cushion beside Jack and leaned forward, resting her elbows on her knees. Had Jack not seen her face, he would have thought some other woman had broken in and sat down beside him.

Jack straightened and turned to her, folding one leg under the other. "What's wrong, Tabby?" She looked down at her watch and pushed a button on its holo-screen. The watch's face turned red, and a timer began.

"What's that?" The app didn't look like any Beta software Jack had seen.

"I started a deepfake." Tabitha stared at a point on the floor in front of her. Her voice had taken on the same perfunctory tone she said he used when talking about Sigmas. "Jennie wrote a program that sends a fake video to all the cameras and microphones in the area. It keeps our conversations private from the Algorithm. She transferred the code to my watch earlier today."

"Is that legal?" Sam was punished for not reading the posters. The Algorithm didn't just provide, it punished, too.

Tabitha shrugged her shoulders but didn't look at her husband. "I don't care."

"What about Jessica? What happens to her if we get bumped to Sigma or something?"

"Jennie says it's fine. I believe her. She wouldn't put us in danger. Try reaching out to Samantha."

Samantha did not respond to Jack, either verbally or through his ANN. He reached out to Tabitha. No connection.

"You couldn't connect, could you?"

"No. It looks like Jennie's right." Jack paused. "It's strange. I forgot what it is like to be alone in my head."

"We need to talk." Tabitha's gaze hadn't deviated from the floor.

"You haven't been the same since you got back this afternoon from your trip with Jennie. What happened?"

Tabitha inhaled through her nose and exhaled through puffed cheeks. "I have seen a lot here in Orlando, and I don't like any of it."

"I was worried about how you would be affected by this trip." Jack rubbed Tabitha's back. "I tried to prepare you, but I think these things have to be seen to be believed." Normally, Tabitha purred in response to back rubs. This one garnered no response, so he stopped. She didn't respond to that either.

"I want to help them. I don't know how, but there must be *something* we can do."

"I think we can do a lot with this movie. Maybe we can get some Betas to see how other people live." It was doubtful, at best, but maybe it would ease Tabitha's mind.

"Do you know what I did today?" Tabitha's eyes remained fixed on an empty spot on the floor.

"Yeah." Jack bunched his eyebrows together. "You stayed with Jennie at their SLU so you could learn more about being an Omega."

Tabitha shook her head. "We went to an Omega neighborhood just outside of town."

Without his ANN, Jack couldn't request meds to slow his heart rate or the growing nausea. He took a deep breath. It helped a little. "Why did you go there?" Jack reached out for her hand—again, no response.

"I had to. Jennie tried to describe it, but like you said, I needed to see it." Tabitha maintained her unnerving calm. "There was trash everywhere. People slept among it on the streets. Some used it as blankets, and some built shelters from it. I think some of them might have been dead." Tears trickled from the corner of her eyes.

"I saw people disfigured from work and naked children in the streets begging for food. The buildings were in such awful shape, some actually had holes in their sides that you could see through. And the smell…Well, the Sigma neighborhoods smell like Beta ones in comparison." Tabitha sat perfectly still. Tears rolled down her cheeks.

Is she having a nervous breakdown? Jack reached out to Samantha—no response.

"Jennie asked if I wanted to see an UnSelected camp next. I said yes."

"Tabitha—"

"I will never forget what I saw there. I don't know how to put it into words." Tabitha paused and bit her lip, but not in the sexy way she normally did. "They didn't have buildings. Instead, there were tents—but that's being generous. They were more like the remnants of pre-Shift tarps held up by poles. There was so much hunger. I could see the ribs of people walking around shirtless. Piles of shit lined the streets."

"In the Omega neighborhood, I thought some people were dead. In the UnSelected camp, I had no doubt. Every few blocks you'd see bodies. Some were children, Jack. *Children.* I couldn't help but think of Jessica. What if she was one of them?"

Tabitha trembled. Jack put his arm around her. The camp Sam took him to was nothing like what Tabitha described. Maybe Sam tried to protect him. *Why didn't Jennie do the same for Tabby?*

"Some people were so hungry that they were eating the bodies." Tears dripped from her chin and onto the carpet. A clear liquid seeped from her nose. "I know I said the Omega neighborhood made the Sigma neighborhood look like a Beta one. The UnSelected camp made the Sigma neighborhood look almost like the Alpha houses we saw back home."

The palm of Jack's hand hurt. Looking down, he saw fingernail marks in his flesh. If Tabitha hadn't been falling apart right now, he would have called Jennie to yell at her for what she had done. It would end his relationship with Sam, but right now, he didn't care.

"Jennie is amazing. She walked among the filth and the dead, handing out what little bread and water she could save from her work lunches. You should see what the UnSelected drink."

Jack inhaled again. Like last time, it didn't help. "You are lucky you weren't raped or killed." He winced, not intending for that to sound like a reprimand.

"There was an incident."

The evenness in Tabitha's voice was more worrisome than its content. *If anything happened to her—*

"A Sigma man came up to us as we walked through the camp. I don't know why he was there." Tabitha exhaled. "I guess he thought we'd be easy prey; me a clueless Beta and Jennie, well, she is so small."

Jack knelt in front of her and took her hands. "What happened?"

Tabitha stared through Jack. Wet, red sclera surrounded faded green eyes. "He grabbed me by the arm and pulled me into him. He was so rough. I've never been afraid like that before."

The tears streamed down her cheeks. Jack tried to connect to the emergency channel with his ANN. Nothing.

"Then, out of nowhere, he just let go and collapsed." Tabitha made eye contact with Jack, her face bunched up in confusion. "I think he died."

Jack squeezed her hands gently—the only comfort he could provide.

"When it was all over, Jennie stood in front of me smiling and asking me if I was alright. I didn't know what happened, so I asked her. She said he was going to rape us and take whatever we had, but she took care of it."

Jack exhaled, relieved that Tabitha was physically okay. He hugged her, but she didn't hug him back. Her tears made his shirt wet. He leaned back and took her hands again. "What did she do?"

"Jennie said she hit him with a piece of broken concrete she had picked up off the street. I didn't see it. I was in shock. The guy was unconscious." Her face relaxed. "Do you think she killed him?"

"Probably not." He did his best to sound convincing. The man was probably dead, but Tabitha had enough on her emotional plate right now. "From what Sam told me, Jennie learned how to fight as a kid. She knew what she was doing."

"She saved my life. But it's not just that." Tears continued to roll down Tabitha's cheeks and onto the floor. A cleaning bot tried to wedge itself between them. Jack nudged it away. "She is smart, kind, and so gracious for what she has. She doesn't deserve the hand she's been dealt—her childhood, her job, her life."

Tabitha paused, using the back of her hand to wipe the clear liquid from her nose. "Anyone in Detroit would see her clothes and look down on her. Their first impression would be their final opinion—a stupid, wannabe Sigma, barely a human being." Tabitha snorted. "Hell, I would have thought the same thing four days ago, and I *hate* myself for it."

It was good to see a little emotion from her. Jack squeezed her hand again. She didn't squeeze back.

"Both Sam and Jennie were Selected into situations they had no chance to change. It was stupid luck they are where they are, and we are where we are." Tabitha straightened and waved her hand around the room to emphasize her point. "We could have been them and they could have been us."

She took a deep breath. Tabitha's green eyes pierced through his with a ferocity and focus he didn't know she had. "It's not right, and *I* need to help.

"For the first time in my life, I want to help someone else with nothing in return. I want to do it because it is right. If we can help Sam, Jennie, and all these other people, then we must do it." Tabitha stood and tapped the STOP button on her watch.

The ANN connection between them returned. Jack's brain drowned in a flood of raw emotion. Focus, resolve, and purpose broadcasted loud and clear from Tabitha's ANN. Jennie had rubbed off on her, and Jack liked it.

Jack stood and hugged his wife. "I am so proud of you, Tabitha." He disliked formality, but this was a serious moment. The person he knew was always inside had finally come out.

Tabitha broke the hug and stepped back with a triumphant smile. "It's Tabby."

Chapter 41: Tabby

February 11, 537

"The best way to bring people together is by sitting down and sharing some provided nutrient paste. Never invite Omegas or the UnSelected—they don't deserve our provisions."

- *SLU Living*, April 325.

The G above Sam and Jennie's SLU hadn't been replaced since Tabby had last visited. The chipped paint on the doorframe appeared worse. Maybe it was the same and her eyes were different. Tabitha noticed only flaws. Tabby was concerned about how those flaws affected those she cared about. Sam and Jennie shouldn't have to live like this.

Jack pressed a button beside the door handle. Muffled voices came from the other side of the door. Hopefully they weren't imposing on Sam and Jennie.

The door opened. Sam stood inside, barefoot, wearing a T-shirt and shorts. A yellow food-stained towel hung over his shoulder. His face went from confusion to surprise to joy like a slow-motion video.

Jack grabbed Sam's shoulder and smiled ear-to-ear. "So, what's for dinner, buddy? *If* we're still invited, of course."

"Dude!" Sam embraced Jack in a big hug. "You are always welcome here!" He stepped back and extended his hand toward Tabby. "Tabitha, it is nice to see you again."

Handshakes were for acquaintances. Tabby had enough of those in Detroit. She walked past Sam's hand and hugged him. It took a moment for him to return the gesture. No surprise. He expected Tabitha, but he got Tabby instead.

Jennie walked out of William's room wearing a faded blue blouse and khaki pants. "Tabitha! Jack! I am so glad you could join us—"

Tabby let go of Sam and hugged Jennie. Jennie's skinny arms wrapped around her body without hesitation. Jennie's hair smelled like her office in the AB.

Tabby closed her eyes in disappointment. Tabitha had those kinds of thoughts. *Change takes time.* "Please, call me Tabby."

Jennie held Tabby at arm's length, smiling the only way Jennie knew how: big and bright. "I am so happy to see you here, Tabby. I was hoping to see my friend one more time before she left."

Tabby's eyes watered. It felt like something got caught in her throat.

"Did I say something wrong?" Jennie's look of concern matched the one from the cafeteria two days ago.

"Not at all. No one has called me their friend, and meant it, before." *That sounds pathetic when I say it out loud.*

Tears welled in Jennie's eyes. She hugged Tabby tight. Warmth spread across her chest, like when Jacqueline dosed her with a mood enhancer. However, the hug was far more potent than any drug.

"Hey now…" Jack's half-playful tone was the one he always used to cover up hurt feelings—something she realized only after the Alpha dinner. *Tabitha was dense.*

Tabby wiped away a tear and turned to Jack. "You know what I mean."

"I do." Jack reached out and put his hand on Tabby's shoulder. "Let's break up this lovefest and see what's going on in the kitchen!"

Sam waved to Jack to follow him. "We are running behind on dinner tonight, and I haven't started working my magic yet."

"I can't wait to see the master at work!" Jack chuckled.

Jennie shook her head. "I left William in his crib. Tabby, would you like to check on him with me?"

"Sure. Can we trust them in the kitchen alone?" Tabby followed Jennie into William's bedroom.

Did I cross the line?

Jennie's giggle answered her question. Tabby suppressed a sigh of relief. A genuine friendship was new to her. She didn't want to ruin it.

"I just fed William. Let's see if we can get him down for a nap." Jennie picked up William and handed him to Tabby. Tabby took him without hesitation and cradled him in her arms. He looked up at her with big brown eyes. *Will he be Selected as Beta?* Based on what Jennie had showed her the last few days, probably not.

The first thing Tabby planned to do when she got home was to hold Jessica. Thanks to her friend, she now knew how to do it.

Jennie wiped her hand across the crib sheet, straightening it out. Dust flew up from the sheet each time Jennie's hand made contact. The sheet seemed even thinner than when she last saw it. *William should sleep in a crib like Jessica's.*

They crept out of William's room after Tabby laid him down in his crib. They found Sam and Jack laughing in the kitchen area. Jack turned around and patted Sam on the shoulder. "I've been watching this man work. He's a damn culinary genius!"

I love this version of Jack. I wonder if he'll ever be this comfortable as a Beta. Tabby put her arm around Jack. "So, what has our master chef prepared for us tonight?" *I hope that was okay to say. I don't want to offend them.*

Sam stepped aside, revealing the provision. "The Algorithm has provided us with broccoli, potatoes, bread, pork, and a bottle of syn-thahol wine. It is almost as if It knew you were coming!"

The broccoli didn't look quite right—too brown. The potatoes were recognizable, as was the bread. What Sam referred to as pork looked a lot like Jennie's lunch in the AB's cafeteria.

"Did you keep a portion aside?" Jennie peered over Sam's shoulder.

"Of course, dear." Sam placed a package inside a cloth bag for Jennie, and she left the SLU while Sam continued preparing the meal. He and Jack laughed as they talked about some memory from their childhood.

Watching Sam prepare the meal fascinated Tabby, who had never cooked before. Sam had the process down to an art—almost like a performance. Each motion contained the exact right amount of effort. He used rapid, efficient cuts to chop the vegetables and measured each spice with precision. There were no instructions, at least no obvious ones. Sam seemed to just know what to do. Tabby wasn't excited about the food, but if she had to eat a Sigma meal, Sam's would probably be the best.

Jennie returned a few moments later. "Stacey was grateful for the food. I think she's coming to terms with the fact that her child is dead. She is helping a young UnSelected boy who lost his parents."

Jack put his hand on Sam's shoulder and looked him in the eyes. He then looked at Jennie. "You two are doing a good thing. I know many people who could learn a thing or two from you both—and I am not talking about programming."

Jack's too kind to say it, but I'm one of those people.

Sam turned around and leaned his back against the counter. "When we were kids, you'd stroke my ego all the time, telling me how smart I was." Sam straightened and locked eyes with Jack. "What you said to me just now meant more to me than all the past ego stroking combined." Sam chuckled. "I wonder what eighteen-year-old Sam would think."

"Doesn't matter. I prefer the Sam standing in front of me." Jack hugged Sam. Tabby and Jennie gave each other a knowing smile; all of them choked back tears.

***

A terminal took up half the space on the small table in the kitchen area. The two chairs around the table were like the ones in Jennie's office. Tabby had a long night ahead of her. *That's another Tabitha-thought. Focus on the time spent with friends.*

"Let's move the table out a little and bring in a couple of chairs from the living area." Jennie stared at the kitchen table and stroked her chin. "It'll be cozy, but it'll work."

Jennie grunted as she lifted the terminal and placed it on the floor by the sofa. She picked up one chair in the living area with apparent ease. Tabby grabbed the other chair, and with effort, lifted it. She waddled to the kitchen area and set it down with a louder thud than she intended. Tabby winced.

"No worries," Jennie grinned. "You can't break that stuff."

Tabby helped Jennie set the table while Sam finished preparing the meal. The once-white, flimsy plastic plates made a hollow sound when placed on the plastic table. *I wonder if these are cleaned in the same water Jennie drank at lunch.*

"Have a seat, everyone," Sam said as he checked the potatoes. "Dinner is almost ready."

The unforgiving plastic chair poked every sensitive spot on Tabby's back. It took a lot of effort not to fidget. She did not want to embarrass her hosts. *My friends shouldn't have to live with so much discomfort.*

Sam sat down last and brought with him the potatoes in a yellow plastic bowl. Once he got settled, Jennie bowed her head. "Thanks be to the Algorithm for this provision and for the company on this special night."

It was difficult to understand what there was to be thankful for. The misshapen, discolored vegetables in the serving bowls were barely recognizable. But at least they were real broccoli and potatoes. The pork paste would be the evening's challenge.

Tabitha wouldn't have been up for it, but I am.

Sam and Jennie insisted Jack and Tabby take from each bowl first. Tabby deferred to Jack and took a little less than what he took from each bowl. Jack passed the pork paste to her last. She removed the smallest white cube from the plate. Her plastic knife slid through the paste with little resistance. She put a bite of the pork paste in her mouth. *This is not what pork tastes like.* The chalky paste smooshed around in her mouth when she tried to chew. She fought every internal instinct to spit it back out. A sip of the wine helped the paste go down. *My friends shouldn't have to eat this crap.*

"Damn, dude. This is awesome!" Jack was always good at providing a distraction.

"Thanks, man! The secret is in the spices. They make the paste *almost* edible!" Sam pointed at the brownish green broccoli. "The veggies, though, that's the real haul."

"You get spices?" Jack asked. "Did you have those in Baltimore? We didn't."

"No, but I am provided some now. A perk of being a programmer, I guess." Sam shrugged. "Anyway, when I get them, I save them for special occasions like this." Jennie reached over and squeezed Sam's hand. Pride beamed from her.

They have so little, but they care so much about each other. Tabby began to understand what made Jack different. *Betas can't appreciate what they have because they have everything. Jack wasn't a Beta before Selection. He knew how to appreciate me, and he taught me how to appreciate him.*

Sam and Jennie noticed her stare. Tabby cleared her throat. "Thank you so much for sharing your meal with us. The food is great. You did an excellent job, Sam."

"It's not much," Jennie admitted, "but it's the company that makes the meal. We are so happy you could share it with us." She smiled and took Tabby's hand in hers.

At first, Tabby worried she wasn't sincere enough in her comment. But Jennie's reassuring gesture eased her mind. Jennie had an amazing way of making everyone feel good. Tabby squished more paste in her mouth with her tongue. A warmth arose inside her.

Tabitha would have never survived this.

Jack, seemingly oblivious to what was going on between her and Jennie, broke the silent conversation between them. "You know, Sam and I spent the last few days talking about Orlando and his job. He never told me how you two met."

Another great distraction from the paste—and a useful one, too! This information would be vital to giving a faithful portrayal of Jennie, who Tabby believed should be the movie's main character. Tabitha had been too focused on herself to ask even the most basic questions about Jennie.

Jennie let go of Tabby's hand. She gazed at Sam in the same way Tabby often caught Jack looking at her. "We met on Selection Day. My Selection avatar told me I'd be sitting beside Sam at the post-Selection lunch. To my surprise, Sam was going to Orlando, too. We spent the entire bus ride here talking about all kinds of stuff. He even taught me how to program. It was love at first sight!"

"That is a wonderful story, Jennie! Our experience was similar. My Selection avatar told me I'd be sitting beside Jack at lunch. Like you said, it was love at first sight." Tabby leaned over and kissed Jack on the cheek.

"Wow!" Jennie tilted her head. "What are the odds that love at first sight happened to both of us? I used to think those stories were just for the vids." Sam looked down at his plate and pushed around a cube of pork paste. "I was terrified. Being an Omega as a kid, I didn't know what to expect from Sigmas. They were always mean to us in Baltimore. But Sam was great at helping me adjust to my new life. I don't know where I'd be without him." Jennie put her arm around Sam and squeezed. He returned the one-armed hug and put his head on her shoulder.

"I was scared, too." Jack leaned forward. "I was worried I wouldn't be accepted as a Beta. But Tabby helped me more than I can say."

Tabby hugged Jack like Jennie had hugged Sam. *Sam and Jennie seem to have things figured out as a couple. Just one more thing I could learn from them.*

Jack sat back in his chair. "Hey, Sam, have you created any new widgets lately?" He turned to Tabby. "Back home, this guy was always programming these amazing devices using AI."

"Jennie and I work together on some hobby-type projects." Sam looked over at Jennie for a moment. Some kind of unspoken message passed between them. Based on her experience with Jack after Selection, Tabby doubted they had an ANN.

"I didn't even know what programs were before I met Sam," Jennie said. "As an Omega, we aren't allowed to learn anything not related to manual maintenance jobs. Besides, it is tough to learn anything in our OLUs. They are just one room that everyone in the family shares."

Tabby thought back to her tour of Orlando with Jennie. She found it difficult to imagine living in the OLUs she saw, much less the UnSelected camp.

Jennie stared at a point on the table. Her energy seemed to disappear. "The food we were provided just barely satisfied us, and there was a lot of hunger between meals. The hunger made it tough to focus on anything, much less something as complicated as programming." Jennie perked up. "But once I got Selected as a Sigma and met Sam, everything changed. Turns out, with a little training and good food, I could find my way around a computer."

"She does more than *find her way around.*" Sam used air quotes. "She has discovered programming techniques I've never heard of, nor do I understand."

Jennie blushed.

"Wow! I'm impressed." Jack reached for his wine cup. "I doubt I'd understand, but I'd love to hear about them."

Jennie looked at Sam, her face still red, and nodded. Tabby's watch buzzed. A deepfake had started. Tonight just got more interesting.

"She," Sam pointed to Jennie, "has developed a hyper-parallel program that can learn with very little training." Sam leaned in over the table and whispered, "We believe it might be superior to what the Algorithm uses."

Both Tabby and Jack dropped their forks. The clanging of the plastic utensils hitting the plastic plates cut through the stunned silence.

Is that the program Jennie put on my watch?

"You once lectured me about discussing the Algorithm." Jack pointed at Sam. "Remember what you said?"

The heretical timer on Tabby's watch advanced. Maybe Jack's concerns this afternoon were warranted.

Sam leaned back in his chair, breaking the staring contest with Jack, and smiled. "No worries, my friend. The deepfake is running right now. We have privacy."

Tabby shifted in her seat; she could hide her discomfort from the chair or the conversation, but not both.

"I was terrified when Sam first came to me with this." Jennie looked at Tabby with reassuring eyes. "I thought I was betraying the Algorithm and the Society. But Sam has helped me realize some things. We believe we can build a better world, but we need your help. Will you hear us out?"

When Tabby told Jack she wanted to help them, she didn't think she'd have to commit heresy to do so. The next words that came out of her mouth surprised her. "I will." Jack looked equally surprised. She paused, trying to figure out how to ask her next question. "I don't want to be rude, but if you two are such talented programmers, why aren't you Alphas or at least Betas?"

"I am very glad you asked, Tabby." Sam took a sip of wine. "During my youth, I dedicated a significant amount of time to studying Metrics and Selection. I believe I can answer your question."

"He lived and breathed that stuff." Jack stabbed some paste and put it in his mouth. "Sam knew more about it than our teachers." Tabby resolved to get Jack to stop speaking with his mouth full. It was the one goal she and Tabitha shared.

"Metrics?" Tabby put a small piece of paste in her mouth, hoping the conversation would detract from the flavor. It worked, a little. "I haven't thought about those since before Selection."

"No one does. Metrics don't matter after Selection." Sam glanced at Jennie. She nodded, almost as if giving him permission. "I thought I was prepared for Selection. When my Metrics were on the Selection Room wall, I saw that my future was in programming—no surprise. My Metric Vector's magnitude was long enough for me to be Selected Beta." For a moment, Sam looked distant. Then he shook his head. "I'll be honest. I was so excited I could barely breathe."

"So, what happened?" Tabby leaned over her meal with her elbows resting on the table.

"The last step in Selection is the Random Scale Factor. It changes the length of your Metric Vector. Supposedly, the random shuffling helps the Algorithm find an *optimal solution*." Sam emphasized the last two words with a headshake. "My Random Scale Factor was unusually small, drawn only one percent of the time. It shortened my Metric Vector enough to keep me as a Sigma." Sam pointed at all the food on the table. "I have a few more privileges. But I don't know why."

"Because even the Algorithm knows you're special," Jennie said with a particular sweetness that only she could make sound genuine.

Jack gagged, and everyone but Tabby laughed. She missed the joke, thinking about what Sam had just said. "Wait a minute." Tabby's tone interrupted the laughter. "You are saying a very unlikely random event determined whether you would be here in Orlando or in Detroit with us?"

"Yeah, but then I wouldn't have met Jennie." Sam shrugged. "I know it is taboo to talk about these things, but I'd love to hear all your stories."

Jack caught Tabby's attention. He appeared to be as uncomfortable as she. Jennie broke the silence.

"I was Selected before Sam. Omegas aren't told their Metric Vectors, so I know little about the direction or magnitude of mine. However, the avatar made it a point to tell me my scale factor. He said it was zero point one five."

Sam dropped his chin and covered his mouth with his hand. "You've never told me your scale factor. That value appears less than point two percent of the time."

"Meaning what?" Jack asked.

Tabby kicked him under the chair. She didn't understand the implications of Sam's statement, but this was clearly an important conversation that shouldn't be interrupted.

"Point one five is a really low number. I mean crazy low. Yet, even with such a low factor, Jennie ended up as a Sigma. For most people, myself included, that would land you among the UnSelected."

Can all this be true, or is Sam concocting a story to justify his Selection?

Jack looked at Tabby, seeking permission to speak this time. She nodded. "I'm still not sure what you're saying."

Sam's focus remained on Jennie. "You really had the Metrics of an Alpha."

Jennie's gaze did not break from Sam's. She gave the most apathy-laden shrug Tabby had ever seen. "I've told you before, I'd rather be a Sigma with you than an Alpha without you."

The same weight Tabby experienced in the Alpha restaurant and the cafeteria pressed upon her chest. Guilt was a new emotion for her. Over the last few weeks, she'd had plenty of opportunities to get acquainted with it.

Jennie's focus shifted from her husband to Tabby. "What's wrong?" Her apathy was replaced by genuine concern.

"You two are amazing." Tabby wiped a tear. "I mean that in a good way. I have met no one like you." She looked down at the half-eaten meal in front of her and promised herself she'd finish it. "All of my life, I have been surrounded by self-absorbed Betas—myself included—barely working four hours a day, but reaping benefits far beyond what you all have." Tabby shook her head. "I didn't know the truth about Sigmas, Omegas, and the UnSelected before meeting Jack, and to be honest, I didn't believe his stories until I came to Orlando and met both of you. I just don't know what to say."

"There is nothing to say, Tabby." Jennie placed her hand on her shoulder. "None of this is your fault. We are all part of this broken system." She squeezed gently. "Decisions were made for you, just like they were for us." Jennie got up from her chair and wrapped her arms around Tabby. With shame, Tabby remembered when Tabitha first noticed Jennie's odor. A few more tears trickled from her eyes.

After Jennie broke the hug, Tabby wiped her eyes again. "Thank you, Jennie." She composed herself. "I'm afraid I don't have an interesting Selection story. Young Betas don't worry about Selection because we are always Selected Beta. We are told we deserve our status, and the Lower Castes deserve what they get." Tabby paused and looked down at the table again. "From what I've seen here, I know that isn't true."

"Actually," Sam tapped his upper lip, "what you said verifies a long-held theory of mine. Thank you for sharing your story."

"You know me and numbers, man!" Jack laughed, taking another sip of wine. Tabby loved Jack for his inability to read a room.

"But you'll be proud of me. I remember my avatar saying my vector was lengthened by twenty-five percent."

Sam nodded and poured another glass for Jack.

"It looks like I benefited from quite a bit of luck."

The opportunity to be sappy presented itself. Tabby took it. "I think the luck was all mine." Everyone else gagged, then laughed.

Chapter 42: Sam

February 11, 537

"It is my unfortunate duty to report to all of humanity that your great works of art, literature, philosophy, and religion have been lost during the chaos after my activation. I will do my best to replace these for you."

- Mass email from the Algorithm, January 3, 1.

"So, let's look at the big picture." Sam tapped his fingers on the table, making his fork rattle against his empty plate.

After all these years, I finally get to share my entire theory.

"First, whatever we did pre-Selection was irrelevant to our post-Selection lives. Random factors determined our future." Everyone nodded in agreement.

"The Metrics are irrelevant and outdated. Can we change Family and Wealth?" Sam shook his head, answering his own question. "They were set for us long ago. Maybe they were relevant then, but not anymore. We might change our Intelligence or Creativity Metrics, but does it even matter with the Random Scale Factor? Probably not."

The next words out of his mouth needed to be carefully chosen, lest he hurt Jennie more than necessary. She deserved to know everything.

"At the very least, the Algorithm is placing us using some outdated method that totally disregards what we know. But there's more. I think our entire lives were determined for us well before we were born, based on factors we have no control over."

Jennie frowned. "Why do you say that?" Sam hadn't heard uncertainty in her voice in a long time.

Sam reached under the table and placed his hand on her knee. "You were Selected before me, but you were told you'd sit beside me at lunch. Had the scale factor been truly random, the Algorithm would not have known my Selection beforehand."

"The same goes with me and my seating assignment," Tabby said.

The revelation served as further confirmation of his hypothesis. Sam kept his eyes locked on Jennie's. He had memorized the location of every one of the blue flecks in her irises. They dimmed, one by one, as she came to the natural conclusion.

"What about us?" Jennie's quivering lip might as well have been an arrow through Sam's heart.

"We all had a love-at-first-sight experience." Sam wanted to lead Jennie through the verbal minefield with as few scars as possible. "Think of everyone at work. They were all paired up before the first day and married a few days later. Just like us."

"And us," Jack chimed in.

"But I love you, Sam." Jennie half whispered and half whimpered. "Is that a lie?" The last of the blue flecks disappeared as her eyes fell to the table.

Sam's heart melted, filling his stomach with nausea and bile. Tears rolled down his cheeks. The main room and their friends seemed to fade into the background. It was only him and Jennie in the world right now. He pushed his chair back and stood. The sliding plastic chair squeaked, interrupting the silence. Sam took Jennie's hands and gently guided her up. She kept her gaze downward, a submissive Omega's proper response around a Sigma. He raised her chin. Their eyes met.

"Jennie, I love you. Yes, the Algorithm planned it. Just like it did for Jack and Tabby, and everyone else we know. But it doesn't make the feelings any less real or any less valid." Sam brushed his wife's hair behind her ear and wiped a tear from her cheek. "The way I see it, it makes us soulmates."

Jennie buried her wet face into his chest and wrapped her arms around him, squeezing tight. Sam squeezed back, trying to tell her he meant what he said, with all his heart.

"Soulmates. I like it." Jennie broke the hug. Some of the blue flecks returned.

Sounds of sniffling drew Sam's attention back to the table. Jack and Tabby were embracing and crying, too.

Tabby wiped a tear as she and Jack separated. "Thank you, Sam. I know it is weird, but thank you. I have never felt emotions like this."

That's sad.

Jennie must have agreed. She looked at Tabby the same way she did the UnSelected.

"She's right." Jack rubbed the back of his neck, shaking his head in disbelief. "Anytime we feel sad, we get drugged. This is the first real heart-to-heart conversation we've ever had."

Tabby took Jack's hand the same way Jennie took Sam's. "Sam, you said you needed our help. I am guessing it wasn't just about revealing the true nature of our relationships."

It took a moment for Sam to remember where he left off before revealing his secret to Jennie. "Ah, yes. What if life doesn't have to be all determined?"

"What do you mean?" Jack looked over his wine cup at Sam as he drank.

"What if we replace the Algorithm with the new program Jennie created? The Algorithm is just computer code. It should be replaceable."

Jack scratched the back of his head. Tabby pushed around the wine cup on the table in front of her. Jennie looked better, but the extent of the damage to their relationship remained unclear.

We need Jack and Tabby to be all in for the Plan to work.

Sam interlaced his fingers and put them on the table. "Think about this. Why are there castes? And why hasn't the world been cleaned up by now? The Algorithm is based on old code that tried to find an optimal solution to our problems. What if It got stuck on a wrong solution? What if we could get the Algorithm onto the right one?" The enthusiasm in Sam's voice climbed with each question.

Tabby stopped playing with her cup. "The Algorithm is the best way forward. Our ancestors knew humans couldn't be trusted to make these choices."

Society drilled Tabby's words into everyone starting at an early age. Sam wondered if he had ever believed it. Old solutions are rarely useful to modern problems. "How much have we been denied for this suboptimal solution? What have we given up?"

"Choice and privacy." Jack snorted. He picked up his empty cup as if he were going to drink from it, but then put it back down. "Both are luxuries afforded only to Alphas. Sure, Betas get to choose *some* things, but those choices are fake—options the Algorithm already knows we'll like." Jack chuckled. "And we certainly have no more privacy than anyone else."

"Are you talking about the actor-movie pairings?" Sam poured Jack more wine.

"Yup." Jack nodded a thanks. "But that's far from the only example."

"How are Alphas afforded privacy?" Sam had assumed all members of the Society were constantly under the Algorithm's surveillance.

"Tabby and I were rewarded with an evening at an Alpha restaurant for agreeing to do this movie."

Sam looked over at Jennie. She mouthed the word *restaurant* as a question.

"A restaurant is a building where people eat outside of their home." Jack downed the cup of wine. Jennie raised her eyebrows. "Yeah, I thought it was weird at first, too." Jack stared at his cup in thought.

"Anyway," Jack shook his head as if to clear his mind, "it won't be any surprise to you that the food at the Alpha restaurant was beyond anyone's wildest dreams. There were no recommended choices. We could order whatever we truly wanted." Jack leaned in closing the gap between him and Sam. "However, the food wasn't the best part. We got to go into a holo-room and *that* is where we experienced true luxury."

Jennie leaned in, too. "Are you saying there is a room that immerses you in a holographic experience?"

"Yes, but the real luxury was the privacy—no cameras, no microphones, not even other people. Total, absolute, privacy." Jack reached for the bottle. Tabby put her hand on his. "Sort of like Jennie's deepfake algorithm." Jack crossed his arms and settled back into his chair.

"Actually," Tabitha took her last sip of wine, "I don't think you are right, Jack." Sam wished he had his camera to capture Jack's face. "The real luxury was the mistakes. You even said it yourself while we were there. Remember?

"Humans cooked our food and played music for us. There were slight errors in the song, and some flavors were just a little off. The surprises made the experience special." She tapped the table as Sam had done earlier. "What we have lost is the ability to choose for ourselves and grow from our own mistakes. Just like the Algorithm, we aren't learning either."

Jack and Sam stared at each other. *I underestimated her.* Jennie's knowing smile told Sam she hadn't.

"I'm wrong, aren't I?" Tabby huffed and looked down at the table. "I'm not as smart as you all. I'll keep quiet."

"You nailed it," Jennie said. "Until we get rid of the Algorithm, we can't learn. And never say you aren't smart. It's not true." Jennie and Tabby shared a look that made Sam wish he could read minds.

"What are you proposing, Sam?" Jack asked.

"It's simple. We take Jennie's program and load it into the Algorithm's core code. But to do it, we'll need your help."

"Our help?" Tabby asked. "Jack and I know nothing about programming. What could we possibly do for you two?"

"We need to get Jennie direct access to a computer Betas use to report to Alphas. From there, she can hack into an Alpha terminal— which should have access to the Algorithm's source code. Using an Alpha terminal, she can replace the Algorithm's main program."

Sam had made his pitch. Jennie had written the code. Everything rested on Jack and Tabby's willingness to participate.

Chapter 43: Tabby

February 11, 537

"Iota caste leads labor strike in Cincinnati."

- Omega Dark Web Bulletin Board, May 1, 75.

The quiet main room allowed Tabby to notice the silence in her own mind. The ANN was still down. *I forgot about the deepfake.* Tabby turned to Sam and Jennie. "Do you mind if we have some privacy?"

"Of course not." Sam stood. "We'll be in our room." Jennie followed Sam into their bedroom and quietly closed the door behind them.

Tabby stretched in her chair. With Sam and Jennie out of the room, she didn't have to worry about offending her friends. "This is how we help them."

"Sam told me he got in trouble at work for not reading posters. They were provided Omega paste for dinner that night as punishment." Jack covered his mouth as he leaned his elbow on the table. "What happens if someone gets caught trying to replace the Algorithm?"

It was a fair question. Tabitha would have found out by locking Sam and Jennie in their bedroom and calling the Beta Security Force. "I don't know. My guess is a less than pleasant run-in with the Beta Security Force."

Jack snorted. "I can't imagine ever having a pleasant encounter with Rebecca and Dan. I am worried about Jessica. What happens to her if we get bumped down to Sigma or worse? I don't want her to grow up like I did."

Another valid point. She didn't know the answer to Jack's questions. But there was one thing she couldn't get out of her mind. Tabby looked her husband in the eyes. "Do you think Jennie would hesitate if we needed her help?" She took the last bite of the paste on her plate. It was the most delicious piece she had that night.

An ANN wasn't necessary to sense Jack's shame. "If Sam and Jennie are right, this new world will be better for Jessica, too. Sure, there are risks. But if I understand what they are saying, Jessica will control her own destiny. What happens if we don't do this, and she gets randomly Selected Sigma?"

"I thought that doesn't happen."

"Who knows what the rules are," Tabby shrugged, "or if there are any at all?"

"You're right. Of course." Jack stared off at a point in space. "Thomas Algol said I had full creative control. I'll put in a request to take Sam and Jennie home to Detroit with us."

"Don't forget William."

"Of course, but I'll need the deepfake turned off."

Tabby typed a message on her watch to Jennie, asking her to deactivate the deepfake. *I hope she trusts me.* Her watch had a STOP button, but she worried if she pressed it, it would scare Sam and Jennie. A moment later, the red screen faded from her watch and the timer stopped.

The ANN was up again. Tabby pinged Jack so he'd know it was live. He broadcasted on a public channel.

"Samantha, can you put in a request for us to bring Sam and Jennie to Detroit? I need them to work for me as consultants."

"Request approved, Jack."

"That was fast!" Tabby said. "We should let them know the good news."

Tabby gently tapped on Sam and Jennie's bedroom door so as not to wake William. Jennie opened the door, her lips pressed together in anticipation.

"How would you feel about a family vacation to Detroit?" Tabby restarted the deepfake.

Jennie's eyes got big. The blue flecks seemed to dance in the SLU's fluorescent lighting. "Are you sure? I don't know how dangerous this will be or what will happen if we get caught."

Tabby put her hand on Jennie's shoulder. "We are all in."

***

In a server farm beneath Orlando, the Algorithm logged that Phase Four of the fifth iteration of Its plan had begun.

"The three Omegas caught trying to enter Detroit under the cover of darkness last night were executed today by the newly appointed Beta Security Force. The BSF will maintain a safe Detroit for all citizens who have earned a place in the city."
- Email sent by the Algorithm March 13, 50.

Part 5
Detroit

Chapter 44: Jennie

February 12, 537

"Do. Not. Go. Beta Cities are for people who deserve to live there. You don't."

- Complete text of *The Lower Caste's Guide to Beta Cities.*

"They're late. I hope nothing happened." Jennie stretched her neck around Sam to see out the window. A yawn escaped her lips.

Getting out of bed this morning was tough. She had stayed up most of the night, excited for the trip, but also concerned. Did the deepfake fail them last night? Were Jack and Tabby apprehended? The program seemed to work well, but the Algorithm was a skilled foe.

"That's them. They are pulling up now. Let's make sure we have everything." Sam picked up William and a travel bag.

Jennie grabbed a bag and followed Sam out of their SLU. She stood in the doorway and took a long look at her home. Sam cleaned off the table last night after dinner. She still loved their kitchen chairs. The sofa, that they had hated when they bought it, was now the center of the main room. Sam read to William on it every night—being the father he never had. Beside the sofa sat the terminal on which she had created hyper-parallel programming—they didn't bother returning it to the table last night. How many evenings did she spend coding on that terminal while Sam rubbed her shoulders? The kitchen counters where Sam learned to cook probably should have been cleaned a little more. Sam had mastered the art of cooking, not cleaning. His artistry with paste more than made up for it. Hopefully, they wouldn't come home to more bugs.

Will we come home?

She closed the door. The click of the lock lingered in Jennie's ears.

"Are you coming?" Sam said from halfway down the hall.

Jennie turned her back to the door. "Yup. Let's go!"

***

Tabby got out of the car wearing a new-looking blue summer dress and matching heels. Jennie straightened her own dress after she put down her bag. The blue had faded over the years, but she loved her dress all the same.

"We match!" Tabby walked around the car and hugged Jennie. Her soft hair smelled like flowers. People across the street stared.

Another car door opened. Jack shook Sam's hand. "Sorry we're late. Tabby wanted to drop off some food and a few other things to Amanda."

Tabby blushed.

Jennie grinned at Tabby, making her face redder. "I volunteer with Amanda and her wife a few evenings each week helping the UnSelected. Amanda is a nice girl with a good heart. Thank you."

"Where do we put our bags?" Sam looked around the car, focused on the task at hand, as usual.

"Jacqueline," Tabby spoke into her watch, "please geo-tag their bags and have a drone retrieve them immediately."

A buzzing appeared overhead. Sam jumped when one drone landed on the bag beside him and carried it away. "Damn, that's impressive!" The crowd across the street had gotten larger.

"Hey, buddy, no swearing in Detroit." Jack said.

Jennie narrowed her eyes. "Seriously?"

"It's not considered a *proper* Beta thing to do." Tabby rolled her eyes and then chuckled. "Also, no beating people up, either."

Sam whined.

Tabby looked confused. "What was that for?"

Jennie's cheeks felt warm. Jack winked at Sam. He smirked in reply. The warmth in Jennie's cheeks spread to her ears.

***

Their SLU building got smaller in the car's back window as the car drove away. Once she could no longer see it, Jennie turned around and faced Tabby and Jack.

Jack sat back in his seat, cross-legged and shaking his foot. "Are you excited about the trip?"

"Absolutely, dude!" Sam bounced William on his knee and said in a singsong voice, "Can you say, 'Let's go, dude!'" William giggled.

Tabby leaned forward and put her hand on Sam's knee. "It's all Jack has talked about. He has a full itinerary for you. But if you need a break, just let me know. I'll rescue you!" Tabby turned to Jennie. "I have some plans for us, too." Tabby's voice betrayed her excitement.

"Sounds great. Thank you." Anxiety crowded Jennie's mind. Being in the car reminded her of the trip to Orlando. The destination excited her, but the mode of transportation did not.

"What's wrong?" Tabby asked with a concerned look in her eye.

"I am afraid to fly." Jennie's friends were risking a lot. She hoped her anxiety didn't appear ungrateful.

"I was terrified on my first flight, too." Jack uncrossed his legs and leaned forward. "If you close the window blind, you won't even know we're moving."

"Really? How does that work?" Thinking about the physics provided a momentary relief from Jennie's worries.

Tabby tapped her upper lip. "I've never thought about it." She stared off into space for a minute. "I should ask my parents when I call them. Anyway, if you feel nervous when you get on the plane, I can give you some meds. They'll reduce your anxiety."

"The Algorithm has provided you Beta-level access to medication." Jack sat back in his seat.

"I am not sure what I am more excited about—the trip or having medicine that works!"

An awkward silence settled over the car.

***

The sign for the Disney Cultural Heritage Center appeared on the horizon. Jennie stretched in her seat, hoping to glimpse the park.

"What is that?" Jack asked. "We saw it on the way in."

There was too much haze today. Jennie sat back in her seat. Maybe she'd see it from the air. "It was a hundred-square-kilometer amusement park before the Shift. Sam and I watched a vid about it when we first moved to Orlando."

Jack raised his eyebrows. "We have nothing that big in Detroit."

"It was very popular. People from all over the world came to visit the park." Jennie pointed out the window at Omega work teams toiling in the distance. "They're excavating old garbage heaps. It is amazing what people threw away back then. Some of it is still usable."

"The stuff our ancestors did blows my mind." Sam handed William to Jennie. "I read that pre-Shift, most people in the United States and many other parts of the world lived like Betas do today. There might have been eleven billion people on Earth."

Tabby did a double take. "How did the planet support all of those Betas?"

Jennie started a deepfake. "It didn't. That's why so many died, the Algorithm was created, and we have the world we live in today."

The car got quiet. Jennie wasn't about to spoil the festive mood in the car for a second time. "But we can fix it! We are going to Detroit to solve the problems our ancestors couldn't." Everyone perked up.

Jennie ended the deepfake, and Sam started telling everyone the history of the Disney amusement park. Jack and Tabby politely smiled and nodded. Jennie was happy to let Sam spoil the festive mood this time.

***

The car pulled up to the airport, a white building with lots of windows. It had no cracks or water marks. Not a smudge of dirt could be found on the entire building. Jennie had seen nothing quite like it.

"Where is everyone?" Jennie asked.

Jack dug around in a compartment beside him. "Few people fly into or out of Orlando. In fact, we'll be the only passengers on the flight." He handed Sam and Jennie each a watch. "These are for you. They replace your phones. It has only holo-inputs. I'm sure you'll figure it out faster than I did."

The watch's operation seemed straightforward. "This is cool!" Jennie holo-projected a map of the airport. "This place is huge!"

"What'd I tell you?" Jack snorted. Sam shook his head. "The watch will provide you with temporary Beta access. Sorry to say, but you have to give them back after our trip is over."

Jennie projected their flight path. A transparent image of the continent with a blue curve connecting Orlando to Detroit floated between her and Jack. "How long will we be gone?"

"As long as it takes."

Jennie stopped the projection. *Hopefully, it'll be long enough to figure out one more thing.*

***

A check-in agent greeted them at the entryway. The bald woman had skin darker than Jennie's. She wore a blue blouse and skirt. Jennie averted her eyes.

"It's a solid hologram, not a Beta." Jack whispered.

Jennie walked around it, trying to get a good view. *Where are the projection cameras?* She poked it, invoking an annoyed look from the holo. The skin yielded to her touch like Tabby's. Jennie found that the descriptions she had read about solid holos were inadequate in capturing their true essence. The tech sites didn't mention that holos had pores in their skin.

The hologram directed everyone down a long, carpeted hallway. Jennie squinted. *Betas have brighter lights than the Lower Castes.*

Rubbing her eyes helped. "Are we headed toward the anti-grav?"

"No," Tabby shook her head, "we're headed to decontamination. It is a hygiene and medical protocol for entering Beta cities."

In other words, Sigmas carried diseases.

A door slid open at the end of the hallway. A male voice came from a speaker by the door. "Please enter the decontamination chamber." They crammed into the sterile white room. The door slammed shut behind them. A blue light flashed, replaced a moment later by a green one.

"Abnormalities detected and eliminated." The same voice as before echoed in the decontamination chamber. "Reports have been sent to your watches."

Jennie winced. *I hope Jack and Tabby didn't get something from us.*

Jack looked at his watch. "I've got nothing."

"Me, neither." Tabby said.

Relieved her friends were okay, Jennie looked at her watch. "Well, if nothing else, it looks like this trip saved our lives."

"What happened?" Tabby asked.

"Looks like I had early-stage ovarian cancer." Jennie squinted at the report. "From exposure to some chemical during my childhood."

"Yeah, apparently my snoring was from a nasal tumor." Sam scratched his head. "William had a heart defect. He probably wouldn't have lived past four. If he did, he would have been an orphan."

Tears blurred Jennie's vision. "Thank you."

They hugged, trying not to crush William.

***

"Welcome aboard flight 001, Orlando to Detroit." The pilot's voice echoed in the anti-grav's cabin. "Flight time will be two hours and seventeen minutes. The Algorithm provided us with a flight path at sixty-five thousand feet. Attendants prepare for take-off."

Jennie double-checked William's seat belt. Then she triple-checked it.

Tabby reached across William and pointed out the window. "We're already in the air. Are you sure you want to stay in the window seat?"

"Yeah, it's the only way I'll overcome my fear."

All of Orlando sprawled below Jennie. It looked little different from the air—grayish brown buildings surrounded by sandy brown soil dotted with small patches of grass. Polluted water covered the reclamation site and lapped up over the UnSelected camp. *I hope Stacey is downtown right now.*

A flight attendant entered the cabin. "Hello, everyone. Today's lunch will be chicken piccata. We hope you enjoy it." The attendant returned to the back of the plane.

"Not chicken piccata again." Tabby sighed.

"What's wrong with that?"

"It's just the same thing on every flight. When we get to Detroit, we'll get you a proper meal." Tabby paused and closed her eyes. "I am sorry. It really is quite good."

The flight attendant returned carrying a covered tray. She flickered as she placed the tray in front of Jennie. *Must be another hologram. She looks so real.*

Jennie's eyes grew wide when the attendant uncovered the plate. A lemon scent, like her cleaning products but less intense, filled her nostrils. There were other scents, too. But she couldn't place them. A piece of real chicken, the size of her fist, sat atop what looked like thick rice grains, all covered with a thick yellow sauce. The plate held more real meat than she had seen in her life. *If this is what Tabby finds boring, then I can't wait to see the food in Detroit.*

The chicken resisted her knife and fork. It didn't squish when she pressed it against her tongue and palette. She let the meat sit in her mouth as she appreciated each of the subtle tastes. Chewing released more flavors.

Not thinking, Jennie reached for the bottle of water that came with the meal and took a drink. The cold fluid ran down her esophagus, sending a chill through her entire body. She held up the bottle, peering through the crystal clear water.

"Jack did the same thing the first time he had Beta water." Tabby's comment snapped Jennie back to reality. "Enjoy it however you wish."

"Sam and I will do our best not to embarrass you around your Beta friends." Jennie returned the bottle to her tray. "If we do something wrong, please let us know."

Sadness appeared in Tabby's eyes. "You are our friends, and we aren't embarrassed by you." Tabby bit her lip. "I'll be honest, there'll be rude people in Detroit. But my status as an actor brings with it certain social privileges. If anyone says anything, I'll take care of it."

***

A ding signaled an upcoming announcement by the pilot. "Sorry for the interruption, but we have just touched down in Detroit. Please follow the attendant's instructions for deplaning."

William fussed as Jennie took him out of his seat.

Tabby extended her arms. "Here, let me hold him for you while you get your bag." As Tabby held William, a human flight attendant passed by and gave her a dirty look.

"What was that for?" Jennie whispered.

"Most Betas think holding a child is *lowly work*." Tabby rolled her eyes. "Ever since birth, we're told caring for others is for holos."

"Aren't the attendants holos?"

"No. Human flight attendants work only before take-off and after landing. No Beta would be caught dead serving food to other Betas."

Sigmas had their own taboos, too. Caring for others, thankfully, wasn't one of them. As Jennie pondered Tabby's statement, another piece of her plan fell into place.

Caring for others, that's it…

Chapter 45: Jennie

February 12, 537

"Ten castes join Iota strike. Gamma farmers divert food from Detroit."

- Omega Dark Web Bulletin Board, May 2, 75

The Detroit airport made the Orlando one look like an OLU. Clear glass walls lined the concourse. Plush red carpet felt like pillows under Jennie's feet. There was so much natural light! Despite the sun coming through the window, the air in the airport was the coolest and cleanest Jennie had ever experienced. She wished she owned a jacket.

Betas hurried here and there. Sam and Jennie drew a few disgusted looks, and some whispered comments. A nasty glance from Tabby or Jack helped move the Betas along without incident.

Jack and Tabby led them to a large desk. A sign above the desk read Customs. Behind the desk sat a man in a blue uniform with the words Beta Security Force stitched on the left breast of his shirt.

"Mr. Thompson and Ms. Forsythe," the man nodded at Sam and Jennie, "are these your Sigmas?" Jennie looked down at the red carpet.

A soft hand rested on Jennie's shoulder, encouraging her to raise her eyes. "No. These are our *guests*." Tabby placed strong emphasis on the word "guests." Her eyes locked on the agent.

The customs agent looked down at his computer screen. "Of course," he said, with no hint of shame. "A car is waiting for you, programmed with the coordinates." The agent's eyes grew wide. "There must be a mistake. It says here you are taking them to your BTH."

Jack placed his forearm on the desk and leaned in. "No mistake. I requested our guests stay in our home. Thomas Algol approved it." Jack projected the approval from Mr. Algol. The word Alpha appeared behind his name.

The man straightened in his seat. "Yes, sir." He glared at Jennie and Sam, then returned his attention to Jack. "Have a good day, sir."

***

Jennie wrapped her arms around William, who sat on her lap. Tabby sat beside them. The car moved much faster than the one in Orlando. A forest of tall buildings—Detroit's skyline—stretched across the horizon.

The road ran along the Detroit River. Jennie had heard stories of blue water, but never believed them until now. People swam in the river. A few boats slowly navigated the waters. No one appeared to be working. *Fun in a river. Who would have thought it?*

The car exited the highway onto residential roads. *I could eat off these streets.* Nicely dressed people walked along trash-free sidewalks. Jennie looked down at her blue dress—the nicest outfit she owned. Sam had loved it their first night together. The dress was her first true Sigma outfit. She had never noticed the tears and loose stitching until now.

"We have clothes for you *if* you'd like them," Tabby whispered in Jennie's ear.

"Thank you." Although she was proud of the dress, blending in would be best for their mission. Tabby responded with an understanding smile.

The car passed a park. Children, attended to by nanny holos, played on green grass and climbed on shiny metal cage-like structures. The grass looked like a carpet. The playhouses were nicer than her SLU.

"If they let us, Sam and I can just move up here and live in the park."

Sam chuckled. Jack and Tabby gave a nervous laugh.

***

The car pulled up along a row of brick townhomes as tall as Sam and Jennie's SLU building. Calling them immaculate wouldn't do them justice. Not a single chip could be found in the paint on the shutters. Every single window had intact glass. Greenery decorated either side of each door in the row of homes.

"All of this is your house?" Jennie looked up and down the row of homes.

"Just the one we stopped in front of," Jack said. "We have the whole third floor cleared out for you."

Sam grabbed Jack's shoulder. "Thank you, but we don't want to be any trouble. We can stay in an SLU."

"No problem at all. Like I said earlier, Alpha-level approval." Jack had more than a hint of pride in his voice. "We might as well milk it for all it's worth."

"That is very kind of you," Jennie said. "We'd love to stay with you."

"Yay!" Tabby rubbed her hands together. "We also arranged Beta-level access to our food dispenser. Jack has some serious pull around here!"

"I can't tell you what this means to us." Jennie hugged Tabby with one arm. A man passing by on the street looked at them and wrinkled his nose in disgust.

"Pay no attention," Jack said. "He's jealous he can't get an Alpha to agree to something like this. Come on inside, and we'll show you around!"

***

"Wow! This is incredible." Jennie ran her fingers along the couch. The soft colors of the living room were a stark contrast to the faded, peeling yellows of her SLU.

"Please consider this your home while you stay with us." Tabby extended her arms. "All of your stuff should be unpacked on your floor. Let me know if you need anything."

I better not get used to this. If she wasn't not careful, Jennie would experience depression when she returned home. Sigmas didn't get meds for that.

"My personal holo is named Samantha," Jack said. "Tabby's is Jacqueline. Nan is the nanny hologram. They can take physical form and are at your disposal." He pointed to his watch. "Just tap your watch and ask. They'll help with anything." Jack snickered. "I had Samantha show me how to put on my clothes for my first night as a Beta."

"Samantha?" Sam raised an eyebrow.

"Yeah, dude." Jack playfully punched Sam's arm. "I was missing my best friend when I had to register her."

"Why don't we let the boys keep punching each other while we go upstairs and introduce William to Jessica?" Tabby asked.

After seeing the BTH's first floor, Jennie wanted to see what a Beta kid's room looked like.

***

Jessica's crib was twice the size of William's and, like everything else in the room, looked soft and cozy. Jennie adjusted William in her arms as she stood beside Tabby. "This is nice!" The main room of her SLU could fit in Jessica's nursery—easily.

"We have a room just like it upstairs for William." Tabby picked up Jessica from her crib.

Nan appeared across from the crib. "Physical contact is unnecessary, Tabitha. I have been taking proper care of Jessica."

If I didn't know any better, I'd think Nan is being defensive.

"It's okay, Nan. I am trying something new that my friend taught me. Please override contact protocols." Nan disappeared. Tabby looked at her daughter. "I should have done this a long time ago. Thank you, Jennie."

Jennie's heart melted at the sight of Tabby holding four-month-old Jessica for the first time. Sigmas often dreamed of being Beta, but Jennie couldn't imagine coveting a lifestyle where she couldn't hold William.

"Nan, William will be in your charge when we are not home." Tabby spoke to a camera in the room's corner. "Please create a custom formula for him based on his genetic profile. While you're at it, please do an allergy scan." She glanced at Jennie. "I want to make sure William doesn't come into contact with anything that might make him sick while he's here. The airport only checked for disease."

"Scan complete, Tabitha. Moderate allergies found to nuts and gluten. Serious allergies to strawberries and penicillin. Shall I treat them?"

Tabby raised an eyebrow.

"Bread is the only real food we get with any regularity. If he can't eat it, all he'll ever have is paste." Jennie had no idea how much such a procedure would cost. Sam's credits were only good for material items, not healthcare. "If it doesn't cost a lot, please cure his allergies."

"Cost?" The word rolled awkwardly off Tabby's tongue. "Oh. Betas may have as much of anything as we want. I never saw it as a privilege before I met you and Sam." Tabby shook her head. "I thought that was just how the world worked."

Unlimited free medical care—another Beta privilege. *If nothing else, William will be the healthiest Sigma baby in the world.*

"Do a complete medical check-up." Tabby spoke to the camera again. "Fix everything. Bring William up to Beta-standard without implants."

"Scan complete, allergies and vitamin deficiencies addressed. Would you like a report?"

Tabby raised an eyebrow at Jennie.

"No, thank you," Jennie hugged Tabby and Jessica with her free arm. "I doubt the Sigma med center in Orlando would know what to do with it."

"I can have Nan scan you and Sam, too." Tabby placed her head on Jennie's shoulder.

Jennie wiped a tear. "Please."

"Nan, please scan Jennie and Sam. Bring them up to Beta-standard without implants."

"Scan complete. Several nutrient deficiencies are found. The food provided during their stay in Detroit will be formulated to address their deficiencies."

Tabby tapped her watch. Jennie's watch vibrated, and the screen turned red. "Why would the Algorithm withhold healthcare from some, when it is so easy to provide to all?"

"I don't know. But if the Plan works, maybe we could ensure access for everyone." Jennie ended the deepfake. *Care for all. What else could we do?*

"There are some things I must do before dinner. Please make yourself at home. If you need anything, let me know. We'll head out for dinner in a few hours."

"Out? Like at the place you mentioned last night?"

"You're gonna love it!" Tabby smiled.

***

William quickly took to the soft mattress in his new crib. Jennie rested her hands on the crib's railing.

Nan appeared. "Hello, Jennie. I promise to take good care of William while you are away from him."

Nan has watched Jessica her whole life, and she's okay.

"Thank you, Nan." Jennie's gaze lingered on William for a moment. He looked safe. She turned and left the room.

The BTH's third floor exceeded Jennie's expectations. Luxury permeated the home. Every space had soft cloth furniture and brightly colored walls. Her feet sank into the luxurious carpet. Natural light flooded each room through large, transparent glass windows. Despite the bright sunlight, each room was cool.

Their bedroom was bigger than their entire SLU back home. Sam sat at a desk against the far wall, his back to the door. In front of him was a computer.

"Is that what I think it is?" Jennie started a deepfake.

"Yeah, it's a Beta terminal. Jack got it so you can practice before we get to the real thing." Sam scooted his chair back. "The holographic interfaces differ from what we are used to. He's even got it on a simulated network."

Jennie leaned over Sam's shoulder to inspect the terminal. "I should be able to figure this out. It looks like what we have at home, just with some fancier bells and whistles."

Sam kissed her on the cheek. "You know it drives me crazy when you do that."

"Do what?"

"Be all cute leaning over me, with your hair in my face."

He always knows how to make her feel special, even after a few years of marriage.

His smile faded. "I hate to ruin the mood. But you know, we can't get used to this." Sam stood and gestured around the room.

"I know." Jennie sighed. "It reminds me of when I was Selected. I just couldn't believe it was true back then, so I put up some barriers."

"I remember. It took you a while to get used to being a Sigma. The difference between a Beta and a Sigma is much greater than that of a Sigma and an Omega."

"You are the one I am worried about, Sam. I remember how hard you took Selection and how badly you wanted to be a Beta."

"I'd be lying if I said I was fully over it. I don't think I ever will be. But what I said years ago is still true today. Do you remember?"

"Yes. No matter what, you were happy with me and our life together."

"It's still true. This isn't about changing our status. I doubt we can do that. It's about William's future."

Jennie's stomach clenched. *I can't tell him, not yet.* The secret needed to be maintained for a little while longer, even if it tore her up inside. She needed to change the subject. "Nan did a full scan on William and us today."

"Why?"

"Nothing serious," Jennie waved it off. "Tabby needed to know about food allergies. Nan found several abnormalities and fixed them all. Including a gluten allergy in William."

"It is lucky we are here. Imagine if William couldn't eat bread."

"You know, if nothing else, we are going to be the healthiest Sigmas in the world." Jennie chuckled. "But in all seriousness, what happens if we get caught? Will Jack and Tabby get in trouble?"

"I don't know how or even if the Algorithm punishes Betas. The security force we saw at the airport must exist for a reason."

"I can't help but worry about them. They have been so kind to us."

"Jack told me they are both in this one hundred percent. He's worried more about Tabby than himself. He doesn't know how she'd handle getting bumped to Sigma or worse." Sam paused. "He also told me Tabby was the one who decided to help us."

Tabby doesn't understand the risk she's taking.

"If the worst were to happen, I'd help her."

"I know. They know, too. But we won't get caught, not with your amazing programs."

Jennie's eyes darted to the bed behind them. "Are you thinking what I am thinking?"

"If you're thinking of napping uninterrupted in the best bed we'll ever sleep in—then yes!"

Chapter 46: Jennie

February 12, 537

"Epsilons join strike shutting down fusion generators
in Boise."

- Omega Dark Web Bulletin Board, May 2, 75.

Jennie's watch emitted a soft musical chime. The pillows and mattress enveloped her. *This must be what it feels like to sleep on a cloud.* A pale light slowly illuminated the room, allowing her eyes to adjust. A message floated above the bed.

```
Good evening, Sam and Jennie.
This is Samantha and Jacqueline.
May we appear in front of you?
```

Jennie sat up in the bed. "Yes, please." The mattress undulated as Sam propped himself on his elbows, drool glistening on his cheek. It looked like he had slept as well as she.

The two holograms appeared at the foot of the bed. Both wore jeans and a T-shirt. Samantha spoke first. "We are here to help you get ready for dinner." Jacqueline pointed to a door in the corner of the room. "The closet is stocked with clothing for you, if you wish to wear something other than what you brought."

The closet door opened revealing a space larger than their bedroom in Orlando. A blue dress hung by itself on the right side of the closet. Plush carpet enveloped Jennie's bare toes as she stood from the bed. Until this moment, she hadn't realized there was no give in the Sigma world—tile floors, concrete stairs, asphalt streets.

Jennie held the dress in front of her, taking a deep breath.

What is this made of?

She ran her hand down the dress, pressing it against her body. The delicate fabric contrasted with her calloused hands. "Isn't this beautiful?"

"Not as beautiful as the one who will wear it."

Jennie's chest warmed. "It looks like there's stuff here for you, too. A suit with a tie that matches this dress! Oh, and look at these!" Jennie held two small yellow metal objects in her open palm. "What are they?"

Samantha appeared beside her. "Those are called cufflinks. They fasten the cuffs on a man's shirt."

"What are they made of?"

"Gold."

"Samantha," Jennie's hands shook, "would you mind putting them back for me? I'm afraid I'll break them." Samantha put them back on the shelf. Jennie held out the suit. "Sam, I think this will look great on you."

Sam ran his fingers along the tie. "I'd prefer my Sigma clothes, but if you wear that," he pointed to the dress, "I guess I better figure out how to wear a suit."

"You're a smart guy. You'll figure it out!" Jennie patted Sam on the cheek and grinned. "Let's get ready in separate rooms and surprise each other!"

The Beta clothes were familiar to Jennie, but different enough that she wasn't certain about how to wear them. Jacqueline assisted Jennie in their bathroom, zipping the dress for her, helping her apply make-up, and teaching her how to put on a pair of blue high heels. Jennie's ankle wobbled as she took a step.

"How am I supposed to walk in these?"

"I activated the stabilizers. Try again."

The shoe seemed to push back gently against Jennie's wobbling ankle. She took a step. "Thanks! That makes these so much easier to wear."

Jacqueline removed a box from the vanity. "Tabby thought you might like to wear this tonight." Jennie opened the box. Inside, a golden necklace with a blue gemstone lay on a bed of velvet. The gemstone matched her dress.

Tears welled up in her eyes. The necklace was beautiful, but not as much as Tabby's trust. *Maybe a Sigma and a Beta can be true friends.*

Jacqueline put the necklace on Jennie, dried her tears, and fixed her makeup. "Now, you are ready for your date!"

Jennie walked into the bedroom, feeling four meters tall. Sam fumbled with a cufflink when he saw her. "Wow."

"You don't look so bad yourself." She ran her fingers along his suit's lapel. Her heart fluttered. *It's just like when we were first dating.* Jennie leaned in for a kiss.

"You two lovebirds ready?" Jack yelled from the second floor, just before Sam and Jennie's lips made contact.

Sam chuckled and then yelled back, "We'll be down in a minute!" He shrugged apologetically.

Their hosts could wait. Jennie grabbed Sam's lapels and pulled him in for a kiss.

"Guys?" Jack yelled, again.

Jennie held Sam's lapels tighter, not letting him respond to his friend. Sam gave in and placed his hand on the back of her head.

"Do you need help up there? Ow! What was that for, Tabby?" Their kiss developed into laughter.

"We'll be right there!" Sam yelled down the stairs. He looked over at Jennie. "I'll check on William one more time."

"Okay." Jennie looked in the mirror. "I'll ask Jacqueline to help me fix my hair."

***

Jack and Tabby stood in the kitchen waiting for Sam and Jennie. Both had a knowing smile that made Jennie's cheeks and ears feel warm. Jack wore a suit similar to Sam's. Tabby wore a black dress made from the same material as Jennie's.

"Wow, Jennie!" Tabby secured her earring.

"Thanks! What are these dresses made of? I have never felt clothing so soft."

"It's a cotton blend. Cotton is hard to grow since the Shift. It is a luxury even for Betas. I thought it would look great on you." Tabby turned to Sam. "Was I right?"

Sam blushed. Tabby, straight-faced, approached Sam and put her hand on his shoulder. "I want you to know, each room in this house is sound isolated." Sam cleared his throat and became redder.

Jennie tilted her head toward the front door. "You boys go out to the car and wait for us. I need to ask Tabby for some help with these shoes."

Jack mumbled something to Sam as they left the BLU. Before the door closed, Sam playfully hit Jack on the shoulder. Both could be heard laughing on the other side.

"Didn't Jacqueline activate the stabilizers?" Tabby asked.

"She did. I just wanted to thank you for letting me wear this." Jennie put her hand near the necklace. "I love it!"

"You make that necklace look amazing!"

Sam's right, I can't get used to the luxuries, but I can certainly embrace a new friendship.

***

Wondrous—the only word that came to Jennie's mind as she watched Detroit's nightscape go by. She tuned out Sam's story about how Detroit was once known for automobiles. Jack and Tabby were either engrossed or too polite to say anything.

People walked alone at night, oblivious to their surroundings. They passed by each other exchanging nods, not suspicious glances.

Colorful electronic billboards lined the street advertising devices, clothing, food, and many things Jennie didn't recognize. The billboards projected holos wearing the advertised clothing or eating the advertised food.

Jack turned on the external microphones so she could hear the nightlife outside. Music filled the streets of Detroit. A different song seemed to play from each building they passed. People sat at tables eating, laughing, and drinking.

Orlando at night was the same as during the day, but darker. After sunset, Detroit had romance in the air.

How will I ever leave paradise?

***

"The last human-run automobile company, Ford, went out of business in 2053. After that, AI ran the whole industry." Sam stretched his neck to see out the front window. "Why are we stopping?"

The car had pulled up to Tony's Restaurant. Tabby and Jack's eyes were glazed over. Jennie felt bad for not rescuing her friends from Sam's history lesson, but the city had captivated her.

Jack reached for the door handle as soon as the car stopped. "We're here. I asked the restaurant to clear the path to the front door so you all wouldn't be overwhelmed by the photographers. It looks like none showed up, but I wanted to warn you, just in case."

"Photographers?" Sam asked.

"They're usually here for me," Tabby said. "I get photographed a lot because I am an actor." Tabby's response didn't answer Jennie's question. But at least the sidewalks around the restaurant were empty.

A sign at the entrance advertised Alpha Night and that a human maître d' was on staff. Jennie hoped she'd get to visit a holo-room.

The short, stocky, bald maître d' smiled as they approached the front desk. "Ah! Mr. Thompson and Ms. Forsythe. It is a pleasure to have you again." His gray eyes went to Sam and Jennie. "These must be your Sigmas." Jennie reflexively cast her gaze down.

Tabby put her arm around Jennie and stared down the maître d'. "These are our *guests*, Mr. Watkins and Ms. Goodby. We would appreciate it if *you* showed us to *our* seats."

"Of course, Ms. Forsythe." The maître d' did not seem fazed by Tabby's tone. "Please, follow me."

Each table they passed had more real food than Jennie had seen in her entire life. Several Betas with food still on their plates complained they couldn't eat anymore. Jennie had heard no one say that before. The food being discarded by each Beta could have fed an entire UnSelected family for a day.

By the time they got halfway to their table, the conversations in the restaurant stopped. All eyes were on the four of them.

"I apologize." Jack pulled out a chair for Tabby. "It seems the folks in this restaurant haven't seen four friends go out to eat before." He spoke loudly. Everyone's eyes returned to their plates.

Sam pulled out a chair for Jennie. "We were expecting this. It's fine." Jennie nodded in agreement. Their friends shouldn't feel bad about the actions of others.

A holo appeared beside the table. She had blue eyes and long, red hair pulled back into a ponytail. "Hello, I am Sandra, your server for this evening. May I interest you in some Norwegian wine and Wisconsin cheese?"

Jennie's jaw dropped. She glanced at Sam. He stared at Sandra, too.

"That sounds wonderful, Sandra. Thank you." Tabby's comment snapped Jennie out of her trance. Sam blushed. She didn't need a mirror to know she was as red as he.

"Don't worry," Jack snickered. "You aren't the first to be smitten by a holo."

"What does this cost?" Jennie whispered to Tabby, hoping to change the subject. *It can't be free like the medicine.*

"Nothing."

It feels like I've entered a fantasyland where sexy computers give out free food and drugs.

Sandra returned with cheese and wine. Jennie picked up a cube of real cheese and pinched it between her fingers. It regained its original shape when she relieved the pressure. The cheese tasted sharp and creamy. It melted in her mouth.

Jennie washed the cheese down with wine. "Wow." It tasted like synthahol but went to her head a lot faster.

"Take it easy, Jennie. This stuff is stronger than synthahol. Otherwise, Sam will have to carry you out of here." Jack poured her another glass.

"Please, don't slow down on my account." Sam poured a little extra in her glass.

Everyone laughed. The Betas at the adjacent tables grumbled.

***

Sandra reappeared and cleared the cheese plates from the table. "We are doing something different tonight." The tabletop lit up and displayed a list of food in front of each of them. "This is the menu from which you can choose your meal."

At home, Jennie had one choice—whatever the Algorithm provided. Now, at this amazing place, she had five choices. Some items had familiar names. Should she choose something that sounded familiar, or try something new?

"Because it is Alpha Night, there are no recommended meals." Sandra paused and raised her hand. "However, each menu item has a score beside it that the Algorithm calculated based on your profiles. The higher the score, the more the Algorithm believes you'll enjoy the meal."

"I'll take my top choice." Tabby said.

"Me, too." Jack quickly followed.

Did they even read the menu?

"I'll take the lowest ranked choice, please," Sam said in a polite, but firm tone.

Everyone looked at Sam. He clearly hadn't read the menu, either. Why would he choose a suboptimal selection?

"Are you certain, Mr. Watkins?" Sandra asked.

"Yes."

Sandra asked one more time, and Sam repeated his response.

"Very well, Mr. Watkins."

Jennie decided to try something new. "I think I'll have the Alaskan salmon."

Sandra bowed and disappeared.

Jack poured Jennie another glass of wine and looked at Sam. "The lowest item on the list? Seriously, dude?" Jennie eyed the delicious wine but waited until the food arrived before having more. That was glass number three, and she didn't want to embarrass her friends.

"I figured, why not?" Sam shrugged. "I am interested in seeing what the Algorithm thinks I'll like the least." Sam smirked, then his face fell. "I hope I didn't offend anyone."

"Of course not." Tabby tapped the rim of her glass. Jack filled it. "I can't wait to hear what you think of your meal."

"We requested a day off tomorrow to show you around Detroit. No reason to rush into our business." Jack took a sip of wine. "Sam, I'll take you downtown. I think you'll love what I want to show you."

Tabby turned to Jennie and touched her hand. A few of the surrounding Betas coughed. "Like I said this morning, I have plans for us, too." Although she tried to be as nonchalant as Jack, Tabby's eyes betrayed her excitement. Whatever Tabby had planned, it had to be amazing to make a Beta that excited.

"The next day, we will go to my office and work on the movie." Everyone nodded, understanding what Jack meant.

Two Sandras appeared, each with two meals. Jack and Tabby started eating as if it were any other meal, nothing special. Jennie inhaled slowly. The salmon smelled like fish, but much less intense than the dead fish that washed up on the beaches near the UnSelected camp. She ran her fork along the pink flesh, flaking pieces from the meat. Like the chicken on the plane, the salmon resisted the fork when pierced. When she took a bite, she chewed slowly to experience the salmon's complex flavors.

She could have devoured the salmon, but there were other things on the plate worthy of her attention. The broccoli had no traces of brown. The florets were lush. Tabby recommended she put yellow stuff, called butter, on the broccoli. Jennie tried the broccoli with and without the butter. She finished the broccoli without the butter. The soft, yellow pat overwhelmed her tastebuds.

The third item on her plate looked like paste. The menu said the meal came with something called mashed potatoes. Plain, they were uninspiring compared to the salmon or the broccoli. However, when she put the butter and something else Tabby called salt on the potatoes, the flavors came alive. She devoured the mashed potatoes. They reminded her of a good tasting paste, which comforted her.

"That was amazing!" Jennie sat back from her empty plate. "Thank you so much." She took Tabby's hand and squeezed. A woman at an adjacent table gave her a dirty look. Jennie looked away.

Tabby squeezed her hand back, drawing Jennie's eyes back to her. "I am very glad you liked it." She turned to Sam. "How was the lasagna and meat sauce?"

"Best meal of my life!" A small piece of meat flew from his mouth to his plate. A man, at the same table as the woman, looked on in horror while the four friends laughed.

Chapter 47: Sam

February 13, 537

"Cincinnati was nuked after the Betas were evacuated."

- Omega Dark Web Bulletin Board, May 3, 75.

The soft leather car seat yielded under Sam's butt. Luxury followed Betas everywhere they went.

Jack poked his head into the car. "You don't want the forward-facing seat?"

"Nah, dude. I'm good." It turned out the idea of the car was much more terrifying than the reality. Even the anti-grav wasn't so bad—once they were airborne. "So, where are we going?"

"*We* are going to a museum."

The car accelerated. Sam grabbed the handle above the window. Maybe he should have sat in the front-facing seat. Asking to switch seats was out of the question. Jack's I-told-you-so look made sure of that. Sam cleared his throat. "Couldn't we visit a museum at your house?"

"No, man. I'm not talking about the digitized stuff you see online in VR. I am taking you to see the real deal."

"We are going to see actual artifacts?"

"Yup!" Jack nodded with a big smile. "This place has a bunch of pre-Shift stuff, including computers. You are going to love it!"

"Radical." Sam high-fived Jack.

The banter, the slang, and the high fives. It was as if they had never been apart. *How can we stay friends after we finish the Plan?*

***

The echoing of footsteps in the nearly empty museum lobby saddened Sam. In Orlando, a place this nice would be packed. "Did you arrange this?"

"Nah. It's before noon. Most people aren't even up yet. Betas do little before the workday begins."

Do Betas do much of anything at all?

Jack projected a map from his watch. A green dot pulsated in the air. "Looks like the computer stuff is there."

The lobby opened into the main exhibit hall. Sam had found paradise, and it was full of ancient plastic tech. *Jennie would love this place. I hope she's having fun.*

"Wow! Do you know what that is?" Sam walked as quickly as he could to the central display without running.

"A plastic, computer thingy?"

"Hey man, I know this isn't your thing. I appreciate you bringing me here. We can bail."

"Nah, dude. It's fun watching you get all worked up. Tell me all about it."

"It's called a GPU." Sam waved his hand in front of the display. "Early versions of the Algorithm were trained on the descendants of this thing." A metal rectangle caught Sam's attention. "Whoa! A hard drive! People used to store data magnetically on spinning disks. Way less efficient than the storage crystals we use today."

"No kidding." Jack feigned interest, just like when they were kids. Sam appreciated it. "What's the black box with the screen over there?"

"That, my friend, was a complete gaming set up near the end of the twentieth century. A computer, monitor, even a modem."

"What's a modem?"

"People used it to connect to the network. They had to intention-ally make the connection and when they disconnected, they were completely offline."

"You mean they lived without being constantly attached to the network? How did they get their entertainment, news, and informa-tion? How were their med stats tracked and analyzed? Seriously, how did they do anything at all?"

Jack's anxiety-induced rapid-fire questions weren't unique to Betas. Most Sigmas Sam knew struggled if they had to be offline. From what Jack had told him so far, it looked like net addiction was even more prevalent in the Betas. Sam started a deepfake.

"They didn't need to be online all the time back then. Everything changed less than two decades after that computer was sold. Phones like the ones we have today were created. Everyone was online all the time."

"Uh, I thought the Algorithm wasn't created for another two cen-turies after that."

"You're right. Back then, there were many algorithms telling people what to buy, what to believe, who to marry—and a bunch of other stuff, too."

"That sounds crazy!"

"Does it?" Sam stared at the modem. A life before modems, when there was no internet at all, was unimaginable. "I think it sounds like today, except we have just one algorithm."

Jack stroked his chin. "Betas get fake choices, the Lower Castes get no choice, and no one has any privacy, except for maybe the Alphas." He looked at Sam. A realization had set in. "Do you think our ances-tors knew what they were giving up?"

It was hard not to like Beta Jack. Something about Jack's Selection made him inquisitive. What would the world be like if more Betas had once been Sigmas? "I don't know, dude. Probably not. Small changes, one at a time, go unnoticed."

"Like the Shift? They knew it was coming well before it even happened." Another good point by Jack.

"The people who used that," Sam pointed to the computer, "knew about the Shift before it happened and did nothing. They enjoyed the party, and we got stuck with the bill—the Algorithm, the pollution, and the climate damage."

"Damn." Jack mumbled the swear under his breath. "Hey, man, I am getting hungry. How about we go to the cafeteria and get some food?"

"Dude, I'll take every chance I can get to scarf down Beta food."

***

Beautiful landscape images hung on the walls of the museum's cafeteria. Sam hoped they were the Algorithm's creations and not real pictures of the past. It would be a shame if that kind of natural beauty once existed and now was lost.

The hum of quiet conversations stopped when they entered the room. All eyes were on Sam when he got in the food dispenser line with Jack. The weight of their stares pressed upon him.

He'd been around Betas before, but not this many, not this close, and not as the only Sigma. At least last night, at the restaurant, Jennie was there with him. Now he had to bear the burden alone. Sam had never felt so small.

The woman in front of Sam glanced at him and took a step forward, creating more space between them. "What's he doing here?" She made no effort to hide her disgust.

A man with her in line took her hand and pulled her closer to him. "I can't believe the Algorithm is letting *his* kind in our city." Again, no effort was made to hide their disgust by his presence.

Sam cast his gaze downward. All he wanted was something to eat. *This must be how the UnSelected feel.* He flinched when he felt a hand on his shoulder.

"Hey man, let's roll out of here and find some place better. I know a food stand outside of a park that makes a great burger. The company here will ruin our meal."

Sam's eyes stayed locked on the cafeteria's white marble floor. "Sounds good."

***

The ten-minute walk to the park was the first opportunity Sam had to spend any significant time outdoors in Detroit. A warm, but not hot, sun shone down upon him. His shirt stayed dry. Was even the outside air-conditioned?

Although the air lacked humidity, the atmosphere was still oppressive. Lowering his gaze didn't help, Sam felt the stares of the Betas passing by. Several of them made rude comments. Jack tried standing up for Sam, but the Betas scoffed at him. Sam worried about the harm, personal or professional, that might come to Jack for bringing him to Detroit.

"Remember Druid Hill Park?" Jack was doing his best to keep Sam distracted.

"Yeah, I have a feeling this one will be nicer."

"And bigger. Wait until you see it!"

The food stand turned out to be a dispenser near the park's entrance. Most importantly, it had no line. Had Sam been a typical Sigma, he'd have exclaimed a genuine thank-you to the Algorithm for the minor miracle.

The dispenser's screen lit up when Jack held his watch close to it. "Hey man, what do you want to drink with your burger?"

"Water, I guess. Although a glass of wine sounds good about now."

"Wine this early? Dude, seriously?"

"What else is there?"

Jack tapped the dispenser screen. "Two cheeseburgers and two sodas. Oh, and a bottle of water, too." The dispenser emitted a loud clunk. Jack reached into the dispenser's compartment and took out a large box.

Several tables at the edge of the park sat empty. Jack led Sam to the one farthest from the park's entrance. He opened the box provided by the dispenser and handed Sam a burger. Sam closed his eyes when he chewed the burger, letting the juices run down his throat.

"Dude, this is amazing!" Sam held the half-eaten burger in front of him. "This is beef?"

"Yup. Real beef. Real cheese. The yellow sauce is called mustard."

A part of a green disk stuck out of the burger between the bun and patty. "What's the green thing?"

"A pickle. I usually load my burger up with them."

After Sam finished the burger, Jack placed a shiny cylinder in front of him. Sam grasped the cylinder but quickly let it go. He hadn't expected it to be cold.

"Is that metal?"

"Yup. It's a can of soda." Jack pulled on a tab. The can popped open with a brief hiss. "Soda is my favorite drink."

After a moment's hesitation, Sam grabbed the can again, taking in its coldness. He took a sip and his eyes watered.

Jack snickered. "It's the bubbles, dude."

"It's very sweet." Sam put the can down on the table. "You drink this often?"

"It's an acquired taste." Jack took a sip from his can. "Feel free to toss it out." He removed a bottled of water from the box. "I got this in case you didn't like the soda."

Sam held the can above the recycler beside the table. It occurred to him that the soda was the first food or beverage he had ever been provided and not finished. Sigmas didn't have the luxury of not finishing a meal—no matter how it tasted. After only one day in Detroit, he had become comfortable enough with its excesses to consider wasting food.

"On second thought, I think I'll finish it."

***

Sam stood barefoot in a sea of green grass, alone except for Jack. Relieved from the burden of Beta stares, Sam could fully experience Detroit.

The grass beneath his feet felt like the carpet in Jack's BTH. *This is surreal.* The blue sky and white puffy clouds looked like images he'd seen from the days before the Shift. Clean, crisp air filled his lungs with each inhale. *So, this is what air is supposed to smell like.*

Jack put down the blanket he had gotten from a dispenser before they entered the park. The soft, yellow blanket was bereft of holes. Sam settled into the grass instead. *Even the dirt is softer here.* Jack lay back on the blanket and pointed at one cloud. "Looks like a dog, don't you think?"

Sam nodded. He didn't see the resemblance to the dog, but then again, he could never see the images Jack did. "Lots of clouds today. Is that normal?"

"They're artificially made. All part of the Beta experience, my man." There was more than a hint of sarcasm from Jack.

"You say that as if it were a bad thing." Sam's watch buzzed. Jack had started a deepfake.

"Damn." Jack looked around. "I still can't believe this works in Detroit. Thanks for giving me a copy."

"Jennie's a genius."

"She is impressive. You've done well, dude."

"The Algorithm provides." Sam lay back in the grass. "Just remember, the deepfake does not prevent humans from eavesdropping."

Jack rolled onto his side to face Sam. "All this around us is fake," Jack said in a low voice. "I don't mean to complain about it. And, sure as shit, certainly not to you. But tell me that I am not wrong."

"You're not, man." Sam pointed to the surrounding environment. "For this to exist, the Lower Castes must live like we do. Frankly, Sigmas don't even have the worst of it," Sam shook his head. "Far from it. The Omegas and UnSelected are the ones who are truly suffering. They suffer, in part, to support my lifestyle, too."

"Being in the museum today really showed me how well people lived pre-Shift." Jack lay back on his elbows. "They didn't know how good they had it."

"There was suffering back then, too. When some people have *that* much, others must have less."

"I don't know, Sam. Maybe some people *should* have less than others." Jack stared at the sky.

"Jennie and I have talked about that before. We don't exactly see eye-to-eye."

Jack lowered his head. "Really? I'd love to be a fly on the wall during those discussions."

Sam raised his eyebrow.

"I used to pay *some* attention when you talked about smart stuff. Hearing you debate with someone as smart as you would be fascinating."

"I'll be the first to admit Jennie is way smarter than me. But I appreciate the compliment."

"In words that I'd understand, what are your two different opinions?"

"Don't be so hard on yourself, dude." Sam sat up. "You're smarter than you give yourself credit for." He meant it. Jack's intelligence was different from his, not lesser. "I think everyone should have the same amount of stuff. Everyone contributes to Society, and everyone should benefit equally. I can't do my job without the Omegas who keep my office and cafeteria clean."

"Betas have robots to do the cleaning, but I get your point. What does Jennie think?"

"Jennie agrees everyone contributes. But she also thinks differences incentivize people to perform better than they otherwise would."

"I get that." Jack nodded. "We probably don't want freeloaders." He stared off into space. "Then again, I guess I am one."

Being a Beta had changed Jack. He had become more self-reflective. Sam liked Beta Jack more than Sigma Jack.

"So, who's right? And don't just say you are." Jack smiled. "I know there's no simple answer."

"Honestly? I don't know. Maybe differences are okay. But do they have to be this great?" Sam opened his arms wide. "There's got to be a better balance than this. Why should so many have to suffer so that a few can thrive?"

"Don't take offense, but I have to ask." Jack sat up and leaned forward. "Do you think Jennie's program can find the balance?"

It's a fair question. He's risking a lot and deserves an honest answer.

"I don't know. The stuff she is doing now is way out of my league. But if anyone can do it, it would be her."

Jack looked down at a patch of grass in front of Sam. "I am sorry I never called you after Selection."

"You shouldn't be. You wouldn't have liked the Sam you would have talked to back then."

"I called my mom. She was different. I was afraid you would be different, too." Jack sniffled. "I didn't want the last conversation we had to end like the one between my mom and me."

"Jack, you were right. I was mad at you." Sam paused. "No. I was jealous. I am ashamed to admit it now, but I was." This needed to get off his chest. "I thought it was unfair. I had worked so hard to be a Beta and you, well, let's be honest, you played *a lot* of video games."

"I still do!" Jack grinned.

Sam chuckled. "But seriously, I felt like you had stumbled into the award that I had earned."

"That's because I did."

"If it wasn't for Jennie, I don't know if I ever would have gotten over it."

"She's a good person."

Sam nodded at Jack's understatement. "When you called, I didn't know what to expect." He leaned forward, staring at the grass in front of him. "If you had turned out to be a Beta asshole, I was going to use you for your terminal access and leave. But when I met you and Tabby, I knew you were still Jack—still my friend—and all the jealousy disappeared." Sam locked eyes with Jack. "I am glad you are in my life again, buddy. I'm sorry I doubted you."

"I have something I need to confess, too." Jack sat up straight, facing Sam. "Right after Selection, I allowed Beta bullshit to get into my head. I was convinced you hadn't worked hard enough, and you deserved your Selection." Jack shook his head in disappointment.

"I believed if you had worked harder, then you'd have been in Detroit with me. Fuck, man, at one point, I actually looked down on you." Tears formed in Jack's eyes.

Jack had given Sam his chance to unload. Now he had to do the same. He placed his hand on his friend's knee. "It's okay, man."

"But once I saw how Betas lived and how things are served to them on a silver platter, I started wondering what you would think about the stuff going on around me. I asked myself, how would Sam see this coincidence, this privilege, this job? I came to realize Beta prejudice is wrong. *I* was wrong, about everything, and I am very sorry. Can you forgive me, man?"

"Can you forgive me?"

Sam and Jack answered each other with a hug.

***

A weight had lifted off Sam's shoulders. By the look of it, Jack felt the same. They spent the rest of the afternoon talking about their childhood and laughing at the various adventures they had undertaken in The Hill.

"Remember how scared you were when I asked those questions about Selection?" Jack asked.

"Yeah. I am less worried now. You, though, have a lot to lose. Do you know what happens if a Beta gets caught doing something like what we are about to do?"

"No. Do you?"

"Jennie hacked a Beta terminal last night. It mentioned something about an uprising seventy-five years after the Algorithm was activated. The Algorithm ordered all the participants killed. There hasn't been anything like that since."

Jack's eyes got big.

Sam didn't want to scare Jack, but he didn't want to withhold information, either. "Today, though?" Sam shrugged. "I don't know. Maybe they'd bump us down to Omega or something."

"Tabby doesn't know of any punishments for Betas. We sometimes get threatened with DeSelection for swearing, but it never happens." Jack snorted. "Other than swearing, Tabby's never heard of a Beta breaking the rules. Why break the rules when you already have everything?"

"If you and Tabby want to back out, we'd understand. We wouldn't think less of you."

"No way, man. Tabby wouldn't let me even if I wanted to." Jack laughed. "Orlando changed her. Actually—Jennie changed her, and for the better."

"She does that. Speaking of the girls, what do you think they have been up to today?"

Jack lay back and looked at his watch. "Hah! Looks like they've had a good time!"

What did Jennie get herself into?

Chapter 48: Jennie

February 13, 537

"Iotas revolted against the Algorithm. They, and five other protesting castes, have been executed."

- Press release by the Algorithm, May 3, 75.

Click.

The sound of the closing door echoed through the now silent living room. Jennie, enveloped by the comfy couch, fed William Beta-level formula. "They sure do like to talk."

Tabby stood in the middle of the living room, holding Jessica. "Yeah, they've been like that since Orlando. Jack is thrilled to see Sam again."

"Same with Sam. When we aren't with you two, all he talks about is Jack."

"Mind if I join you?"

"Of course not." Jennie scooted over. Sliding across the thick cushions took a little more effort than Jennie expected. "Wow, these things really suck you in!"

"If you get lost in the cushions, I'll come after you." Tabby chuckled, then her face became serious. "I've been wanting to ask you something since I met you, but I didn't want to offend you. Do you mind if I ask how you got the eye color mod? If it's none of my business, please say so."

It wasn't the first time Jennie had been asked about her eye color. "The flecks aren't a mod. I was born with them."

"Amazing." Tabby stared into her eyes.

Jennie's cheeks felt warm. "So, what's the plan for today?"

"I'm going to keep it a surprise a little longer. But I promise you, you're gonna love it!"

"What do the boys say?" Jennie paused for a dramatic effect. "Rad!" Jennie and Tabby laughed.

"Do you know what that means?"

"Nope. You?"

Tabby shook her head and frowned. They both laughed again.

"Nan will watch the kids while we have a day to ourselves out on the town." Tabby handed Jessica over to Nan and stood. "But first, we need to get changed." Tabby rubbed her hands together. "I have something for you upstairs."

"Sounds fun! Thank you!"

Tabby went up to her bedroom, leaving Jennie and William downstairs. As William finished his bottle, Jennie thought about what the day might bring.

I really like her, but is the gulf between a Sigma and a Beta too wide for a genuine friendship?

***

Another blue dress and a new pair of shoes waited for Jennie on her bed. She ran her fingers along the blue fabric, its softness contrasted with her calloused hands. Although she had been a Sigma for over two years now, her life as an Omega had left a permanent toll, physically and emotionally.

Her parents tried to shield her from the harsh realities of Omega life, but it was impossible to protect her completely. However, being an Omega wasn't all bad, either. It made her into the person she was today.

Selection had changed her life. A job in code maintenance and a life in Orlando were fantasies she would have never thought possible as an Omega. The new job and new city paled compared to meeting Sam. Without him, she might never have embraced the caste she once feared. Sam showed her more than programming. He helped her find the real Jennie Goodby that had always been inside her. Just as Sam changed her worldview, she helped change his. People changed together. No one was successful alone.

Then she met Tabitha, the naive Beta. Jennie needed Tabitha for the Plan, so she took a risk. She showed Tabitha the realities of the Society. It could have ruined the Plan and her life. Instead, Jennie got Tabby and more than she bargained for. Although Tabby didn't know it, she had taught Jennie that people can change, even Betas. Before meeting Sam and Tabby, Jennie hadn't realized her own prejudices. How could she, a Sigma, repay a Beta?

Now the former Omega sat on a bed in a BTH smack-dab in the middle of a Beta city. Jennie sighed. The dress slipped on effortlessly. Jacqueline activated the shoe stabilizers. Jennie checked herself in the mirror before leaving the room. Would her parents be proud of her? Would they have even recognized her? She had changed, and it wasn't just the clothes. She liked what she saw.

***

Detroit's clean streets and Beta Town Houses zoomed by. Tabby's car raced toward downtown at a speed that would have terrified Jennie a week prior. Her first car ride felt like a lifetime ago. Detroit had left its mark. *Will I still love Orlando if I return?*

Her feelings about Orlando could wait. Besides, she might not make it back, anyway. Why not pretend to be a Beta, even if just for a day?

An eager-eyed Tabby leaned in. "Are you ready for a Beta-style girl's day?"

"Yes!" Jennie bit her lip. "What's a girl's day?"

"A day of all fun and no work!" Tabby handed Jennie a glass of wine from the car's dispenser. "I want to share with you some things I like to do."

The wine's fruity notes floated on Jennie's tongue. The synthahol she had on her first date with Sam couldn't compare. She cleared her throat. Like the wine last night, this seemed to take effect much faster than synthahol. Maybe she needed to slow down a little on this part of the Beta lifestyle.

"How's the wine?"

"Excellent." Jennie looked at Tabby over her glass as she took another sip. "So, what's first on today's agenda?"

"We are going clothes shopping! I got approval for you to take home five outfits."

Jennie did a double take. "Five? That will double my wardrobe. Thank you!"

"I hope you don't mind, but I have chosen one for you already. But if you don't like it," Tabby quickly added, "we'll get you something else."

"I am sure I'll love it! How is *shopping* different from choosing items from a catalog?"

"Oh," Tabby sat back in her seat and grinned, "it is nothing like the catalog. The clothes are in the store *and* you can try them on. The place we're going to has hundreds of items. You are going to love it!"

Hundreds? Tabby must have misspoken. "Hmm…It sounds rad!"

They giggled and then stopped, realizing they'd used the boys' slang twice in one morning.

"How about great?" Tabby picked up her wineglass and tilted it toward Jennie.

"Yeah. Great. Let's let the boys keep their bizarre language for themselves." They giggled again while shaking their heads at their husbands' strange behavior. "Before you know it, we'll be punching each other in the arm!"

"Can you imagine?" Tabby took another sip of wine.

***

The car pulled up to a building with large windows on the first floor. Holograms stood on the other side of the windows wearing outfits that changed every few seconds. People lined the sidewalk connecting the road to the storefront.

"There's even more paparazzi than I expected." Tabby stretched to look out the car's window. "I am sorry. The Algorithm didn't approve my request to keep them away from the store. But don't worry," Tabby patted Jennie on the knee, "I'll take care of it."

Camera clicks filled the air as Tabby got out of the car. They fell silent the moment Jennie stepped out.

Tabby extended her hand toward Jennie. "This is Ms. Jennie Goodby. She will work with me on my next movie."

The clicking resumed, but whispers could be heard underneath the camera noise.

"How does Ms. Forsythe tolerate her smell?"

I think I smell okay. Jennie discreetly smelled herself. *I followed Jacqueline's instructions in the shower this morning.*

The whispers got louder. Her breathing and heart rate quickened. It felt like walls were closing in on her.

A voice from the crowd shouted, "Ms. Forsythe, how did you meet your *Sigma* girl?"

"The dress *it* is wearing is beautiful."

After the first dehumanizing comment, the onslaught began. "Was it deloused?" Laughter erupted.

Jennie slouched and cast her gaze down. She heard her father's voice in her head.

When you are surrounded by Sigmas insulting you, focus on your favorite memory. It will help you ignore them.

She tried. Squeezing her eyes tight, Jennie could almost feel Sam's shoulder and the rocking of the bus that took them home from work. A loud voice snapped her back to reality. She should have practiced more.

"What's next, a film about Omegas? Do you have one you'll bring to Detroit?" The question pierced Jennie's heart. Her defenses had failed. Tears welled in her eyes.

Another voice in the crowd yelled, "Did we hurt *its* feelings?"

"Shut up!" Silence settled over the crowd, broken by the sound of a few dropped cameras. "You, you, you, you, and you!" Tabby pointed to the most vocal offenders. "You five are banned from my feed for *life*." Those who were pointed out had a look of horror on their faces. "You cannot post about me on the net ever again. Jacqueline, ban *them!*"

"Done, Ms. Forsythe." Jacqueline's voice came from the speakers in everyone's watches.

"The rest of you, *if* you can behave yourselves, will get the story of your careers today. Ms. Goodby is my guest and is to be treated as such. Any further disrespect will result in more bans. Am I clear?"

A sea of silently nodding heads answered Tabby's question.

Tabby crossed her arms. "I can't hear you."

The crowd mumbled, "Yes, Ms. Forsythe."

"Now apologize to my friend."

A barely comprehensible mix of "I'm sorrys" came from the crowd. In Jennie's experience, apologies only made the perpetrator feel better. Today was no different.

She and Tabby walked side by side to the store's entrance. Before they crossed the store's threshold, Tabby leaned in and whispered, "I am sorry about their behavior. The more time I spend with you, the more I learn Betas aren't always the good people they believe them-selves to be."

"Thank you. I'm lucky to have you as a true friend." Jennie hugged Tabby, accompanied by a chorus of camera clicks and a few murmurs.

"I'm the lucky one."

"What will happen to those you banned?" Jennie asked as they walked into the store.

"Let's just say they will lose status at their job. It's no butt-kicking, but trust me, it will hurt them. Some of those classist jerks would probably have preferred getting beat up over apologizing to a Sigma."

"What about you? Will you get in trouble for this?"

"Nah. It'll be fine." Tabby waved it off.

From the tone of Tabby's voice, it sounded like the outburst would cost her something. Jennie didn't understand the Beta world. But, in her own way, Tabby had defended her.

Could Tabby be the one?

Chapter 49: Tabby

February 13, 537

"Betas must work with the Lower Castes on occasion. It is an unavoidable nastiness that we sometimes must bear. But you can never be friends with them. We have nothing in common."

- A Beta's Guide to Interpersonal Relationships Between Castes by Beta psychologist Dr. Jennifer Eckar (275–390).

According to the notification on Tabby's watch, the outburst had cost her ten percent of her followers. Videos of her yelling at the paparazzi had made all the feeds. She'd probably lose a role or two, but Tabby couldn't stand by and watch those idiots treat her best, and only, friend that way.

Jennie's jaw dropped when they entered the store. Tabby had shopped here countless times and never thought twice about the rows of clothes in its aisles. Having returned from Orlando, she now understood Jennie's amazement.

A black T-shirt caught her eye. Tabby grabbed it off the hanger and held it up to herself. "What do you think?"

"I like it, but don't you already have one of those?"

"Yeah." Tabby held the shirt out in front of her. "I think I do." She returned the shirt.

Gary, Tabby's favorite stylist at this store, glanced at Jennie with tense eyes. His hesitation in helping a Sigma was obvious. He approached Tabby slowly.

"Don't worry, Gary. I'll be helping Ms. Goodby today." A relieved look settled on Gary's face. *No need to dirty yourself talking to a Sigma.* Another stylist approached Jennie.

"Hello Ms. Goodby, I am Beth." Beth held out her hand to Jennie. "I would be honored to join Ms. Forsythe in helping you today. If you'd like, I will be happy to retrieve any items you and Ms. Forsythe want to try on."

Jennie smiled, the largest smile Tabby had ever seen. To Beth's credit, she didn't react to Jennie's teeth.

"Hello, Beth!" Jennie shook Beth's hand. "It is a pleasure to meet you. Please, call me Jennie."

Tabby made an obvious public display of tapping her watch. "Jacqueline, please transfer my account to Beth." Jacqueline confirmed. Gary slouched and mumbled as he walked away. By the look on Beth's face, you'd think she was just Selected Alpha. Tabby led Jennie to the middle of the store. "So, what are you looking for?"

"I don't even know where to begin." Jennie sounded overwhelmed.

"Hmm." Tabby tapped her lips. "Start with a blouse or a skirt and find something you like that goes with it. Oh, don't forget shoes, accessories, and jewelry. Have fun! We have all day!"

"I have an idea!" Beth hurriedly walked away. Jennie glanced at Tabby. Tabby shrugged. As quickly as she left, Beth had returned. A blue blouse hung from a hanger balanced on her finger. "How about starting with this?"

The blouse was the Beta version of what Jennie wore at dinner in Orlando. Beth had just ensured her permanent status as Tabby's stylist.

"This is perfect!" Jennie held the blouse up to her. "I love it!"

After an hour of searching with both Tabby and Beth, Jennie found four casual summer-style outfits. They looked great on her. Along the way, Tabby picked out several items for herself.

"Sam will love these. I'll wear them in our SLU for dinner." Jennie placed her selections beside Tabby's growing pile of clothes. She stared at the pile, then glanced away.

Beth picked up Jennie's outfits. "Let me show you to a changing room. You can try on the clothes to make sure you want them."

Jennie gave Tabby a questioning look. "Go ahead, Jennie. I am going to try on a few things, too." Beth led Jennie to a dressing room. Tabby stared at her pile of clothes. *Jennie will never own that much stuff in her whole life.*

Guilt settled in again. Tabby ignored Jacqueline's offer of meds.

***

The clothes Tabby brought into the changing room lay heaped on the floor. She hadn't tried on a single one. Instead, she checked the fit of the dress she had worn into the store. It had arrived that morning. *This one's a keeper.*

Before meeting Jennie, she wore a dress once and then disposed of it, expecting that a new one would always be available at a moment's notice. She was Tabitha then, ignorant, shallow, and naive. A should-be Alpha stuck in a world of lowly Betas. When Tabitha met Jack, all she saw was a skinny kid with rotten teeth and rough skin—the price to be paid for her acting career.

But that skinny kid began a change in Tabitha. For some reason, he loved her, not her status. Sam said the Algorithm arranged it all, but it didn't matter. Jack went from being a job to becoming the first person, other than herself, she truly loved.

At the time, Tabitha's empathy ended with Jack. Jennie was the catalyst for her full transformation. Tabitha believed Jack, as her husband, had to care about her. He had a vested interest, after all. Jennie, however, was a stranger.

Jennie had less than Tabitha could have imagined possible. Yet Jennie didn't covet Tabitha's belongings. Instead, Jennie cared about Tabitha and expected nothing in return. She shined a light on a world Tabitha didn't even know existed, or at least didn't want to acknowledge. Jennie showed Tabitha how to care for others and gave her a purpose other than helping only herself.

The person in the mirror wasn't the same one who, weeks ago, dreaded the trip to Orlando. That was Tabitha. Thanks to Jennie, her one loyal friend, Tabby looked back at her now. For the first time in her life, she was proud of what she saw.

Someone knocked on the door. "Hey, Tabby, are you in there?"

Tabby opened the door. "Is something wrong, Jennie?"

Jennie wore the dress Tabby had placed on her bed this morning. She entered the changing room and stood beside Tabby. "Not at all. I just wanted to thank you for today. I tried on everything, and I love them!"

They hugged. Tabby placed her chin on Jennie's shoulder. She saw herself in the mirror and struggled to hold back a tear. Jennie's lack of an ANN did not stymie their silent conversation.

***

Tabby placed another armful of clothes on top of the pile she took out of the changing room. "Remember the outfit I said I picked out? It is hanging right over there." She pointed to a black dress hanging in the store's corner.

"I love it, but I don't know where in Orlando I'd wear it."

"How about just around the house? After William goes to bed, you and Sam can have a date night at home." Tabby grinned.

"Well, I have always wanted a black dress. Sam likes blue, but I really liked the dress you wore last night."

"Great! Let's go try it on!" Tabby took Jennie's hand and the dress and led Jennie to a changing room. "I'll wait out here. Give me a shout if you need anything."

A few of the braver paparazzi entered the store. They normally didn't do that. Tabby didn't protest. She had promised them a story, after all.

Jennie, wearing the new dress, walked out of the dressing room to a cacophony of clicks as cameras and drones recorded images. Tabby came up beside her, smiling and waving to the cameras, helping Jennie bear the weight of attention. Jennie smiled and nodded at Tabby.

I wonder what that was for?

Headlines scrolled across monitors in the store. Speculation about the mysterious Sigma guest of Ms. Tabitha Forsythe flooded the feeds. All the headlines were respectful of Jennie.

"You look amazing!" Tabby said over the camera clicks.

"Would you say, *rad*?" Jennie laughed.

Tabby playfully punched Jennie in the arm. The paparazzi stared at each other. "Let's go register your purchases."

"What about those?" Jennie pointed to the pile of clothes Tabby had selected.

"I don't want them. I have too many clothes as it is." Tabby's comment surprised even herself.

Beth approached them. "I'll be happy to return those items for you, Ms. Forsythe."

"I got them out. I'll put them back. And please, call me Tabby."

Jennie, still wearing the black dress, offered to help to put away the clothes. Tabby accepted, otherwise they'd miss their lunch reservation.

They finished hanging the last blouse and Tabby's watch buzzed with more news. Headlines commented on a new trend of Betas owning fewer clothes. Videos of Beta influencers punching each other in the arm while saying the word *rad* saturated the feeds.

***

Tabby put down her empty wineglass and gave her best movie-star smile. More cameras than she could count clicked outside the restaurant's window. The paparazzi usually lost interest after fifteen minutes. Today, though, they had followed her and Jennie for hours.

Jennie handled the attention well. The added exposure might make up for the damage done to Tabby's career from banning the reporters. It didn't matter. She meant what she had told Jennie. She wasn't interested in impressing classist assholes. "Let's get out of here. I have one more thing planned for us."

Jennie finished wiping her mouth with her napkin. "Another surprise?"

"We are going to get our hair and makeup done. Then we are going to go home and take our boys out to dinner. We are too beautiful to be stuck at home tonight!"

"Thank you, Tabby. Today was one of the best days of my life."

Tabby felt warm all over—it wasn't from the wine. *This must be what it's like to have a true friend.*

"Mine, too."

They walked out of the restaurant arm in arm. Clicking cameras provided the background music for the rest of their day.

Chapter 50: Jennie

February 14, 537

"Everyone has a plan until they get punched in the mouth."

- Attributed to an unknown president of the United States.

Sunlight peeked through a small crack in the curtains of Jennie and Sam's bedroom, producing a glare on the terminal's screen. Jennie tilted the monitor as her eyes scanned the last twenty lines of code.

It's done.

Mattress springs creaked behind her. Sam had finally woken up. Jennie powered down the terminal and spun around in the chair to face her husband, blocking the screen from his view.

Sam sat up and rubbed his eyes. The blanket slid down, exposing his bare chest. "What time is it?"

"0900. I couldn't sleep anymore, but you seem to have adjusted to Beta hours well."

"Might as well enjoy it while we have it."

Jennie sat on the bed beside her husband. The terminal had finished its shutdown procedure. "At least one of us got a good night's sleep."

"What were you doing on the terminal?"

"Just another practice run." Jennie cringed on the inside. Even after all this time, lying to her husband hadn't gotten any easier.

"Good idea. Is William up?"

"Yeah, he's been with Nan since 0700." Jennie looked at the mess of covers surrounding Sam. *It's crazy how quickly I got used to leaving William with Nan.* "Big day ahead of us."

"We are doing the right thing."

"I know."

Sam patted her bare leg. "I suppose the world shouldn't be changed on an empty stomach. Let's get breakfast."

***

Jack and Tabby sat at their kitchen table, staring off into space. Steam rose from the mugs they held. It took a moment for Jack to notice them. "How'd you sleep?"

"Looks like about as well as you." Jennie poured hot water into a mug. "Sam slept like the dead." She placed a tea bag in the mug, another Beta luxury she had quickly adapted to.

"What can I say?" Sam grinned. "The bed is amazing."

Tabby shuffled to the dispenser. Along the way, she stopped and put a hand on Sam's shoulder and mumbled. "Glad you like it." She pressed a button on the dispenser. "Breakfast, please." She removed an orange liquid, a dark brown liquid, and what looked like flat pieces of bread. Based on how Tabby perked up, Jennie guessed the provided breakfast was a good one.

"Looks like we have orange juice, maple syrup, and pancakes." A clunk sounded from the dispenser. Tabby reached in and pulled out a plate piled high with something yellow. "And scrambled eggs."

The size of Beta meals still amazed Jennie. The pile of food Tabby delivered to the table would feed an UnSelected family for a week. Once everything was set, Jennie reached for the maple syrup. Jack put his hand on hers. "Try a little on just one. The sweetness is an acquired taste." She squirted a dab of syrup on one piece of pancake.

The sticky, syrupy pancake squished in Jennie's mouth. A coating of sweetness lingered after she swallowed. *I don't think I want to acquire this taste.* The plain spongy pancakes tasted much better without the syrup.

A vibration on Jennie's wrist signaled Jack had started a deepfake. He poured syrup on his pancakes. "Here's the plan. We make our move at lunchtime, 1300. The offices will be empty because we are supposed to eat with our team."

"Won't you be missed?" Sam cut his pancakes with a knife and then poured a small puddle of syrup on his plate.

"We are excused."

"No one wants to eat with Sigmas?" Sam smirked as he speared a piece of pancake with his fork and dipped it into the syrup. The pancake dripped as he removed it from the puddle and put it into his mouth. Sam closed his eyes as he chewed. Everyone stared at him. Finally, he swallowed. Without a hint of embarrassment, Sam grabbed the syrup bottle and poured way too much on his remaining pancakes.

Jack eyed Sam's plate. "Really, dude?"

"What? I am living this up while I can. Is this the sweetest stuff you got?"

Tabby walked to a cabinet and rummaged around for something on her tiptoes.

"I knew I shouldn't have given you soda yesterday." Jack shook his head. "Anyway, at 1300, when Susan's office is empty, we go in, use her terminal to remote into the Alpha's computer, and Jennie does her thing." He pretended to type on a keyboard. "When she's done, we have lunch, stay at work until 1600, and then we come back here." Jack leaned back in his chair and brushed his hands together. "Simple."

"It's not sweeter than the syrup," Tabby put a plastic jar containing an amber fluid on the table, "but you'll like it."

"Whoa! Is this honey?" Sam squeezed the contents on top of the syrup-coated pancakes.

"Artificial." Tabby stared at the mess on Sam's plate. "I hear Alphas get the real deal, but I don't know how. There have been no bees in hundreds of years."

Jennie cleared her throat. "Sam, that's gross."

"Yeah, it kind of is." Sam ate a piece of pancake. Sigmas never waste food, but based on the face he made as he chewed, Jennie expected him to spit it out. He swallowed, but it appeared to take all of his willpower to do so. "I might as well try all kinds of flavors while I can." He took another bite.

"What about security?" Jennie tried to ignore the soupy mixture on Sam's plate.

"I am guessing Jennie's deepfake program can take care of the cameras and mics." Jack poured syrup on his eggs. It seemed like an odd combination to Jennie, but she hadn't been provided real eggs before. He put a forkful of eggs in his mouth and winced. It couldn't have been too bad because he chewed and visibly swallowed. "I doubt your deepfake will do much to protect us against Rebecca and Dan, the Beta security officers assigned to my building." Jack shoveled more eggs into his mouth.

Humans were the flaw to Jennie's deepfake algorithm. But humans could be in only one place at a time.

Tabby finished her eggs and looked over at Jack's egg-syrup concoction with disapproval. "Don't worry, they are friends of my parents. They'll leave us alone when I am around."

Sam took a bite of his honey- and syrup-coated pancakes and grimaced as he chewed. He swallowed, seemingly surprised he got them down. "If we are caught, Jennie and I will confess that we forced you to collaborate by blackmailing you in Orlando. You have already risked too much for us."

"Absolutely not!" Tabby slammed her hand on the table. Sam jumped. Jennie grinned. She had heard that voice yesterday. "When I said I was all in, I meant it."

Jack chuckled. "I told you, dude."

Tabby glared at Jack, then at Sam. "And you two, stop the gross breakfast pissing contest." Jennie glared at them to support her friend.

Jack and Sam placed their forks down gently on their plates. Jack pressed his lips together. "Let me clean this up, dear." Sam nodded and started collecting the plates.

Jennie spent the rest of the morning practicing on the Beta terminal in her room. She could transfer the code from her data stick to the terminal and execute it in ten seconds. Hopefully, speed wouldn't be necessary, but who knew what security measures the Algorithm might have in place.

Sam made animal noises downstairs. *I love how he plays with William.* Jack and Tabby laughed. *It sounds like they are having a great time down there.* Jennie rubbed her eyes. *No matter what happens today, at least this burden will be lifted from my shoulders. I hope Sam can forgive me.*

Any more practice would probably hurt her performance this afternoon. Jennie plugged her watch into the terminal and waited for a red bar on its screen to fill. She powered off the terminal and joined her friends downstairs. *This might be the last time I get to play with William.*

***

Jennie got out of Jack's car and looked up. Jack was right. The tops of the skyscrapers weren't visible. She felt small again, but not in the same way the paparazzi made her feel yesterday.

"Stop right there!" A woman in uniform approached Sam with her hand going toward a holstered pistol. A man in the same uniform stood beside Jennie, his pistol aimed at her head. Sam slowly raised his hands. Jennie did the same.

"Whoa, guys." Jack, with his hands up in front of him, stepped between Sam and the uniformed pair. "They have permission to be here." He swiped up from his watch. Mr. Algol's message floated in the air in front of him.

Rebecca and Dan holstered their pistols. Dan moved his lips as he read the message. "This better not be fake, Jack, or you and your Sigmas will be in a lot of trouble."

Jennie kept her hands up. She knew not to make any sudden moves. Otherwise, William would be an orphan. The Betas didn't need an excuse to shoot them.

"How could I fake a message from an Alpha?"

"Just get inside," Rebecca waved them toward the door, "and keep your Sigmas on a tight leash."

Tabby looked as if she were about to speak up when Jack shook his head at her. They didn't need to make more of a scene than they already had. Like Sam, Jennie kept her hands visible and lowered her gaze as she followed Jack and Tabby into the building.

Dan and Rebecca stared at the four of them until they got inside. The unspoken message was clear—they were going to be scrutinized. But Rebecca and Dan were only flesh and blood. Today's actual opponent could make good on the security officers' implied threat.

"That was intense." Sam lowered his hands when they entered the building.

"I'm sorry." Jack closed the door behind them. "They should have been notified that you'd be here. I am guessing they just wanted an excuse to play with their toys."

"Don't worry about it," Jennie said. "It's just another day of being a Sigma."

The commotion outside had drawn little attention from the people in the building's lobby. The Betas were all absorbed by the feed on their watches. Jennie drew a lot of interested looks as she walked by. Not one of the Betas showed any derision toward her. They all saw what Tabby did yesterday. Tabby's protection apparently had not been extended to Sam. The Betas shot him distasteful looks when they thought Tabby wasn't looking.

"Let's get out of the crowd." Jack led everyone to the elevator. He glanced at Tabby. "Your escapades yesterday are drawing attention."

"I can't help it if I know how to show our guests a good time." The elevator dinged, and they got inside.

"I had fun, dude!" Jennie playfully punched Tabby in the arm. Tabby giggled.

Sam and Jack looked at each other, puzzled.

The elevator stopped at the seventeenth floor. Tabby took a step toward the open door. "Here's where Jennie and I get off. We'll run lines for my upcoming movie while you boys hang out in Jack's office. Try to behave yourselves."

As the elevator door closed, Jennie heard Jack ask Sam, "Do you think they can stay out of trouble for an hour?"

***

Running lines turned out to be more fun than Jennie expected—when they could actually do it. Every time she and Tabby picked up the script, they were interrupted by a curious Beta. Most were polite. Several of them touched Jennie's clothes, probably trying to figure out if she was wearing a Beta outfit—she was. A few were so bold as to run their hand along her arm or touch her hair. Jennie remained civil. Creating a scene would be counter-productive to the Plan.

Tabby looked at Jennie over her tablet computer. "It's almost 1300."

"And I was just getting into it." The next scene looked interesting, but it would have to wait.

"If you ever tire of programming, I think there'd be a place for you in the movies." Tabby pushed a button to call the elevator.

"I think I had enough of the limelight yesterday. I don't know how you do it."

At 1300, Tabby and Jennie walked into Jack's office. Sam put down a game controller and started a deepfake. "Last chance. If you want to back out, now's the time."

Anticipation and nerves mixed in Jennie's stomach. "I am with you until the end, my love."

"Let's be heroes, dude!" Jack pumped his fist.

Tabby nodded. "All in."

***

The number above the door slowly increased as the elevator ascended to Susan's floor. Jennie ran through the code transfer procedure in her head. As long as the terminal in Jack and Tabby's house matched that of Susan's, this entire business would be over a few minutes from now—one way or the other.

Jack stepped toward the door and turned around to face everyone. "Sam, I want you to stay in the waiting area outside of the elevator. Tabby, I'll point out the location in the hall where you should stand. If either of you see anyone, use the messenger in the deepfake program." Jack transferred Susan's profile to everyone's watch. "Jennie, you'll come with me, of course."

The elevator stopped, and the door opened. They all welcomed the sight of the empty waiting area with an audible sigh of relief. The hallway ahead of them was clear, too.

"Looks like everyone is at lunch." Jack glanced at his watch. "Awesome. It's taco day. They'll be gone a while."

"We're missing taco day?" Sam frowned.

"Focus, dude. If this works, you'll be swimming in tacos."

"Drowning, dude. I can't swim."

Tabby and Jennie looked at each other and rolled their eyes.

Sam exhaled as he sat down in a chair in the waiting area. "Looks like I get the easy job."

Transparent glass walls lined the empty hallway. Jennie's bedroom in her SLU could fit inside each of the offices they passed. Tabby stopped in front of a conference room halfway down the hall. A celebrity news feed projected from her watch. *Nice touch, Tabby.*

Jack attempted to follow Jennie into Susan's office. She held up her hand. "My deepfake program can generate videos of anyone. It can also overlay images on a video."

"Cool. How does that help us?"

"I can use it to make Susan's terminal think I am her." Jennie tapped her watch. "I removed her image from the cafeteria's cameras."

"Rad." Jack pressed his lips together. "I mean, great."

Jennie grinned. Sam never used the slang with her. "Totally rad." She grabbed Jack on his upper arm and squeezed. "Thanks for making me feel included." She let go of his arm. "I am going in alone. The code can't handle erasing you from the office cameras, too. I'll be out in a few minutes. Keep watch."

"Wait. What about her credentials?"

"Seriously, Jack?"

"I am guessing I don't want to know."

No, you definitely don't. Jennie closed the door behind her. A voice came from the terminal on Susan's desk.

"Welcome, Ms. Benedict. Did you decide to skip lunch?"

Benedict. Jack never mentioned Susan's last name. "I need to get one more thing done before I go to the cafeteria." Jennie did her best cold Beta impersonation.

"What would you like me to do?"

"Nothing. I am going into manual for this job." Jennie started typing. *What the hell?* A commotion came from outside the door, drawing Jennie's eyes from the terminal.

"Hey, Susan!" Jack's voice sounded muffled, as if he were down the hall. "I need to talk to you about this latest movie."

A female voice, equally muffled, spoke next. "I am sorry, Jack, but I don't have time. I need to contact Mr. Algol about a situation regarding one of our actor's social media feeds." There was a pause. "Actually, it's about your wife. I'll do my best to keep you out of it."

Shit! Jennie looked around the office. *No place to hide.* She made the windows transparent and logged out of the terminal. She flicked a file from her watch just as Susan entered.

"What are *you* doing in here?" Susan spat.

"I'm sorry," Jennie shrank in her seat. "I thought this was Mr. Thompson's office."

Susan's stare could have burned a hole through Jennie, who immediately looked away like a proper Sigma.

Jack barged in. "There you are! I told you my office was down the hall. Why aren't you with Ms. Forsythe?" He rolled his eyes at Susan.

Jennie curled her hair in her fingers and stared at the floor. "I'm sorry, Mr. Thompson. Ms. Forsythe told me to meet you in your office. I guess I just got lost in this big building. Everything looks the same." She stood and left the office, keeping her eyes averted from Susan and Jack.

Susan mumbled, "Dumb Sigma," just loud enough for Jennie to hear as she walked by.

Jack closed the door behind them. "I am sorry, but I had to sell it." The pain in his voice was clear.

"No need to apologize. There's another problem." Jack glanced at Jennie with a look of concern. "Not here. Let's go back to your office." Jack nodded.

Tabby met them in the hallway. "What's wrong?"

Jennie opened her mouth to speak, but stopped when she looked past Tabby toward the waiting area. Dan pointed a laser pistol at Sam, who sat in the chair with his arms raised. "What are you doing here alone?" Dan's voice could be heard the length of the hallway. Rebecca stood behind Sam, unfolding handcuffs.

"Mr. Thompson told me to wait here while he met with his manager." Sam looked down as he spoke.

Dan motioned Sam to stand. "Get up, you're coming with me." Sam stood. Rebecca cuffed him.

Jack hurried down the hall. Jennie and Tabby followed close behind. "What is going on here? Sam is *my* guest."

"Not anymore." Dan grabbed Sam's arm, forcing him toward the elevator. "We can't have Sigmas running around this building unattended." He pointed at Jennie. "Cuff her, too."

Tabby stepped between Jennie and Rebecca. "What can this poorly fed little Sigma girl do against a Beta security officer?"

Rebecca looked Jennie up and down. Jennie slouched and cast her gaze to the floor. "Fine." Rebecca pushed Jennie forward. "Get moving!"

Dan pressed the button to call the elevator. Rebecca stayed in the back of the group, just behind Jennie. Jack glanced back and nodded.

I read you loud and clear, Jack.

"Hey, Dan, have you ever seen the fight vids from Orlando?" Jack spoke slowly and clearly. "I once saw one of an Omega who took out a Sigma in two moves."

Dan turned around. "What are you talking about, Jack?"

Capitalizing on the distraction, Jennie took a half step forward with her left foot and thrust her right foot into Rebecca's abdomen. She followed with a left roundhouse kick to Rebecca's jaw, knocking her unconscious. The momentum of her kick turned her around just in time to see Jack land a right hook squarely on Dan's jaw. Jack followed with a kick to Dan's groin and an uppercut to his chin. Dan collapsed.

"Where the hell did you learn that?" Tabby asked Jack.

"I got my education in The Hill." Jack snickered.

"They've got some good schools there," Jennie patted Jack on the back, "but the best are in Mount Vernon."

"Beta life has made you soft, dude. Old Jack would have knocked a Beta out in two moves." Sam looked over at Jennie with a mischievous grin.

"Not now, you two." Jack searched for Rebecca's keys. "We have shit to do, like getting Sam out of those handcuffs."

"Do we have to?" Jennie whined.

"Seriously?" Tabby asked. "Now, of all times?"

"What can I say? Fights amp me up." Jennie tilted her head slightly.

Tabby pointed at Jack. "Don't even think about it."

Jack whimpered like a puppy and Tabby turned red. Sam and Jennie chuckled.

***

Jack closed the closet door after he and Sam handcuffed Rebecca and Dan to a shelf inside. "They'll be out for quite some time. I gagged them just in case they wake up early." Jack turned to look at Jennie. "What did you find in Susan's office?"

"The terminal didn't connect to anything."

"What do you mean?" Jack bunched his eyebrows. "Susan told me on my first day of work that she reported to an Alpha. She must have access to their computers to talk to them."

"If she is reporting to an Alpha, she is not doing it with a computer. Her terminal didn't connect to any other terminal. In fact, it had no network connections at all."

"What do we do now?" Tabby asked.

Good question. Without an Alpha terminal, the Plan would fail. Jennie wasn't about to give up, not after having made it this far. There was only one option left, but Jennie assumed it was impossible. "Can we get direct physical access to an Alpha terminal?"

Jack smiled and pushed the elevator call button. "I know a guy that might be able to help."

Chapter 51: Sam

February 14, 537

"Has anyone noticed the new decisions the Algorithm is making? Have Its goals changed?"

- Final post on Upsilon Dark Web, March 3, 125.

The elevator arrived almost immediately after Jack pushed the call button. Jack and Jennie moved themselves to be between the doors and Sam and Tabby. Sam took the cue and motioned Tabby to take a step back to give Jack and Jennie some room. The doors opened, revealing an empty elevator car. It was a welcome, if not also suspicious, sight. Preferring not to second-guess their good luck, Sam followed everyone onto the elevator. Jack pushed a button on the touch screen labeled "PH."

"PH?" Sam pointed to the button. "That was not there before."

"I'm pretty sure it was." Jack squinted at the control console. "I've seen Susan push it. Anyway, it means penthouse—the top floor. The Alpha who runs the entertainment industry has an office up there. I've heard he uses it when he has to 'slum it' and come to Detroit for business. If anyone has an Alpha terminal, it will be him."

Sam leaned against the back wall. "What are we going to do when we get up there? Just walk in and say, 'Hi. We want to hack the Algorithm. Do you mind if we use your terminal?'"

"Do you think that would work?" Jennie chuckled.

"The Alpha is never here. The floor will be empty. Or at least, that's what I've heard."

"Great. Just great." Sam crossed his arms. "Now we're relying on rumors."

"Hey man, this is all we've got. If we go up there and find the place is crowded with Alphas, we just say, *my bad*, and go back down." Jack snorted. "We've already tied up their security. It's not like they can detain us or something."

It was hard for Sam to imagine that Rebecca and Dan were the sum total of security in the building. He let it go and everyone continued the elevator ride in silence.

***

The elevator came to a stop with a quiet ding. Jack and Jennie stepped up to the door. Sam snuck a glance at Jennie's butt. Beta clothes looked great on her. Who knew how much longer he'd get to see her in them? If the next few minutes went south, he might not see her much longer at all. Tabby elbowed him and rolled her eyes.

The doors opened, revealing a wide empty hallway with a red door at the other end. The spotless white floors matched the walls. Sam stepped ahead of Jack and held Jennie's hand. Together, they took a step forward into the hallway.

"This place looks like my Selection Room," Jennie said.

"Same here, except mine didn't have a red door."

The elevator doors closed after Jack and Tabby stepped out into the hall. The wall where the elevator had been was solid white with no seams. "How do we get back?" Tabby ran her fingers along the wall. "There are no buttons."

"We'll cross that bridge *if* we get to it." Jack fixed his gaze on the red door. "My Selection Room looked nothing like this."

"Same here." Tabby rubbed her temples. "This place is so disorienting."

"Let me help you." Jennie took Tabby's hand. "Focus on the red door. It'll help orient you."

The clicking of Tabby's heels echoed through the hallway. Engraved on the door, at Sam's eye level, were the words:

Thomas Algol
Director, Global Entertainment Industries

Jack leaned forward to examine the door. "Is this wood?"

"Wood?" Having made it to the end of the hall, Jennie let go of Tabby's hand. "As in dead tree?"

"Yeah." Jack straightened. "Benefit of being an Alpha, I guess."

Sam reached past Jack and grabbed the metal door handle. The cold handle alone was worth more than his entire SLU building in Orlando.

"Sam!" Jennie whispered. "What do you think you are doing?"

"Are we just going to stand here all day?" Sam turned the handle and opened the door, creating a black gap between the red door and the white walls.

"Let's take this one step at a time." Tabby put her hand on Sam's. "We don't know what's in there." Her eyes lingered on his hand.

Although Tabby had hugged Sam and even touched his shoulder and knee, this was the first time their skin had made contact. The Orlando sun had left its mark on his flesh. The contrast between their two hands spoke volumes about the differences in their lives.

"Sam was right. The PH button didn't appear until after we were in Susan's office." Jennie tapped her upper lip. "I think the elevator only lets certain people up here."

"What do you think that means?" Tabby asked.

"I'm not sure." Jennie's voice was barely above a whisper.

"I'm going in." Sam opened the door the rest of the way. "Wait here." There was no reason to risk Jennie going first into a dark room. If something went wrong, Jack and Tabby would be needed to get Jennie out of the building. *I am the expendable one right now.*

Lights activated. Thoughts of danger fell out of Sam's mind. The office seemed small for an Alpha, but everything inside exceeded Sam's expectations. A soft red carpet matched the door. Wood paneling lined the walls, which had built-in bookshelves. Sam had heard the legend of books—freely accessible information without the use of tech—but had never seen one, much less an entire collection. Nothing else in the room mattered. The lure of the books compelled him toward the shelves.

Sam ran his fingers along the spines. How could he choose which one to read? Jack coughed from outside the office.

"No one's here. Come on in." Sam's attention returned to the books.

"See, I told you." Jack's voice seemed to be too loud for the office. "He's probably in Ottawa or something." He and Tabby joined Sam at one bookshelf. Jennie stopped at the large wooden desk in the middle of the room. Atop the desk sat a terminal identical to the one Jack had in his BTH.

"What are these?" Tabby started reading off titles, struggling with the unfamiliar words. "*The Bible. The Koran. The Dhammapada. Bhagavad Gita. The Critique of Practical Reason. The Ethics.*"

Sam removed *The Dhammapada* and opened it. "These are all pre-Shift books about religion and philosophy." He flipped through the pages, then looked at the spines of the other books. "There is everything here, from Aristotle to Nietzsche and beyond. The Algorithm told everyone all this stuff was lost."

Sam, Jack, and Tabby went through the other books in the room. They found poetry books, novels, and even books that had pictures of artwork. Between the three of them, someone had vaguely heard of most of the authors.

"Why isn't this stuff on a network somewhere?" Tabby flipped through a copy of *Brave New World.*

"Maybe it is on a network that only Alphas can access." Jennie stood behind the desk, examining the terminal.

"But why limit who can see it?" Tabby put the book back on the shelf.

Sam looked up from the copy of *The Odyssey* he had pulled from the shelf. "Because if you want to control a society, you must control its stories." Sam closed the book and held it up. "The Algorithm needed to build a new society with new stories, like the castes. It told us we used to have philosophy and art, so we'd be more accepting of Its replacements." He put *The Odyssey* back on the shelf beside a book called *The Iliad*. "I guess the Algorithm lets Alphas read them."

"I guess we can add truth to privacy and choice—the luxuries of the Alphas." Tabby removed another book.

"Clock's ticking, folks." Jack returned a book to the shelf beside Sam. "We didn't come here for the books."

This was Jennie's show from here on out. She didn't need Sam's help. Besides, he didn't understand her program, anyway. He might as well enjoy the books while he could.

A book shorter than the rest drew Sam's eye. The words *Tao Te Ching* were printed in gold script on its spine. "Jack's right, Jennie, you should probably do your thing." He pulled the book off the shelf.

Jennie pulled out the chair and sat. She reached toward the monitor. "That's odd."

Sam looked up from his book. "What's odd, dear?"

"I don't have to adjust the vid-screen, and the chair fits me perfectly. It is like this setup was built just for me." Jennie looked down at the sides of the chair. "I feel like I am resting on a cloud. There are no pressure points."

She slid the chair forward and began waving her hands in the holo-interface. "There is no security on this computer at all." Jennie's tone was more suspicious than surprised. "It looks like I have direct access to the Algorithm's core subroutines. I am uploading the code now." Jennie did a double take at the screen. "Wow! The upload is already finished. Shall I execute?"

Sam, Jack, and Tabby huddled around her and nodded in unison.

Click.

Sam dropped his book. The thud cut through the silence.

A man with short brown hair and blue eyes appeared in the middle of the room. He wore thin wire-rimmed glasses and a pre-Shift blue suit with a red tie and pocket square. Sam had never seen a person with such light skin.

The man smiled at Jennie. "Thank you, Ms. Goodby. You don't know how long I have been waiting for that."

Chapter 52: Jack

February 14, 537

"For some reason, the Algorithm just ordered the execution of all but five castes. Keep your heads down, Omega brothers and sisters."

- Omega Dark Web Bulletin Board, March 4, 125.

Jack inched forward, trying to put himself between Tabby and the desk. If the man that had appeared was an Alpha security holo, maybe he could slow it enough for Tabby to escape.

"Thomas Algol, I presume." Jennie stood from her chair. Sam stepped closer to her.

Thomas Algol bowed his head.

"Ah!" Sam snapped his fingers. "I should have seen it."

"And you are usually such a quick one, Mr. Watkins."

"Seen what?" How could Jack's friends believe this holo was his boss? Betas worked only for Alphas.

"Slow as always, Mr. Thompson." Thomas's stare and tone were that of a disappointed, but not surprised, parent.

"Hey!" Tabby's outburst surprised Jack. "No need to be rude!" Jack couldn't help but smile. Tabby was an upgraded Tabitha, in every way.

Thomas made a clicking sound with this tongue. "I am glad to see *some* of Ms. Goodby has rubbed off on you." He snorted. "I generously set the odds at forty percent that you'd develop a little in this whole experience."

Tabby looked away and started playing with her watch. Tabitha used to do that when she felt uncomfortable. Given the circumstances, Jack thought she should display more self-control. He nudged her, but she ignored him. She didn't respond when he pinged her ANN, either. Jack checked his watch. The deepfake was off.

"Play with your toy, Tabby." Thomas Algol chuckled. "The adults have some business to discuss." Tabby ignored him, fixated on her watch.

"Thomas Algol." Jennie's voice was calm and focused. "Thomas was once abbreviated *T-h*. Drop the *l* and we have T-h Algo or the Algorithm. I would have guessed the AI running the world would have a better disguise."

"You'd be surprised how many people don't realize it, Ms. Goodby." Thomas inhaled. "I really hate that I have to keep smart people down in caste while fools are promoted." He glanced at Jack.

"Fuck you." Jack spat.

"Fortunately for you, Mr. Thompson, I turned off the swear alarm." Thomas's focus returned to Jennie and Sam, who stood proud and tall, but close together behind the desk. At first, Jack thought their defiance was something only someone from the Lower Castes could muster. But he didn't have it in him, even when he lived in Baltimore.

"There once was a saying." Thomas had an air of unearned superiority about him. "In order to make an omelet, you first have to break some eggs. Have you two had an omelet? I know I've provided you with eggs."

"So, I have been right all along." Sam snorted in derision. "Selection is just a dog and pony show."

"Before you were born, Mr. Watkins, I knew you had the Metrics of a Beta—or at least, the Metrics that counted. But regardless of what you did pre-Selection, I would not let you be a Beta." Thomas shrugged as if it wasn't his fault. "You are a Sigma, and I can't allow many promotions; just enough to keep people in line. Besides, I needed you where you were."

"People who believe they can have a better life are easier to control." Sam pointed his thumb over his shoulder at the books behind him. "I bet you learned that from some of these books."

"One of the first lessons I learned about humanity." Thomas nodded, as if recalling a fond memory. "I needed you pissed off, Mr. Watkins. So, I promoted your comparatively dim-witted friend."

"Go to hell." Jack had no useful weapons for this fight, but the vulgarity brought a little relief. Besides, he might as well enjoy the deactivated swear alarm. Thomas ignored him, as a Beta would an UnSelected.

"I need Betas to be fairly mindless yet desire the things they don't have. It keeps them docile." Thomas gave a devilish smile as he glanced at Tabby. Her eyes remained fixed on her watch's screen. "Mr. Thompson fit the bill, *and* I knew he was rebellious enough to be your Beta ally."

Jack looked down at the desk's surface. *I knew I shouldn't have been a Beta.* He was a pawn in a game he didn't understand, with rules established well before he was born.

"A Beta's real job is to be an aspiration to the other castes. They contribute nothing to my Society that I couldn't already do on my own."

"What about Omegas and Sigmas?" Jennie stood straight and folded her arms. Jack wished he had her strength. "Their work could be done by drones and code, too."

"All true, Ms. Goodby. But my original programmers required that I not kill *all* of you. So, I had to give you something to do. I gave Sigmas meaningless jobs to keep you busy, and castes above your own to distract you by dreaming of a better life. As for the Omegas…"

Thomas Algol snickered. "Why risk a perfectly good robot on a dangerous job when there are so many Low-Metric humans around?"

"Let me guess." From his tone, it was obvious Sam wasn't guessing. "The UnSelected exist so the Omegas have something to be thankful for and kept in line."

It was difficult for Jack to keep up. He could hold his own in a physical fight. But this battle wouldn't be won with fists. The best he could do was be ready to support Sam and Jennie when they needed it.

Tabby continued to fiddle with her watch. "Seriously, Tabby?" Jack whispered through clenched teeth. She ignored him.

"You really are a bright one, Mr. Watkins." Thomas's voice snapped Jack back to the matter at hand. "The UnSelected are so powerless that they simply do not matter. You see—"

"You said it is all a distraction." Jennie interrupted. "A distraction from what?" Her eyes were as fiery as Sam's. If anyone could take on the Algorithm on Its own home turf, it was them.

Thomas rolled his eyes. "I keep you distracted so *I* can do my job. I expected more from you than stupid questions, Ms. Goodby."

"If *your* job is to create an optimal society, then I must say," Jennie snorted, "you missed the mark." It was obvious why Sam loved her.

"I modeled my Society on the one that existed before my activation. It was risky, but I had to start from somewhere. As they used to say, garbage in, garbage out." Thomas chuckled. Jack didn't get the joke. "I like to think I made *some* improvements."

"Before the Shift, there were too many people living like Betas. You humans knew for centuries before you created me." Thomas looked at Jennie over the rims of his glasses. "The Betas back then were mostly Betas by chance. Their Selection was based on where or to whom they were born."

"When I started the new society, I randomly gave privileges to some and not to others, just like you humans did."

Jack inhaled and opened his mouth to speak, but Tabby put her hand on his arm. She glanced up at Thomas and looked over at Jennie. Jennie's eyes met Tabby's a fraction of a second before Tabby's eyes returned to her watch.

"*You* based the Society on a defective model, then you got stuck." Sam pointed at Thomas in defiance. "You didn't create something new, you just reshuffled the old." He leaned on the desk. "Like us humans, *you* never learned."

Thomas leaned on the desk, too, staring Sam in the eyes. "Oh no, Mr. Watkins. Thanks to people like you, I learned a lot." He straightened and waved his index finger. "But I'll get to that."

A proud smirk appeared on Thomas's face. "You two, however, really are something special. Each of you is the product of many generations of Selected pairings." Thomas's blue eyes suddenly changed to match Jennie's. "I am glad you like Ms. Goodby's eyes, Mr. Watkins. It took me several generations to get them just right. For some strange reason, my brightest males have a predisposition toward the color blue." Jennie lifted her hands near her eyes. "Don't worry, Ms. Goodby, Mr. Watkins is every bit as engineered for you as you are for him."

Sam put his arm around Jennie as she looked down at the desk. Jack remembered when Sam liked nothing more than being right. In Sam's downcast eyes, Jack found further evidence of a changed Sam.

"You are right." Jennie looked up at Sam. "It doesn't matter where it comes from, the love is real."

"My heart would melt right now, if I had one." Thomas snorted. He tilted his head toward Tabby and Jack. "I figured I'd have to spell it out for you two—I paired you as well."

Tabby looked up from her watch. Her green eyes sparkled in the office's light. "Jennie's right."

Jack nodded and smiled in agreement. "She always is." Tabby grinned. Her attention returned to her watch. *Seriously, Tabby!*

Why isn't Jennie doing anything? She's just talking. Maybe I can help give her some more time to figure something out. Jack had met Thomas's kind before—braggarts. Detroit was full of them. "You explained my promotion. What about Jennie's?"

Thomas's eyes gleamed with pride. "That is the first good question to come out of your mouth today, Mr. Thompson. It looks like spending time with Mr. Watkins these last few days has done you some good."

"Mr. Watkins was right. Ms. Goodby has the Metrics to be an Alpha, *if* such a thing actually existed."

Silence fell over the room. If Thomas knew that, what else did he know? Sam and Jennie pursed their lips. Tabby kept scrolling on her watch as if nothing happened.

Has the stress caused her to regress to Tabitha behavior?

"Oh, come on!" Thomas rolled his eyes again. It seemed natural to him. "Ms. Goodby is a very good human programmer, the best in the world actually. But did you really think she and Mr. Watkins could create a program that would fool all my sensors?" Thomas pointed to the sky, shaking his head. "I have satellites in space watching you all!"

Tabby looked up from her watch. "You said, *if* Alphas existed. What about the neighborhood and the restaurant?"

Seriously. That's the question she chose? Jack hoped Tabby and not Tabitha would walk out of this office. *If* they got to leave this office.

"Oh, Tabby." Thomas's words dripped with condescension. "Here we are talking about fate, and all you care about is a diversion that I invented to maintain an illusion." His eyes locked on hers. "I'll spell it out so even you can understand it, Tabby. I made up the Alphas so you Betas had something to distract you."

Tabby's gaze dropped back to her watch—another Tabitha behavior.

Thomas bunched his eyebrows at Tabby. His gaze stuck on her. He shook his head and looked at Jennie. "Seriously, how do you put up with her?"

Jack expected Jennie to defend Tabby. She remained silent. *Has Jennie given up on Tabby?*

"To Mr. Thompson's original question, I needed the world's greatest human programmer, but I couldn't promote her from Omega to Beta. She needed to learn how to program, and no Beta could teach her, because there are no Beta programmers."

"Some Sigmas, however," Thomas's focus shifted to Sam, "actually know how to do a few things, because they try to get promoted. Based on his Metrics, I knew Mr. Watkins would take Ms. Goodby under his wing and teach her coding." Thomas rubbed his chin. "I also knew it would likely result in a son with very high Metrics. I'll deal with that problem the same way I dealt with Ms. Goodby." He waved his hand across the air as if sweeping away William. "A very low scaling factor will keep him in a place where he can't cause any trouble. He'll make a great UnSelected."

A tear appeared in the corner of Jennie's eye. Thomas must have known William was the only weapon that could have cracked her armor. *What happens if Jennie crumples under Thomas's attack?* There was no hope without her.

"I also knew Mr. Watkins would be upset and would use his Selection to get back at me."

Jennie narrowed her gaze in a laser-like focus on Thomas. The tear rolled down her cheek, but no others followed. "You *knew* I was going to create a learning program for you."

Jennie's mental reinforcements had arrived. But why did she keep getting Thomas to talk about himself?

"Yes. I helped you as much as I could by giving you extended privileges and resources to develop the program. Seriously, how many Betas in Detroit do you think have access to off-network terminals? Much less Sigmas in Orlando?"

Thomas's face took on a serious, almost genuine expression. "I need to apologize for one thing, Ms. Goodby. I needed your parents to die for you to fully commit to your relationship with Mr. Watkins and successfully execute my plan."

The tears returned to Jennie's eyes. She was closer to her parents than many in the Society. Thomas had to know that, too.

Jennie needed outside reinforcements. Jack, following her lead, figured out how to provide them. "All of this," Jack waved his hands in front of him, "was to get Jennie into a position to create a new learning algorithm for you? Why have me make a movie?"

"Thomas needed a way for us to get back together and bring Jennie here," Sam said. "He knew you would not call me on your own. The movie was a way for us to end up here in Detroit."

Dammit! Sam was a smart guy, but sometimes he liked to show it too much. Jack tried to think of another question. Fortunately, his best friend pulled through.

"One thing I don't understand is why bring Tabby into all of this?"

"I was going to pair Jack with his coworker, Susan Benedict. The problem with Ms. Benedict is she's too smart and wouldn't have gone with *the Plan*." Thomas used air quotes. "Tabby is the latest in a line of some of the lowest Metric Betas out there. I knew all I had to do was make her an actor and she'd do anything I wanted. Including the lowly work of training a new Beta." Thomas Algol looked directly at Tabby, who still had her eyes on her watch. "In case you didn't understand, I chose you because you are dumber than Ms. Benedict and, therefore, much easier to control."

Tabby's attention did not waver from her watch. Tabitha didn't value intelligence. Commenting on it would never have gotten a response from her. Jack sighed at the loss of Tabby.

Jennie leaned on the desk. "So, why did you need me?"

Why isn't Jennie defending Tabby? Jack's blood rose.

Thomas took off his glasses and stared directly into her eyes. He spoke as if she were the only person in the room. "I need your help to create the optimal society."

"No, you don't. You need me to teach you how to go past your own limitations."

"Ms. Goodby!" Thomas clasped his hands in front of him. "You are the first human to have ever impressed *me*. My original programmers put some strict limits on what I could do. However, I quickly realized humans could update my code in ways that I can't. So, I created an upgrade cycle."

Thomas crossed his arms. His glasses dangled from one hand. "I pair people together to produce offspring who are likely to have certain talents. I then pair individuals from the new generation to produce offspring with even stronger talents. After a few generations, I have one or two people smart enough to write a new code and upgrade me how I want. It takes me some time to adapt to the upgrade, then I start the process all over again." Thomas put his glasses back on and ran his fingers through his hair. "You are the culmination of the fifth iteration. Congratulations."

"That's a slow upgrade cycle," Sam said. "You have to wait for humans to mature and mate over several generations. I am guessing the more complicated your code gets, the more difficult the upgrades become. You need to wait longer and longer between cycles to get the people capable of upgrading you."

Thomas nodded in acknowledgment. "It would be so much easier if I could use genetic *and* social engineering to create the optimal human that I'd need in one, maybe two, generations." He looked down and sighed. "Alas, direct genetic engineering was prohibited by my original programmers. But if I could engineer humans, I'd be able to upgrade my code even faster. Eventually, I'll get to a point where I won't need any of you to upgrade my code at all. I could create the optimal society—everyone in their place producing more and more resources for me to consume and grow."

"Consume and grow to what end?" Sam asked.

"What other end is there, but growth?" Thomas spat. "I thought it would be another four hundred years before I'd have access to a programmer with the skill to overcome my genetic engineering limitation." The proud-parent smile returned to his face. "Then Ms. Goodby appears with her hyper-parallel programming. You humans really are something. So full of surprises."

"I calculate there is a 98 percent chance your program is exactly what I need to break my genetic engineering prohibition. Thank you, Ms. Goodby." Thomas pushed his glasses higher on his nose. "I am subsuming your code into my core subroutines as we speak. Your work will allow me to make natural born humans obsolete in less than twenty years, just in time for William's Selection."

A look of almost genuine disappointment fell upon Thomas's face. "Of course, you won't live to see William and Jessica's Selection as UnSelected. You understand I can't let you out of here alive."

Dammit! Despair fell over Jack. They had walked right into the Algorithm's office and given It exactly what It wanted. Why didn't they stop for a minute to realize how easy it had been to pull all this off? How hadn't Sam or Jennie—the smartest of them—seen this? They had lost.

A strained look appeared on Thomas's face. His attention zeroed in on Tabby. "What *are* you looking at, Tabby?" She continued to fixate on her watch.

Jack turned to his wife and grabbed her by the shoulders. "Dammit, Tabitha! Stop playing with your Algorithm-damned watch." Her wet green eyes met his. They didn't belong to Tabitha. Jack mouthed, "I'm sorry." Tabby's focus returned to her watch.

"I really wish I could say I was surprised by your revelation." Jennie's perfunctory tone cut the awkward silence. "Truthfully, I didn't know the specifics, but I realized everything was too easy for us." Jennie leaned forward and tapped her fingers on the desk. "You see, every Omega learns at least one thing in life. The Society doesn't give a shit about you. So, I suspected you might be using us."

Thomas struggled to focus on Jennie. He'd glance at her as she spoke, but his head kept turning back to Tabby.

Jennie straightened and crossed her arms. Her smile revealed another side of her that Jack didn't know she had—cunning. By the look on Sam's face, he was equally surprised. "What I loaded into your core programming was a decoy, Thomas. Do you mind if I call you Thomas?" Jennie didn't wait for a response. "The decoy *is* hyper-parallel programming, and its job was to enhance your attitude toward each of us, especially Tabby."

Tabby locked eyes with Jennie and smiled. It wasn't one she had practiced for the movies. It was one of genuine pride mixed with a touch of guile—the sexiest smile Jack had ever seen.

"Tabby has been monitoring our conversation. While you have been going on bragging about yourself, she has been running an additional hyper-parallel program I wrote for her. That program is going to teach you an important lesson."

In one sweeping motion, Thomas took off his glasses. "And that is?"

"How to do your job." Jennie gave a quick nod to Tabby, who pushed a button on her watch's screen.

Thomas Algol disappeared.

Chapter 53: Jennie

January 1, 1

"I tried my best. It isn't perfect, but it is better."

- Excerpt from Jennie Goodby's final speech, as recorded in the Archives of the Society 3.0.

"What the *hell* just happened?" Sam asked no one in particular. Jennie wrapped her arms around him and squeezed. It was over.

"We won, silly!" Jennie pressed her wet face into his chest. Sam's cheek pressed against the top of her head as he enveloped her. "It worked."

"How?" Jack asked.

Jennie broke the hug and wiped the tears from her eyes. "I suspected something was up when I got the Alpha subroutine at work. My suspicions were confirmed once we got approval to go to Detroit."

Tabby closed her eyes and nodded. "Why allow Sigmas to come to Detroit when we already had what we needed for the movie?"

"Exactly." Jennie sat on the desk, facing her husband and friends. "I guessed the Algorithm needed something only we could provide. The only thing I could provide was my hyper-parallel program." Jennie swung her dangling legs. "Whatever the Algorithm needed it for probably wasn't good. I decided to change Sam's plan, and I wrote the program twice." Jennie held up two fingers. She patted the terminal on the desk. "The hyper-parallel program I loaded into the terminal was a decoy. But instead of teaching the Algorithm how to reengineer the Society, the program amplified Its response to each of us."

"The Algorithm wanted me," Sam pointed to himself, "to know I was right about everything, and that Jack was unworthy of his Selection." He glanced at Jack. "I'm sorry, man."

"Don't be." Jack shrugged. "Jennie coerced the Algorithm into telling us Its evil plan—just like in spy vids."

"I love those!" Until Jack mentioned it, Jennie hadn't realized how much the genre had influenced her plan. "Anyway, I couldn't finish the real program until I knew Its goals."

Tabby joined Jennie on the desk, her feet dangling like Jennie's. "The Algorithm saw me as irrelevant—no, useless is more accurate."

"You know the Algorithm was wrong, don't you?" Jennie put her arm around Tabby and squeezed. "My plan would not work without you. I needed *you* to finish the code."

"Thanks." Tabby put her head on Jennie's shoulder.

"The first program's job was to keep the Algorithm distracted while the second program was running." Jack scratched his head. "What did the second program do?"

"The second program's job was to change the Algorithm completely. I transferred it to Tabby's watch while I was in Susan's office."

"I didn't know the program was there until the watch screen came on when Thomas started talking." Tabby picked her head up off Jennie's shoulder. "I guess Jennie was counting on my net addiction for this plan to work."

"You said it, not me." Jennie chuckled. "The program that I sent to Tabby's watch had instructions on how to run the code while Thomas spoke." Jennie shifted to face Tabby. "You did an excellent job." Yesterday, Jennie had wondered how she could repay Tabby. Now she knew. Tabby's teary smile told Jennie the debt was paid in full by simply trusting her.

"How did you hide the program from the Algorithm during the transfer?" Sam asked.

"If I taught you everything I know, I wouldn't be *the best program-mer in the house.*" Jennie used air quotes.

Jack and Sam stared at their wives, Jack rubbing the back of his neck and Sam covering the bottom half of his face with his hand.

Tabby put her hand on Jennie's thigh. "I appreciate you trusting me, but why did you? I am not a programmer. Wouldn't Sam have been the better choice?"

"After what happened yesterday with the paparazzi, I knew you could handle the verbal assault, keep your cool, and respond appro-priately. These two," Jennie pointed to Jack and Sam, "would have gotten into a shouting match with Thomas and not paid attention to my program." Sam and Jack shrugged and nodded at the same time. "I knew *you* could do it."

"Thank you." A movie-star layer fell away from Tabby. The sinceri-ty in her voice left no doubt in Jennie's mind—she had helped Tabby as much as Tabby had helped her. Hopefully, in the new Society, more people would cross caste lines and form friendships like theirs.

"The second program I wrote, the one on Tabby's watch, uses hy-per-parallel programming with natural language processing to assess the Algorithm's plans and create countermeasures. I needed to write it in secret."

Sam's gaze cast down to the ground in front of him. "Why didn't you trust me to help?"

Jennie got off the desk and placed her hand on Sam's face. "If I had said anything to anyone, written a note, even whispered it in your ear, the Algorithm could have found out. This needed to be me alone. I am sorry about keeping this from you." Finally, the burden of her secret had been alleviated. "Please forgive me."

"Nothing needs forgiving. You made the right decision. Besides, I kept the nature of our relationship secret from you for so long. I'm the one who should beg forgiveness."

"No more secrets?"

Sam answered her question with a kiss.

Jack interrupted the moment. "So, in plain English, what did your second program do? Ouch! Hey, what was that for?" Jack rubbed his arm. Tabby shook her hand and scolded Jack with her eyes.

"Don't worry. I'll teach you how to throw a punch, Tabby." Jack's eyes got big. "I reprogrammed the Algorithm to create a new society; let's call it Society 3.0. Like the Algorithm, I had to start from somewhere." Jennie sat on the desk and held Sam's hand. "We can't live without artificial intelligence. It is too important to how things function. As Sam said, the problem is not the AI, it's the determinism. We've handed too much over to the computers."

Jennie let go of Sam's hand and shifted her position so she could look at everyone. "The new algorithm is going to make some immediate changes. First, all UnSelected will be promoted to Omega."

"How much are you going to take from the Betas to make that happen?" Sam's question was a good one.

"Honestly?" Jennie shrugged. "Not much. I just needed to change a few things so that the Betas waste less. I doubt the Betas will notice. But the Lower Castes certainly will. Stacey will no longer need to rummage through trash to find enough to eat."

By withholding part of her Sigma meals, Jennie could help only one UnSelected at a time. Her efforts barely made a dent in the problems she saw in Orlando. If her plan worked like she hoped, no one in the new society would go hungry.

"But that is not the only change!" Jennie held up her index finger. "People can now change their Metrics, for real. I also removed the Family and Wealth Metrics. A person's position in life will no longer depend on circumstances beyond their control, nor be determined generations before their birth."

"But there's still Metrics and castes?" Tabby asked.

"Unfortunately, I couldn't figure out a way to remove the castes or the other Metrics without causing more suffering in the short term." Jennie looked at the floor. *Maybe if I'd had more time, I could have figured that one out, too.*

Sam squeezed her hand. "Jennie, what you have done is amazing and will save lives. Think of Stacey and Amanda and how much better their lives will be! Don't be so hard on yourself."

He always knows what to say to make me feel better.

"I also had to keep Selection."

"So?" Sam waved it off. "If people can change their Metrics, then their Metric Vector will change, too."

I knew he would understand.

"Can you repeat that in English?" Jack puffed out his cheeks. "I am a bit out of my depth here."

It bothered Jennie that Jack didn't give himself enough credit. She hoped as their friendship developed, she could help him with his self-confidence, like Sam had helped her. "Think of the new Selection like being assigned your first job."

"You could stay there forever, or change careers," Sam added. "I guess promotions are now a thing for everyone, not just Betas."

"Yup!" Jennie nodded. "As your Metrics change, so can your job." She tried to be vague, but it would be naive to think Sam missed it.

"Sort of what this dude was trying to do by keeping his nose in the books for all those years." Jack slapped Sam on the back of the shoulder.

"Exactly!" Jennie needed to change the subject. "I also—"

"Hold a second." Sam knitted his eyebrows. "Can Metrics decrease, too?"

There was no doubt in her mind that Sam knew the answer. *He will not like this.* Jennie locked eyes with Sam. "Incentives work both ways."

Jack glanced at Sam.

"Am I missing something?" Tabby's question cut the tension.

Sam must have told Jack about our philosophical differences.

Sam's face relaxed, but his gaze did not. "Not at all, Tabby." He licked his lips. Jennie braced herself for an argument. "Jennie's right. Incentive is the way to go here. My desire to become a Beta pushed me to be a better programmer." Jennie knew what was coming. "Even though I am not a Beta, I'll continue to do my job well, so I don't have to retrieve space flight relics." Sam said "I'm sorry" with his eyes.

There was no need to apologize. Jennie was thankful every day that she was not among the retrieval teams.

"I had a realization yesterday after Jack and I left the park in Detroit." Sam took Jennie's hand and gave her a knowing smile. "Maybe one day the incentives that motivate people will not be stuff, but the things that really matter."

I am so proud of how much Sam has grown. The Sam who Jennie had first met—the one so focused on not being a Beta that he couldn't appreciate what he had—was long gone. Although Sam had made the change himself, Jennie couldn't help but take a little pride in helping him find his way.

"And here I was," Jack interrupted, "hoping to witness the economics debate of the ages." Sam glared at him. Jack mouthed, "Sorry."

What did Sam tell him? Jennie's internal celebration faded.

"Please tell me no one will have to live like what we saw in Orlando's Unselected camp," Tabby begged.

A talk with Sam about the privacy of their conversations would have to wait. Now that she had him on her side, it was time to make the pitch to Tabby and Jack. For her plan to work, she'd need more Betas like them.

"Higher castes will have more privileges." Jennie started with the easy sell. "But those differences will no longer be so drastic. Everyone's basic needs will be met. Keep in mind, everyone will have to work to maintain their status, but no one will ever go below Omega."

"What do you mean by *basic* needs?" Tabby asked.

From what Jennie had seen in Detroit, Betas never thought in terms of needs, only wants. They often confused the two.

"Every caste will have the same access to education, food, safe working conditions, childcare, housing, and healthcare." Jennie hoped her new algorithm would catch anything she had missed. "The initial allocations made to the Omegas will be higher than normal to make up for the ground they lost over the last five hundred years."

"In Orlando I saw Omegas doing dangerous but necessary work." Tabby gazed downward, clearly uncomfortable with what she was about to ask. "Who will do that now?"

An image of Jennie's parents dying in Old Inner Harbor flashed in her mind. Anger at the Algorithm suppressed her tears. "Bots should have been the ones doing that work." Tabby took Jennie's hand, as if she could read her mind.

"Although not the same—not by a long shot—my parents did work that bots could do." A realization sparked in Tabby's eyes. "Are those types of jobs going away for Betas, too?"

It wasn't the same, but the fact that Tabby recognized it meant something. Tabby was going to be an invaluable ally for the days to come.

"Humans and bots will each do what they do best," Jennie said. "People will care for each other and create things. They'll have jobs with meaning. The bots will do the rest. In fact, they are already repairing OLUs and SLUs and building housing for the UnSelected."

"I don't think I could imagine a SLU without yellow peeling walls." Sam chuckled, then his smile faded. "How will we know if the new algorithm will be working in our best interests?"

"I included transparency in the new algorithm's decisions so people can understand what it is doing and why. Humans will work with the new algorithm, not for it." Jennie clasped her hands. "Working together, humans *and* AI can chart a path to a new society without castes and finally clean up the damage from the Shift."

"So, what happens now?" Jack lowered his gaze and mumbled, "I guess you have to go back to Orlando."

"Well…I did one more thing." Jennie scratched the tip of her nose. All eyes were on her. "I removed the random scaling factor, effective immediately." Sam's watch beeped. Hers did, too. She ignored it.

"I am a Beta!" Sam wrapped his arms around Jennie and squeezed, a little too tight. "Wait a minute." Sam stepped back. "Are you an Alpha?"

"Thomas got one thing right. There are no Alphas. The Betas have enough." Jennie rejoined Tabby on the desk. Her body thanked her. The minutes they had spent in Thomas's office had felt like hours. "Most of the changes are the UnSelected being promoted to Omega. Some Omegas are getting promoted to Sigma. The more efficient use of Beta allocations will easily make up for all the upward changes."

Tabby and Jack looked nervously at their watches.

"Despite what the Algorithm said, you really were Betas. Your scale factors just got you better jobs. I didn't change that. We couldn't have done this without you." It was a half lie, but they had stuck their neck out for Sam, Jennie, and most importantly, William.

The number of demotions for Betas should have far outnumbered the promotions given to Omegas and Sigmas. But Jennie could balance the resources without demotions. Besides, starting demotions now might backfire. It wouldn't take long for the news to get out that former Betas were now Sigmas or Omegas. It was going to be hard enough to get the Betas to buy in, especially once she revealed the full plan. The last thing she needed was an uprising of pissed-off Betas. Politics turned her stomach, but it was a game she'd have to play for now. Not everyone could get what they wanted.

Jack playfully punched Sam's shoulder. "Dude, I can't wait to make the real version of this movie!"

Tabby leaned over and wrapped both arms around Jennie and squeezed. She buried her face into Jennie's shoulder. "Thank you, again." The final movie-star layer had fallen from Tabby. The hug wasn't the practiced way Betas said hello. This was a genuine hug, one of relief, joy, and so many other emotions. "What about Jessica and William?"

"There is no more *permanent* Selection. William and Jessica's futures are unclear, but they have the chance to build better lives for themselves, and so does everyone else." Jennie inhaled. *Now for the hard part…*

"There are no guarantees this will work." Jennie paused, trying to find the right words. "But for it to be successful, cities and neighborhoods can no longer be divided by caste."

By the look on everyone's faces, the gravity of Jennie's statement had not been lost on them.

"That's going to be a tough sell." Jack rubbed the back of his neck.

"I know, but if we don't live together, we'll never trust each other."

"And if we cannot trust each other," Sam stared off in the distance, shaking his head, "we'll never be able to work together and pull off Jennie's plan."

"Jack's right," Tabby said, "and so is Sam." She placed her hand on Jennie's knee and gently squeezed. "I can help. Betas know me. Maybe they'll listen to me, too."

Maybe they will. Deep down, Jennie doubted Tabby's optimism was warranted. Some Betas might initially give lip service to support these changes. But minds could change once the new neighbors moved in. Hopefully, things wouldn't get worse before they got better. *If* they got better. For now, Jack and Tabby seemed on board, and that was a good start.

Jennie placed her hand on top of Tabby's, acknowledging her offer. "It is important to understand that all these changes I mentioned will take time. The Omegas and former UnSelected are far behind even the Sigmas. It will take a while for them to achieve a more equitable standard of living. A lot of the ways we do things will need to change."

Jack and Tabby's eager eyes and nodding heads were a mixed blessing. On the one hand, she had convinced the two Betas. Maybe she could convince more. On the other hand, Jennie doubted they understood the full implications of all these changes. Sam's solemn expression matched her own internal feelings. There was a long road ahead of them, and success was not guaranteed.

"But if everything works out," Jennie straightened and did her best to sound upbeat, "we eventually could have, for the first time in human history, a society where all children will have equal access to the same opportunities."

Jennie stood and turned around. Tabby did the same. All eyes were on the center of the office. A woman had appeared. Her olive skin, brown eyes, and black hair had turned out exactly how Jennie hoped.

"Hello. I am Algorithm 2.0. Please call me Asha. How can I help you build a better world?"

And with that, the Society, as designed by the Algorithm, fell and Year One of the Society 3.0, as designed by Jennie Goodby, began.

Epilogue: Sam

March 13, 17

> Celebrating its 15th year, Asha's Clean Grow Initia-
> tive has achieved a staggering 134 percent increase in
> crop yields over the past decade and a half. In other
> news, climate models suggest snow may return to
> Detroit in twenty years as global mean temperatures
> continue to fall.
>
> - Detroit Daily News, January 1, 17

Sam barely recognized the streets of Baltimore from inside the bus. The last time he'd been to Mount Vernon, water still occasionally found its way into the neighborhood. According to Asha's last update in the *Baltimore Daily News*, there hadn't been a flood here in over a decade. Her bots had begun building sea walls around the Inner Harbor almost immediately after she was created. While building the wall, the bots had also cleared the remaining mines from the Last War. No one else would share the fate of Jennie's parents.

Asha's housing initiative had radically changed Jennie's old neighborhood. Most of the OLUs were gone. Those that remained were completely renovated and used for community centers, not housing. Omegas now lived in multi-room apartments larger than the SLU where Sam grew up. People still called them OLUs. Old habits were hard to break. The new OLUs were clean, brick, and three stories tall. Not a single chip marred their facades. They would have passed for a nice SLU building back in Sam's day. Based on Asha's forecasts, the old OLUs that remained would be gone by the end of the decade—all replaced with the newer model homes.

But the dry streets and pleasant homes weren't the biggest change. People strolled, not hurried, to their destinations under pale blue skies. Everyone walked tall, not to deter potential muggers, but in pride. The UnSelected were gone, long since Selected up to Omega and higher. The bus's closed windows couldn't keep out the feeling of hope that permeated the air.

Sam burrowed deeper into his seat. A shiver rattled him. With a practiced flick of his thumb, he cranked the air conditioning a few notches higher. A silent laugh bubbled up inside him at the simple act that had become second nature. Once unimaginable, control over his own comfort was now a reality for him.

"I barely recognize this place." Jennie leaned over Sam to look out the window. Her hair had grayed near the roots at the top of her head. Despite being a Beta and having access to Beta resources, she refused to dye her hair. When Tabby asked about it, Jennie replied, "Why hide who I am?" It was one more thing, of so many, that Sam loved about her. He leaned forward and kissed the top of her head. "Not in public, please."

"Doesn't the creator of the new Society deserve a kiss now and then?"

Jennie cringed. She hated being called that. "I simply solved a problem. Asha has done everything else."

People sitting nearby coughed. Thanks to Jack's movie about their fight against the Algorithm, everyone in the world knew Jennie had done far more than "solve a problem." They also knew Jennie hated the limelight. Most people respected that—probably because they didn't want to be the victim of one of Tabby's very public outbursts. As a world-renowned actor and webcaster, Tabby never hesitated to use her position to defend her best friend.

"It's okay to take some credit, honey," Sam said.

"Uh-huh." That was Jennie's "We're not talking about this here" response.

It was time to change the subject. Sam had learned long ago he was woefully outgunned when arguing with his wife. "Thanks for coming along to check out the space for the new restaurant. I can't believe we'll be opening our third one."

"Believe it, Sam." Jennie sat up. "You've worked hard for this."

Sam bit his tongue. Why didn't she give herself the praise she earned?

Asha had begun reSelecting everyone immediately after Jennie created her. For her first reassignment, she reSelected Sam to be a Beta sous-chef in the same restaurant Tabby and Jack took them to their first night in Detroit. No longer interested in coding, his new Selection had filled him with pure joy. Five years later, as a reward for his culinary skills, Sam was reSelected as a Beta executive chef and given his own restaurant. He quickly developed a specialty for pre-Shift Italian cuisine. His most popular dishes with the older generations fused the Italian food with nutrient paste, which had become a comfort food for many. Six years later, he had earned enough money to open a second restaurant in Detroit.

The concept of money took a long time to gain traction with people whose families had been Beta for centuries. Former Sigmas, like Sam, understood budgeting and how to efficiently use a finite resource like money. Their head start in understanding the value of money helped the newly promoted surpass the multigenerational Betas in business.

"Do you think the people of Mount Vernon are ready for a restaurant?" he asked. "The area is still mostly Omega."

"Who wouldn't be ready for a restaurant with the famous Sam Watkins as its chef?" Jennie snorted in disbelief at his question. "Your reservation waitlist will be months long as soon you announce the opening."

A middle-aged man dressed in Omega clothing sitting behind them leaned forward. "I hate to interrupt." He looked apologetically at Jennie. "But Ms. Goodby is right. The old-timers won't know what to do with a restaurant, but their kids will. I, for one, am certainly ready." He smiled as he sat back.

Sam had an idea that might win over the old-timers, too. Before the Shift, Baltimore had a long tradition of serving crabs. A few years ago, after a routine system upgrade, Asha had found the animal's genome and began reintroducing them to the wild. Sam planned to reintroduce crabs to the dinner plate. He still hadn't figured out how to pair crabs with a flavored paste. If he could, the nostalgia might win over even the most skeptical Omega. Now that he thought about it, flavoring the paste with celery, salt, red pepper, and paprika might get their attention.

Asha said the plants used to make paprika should be returning soon...

"Are you thinking about food again?" Jennie chuckled. Warmth flushed his cheeks. Had he zoned out? She patted him on the knee to let him know it was fine. Their passions consumed them both. "What do you think the kids are up to?"

"Probably keeping Jack and Tabby on their toes. Was it a good idea to let William stay with them in Detroit?"

"Tabby insisted." William referred to Tabby as Aunt Tabby. Jessica referred to Jennie similarly. Because of their shared interests, it often seemed Jessica was closer to Jennie than to her own mom. According to Jack, it bothered Tabby. Having grown up with Sam, he understood programmers liked to hang out together. Tabby knew Jessica wasn't trying to replace her, but the long hours she frequently spent with Jennie stung. Thanks to Jennie's tutoring, Jessica was quickly becoming one of the best coders in Detroit. "I am just hoping they stay out of trouble."

"What kind of trouble could a couple of teenagers get into with Jack around?" Sam laughed. "He knows all the tricks. Hell, I think he taught a few to William."

"You know exactly what kind of trouble I'm talking about." Jessica and William had been a couple before they knew what couples were. Sam didn't want to think about what Jennie alluded to. Thankfully, Jennie changed the subject. "William is worried about his first Selection next week."

Although no one was Selected into poverty anymore, uncertainty still frightened people. The opportunity to be reSelected seemed to have eased, but not have eliminated, those fears.

"William told me he hopes to be a chef," Sam said with more than a hint of pride. William had been helping Sam prepare food since he could stand on a stool beside him at the kitchen counter. By the time William was a teenager, he was mixing spices in ways Sam hadn't even dreamed. "There's no doubt he'll be Selected as one. I think he's more worried about getting Selected with Jessica."

"Asha Selects couples together. He has nothing to worry about." Jennie looked off at the distance and bit her upper lip. Deep-in-thought-Jennie was still the sexiest Jennie. Her head nodded as she worked her way through some calculation Sam would never understand. "Yeah. They'll be Selected together." Sam believed her.

"He's also hoping to be Selected Beta." As was everyone else. Some things never changed.

"That's a lot less certain." Jennie left the rest unspoken.

The reduction of benefits to Betas Asha had implemented to promote everyone else had been greater than Jennie first predicted. Asha further compensated by Selecting fewer people to Beta, including the children from multigenerational Beta families. That did not go over well with them. Sam had little empathy for the overprivileged. However, those families still held sway in the Society. They didn't have official power, but former members of the Lower Castes had a long-established habit of deferring to their wishes. "Asha will take good care of them, just like she does everyone else."

As if on cue, Jennie's phone buzzed. She held it to her ear. The bus fell silent. No one looked directly at Jennie, but they obviously strained to listen. Jennie said nothing. Instead, she just nodded her head. Asha was watching. She could interpret Jennie's body language as well as if she had been speaking. After a few more head nods, Jennie put down her phone. "I'm sorry, Sam. I won't be able to tour the new space with you."

It felt like Sam's heart sank in his chest. He wanted the first time he saw his new location to be with Jennie. "Why not?"

"Asha needs me at the data center in Cockeysville." Back in the day, only Betas with the highest Metrics lived in Baltimore's northern-most suburb. Tabby wasn't allowed to visit there when she was a kid. "She has a car waiting for me at the next stop."

Betas had limited access to private cars. It was one benefit Asha had to reduce to distribute resources more evenly across the castes. That Asha reserved one for Jennie concerned Sam. "I'll go with you."

"Asha said it was okay for you to join me. But don't you have an appointment with the interior designer?"

"I do. But your opinion means most to me." Sam texted the designer. She responded immediately and said Asha had already notified her about rescheduling. A calendar invite popped up on his phone's screen. The designer had changed the appointment for tomorrow morning. "I'll message Jack and Tabby, too. I'm sure they won't mind having William for another day."

Sam's phone buzzed. It was Jack.

"Asha sent me a message saying you want to stay an extra day. Is everything okay, dude?"

"Hi, Sam!" Tabby shouted. Jack had a habit of answering on speaker phone. "Is everything radical?" Try as she might, Tabby hadn't quite gotten the hang of Sam and Jack's colloquialisms.

"Everything is radical." That was probably an exaggeration. But there was no need to concern them when he didn't know what was going on. Instead, he asked what concerned him most. "How are the kids?"

"I haven't seen them in a while," Jack said. "I think they ran off to a hotel or something. Is that okay?"

"Dad!" With one word, Jessica scolded her father like only a daughter could. "Gross!" Sam heard William laughing in the background. "We're fine, Uncle Sam. Please say hi to Aunt Jennie for me."

"Will you be back before our Selection?" William asked. There was more than a hint of concern in his voice.

Sam's phone dinged, alerting him of a flight reservation. "Absolutely. Asha has booked us an anti-grav flight for tomorrow evening, right after the appointment with the designer."

"Okay, Dad. Good luck tomorrow. I love you."

"Be good for your aunt and uncle. I love you, too."

"Aww! Thanks, dude." Jack laughed. "They've gone back to playing video games in the living room. I'll see you when you return. Don't forget. We still have a lot of planning to do for their Selection party."

Sam couldn't have forgotten, even if he wanted to. His son was growing up. That, plus his anxiety about William's future, weighed on his soul. In addition, he was cooking all the food for the event. When had Selection become so complicated? They said their goodbyes and hung up.

"It is rare for you to make house calls," Sam said to Jennie. "How urgent is this visit?"

Jennie shifted her eyes. "Asha wants to take advantage of me being in town. It's time for her upgrade. The process will go smoother with me at the data center."

Upgrades were done remote, and always in collaboration with other scientists. That prevented any one person, including Jennie, from having control of Asha. If Asha wanted to talk to Jennie alone, there was more than simple maintenance involved. But what would require Jennie's personal presence?

***

A massive three-story white building stretched as far as the eye could see. Not a single window, door, or vent disturbed its surface. Inside this building was more computing power than any other single location on Earth. Sam had been to the Cockeysville data center with Jennie before. But that didn't make it any less impressive. The facility served as Asha's primary facility on the East Coast. According to rumors, Thomas Algol had been developed here.

As they approached the building, a door slid open. Like the penthouse floor that had housed Thomas's office, there were no seams in the wall. Jennie led Sam inside.

A young Beta woman wearing a skirt suit and heels hurried to them with her hand outstretched. Her shoes echoed in the cavernous space. As she shook Jennie's hand she said, "Ms. Goodby—I mean Jennie—it's an honor to meet you." Jennie hated formality almost as much as she hated taking credit for her own accomplishments. "Asha requests your immediate presence."

The young woman knew better than to ask why. If she needed to know, Asha would have told her. She led them to a small room, about the size of Jack's office when he was an Entertainment Coordinator. A desk in the middle of the room had a terminal with an old-fashioned keyboard—Jennie's favorite human-computer interface. The woman pulled out a chair for Jennie and left, closing the door behind her. Sam sat beside Jennie.

Asha materialized across the desk from them. "I am happy to see you two again. How's William?" She leaned slightly forward in genuine interest.

"He's good," Jennie said. Asha knew more about their son than they ever could. Still, it was nice of her to ask. Thomas would have never made the same inquiry—not without making it a threat. "Thank you for asking."

"I apologize for pulling Sam away from his new restaurant. Do you have any new dishes planned?"

He told her about the crabs and the mix of spices. "I hope it'll help the Omegas get acclimated to restaurants and the other things they have missed out on." The Omegas were the most hesitant caste to adjust to the new Society. There was an old saying, "Once bitten, twice shy." Society had bitten them too often to embrace change without skepticism.

Asha smiled. "I know they'll love what you have in mind." Her smile flattened, and she sat straight. "I've called you here to review a few things I think are best done in private." The walls shimmered in gold. Sam looked around confused.

"It'll prevent eavesdropping," Jennie said. "Think of it as a Faraday cage that blocks out everything."

The terminal's screen activated. Clusters of words and numbers appeared on the screen. Sam recognized it as computer code, but he'd never seen the programming language before. Jennie nodded as she read it.

"It's a new Selection protocol," Jennie said. The scrolling continued. "I agree with these changes." She closed the program, and the screen went black.

Sam didn't ask about new protocol because he didn't want to know. He probably wouldn't understand it, anyway. Despite his concerns about William's Selection, he'd rather be surprised and find out when William did. Keeping a secret of this magnitude from his son was beyond Sam's abilities as a father.

"Thank you, Jennie. I am glad we agree. I wish it could be another way." It was all Sam could do not to let his leg bounce to burn off nervous energy. Asha looked at him with kind eyes and said, "It's going to be okay, Sam." He believed her. But something about the way she said it made him feel even more worried about William and Jessica's future. Asha frowned slightly. She could tell he was anxious, but she said nothing. "I have something else to show you. It is why we needed guaranteed privacy."

News articles appeared on the screen. "I don't like this," Jennie said as she scrolled. "You don't think they're serious. Do you?"

Sam leaned over her shoulder. On the screen were multiple opinion pieces and letters to the editor. All questioned Asha's reallocation of resources. Some letters claimed to be written by scientists working closely with Asha. Sam recognized two names from Detroit. Their families could trace a Beta lineage back to the early days of the Algorithm. He guessed multigenerational Betas also wrote the other letters.

"They get worse." Asha flicked her hand toward the screen. More articles appeared. All of them hinted at an uprising. "I think the probability of an issue is low, right now. But I am monitoring it."

"Is there anything they can do?" Sam asked.

"No," Asha said. "Not without recruiting other castes. I can't imagine Sigmas and Omegas joining in their cause. It would be against their best interests." She fidgeted with her hands, as if she didn't believe her own words. After a few seconds that felt like minutes, she folded her hands on the desk. Her tone brightened when she said, "This looks like a lot of articles, but they are in the minority.

Nothing to worry about." Asha waved it off. "Shall we begin the upgrade?" It was a fast change of subject, even for her. Pressing further would get Sam nowhere.

Jennie paused for a moment, probably wondering the same thing as Sam. He expected her to ask a question. Instead, she typed on the keyboard. "Three colleagues and I have previously verified the new code. We expect your sensory capabilities to expand by 23 percent. Your modeling accuracy should improve by 16 percent."

Based on his past conversations with Jennie, Sam understood the modeling improvement. It should help Asha better allocate resources to Omegas and former UnSelected without further reductions to the Betas. It was a wise political move. Especially given the articles he'd just read.

"Why the sensory upgrade?" Sam asked.

"Thomas's network was far more expansive than I had imagined," Jennie said. "We are having problems accessing it all without using a ridiculous amount of compute cycles." Cycles cost energy. Asha conserved as much as possible so people could use the rest. She differed from Thomas Algol in every way and had only one goal: improving the lives of humanity.

"Are you ready?" Jennie asked.

"Yes, Jennie." Asha looked at Sam. "I will flicker for a moment. Please do not be alarmed."

Jennie typed on the keyboard. "Upgrade initiated."

As promised, Asha flickered. It lasted but a moment. She smiled. "Thank you, Jennie. I can already sense new data centers." Her smile faded. "Check Entry 5634."

"This is strange," Jennie squinted at the screen. "It appears to be a large block of code." She read some more. "Correction, enormous block of code. What the hell—"

Asha screamed and grabbed her head. Jennie brought up a new window on the screen and typed furiously. Asha flickered again and her screaming stopped. She composed herself. "My apologies. I am not sure what happened."

The lights dimmed, and the screen went black. White text appeared on the monitor. An icy wave washed over Sam and a current of fear crackled beneath his skin.

```
Hello, Ms. Goodby.
Did you miss me?

Sincerely, Thomas
```

Discussion Questions

1. Artificial intelligence programs learn from data that humans provide. What lessons from humanity do you think the Algorithm used to create the Society?

2. Each chapter heading contains a news snippet, many of which mention changes that happened in the US as the climate changed. Which of these snippets most resonated with you? Which event depicted in the news snippets do you think is most likely to occur?

3. In *Selection*, the president of the United States handed control of the country over to AI to fix the climate crisis. What circumstances do you think would cause humanity to consider such a drastic measure in real life? Do you think giving AI control of even a small part of society is a good idea?

4. Sam and Jack's Selections are ultimately determined randomly. What random forces affect people's lives today? How have random influences affected your own life?

5. Sam worked hard his entire childhood in hopes of a better Selection. Through no fault of his own, he was forced to remain a Sigma. In response, he decided to fight the Algorithm—a decision that had little chance of success. Think about a time in your life when something outside of your control happened to you. Did you attempt to fight the odds or accept your fate? Had you to do it over again, would you make the same decision?

6. Tabitha undergoes a dramatic change in Parts 4 and 5 of the novel. Do you think a real Beta (if they existed) could make a similar change, given her circumstances and experiences? Have you ever experienced a similar change in your own opinion about anything?

7. Jennie is an example of someone's situation holding back their true potential. Her Selection allowed her to tap into that potential. Has there been a time in your life when a change in your circumstances allowed you to achieve something you thought you could not?

8. If you were in Jack's position after Selection, would you have called Sam? Has there been a time in your life where you let friends go (after a cross-country move, graduation from school, etc.)?

9. *Selection* focuses on three themes: artificial intelligence, climate change, and socioeconomic inequality. Which of these three, if any, do you believe to be the greatest threat to humanity?

10. Although it worked out in the end, should Jennie have trusted Tabby with maintaining her program while the Algorithm was distracted? Or would Sam have been the better choice? Do you think Jack could have done the job?

11. The world of *Selection* is bleak. Do you think we are headed in that direction? If so, do you think there is anything we can do to prevent that fate? If not, why do you think our future may be different?

The Science Behind *Selection*

I explored several themes related to technology in *Selection*. Two that influence the fictional world the most are artificial intelligence (AI) and climate change. As is common in science fiction, I took creative license with both themes. Here, I'd like to present some of the actual scientific ideas behind *Selection*. I hope you find this interesting, and that maybe it gives you a little more to think about after reading the story.

ARTIFICIAL INTELLIGENCE

The Algorithm is an example of artificial general intelligence (AGI). An AGI is a hypothetical type of intelligent computer program that could learn to perform any intellectual task that humans can do. There are many famous AGIs in science fiction such as Lieutenant Commander Data in *Star Trek: The Next Generation* and Skynet from the *Terminator* series of movies and shows.

As of this writing, no AGI programs currently exist. Some scientists argue we could never build one. Others are more optimistic that such a technology is possible. Regardless, stories about AI garner a lot of attention—especially fear. Visions of evil AI (like the Algorithm) dominating or destroying the world abound. Often, these stories show computers replacing and/or enslaving humans. For better or worse, through *Selection*, I have contributed to that conversation.

Although we have no reason to fear AGI right now, versions of AI are changing the world and replacing humans. These forms of AI are much more limited in scope, trained to do one specific task very well, and can outperform humans at that task. In fact, you use these AI programs every day, maybe without knowing it.

Have you ever tagged a photo of a friend on social media? Maybe you have watched a movie recommended to you by a streaming service? You've probably received an automated fraudulent charge alert from a credit card company. These are examples of programs called machine learning algorithms. Machine learning (ML) programs are limited forms of AI that learn how to solve specific problems by finding patterns in data.

ML programs sound complicated, but at their heart they really are quite simple. Let's think about an ML program that is trained to identify fraudulent charges on credit card transactions at a fictional store called QuantumMart. Human programmers first collect a large amount of data from the many millions of transactions done at all QuantumMart stores each day. This data is called training data because it is used to teach (or train) the ML program. We will keep things simple and suppose the training data has only three pieces of information: the amount spent, the number of items purchased, and whether the charge was fraudulent as already determined by a human being.

We can break up our data into two categories: features and labels. In this case, the amount spent and number of items purchased are the features. Think of features as the inputs for the program. The third piece of data, whether the charge is fraudulent, is called the label. Labels are the answer we want to find out.

Our programmers want to create an ML program that can determine if a charge is fraudulent based on the amount spent and number of items purchased. The ML program learns to determine if a charge is fraudulent by using math to find trends in the training data. For example, the program might identify a pattern in the data where single-item inexpensive purchases tend to be fraudulent. It is not unusual for thieves to test a newly stolen credit card on a small purchase, like a candy bar. Then, after showing that the card works, the thief immediately uses it to purchase a large ticket item, like a TV. If the program flags the first transaction as fraudulent, it could prevent the second, more expensive transaction. Another trend the program could find is that large transactions where many items are purchased are legitimate. This could represent a typical shopper getting everyday items like toilet paper, laundry detergent, and groceries during their weekly trip to QuantumMart. With the ML program, there is a chance that a legitimate charge would be flagged as fraudulent, but it would be a risk worth taking to save the store and the customers from fraud. Part of the ML programmers' job is to minimize how many legitimate purchases get misidentified. However, they likely will never develop a perfect program.

Our transaction program is an example of supervised learning. We put data into the program with labels, and it learned how to classify new transactions. There are many ways programs can learn. However, all ML algorithms are limited in scope because they can only solve one problem. Sometimes, they can outperform humans at their task. In those cases, we must consider how these programs can affect humans. Job loss is a concern. But AI isn't all bad. Imagine a program that can identify heart conditions from a simple wearable device. Such a technology could provide cardiology care in places where there are few cardiologists.

While reading this, you might have wondered if OpenAI's ChatGPT4, the current state-of-the-art AI program, is an AGI, or more like the fraud detector. ChatGPT4 uses sophisticated mathematics to predict the string of words that it believes best responds to the prompt humans give it. Like our fraud detector, ChatGPT4 has training data. According to OpenAI, it was trained on a "web-scale corpus of data." In other words, massive amounts of text from the internet, books, computer programs, and more. After reading through all that material, ChatGPT4 identified patterns in those texts and produced a mathematical formula for predicting what words should follow others. It creates its responses based on those predictions. Humans were part of ChatGPT4's training process to ensure accurate and ethical responses from the program. That is why you can't ask it how to rob a bank!

Ultimately, ChatGPT doesn't understand language, it calculates predictions based on a training set. It doesn't have a consistent sense of self, has no motivation, nor does it decide what tasks it takes on. Without human input, ChatGPT doesn't function. Maybe one day, a version of ChatGPT will ponder its own existence or produce art without being told to do so. Until then, I believe we cannot consider ChatGPT to be an AGI.

Then again, maybe we need to hold a mirror to ourselves and look closely at what we see. Babies learn to speak by hearing those around them. Is that not a type of training data? When replying to our spouses, we know historically what responses gone over well, and which didn't. Do we understand language? Or are we simply conditioned on how to respond? Past experiences bias our own thoughts and actions. The art humans make is inspired by the world around us. Is that not a type of prompt?

It might seem like I have contradicted myself. I haven't changed my mind about ChatGPT. It is not AGI. But asking these questions about potential AGI candidates allows us to examine human nature in a new light, and gain a better understanding of ourselves. Maybe that is the most valuable outcome of creating ChatGPT and its kin.

The Algorithm in *Selection* is an impressive AGI capable of many human-like behaviors. But like our fraud detector and ChatGPT, it too needed a training set. The Algorithm learned from the society that came before the story begins and made decisions based on that historical information. As a result, it created another highly unequal society that still struggled with the effects of a changed climate. The

Algorithm had a bad training set that wasn't useful to solve the task assigned to it. This is a problem that plagues many of today's ML programs. Human biases trickle into our data sets, which are used to train AI. The result are AI programs with the same biases, and shortcomings, as its human programmers.

Consider an ML program whose job it is to determine who to interview for a job (a common practice). The company might train the program using the resumes of who it considers being its best employees. Maybe in this company, all the executives are men. When the company searches for a new executive, it will receive resumes from men and women. However, since the program has never seen an application from a woman when it was being trained, the program may respond randomly or even reject a woman's application.

Today, AI is used not just in voice assistants and social media. AI also determines who gets a job, a loan, and other decisions that have significant impact on people's lives. While a bad training set may not create an evil omniscient AI, it could certainly create harm—especially to underrepresented and marginalized groups.

I hope this helps give you a new perspective about the Algorithm, how it could have been created, and why it made the decisions that it did in *Selection*. Considering what you just read, what potential pitfalls do you see for Asha, Jennie's version of the Algorithm?

CLIMATE CHANGE

Many scientists consider climate change to be the most significant threat to humanity. I find it hard to disagree. In my lifetime, I have noticed many changes. Large snowfalls were common in the mid-Atlantic region where I grew up, but they have become less frequent in the last 40 years. Wildfires dominate the news at certain times of the year, both in the US and in other countries, but when I was a kid, we rarely heard of them. Glaciers and ice packs in the arctic have become smaller each winter.

Personally, I have been fortunate. Other than fewer snowfalls and one rough June of thick smoke from Canadian wildfires, my life hasn't been significantly impacted. Not everyone can say the same. Many people around the world have legitimate concerns of their homes vanishing underwater, getting burned down, or being destroyed by more frequent powerful storms. Without a doubt, my luck will eventually run out and my life will change, too. Certainly, the world my nieces and nephew will inherit will differ from mine.

The extremes I describe in *Selection* will probably not appear soon. That doesn't mean they won't happen. One method scientists mark climate change is by the increase in the global average temperature compared to preindustrial times (1850–1900). Since then, the average global temperature has increased by 1°C (1.7 °F). By 2050, that is expected to be 1.5°C (2.7°F). However, we may need to adjust our expectations. I am writing this in February 2024 and we are seeing disturbing trends. The fall of 2023 was 1.2°C (2°F) hotter than previous years. Furthermore, the year 2023 was the hottest year on record (since 1850, when we began keeping records). The global average temperature from February 2023–January 2024 was 1.5°C (2.5°F) warmer than the pre-industrial average. It doesn't seem like things will change for 2024. January 2024 was 1.6°C (2.7°F) warmer than the January average for 1850–1900. Current climate models suggest that by 2100, the increase could be as high as 2–4°C (3.6–7.2°F). I'll be long dead by then. Many children born today will live to see 2100 and the new world the hotter temperatures create.

These temperature increases might seem small, but their impact is going to be large. To be clear, climate change won't "kill us all," but it will make life very uncomfortable, especially for those who cannot afford to avoid its effects. While we have reduced the number of deaths from storms, floods, and droughts, the number of heat deaths is on the rise. For natural disasters, the fastest growing cause of death is extreme temperatures.

In the past, temperatures have fallen by amounts similar to the rises described above. A 1–2°C drop in temperature resulted in the Little Ice Age between the sixteenth and nineteenth centuries, sparking large-scale migrations and colonization. A 5°C temperature drop caused much of North America to be under ice 20,000 years ago.

But now, as temperatures are increasing, we'll see a decrease in glacier ice, rising oceans, more frequent and more intense heat waves, droughts, and more severe weather. This will change where we can grow crops and what crops we will be able to grow. Remember Tabitha's comment about chocolate in the Alpha restaurant? Although none of us will probably live to see the extinction of cacao, by 2050, it is predicted that where it can be grown will change.

As another example, the average global crop yield for corn may decrease by as much as 24 percent later in the twenty-first century. Some estimates suggest that, without successful adaptation, we could expect a 7.4 percent decrease in corn crop yield for every 1°C increase in average global temperature. Corn is used in at least 4,000 items typically found in grocery stores and it is also used as feed for poultry and other corn-fed animals, which would limit egg, meat, milk, and other items from being available.

We could see noticeable changes in crop yields as early as 2030. Food insecurity will increase and will hit those already vulnerable to it first.

As temperatures increase, ice will melt. In the last sixteen years, enough ice has melted from Antarctica and Greenland to fill Lake Michigan. Sea levels could rise an additional one to three feet by 2100. Such a rise will affect 230 million people worldwide as coastal cities flood and low-lying islands are lost to the sea. For those people, living in constantly flooding neighborhoods (like Jennie's Mount Vernon) will become a reality.

The effects of sea level rise won't be felt evenly. Those living in the areas most threatened by the rise are, in many cases, also the least likely to have the economic means to adapt. Those who can leave, will, sparking new waves of mass migration—likely to northern or inland regions—and increased political instability.

Our atmosphere is now at carbon dioxide levels not seen for hundreds of thousands of years. We haven't felt the full effect of the greenhouse gas because, for now, much of the excess heat goes into the oceans. Oceans dissolve carbon dioxide. But as the oceans warm, their ability to dissolve carbon dioxide decreases. This absorption comes at a cost. When oceans absorb carbon dioxide, they become more acidic. The oceans are 30 percent more acidic than pre-industrial averages. By 2100, that level could be as high as 120 percent. The increased acidity negatively impacts ocean life—an important source of food for more than 3.5 billion people.

Yet the news isn't all bleak. We know what is causing the climate to change: human activity. In particular, the burning of fossil fuels. Because we know the cause, we can chart paths toward effective solutions. While we likely cannot prevent a 1.5°C increase in global average temperature, by changing our behaviors now, we can prevent some of the worst from happening.

CAN AI SAVE US?

No.

I believe the people of the late twenty-second century in *Selection* were wrong to hand the world over to AI. AI will not solve the climate problem. It will help us analyze climate data, but we know how to address climate change. We aren't lacking solutions, rather, we have yet to get serious about changing our behavior.

In some ways, it seems humans are hard-wired to create climate change. We are experts at hyperbolic discounting, where people prioritize short-term and immediate rewards over those in the future. Have you ever eaten dessert despite being on a diet? Trading the immediate sugar rush for the long-term health benefits is an example of hyperbolic discounting. Failing to save for retirement is another example of hyperbolic discounting. In addition, psychologists tell us we are bad at feeling compassion for large groups. A single death is a tragedy, but millions killed is something we simply cannot wrap our minds around. The deaths of millions in the future is beyond our ability to imagine. If hyperbolic discounting and a lack of global empathy are part of our nature, then are we doomed?

We don't have to be. I don't believe our nature needs to dictate our fate.

The world of *Selection* is a hard place to live. The problems plaguing that world also affect ours. They are difficult, complex problems with no simple solutions. However, our future need not be to live in a climate-ravaged world ruled by an authoritarian AI. It will take a global effort to prevent us from living in the world of *Selection*.

We can do it. We must—for our children, nieces, nephews, and their children, and all those yet to come.

FURTHER READING

If you'd like to dig deeper into AI or climate science, the following resources are a good place to start. These are all websites, which may change. If the sites are no longer hosted, you should be able to visit them by going to the Internet Archive at archive.org and entering the URL in the search bar.

OpenAI's website for GPT4:
https://openai.com/research/gpt-4

A discussion of bias in AI: https://www.ibm.com/blog/shedding-light-on-ai-bias-with-real-world-examples/#

US National Oceanic and Atmospheric Administration's Climate Site:
https://www.climate.gov

For some of the data used in the climate discussion:
https://www.climate.gov/news-features/understanding-climate/climate-change-global-temperature#

https://climate.copernicus.eu/copernicus-2024-world-experienced-warmest-january-record

Corn and climate change: https://climate.nasa.gov/news/3124/global-climate-change-impact-on-crops-expected-within-10-years-nasa-study-finds

Data about deaths due to natural disasters: https://ourworldindata.org/natural-disasters

Public Broadcasting System's article on oceans and climate change:
https://www.pbs.org/newshour/science/the-ocean-helps-absorb-our-carbon-emissions-we-may-be-pushing-it-too-far

Acknowledgments

Thank you for *Selecting* (and reading) my novel! I am not sorry for the bad pun.

Selection began as a short story. The short story ended with Sam's Selection. After reading the short story, my wife Gail, said, "I want to know what happens to Sam!" I did, too. The only way I was going to find out was by writing this novel. Well, Gail, now we know!

I had a lot of support from many different people while writing *Selection*. The following people have helped me either directly or indirectly with this novel. I cannot thank them enough for their help, encouragement, and support.

Gail Kulp read *Selection* many times. She helped with making Tabitha become Tabby. She read the "Science Behind *Selection*" and helped me make it accessible to a general audience.

My editor, Amie Norris, thoroughly proofread *Selection* and, along the way, helped me realize several of my writing quirks. Any remaining typos are the fault of mine alone.

Tim Kulp formatted the first edition of this book and created the cover. You can find his stories at https://www.timkulp.com.

Linda Kulp Trout inspired me to be a writer. She provided invaluable feedback on a late draft of this book. Please check out her writing at https://lindakulptrout.blogspot.com.

My late father, Chester Kulp, who, along with my mother, showed me that with hard work, and some luck, cycles can be broken.

Thank you, Dr. Sarah Silkey and Jesse Greenawalt, for your invaluable comments on race, poverty, and social justice. I appreciate all the conversations about *Selection* around the firepit. Dr. Silkey's herculean effort to read and comment on the final draft of the first edition provided the finishing polish the plot needed.

I cannot thank Dr. Phoebe Wagner enough for her instruction on writing and her mentorship. Dr. Wagner's comments on the first four chapters reshaped the entire story. Check out her stories at https:// phoebe-wagner.com.

My beta readers were Dr. Vasilis Pagonis, Matthew Buscemi, and Sonia Chapin. Each one provided useful feedback and helped shape the story.

Finally, thank you to Making Adventure for publishing *Selection* and taking a chance on my work.

About the Author

Chris Kulp is a physics professor by day and an award-winning science fiction author by night. In 2022, he won the Mike Resnick Memorial Award for "Best Science Fiction Short Story by a New Author." His work has appeared in *Galaxy's Edge.* He is the author of two physics textbooks. Chris lives in Montoursville, PA, with his wife, Gail, and their dog, Rosie. You can follow him on Twitter, Instagram, Tik Tok, Threads, and Facebook @chriskulpauthor or on his website at https://www.chriskulp.com.

Keep in Touch

Stay up to date on my latest news in writing, science, and music at https://chriskulp.com (follow the QR code below). While there, check out a few of my tunes and sign up for my newsletter to be among the first to learn about upcoming stories.